The Very Thought of You

The
Very Thought
of You

Lynn Kurland

JOVE BOOKS, NEW YORK

THE VERY THOUGHT OF YOU

A Jove Book / published by arrangement with
the author

The Penguin Putnam Inc. World Wide Web site address is
http://www.penguinputnam.com

ISBN: 1-56865-753-6

A JOVE BOOK®
Jove Books are published by The Berkley Publishing Group, a member
of Penguin Putnam Inc.,
200 Madison Avenue, New York, New York 10016.
JOVE and the "J" design are trademarks belonging to Jove
Publications, Inc.

PRINTED IN THE UNITED STATES OF AMERICA

To Elizabeth Moira,
our little bundle of joy

and

to her father, Matthew
who makes all my best wishes come true

Acknowledgments

The author gratefully and with proper auntlike pride acknowledges the aid of Jana Clara Gardner, a paragon of little girldom, a former toddler of unparalleled cuteness and intelligence, who taught the author most of what she knows about three year olds.

The author is also quite grateful that Jana forgave her for cutting off her ''long, pwetty bwown hay-uh,'' something the author's husband has yet to do.

And lastly, but by no means leastly, a hearty thanks must go to the author's husband who was, despite his insistence on referring to Margaret of Falconberg's minstrel as ''Bardric the Bald,'' a veritable font of poetic inspiration.

The
Very Thought
of You

One

❧❧❧

THE HIGHLANDS, SCOTLAND
FEBRUARY 1998

THE HORSE SCRUNCHED UP HIS NOSE, TOSSED HIS HEAD IN obvious discomfort, and then sneezed.

Alexander Smith opened his mouth to curse, then realized the precariousness of his situation. He grasped the top edge of the stall door and very deliberately clamped his lips shut. He blinked furiously to clear his eyes of a substance he didn't want to examine too closely.

He should have stayed in bed.

He'd known that, of course, from the moment he'd woken. His first clue had been the sound of rain on the roof—day fifty-six of the Scottish deluge. His next warning had been shivering through a cold shower, courtesy of his younger brother. The final straw had been counting on a breakfast of sausage, eggs, and fried potatoes only to find nothing but dangerously aged cottage cheese and on-the-verge-of-turning-green bread in the fridge. By the grease stains on his brother's chin, Alex had known immediately where to lay the blame.

And now this.

He looked down at his snotty shirt and wondered just how long it would take for it to crust over so he wouldn't drip all over the house.

His horse, looking much more comfortable and rather contrite, bumped him companionably with his nose.

"Beast, Beast," Alex said, carefully dragging his sleeve across his mouth, "do you really think I can go out looking like this? What if we run into some beautiful Scottish girl? What kind of impression are we going to make?"

Beast ducked his head in obvious shame.

Alex grunted. "That's right. Well, have a nice day. I'm sure you will, now you can breathe again. I'm going back to bed."

It seemed the safest alternative.

He wiped his face with a patch of clean shirttail, then left the stables and walked across the courtyard. The castle rose up before him, an impenetrable wall of gray stone relieved only by a few windows on the second floor. His brother-in-law Jamie had spent a fortune seeing the keep restored and the results were chilling. Alex could almost see medieval Scottish clansmen bursting out the front door in their plaids, brandishing their swords and screaming like banshees.

Alex entered the hall and pulled the door shut behind him with a bang. Once his eyes adjusted to the interior light, he saw his younger brother sitting in front of the hearth, warming his toes by the fire. Alex marched across the great hall, prepared to give the runt a second installment in the berating he'd given him earlier. He didn't want another Saturday starting out like this—*sans* hot water and saturated fat.

Zachary glanced up from his book, took one look at Alex, and started to laugh.

"Gggrrrr," Alex said, wondering if strangling his brother would be half as satisfying as just contemplating it was.

"Good grief," Zachary gasped out between guffaws. "What'd you have—an encounter with the Blob?"

Alex gritted his teeth. "How'd you like to have an encounter with my fists?"

"Eeuw," Zachary said with a shudder. "Maybe after you clean up."

"As if I could," Alex growled.

"What's your problem? I had plenty of hot water."

"I know!"

Zachary only blinked innocently. Then he rubbed his disgustingly well-fed belly. "There's nothing left in the fridge, you know," he said.

"And whose fault do you think that is?" Alex demanded.

Zach sighed again, the mournful sigh of a man left home alone with nothing to graze upon. "Man, I hate it when Jamie and Elizabeth go out of town. The least they could have done was leave Patrick or Joshua behind. Josh makes great desserts." He looked at Alex narrowly. "Why'd I get stuck with just you? You won't even keep the fridge stocked."

Alex relived briefly in his mind some of the more choice experiences he'd had pummeling his baby brother. His irritation momentarily soothed by those warm and fuzzy memories, he managed to speak very calmly. "And what's wrong with you that you can't go to the store?"

Zach settled himself more comfortably into his chair and moved his toes closer to the fire. "I'm too busy. You go instead. And get something good. None of that health food garbage."

Alex mentally counted to ten. When that didn't work, he set his sights on a larger number.

"Oh, and Alex? I'd go shower first if I were you." He looked at Alex and started to grin again. "Really. I think it would be the right thing to do."

Alex wanted more than anything to wring his brother's neck in payment for ruining his Saturday morning and to stop the brat's giggles. Unfortunately, his shirt was beginning to crust over and he was starting to itch.

"I'll go to the store later," he growled, contenting himself with giving Zachary a murderous look and a smart cuff to the ear on his way to the stairs. With any luck there would be hot water by now.

He rummaged around in the armoire for clean clothes, then headed for his bathroom. He was just reaching into the shower for the taps when the phone started to ring. He ignored it and turned on the water. He hesitantly put his fingers under the spray and smiled in faint surprise at the increasingly warm temperature. Maybe things were starting to look up.

He started to strip when he realized he had no towel. He had a vague memory of having flung it into the hamper in disgust after his earlier foray into chilly waters. After turning off the shower to conserve what precious hot water there was, he opened the bathroom door only to hear the phone still ringing. Alex growled in frustration.

"Zach, get the phone!" he yelled.

The phone continued to ring. Alex cursed as he gingerly rebuttoned his shirt, then made his way into his brother-in-law's study.

"What?" he barked into the receiver.

"Nice to talk to you, too, buddy," a male voice said with a laugh. "All that lovely Scottish scenery getting to you?"

Alex rolled his eyes heavenward. His day had just taken a decided turn for the worse. "Tony, what do you want?"

"What, no chitchat?"

"Not with you, thanks anyway."

"How's Elizabeth?" Tony continued. "The baby? Your barbarian brother-in-law?"

"My sister's fine, her baby is fine, and Jamie is fine. Now what the hell do you want?"

"Well, since you asked," Tony said with a strained laugh, "I'll get right to it. We need your services."

Leave it to Tony not to mince words. Alex took a deep breath.

"Tony, I quit eight months ago. I haven't changed my mind."

"But you haven't heard the deal on this one, my friend."

"I don't want to hear."

Tony made a sound of impatience. "It's the sweetest takeover I've ever seen. Smooth, easy. They'll never see it coming. I've already got controlling interest. I just need you to come in and close the deal. It will make you richer than your wildest dreams."

"I'm already richer than my wildest dreams, Tony."

"You can always use more—"

"No. Don't call me again."

"Alex—"

"Don't." Alex hung up the phone.

He leaned back and let out his breath slowly. Was it possible he had ever enjoyed any of this?

Unfortunately, he could remember all too well just how enjoyable it had been. And he remembered just as clearly how it had all started. Anthony DiSalvio had hired him fresh out of law school, when Alex had still been green and full of chivalry. He'd become a lawyer to save the world from injustice. And then Tony, a senior partner, had come to him with a special assignment. Alex had been flattered beyond belief. A little corporate raiding, a take-over done by the book; it had been a rush. He'd saved all the little guys by getting rid of the big bad guys.

He'd been a smashing success.

It had gone to his head.

He'd woken up seven years later. It had taken his sister's mysterious disappearance to make him take a good hard look at what he was doing with his own life; he hadn't liked what he'd seen. He had become a pirate—a very rich pirate, but a pirate nonetheless. The little guys had become lost in the shuffle. Alex had raided just for the sheer sport of it, and for the money. He'd started out to save the world from injustice; instead he'd wound up being the cause of more injustice than he cared to think about.

So he'd walked away. Far away from New York and London and all the places where he'd hoisted the skull and crossbones. Leave it to Tony not to take his blunt and offensive resignation seriously.

"I need a change of scenery," he said to the contents of Jamie's study. "To somewhere sunny, like the Bahamas."

Maybe Jamie had a few travel books on the shelf above his desk. Alex put off his shower a few minutes more in deference to Jamie's private library. Surely there was some destination detailed there that would interest him. He had the time for a vacation. He certainly had the need for one.

He ran a finger along the spine of each book above Jamie's desk, mentally checking off the ones he'd read.

Then he stopped.

Trails Through Time. Now, this was a new one. Alex pulled the book down and opened it. He read the inside jacket. "In *Trails Through Time* author Stephen McAfee takes the reader on a marvelous journey down roads in Britain, from Roman times to the present day."

Interesting. Alex flipped through the pages, then stopped when something slipped out and landed on the desk with a soft *plop.* Alex put the book aside and reached for the folded piece of paper. It was very worn, as if it had been folded and unfolded dozens of times. He gingerly straightened it out, then looked at it in astonishment. It was a treasure map. Considering the day he was having, he was fairly impressed with his ability to recognize that.

Not that he should have been surprised. He'd been an Eagle Scout, after all, and one famous for his mapmaking skills. Add to that the board and plunder skills he'd acquired after law school and he had the piracy category all sewn up. This was, however, one of the oddest maps Alex had ever seen in his long and illustrious career.

There were the normal things, of course: requisite directional arrows, landmarks aplenty. In fact, the landmarks looked suspiciously like the surrounding countryside. Yes, Jamie's mountains were there to the north. The castle sat prominently in the middle of the map, with the meadow below it due south. There was the forest to the west and another part of forest to the south. And that squiggle over there had to be the stream that fed into the pond not far from the garden. Alex stared at it for several minutes wondering what looked so strange.

Then it hit him.

There wasn't just one X marking the spot. There were several.

To another man, such a flagrant disregard for treasure-mapmaking standards might have only indicated slight befuddlement on the part of the mapmaker. But Alex wasn't just another man. And the mapmaker was his brother-in-law, James MacLeod. And Jamie wasn't befuddled, he was an honest-to-goodness, former mediev—

Alex put on the mental brakes before he traveled any further down that well-worn path. Traveling down *any* path Jamie was associated with was hazardous to one's health. Maybe Jamie had just been scribbling in his spare time.

Unfortunately, those didn't look like scribbles. Alex looked at the map again and frowned at what was very deliberately scrawled next to the X's in Jamie's bold handwriting.

Medieval England.

17th Century Barbados.

The Future.

It couldn't mean what he thought it meant. The map was just Jamie's doodles. People didn't just walk over certain spots in the ground and up and disappear.

Though Barbados didn't sound too bad at the moment. At least it would be sunny there. And look, there it was, due north of Medieval England. Alex left the map sitting prominently on top of the book where Jamie couldn't help but notice that Alex had seen it. He would realize he'd been caught, and Alex would enjoy the opportunity to give Jamie a thorough ribbing. Heaven knew he deserved it.

Could it be true? Alex turned the possibility over in his mind. Barbados at least would be a pleasant change of scenery. What could it hurt to just go have a look and indulge in the fantasy for an hour or so? He had a great imagination. He could hang out under a tree and pretend he was loitering on some sunny beach. Maybe he'd even pretend he'd traveled there, just to see if he could rattle Jamie. Yes, the morning was starting to shape up nicely.

Alex left the study, grabbed his coat, and headed down-stairs. He was still covered with horse snot, but there was no sense in getting cleaned up now. He wouldn't need his shirt much longer because he'd be sunning himself on a nice beach, watching bikini-clad women strut their stuff in front of him—or at least pretending to do so. Given the fact that he hadn't seen blue Scottish sky in weeks, Bar-bados was starting to sound mighty nice.

If there just wasn't that disconcerting seventeenth-century business attached.

Alex plowed into his brother at the bottom of the steps.

"Hey," Zachary said, annoyed, "watch it. You're going to get me dirty and I have a date."

Alex steadied himself with a hand on the wall. Zachary had a date? Alex hadn't had a date in eight months, and he was the owner of a huge portfolio and worked out every day to keep his body from turning to fat. Zachary was a semi-starving former student who ate junk food in front of the television and grew things on paper plates under his bed. How was this possible?

"With whom?" Alex asked, stunned.

Zachary smirked. "Fiona MacAllister."

Alex reeled like a drunken man.

"Fiona?" he gasped.

"Yeah," Zachary said with a shrug. "You snooze, you lose, bro. And *I* wasn't snoozing. I gotta go get cleaned up." He gave Alex's crusty shirt a pointed look before he mounted the stairs and disappeared out of sight.

Alex shook his head. Fiona MacAllister was the grocer's daughter. Alex had been planning to ask her out for weeks. He'd just been waiting until he thought she might be used to him. After all, he was a rich and powerful former cor-porate raider, and he hadn't wanted her to want him just for his money.

Alex pushed away from the wall. There was something very wrong in the world when his brother could get a girl to go out with him and he couldn't.

He made one last detour to the kitchen on the off chance

that some undiscovered cache of junk food was hiding there. He rummaged through the pantry and found his secret box of Ding-Dongs still safely hiding behind a container of oatmeal and a bag of rice. It was a good thing Zachary never came close to anything resembling a raw ingredient. Alex indulged himself immediately and tucked a second snack into his coat pocket. One never knew what one might find for dinner on the beach. No sense in not being prepared.

He shut the hall door behind him and put on his coat. As he walked across the courtyard to the stables, the rain increased with every step he took. It wasn't a good sign, but he ignored it. Within minutes he had Beast saddled and was heading out the front gate.

He turned back to the north to look at the mountains behind the estate, with their last dustings of snow. Spring was right around the corner. He could smell it. He followed his nose as it pointed him to the west where a little stream ran into the pond which sat serenely next to the garden. Jamie had certainly done a good job reproducing that stream on the map. And there lay Barbados just past Medieval England on the other side of the pond.

Alex felt an uncomfortable tingle in the air and frowned. He could believe anything of the forest on the other side of the keep, but this bit of ground in front of him? There were no gateways to the past lurking under those boughs. Maybe his sister Elizabeth was just using the map for one of the romance novels she wrote.

Alex urged his horse forward, wondering as he did so just what he thought he was doing out in the rain on a horse who had a cold, following directions on a map made by his lunatic brother-in-law. He was losing it. It was the only answer. His breakfast of fermented cottage cheese had obviously had adverse effects on his common sense. Even the thought of mentally spending a morning in Barbados was starting to sound unappealing. He would probably be better off calling a travel agent.

But he had already come this far; there was no sense in

turning back now. He continued on his way under the boughs of the rowan trees. The silence was palpable. A chill went down his spine. Alex pulled his collar closer to his neck and gave himself a hard mental shake.

All the same, he wondered just how Jamie had discovered all that business about those little gates.

Probably better not to know.

The trees thinned and suddenly gave way to an intimate little glade. The forest floor was carpeted with moss and clover and a large circle of plants. Elizabeth called it a faery ring. Alex looked narrowly at it. Was this the gate? Was it possible? He shook his head. It just couldn't be anything more than a very simple ring in the grass.

Right?

Alex pulled out his spare infusion of chocolate and lard and munched thoughtfully. He'd traveled back to the fifteenth century through Jamie's forest, but he didn't remember having felt this kind of tingle in the air. Though at the time he'd been too worried about keeping his head on top of his neck to think much about the mechanics of the process.

Alex looked at the silver ball of foil in his hand and smiled faintly. It could be his version of the breadcrumb trail. He dropped it outside the ring, then patted his gelding's neck.

"Well, Beast, we're here so we may as well give this a try. We'll sit here for a few minutes, pretend we've hiked on over to blue ocean and white sands, then we'll go home and see what we can do about putting Zach out of commission. I'll run to the market myself and take some action on this thing. Maybe Fiona just needs to know I'm interested. And if by some miracle we wind up on the beach, maybe Jamie will see our Ding-Dong trail and come get us. But not right away," he added, nudging Beast forward until they were standing in the middle of the circle. "I could really use a dose of sunlight."

Something whistled past his ear and Beast reared. Alex fought to stay mounted but it was a hopeless battle. He crashed to the ground, feeling a sharp pain in the back of his head. Then he saw stars, lots of them. He gritted his teeth as he struggled to stay conscious. He should have told Zach where he was going. Well, at least his brother would eventually realize Beast was gone. Maybe the brat would have the good sense to come after him before he drowned in the rain.

Through the haze that clouded his vision, he could have sworn he saw an arrow quivering in a tree above him.

This was not a good sign.

He felt the definite nudge of a foot in his side. A booted foot. A very ungentle foot.

He tried to focus, but the pain in his head was blinding. Then he felt cold steel press against his neck. Now he *knew* he was losing it.

"You trespass on my lands," a husky voice snarled. "Give me your name and your business."

Alex blinked against the rain that had suddenly started up again with renewed vigor. All right, so some yahoo had wandered onto Jamie's estate and had decided to rob him. If he could just buy time enough to let his head clear, he could deal with this. He started to sit up, then got help. He was hauled into a sitting position by the front of his jacket and he groaned involuntarily at the agony the motion sent flooding to his brain.

"Just a minute," he said. He put his hand on his attacker's shoulder to steady himself and forced his eyes to focus.

Big, brown eyes stared back at him from the shelter of a chain-mail coif.

A *chain-mail coif?*

Alex took in the rest of the boy's outfit. He was sporting chain mail head to toe, topped by a surcoat, leather cross-garters over boots, and crude leather gloves. One gloved hand currently gripped a sword. Alex looked back at the young man's face. It was a face far too beautiful to have been wasted on a boy. Maybe the kid got teased a lot.

"Your name, you fool!" the boy demanded.

It was then that Alex realized fully that something was
dreadfully wrong. He was still cold, there were still trees
around him—but he was being shaken by what looked to
be a knight in full battle gear.

"Hey," he said, "I was heading for Barbados!"

"If that is your word for hell, then indeed that is where
you will be going if you do not answer me!" the young
knight said angrily. "Must I cut your name and business
from you?"

Alex was too stunned to answer. Damn it, he'd wandered straight into Medieval England!

"Just let me sit here for a minute, okay?" Alex said.
"And stop shaking me!"

The knight shook him again anyway. "I should slit your
throat to save myself the trouble of having you on my
land."

Alex watched the boy lift his sword to do that, when
from the trees behind the knight there came the sound of
merry whistling. His captor released him so quickly that
he fell back again, smacking his head smartly against the
ground.

"Count yourself fortunate you are so near the border,"
the young man snarled, "else I would slay you and not be
sorry."

Alex was vaguely aware of the knight leaving the clearing. He stared up at the sky and let the rain fall on him
unimpeded. Well, at least it might eventually soak his shirt
enough to get it clean. No sense in time traveling when he
was looking less than his best.

His horse ambled over and nudged him with his nose.

"This is all your fault, Beast," Alex said. "If you
hadn't had a cold, I never would have gone into the house
and never would have found that damned map." Alex tried
to sit up, but it was just too much effort. "Just a few more
minutes," he promised himself. "I'll lie here for a few
more minutes."

He frowned as the singing came closer. This bozo
couldn't carry a tune in a bucket. The singing stopped

abruptly to be replaced by a gasp. Alex heard the snorting of another horse and the jingle of spurs. Alex stared up at the sky until the gray was blocked by the sight of another man in chain mail.

"This is merely hypoglycemic trauma brought on by lack of junk food," Alex said firmly, closing his eyes. "I need Twinkies. I need Moon Pies." He groaned. "Damn it, Jamie, I'll get you for this!"

"My lord, allow me to assist you."

"Go away," Alex said crossly. "And stop singing. You suck."

Soft laughter greeted his ears. "Good sir, you've had a fall that has addled your wits." The scrape of metal and creak of leather preceded a firm hand on Alex's shoulder. "Can you sit?"

"The question is, do I want to? And the answer is no."

"You certain do not wish to remain here. We are too near Margaret of Falconberg's land. Very fortunate are you that she hasn't sent one of her men to slay you already."

Alex was torn between wanting to laugh and wanting to cry. Damn it, why hadn't Jamie locked that map up? Or at least put some kind of decent warning on it? Alex decided that when he managed to make his way back to 1998, he would strangle his brother-in-law and enjoy every minute of it.

With a heavy sigh he opened his eyes and looked up. "Who the hell are you?"

The man's smile deepened into a grin. "Edward of Brackwald, at your service. Be you thankful I am so even-tempered, else your insults would have forced me to challenge you." His grin didn't fade. "Fortunately for you, I committed adultery with the countess of Devonshire a se'nnight past. My penance was to do a good turn for one in need."

Alex sat up with a groan and gingerly touched the back of his head. "If ever there were a man in need, it's me." He looked at Edward of Brackwald and winced. Chain mail. A surcoat. Cross-garters covering hose and boots.

Alex sighed. "Let me guess. England, right?"

"Ah, you're one of King Richard's lads, eh?" Edward said with a soft laugh. "No Saxony or Normandy for you and your kind. Though I daresay you speak English with the lack of skill only a Norman could boast of."

"My French is even worse," Alex sighed. He rubbed the back of his neck with his fingers, grimacing at the pull. "Well, the scribbles didn't lie. Twelfth-century England. Jamie did this one up right."

"Who is Jamie?"

"My brother-in-law. It's a very long story."

"I have nothing but time on my hands. Let us return to my brother's hall. I can see by the condition of your garments that you've been traveling for quite some time."

Alex didn't bother to correct him. "I'd really love to, but I need to be getting home." He closed his eyes and conjured up an image of Jamie's keep.

No, that wasn't working. All he could imagine was his fingers around his brother-in-law's throat. Satisfying, but not very positive. He turned his thoughts to his car, but all he could see was it wrapped around a tree with Zachary standing next to it looking sheepish.

'Tis my experience that a body cannot come home until his task in the past is finished.

Jamie's words hit Alex with the force of a wrecking ball, and he gasped in spite of himself. If what Jamie had said was true, the ramifications were startling.

First, he might not be able to get home until he'd done what he was supposed to do in medieval England.

Second, Jamie had been doing more research on the subject than was good for him.

Either way, Alex knew he was doomed.

"My lord?"

"I think I would appreciate some help. For the moment," he said, as a reminder to himself. He'd get rid of his headache, then he'd go home and kill Jamie.

"What is your name, my lord?"

"Alex."

"Of?"

Alex smiled. "Of Seattle, originally." Maybe it was just as well he didn't admit to any Scottish connections for the moment.

"Ah," Edward said wisely. "From the continent, I assume. Very well, then. Let us speak French. That will soothe my brother. He's of a mind that the English tongue should be executed along with its Saxon speakers."

Then he launched into a long, drawn out tale only a portion of which Alex caught. He might have been fluent in Gaelic and fairly respectable in Old English, but his French was so poor as to be almost nonexistent. Too bad he hadn't landed in ancient Rome. His Latin was excellent. Next time he would head over to that X. Damn, but he'd really wanted to wind up in Barbados. If he'd known the map was accurate, he would have worked a little harder at following it. White beaches, naked women, tasty rum. Why hadn't he headed north instead of south?

"Sir Alex? Or should I call you lord? Is your father a nobleman?"

Alex had the distinct feeling Edward wouldn't understand if he learned Robert Smith was a pediatrician. Best not to explain. Indulging in delusions of grandeur couldn't hurt, could it?

"My father is a very important man in, ah, Seattle."

"Ah, a nobleman. Then you are a knight?"

"Um, sure," Alex lied. No sense in labeling himself as a serf from the start.

Edward looked at Alex's feet. "But where are your spurs, Sir Alex? And your sword? By the saints, have you been robbed?"

"Well, not exactly. I sort of left them at home."

"Ah," Edward said, "I see. A dangerous way to travel, to be sure, but each man must act as he sees fit. Let us away to Brackwald and perhaps other gear can be found for you there."

"Sounds good to me," Alex said as he accepted Edward's hand up. He heaved himself up into the saddle and gritted his teeth at the flare of pain in his skull. Edward started babbling again in French.

"Not so fast," Alex begged. "My French is very poor."

"How can that be," Edward asked, "if your kin are from the continent?"

"I've been traveling most of my life."

Edward's ready smile was back. "Of course, Sir Alex."

Alex followed Edward's lead and poured all his energies into staying conscious. He was stuck and Jamie was responsible. Medieval England. Of all places.

Well, maybe it wasn't a complete loss. He'd hang around for a few days, soak up some culture and then head back to the faery ring. He would blink a couple of times, mumble a few old Celtic names as a spell, then be home. Jamie probably was just theorizing about that whole task in the past business. Damn him and his Scottish philosophizing. Alex pushed thoughts of bodily harm out of his mind and concentrated on his return. Maybe he'd manage to get home in time to head off Zachary before he went on his date with Fiona.

He felt himself begin to slip from the saddle, but found he didn't have the energy to do anything but go with it. He landed in the mud with a bone-jarring thump.

As his last coherent thought flashed across his brain, it occurred to him that Jamie and Elizabeth had been coming home after long weekends looking quite tanned. Alex had the feeling he knew just where they'd been going on their little overnighters.

Sunny Barbados.

And here he was in soggy old England.

Damn them both!

Two

❦

MARGARET OF FALCONBERG STOOD ALONE ON THE BAT-
tlements and looked out over the countryside before her.
She stood perfectly still in spite of the cold—and the fear
she refused to acknowledge.

As far as she could see was the land her grandfather had
claimed for his own. Her father had then held it in turn,
adding to it with his skill and wits. Now, despite how any
number of men might view things, it was all hers, to hold
or lose. And hold it she would, or die in the attempt.

She shielded her eyes against the setting sun. The view
might have been pleasing at another time. Even tonight it
might have been a fair sunset had it not been for the smoke
from fires which obscured the evening sky. Damn Brackwald! He grew bolder with each passing week. A fortnight
earlier he had stolen a quarter of her herd. The sheep had
been recovered but at a cost. The animals had been sent
back intact, herded by sheared, naked knights. The five
men had been so humiliated, she had released them early
from their yearly turn of service to her.

And now the peasant huts. Only two of them, but even
that simple act had displaced two families. Nine people
who had been given temporary shelter in the keep. It was
just another in a long line of injustices wrought upon her
and her people.

Perhaps what was most insulting was that Ralf of Brackwald did not simply come at her openly. That she could
have borne. Indeed, she could have retaliated with an of-

fensive that would have made the king himself take notice. But Brackwald didn't intend to lay siege to her holdings. He'd made it painfully clear that he found her too unworthy an opponent to do the like. Nay, petty thievery and thinly veiled insults were what he thought she deserved. He thought to wear her down, belittle her so much and for so long that she finally broke down and threw herself, weeping, at his feet to pray for his mercy.

"Bastard whoreson," she muttered under her breath. She would *never* give him the satisfaction of seeing her cower. She might have been born a woman, but she had the courage and stamina of a man. Neither her father nor her brothers would have given in to Brackwald; she wouldn't, either.

At least the fires were beginning to die out. There would be more. Brackwald wouldn't stop until he had all her lands and the very mail off her back. She lifted her eyes and shook her fist toward the east, where Brackwald lay. Let him try. He would find out that the last of the Falconbergs was not the least by any means.

"Lady Margaret?"

Margaret turned to find her garrison captain standing some ten paces from her. His weathered face sported a crusty frown. Margaret sighed silently at the sight. What new havoc had Brackwald wreaked?

"Aye?" she asked.

"The peasants have been settled and men sent to reconstruct their homes. A score more sheep were lost and a field looted. This was pinned to a tree with an arrow."

Margaret took the missive and struggled by the last light of day to make out the words she already knew would damn her.

Lady Falconberg,

Spare yourself and your people while you still can. A woman is not capable of standing against a man; something your father should have taught you. I have been

*gentle in the past, out of respect for your gender. I will
be gentle no longer. A month is all the time you have
to resign yourself to your fate. At that time I will expect
to see you open your gates and meet me, dressed properly. I have spoken to Prince John regarding the matter
and he has agreed 'tis well past the time you had a
husband to control you. He has agreed I should be that
man.*

Your servant,
Ralf de Brackwald

"My lady?"

Margaret looked at her captain. "He has gone to John,"
she said flatly.

Sir George made a noise akin to a grunt. Margaret
wasn't sure how he did it, but somehow he managed to
convey without words his opinion of her and her situation.
Unfortunately, she knew exactly what he thought, for he'd
told her often enough.

Each time she held a sword in her hands, she knew he
would rather she were holding a needle. Each time she
planned a stratagem, she knew he thought she ought to
limit herself to planning the meals. He believed her place
was sitting at a tapestry frame, not a council of war—no
matter that he'd watched her learn the arts of warfare right
along with her brothers, and no matter that she'd taken
over the running of the keep after her brothers, one and
all, had perished and her father fallen ill.

But, despite his thoughts, he had never once failed to
stand behind her. When her father had died, he'd turned
to her without so much as blinking, gone down on one
creaking knee and held out his sword hilts to her. To her,
a fifteen-year-old girl who had no spurs. She'd never said
it, but that act of trust had given her the confidence she'd
needed over the years to keep to the path she'd chosen.

And keep to it she would. Because of Sir George's fealty
and in spite of his grunts.

"Bloody hell," she said, staring out over her fields. "The wretch hasn't the spine to come against me openly. How dare he go behind my back to the prince!"

George leaned his elbows on the wall next to her. "You'll have to wed eventually, my girl."

"Not to him. George, he'd beggar Falconberg inside a year!" She shook her head. "Even if I wanted to wed, which I do not, I would never choose Ralf of Brackwald. By the saints," she said, slapping her hand down atop the rock wall, "I can hold this keep without a man's aid!"

George grunted. "Hardly among the skills a chatelaine should possess."

"But they're *my* skills, and I've paid dearly for the learning of them."

He inclined his head just the slightest bit. Margaret knew, because she'd been watching closely enough for it.

"A pity men are too stupid to appreciate my training," she said tightly, "else they might send me their sons to page."

George cleared his throat. "We do well enough with what we have. Now, how is it you see yourself escaping from this plight?"

"I'll stave him off 'til Richard returns."

"And if the rumors of the king's return are false?"

Margaret looked over her land and felt the noose begin to tighten about her neck. "Then I'll beggar Falconberg myself to buy John's favor. Bribing his henchmen has worked well enough so far. Not a one of them has ever demanded to see my father. If Ralf hadn't discovered the truth of it himself, I would still have my peace."

George shook his head slowly. "Lucky you are that both Ralf and John think your sire has only recently passed on. How we've managed to keep his death a secret all these years, I don't know." He looked at her. "It couldn't have lasted much longer, Margaret."

"Then I will find another way," she said firmly. "I have yet a pair of fortnights to think of a scheme. I must, for I've no intentions of wedding with that wretch. If only I hadn't bested all my potential allies in the lists—''

"My lady, my lady! Come quickly!" A young page stood at the tower door. "He's begun again, and we've had no time to prepare."

Margaret whirled toward the kitchen lad—nay, the page, she corrected herself. Timothy had seemed a promising enough young boy. The saints knew it wasn't as though she had that many to choose from. Others would scorn her for whom she trained as pages and squires, but she did what she could with what she had.

"My lady, please!" Timothy called frantically.

Margaret wanted to throw up her hands in despair. First Brackwald, now this. What could the day possibly throw at her more before complete darkness fell?

"Come, George," Margaret said, with a sigh. "We may as well descend before the hall is littered with piles of thread."

"I'll wait here," George said, clinging to the rock wall like so much stubborn lichen. "Just to save your place," he added.

"You will not," she said, grasping him by the elbow and pulling. "If I must go, then so must you."

"I'll be of no aid," George protested.

Margaret glared at him. "If I must endure the rampage that awaits below, then so must everyone else in the keep, including you."

She thumped down the stairs as quickly as possible, sprinted down the passageway with as much haste as her mail would allow, then descended the final set of circular stairs to the great hall. She pulled up short at the silence there, a silence only broken by George's huffing as he tromped down the steps behind her.

"Oof," she muttered as he plowed into her back. She threw out a hand to steady him and to cut off his apology. By the saints, she should have been more attentive. It was obvious by the looks of strain on the faces of those gathered in the great hall that she had indeed come much too late.

Baldric the Bard was atop his small stool, scratching his wrinkled, stubbled cheek. Aye, 'twas a very bad sign indeed.

Margaret started across the hall floor slowly, so as not to bring notice to herself, nor interfere with the bard's concentration.

He was rubbing his jaw now. By the saints, 'twas an action of evil portent!

"Flower?" she offered as she came to stand near his stool.

He looked down at her with annoyance and gave forth a disdainful huff.

"Sword thrust?" she ventured, watching his expression for any sign of hope.

He shook his head.

Margaret swept the other souls gathered there with a questioning glance. To a man, they looked back at her helplessly.

"My lady," Timothy whispered up at her, "he begun 'afore we could gather. No warnin' at all. Just up on his stool, he was, and halfway through 'afores I could blink."

Baldric looked down at her with a frown. "You missed the start of it," he announced, sounding rather put out.

Margaret dredged up a look of contrition. "Other concerns kept me, good Baldric."

"Womanly concerns," he said with a scowl. "By the sweetest of saints, you women are too troubled by such things!"

She nodded. "Aye, 'tis true. I beg sincere pardon, good sir, for surely 'tis my fault we were not properly gathered before you chose to delight us with another verse or two. Perhaps you would begin again?"

Baldric considered.

"My heart breaks that I did not hear the beginning of your song."

"Hmmm," he said, sounding slightly appeased. "Very well, then." He cleared his throat, hacked, and then spit over his shoulder into the fire.

Margaret resisted the urge to put her face in her hands and groan. Why one of her brothers hadn't taken Baldric crusading was a mystery. Not only had she inherited her father's estates, she'd inherited his minstrel—who was as daft as a duck. He had long since ceased to have any sense. The saints only knew from which font of madness he dredged up his verse forms, for they were like nothing she'd ever heard before. But create such verse he would, if it killed them all to listen to them.

"Ahem," Baldric repeated, looking at her sharply.

Perhaps he wasn't as daft as all that, Margaret thought with a wince.

> *One bright shining morning in June,*

he began,

> *Young Margaret her true love did seek.*
> *She roamed over hill and o'er dale,*
> *And in every small stream she did peek.*

"Sounds as if you've gone bloody fishin'," George muttered from behind her.

Baldric shot George a look that could have wilted a hardy bloom at fifty paces. Margaret heard her captain grumble something under his breath, then felt him move behind her, out of Baldric's sights. Margaret couldn't find fault with that, for she surely wished to do the same thing. By the saints, she had no stomach for listening to lays about her searching for a bloody lover!

> *Along came a man swathed in black,*
> *Who wielded his sword with great skill.*
> *He clapped eyes on our wandering lady,*
> *As searched she atop a small hill.*

> *As on yon sweet maiden he gazed,*
> *A smile soon replaced his dark frown.*

> *He said, off with us to a priest!*
> *And our Meg said . . .*

" 'I'd sooner drown,' " Margaret muttered.
Baldric harumphed, sounding thoroughly offended.

> *And our Meg said, I fancy men in brown!*

He finished the verse curtly, casting her a withering
look.
Margaret struggled to appear contrite, but it was all she
could do not to turn tail and flee. Why, by Saint Michael's
gnarled toes, had Baldric chosen this subject for his verse
today?

> *He offered our lady his sword,*
> *And told her to take him by force,*
> *For have her he would or feign perish,*
> *She said, "Nay, but I'll have your horse."*
>
> *So Margaret rode home with his mount,*
> *And thought the day quite a success,*
> *When home, she fed dear Baldric all the*
>   *sweets he loves best for he was a very*
>   *fine poet,*

Margaret held her breath. Already he was losing his
sense of meter. The saints only knew what would come
next.

> *Then she said to herself, I am . . .*
> *I am . . .*

Baldric frowned in concentration. The entire group
leaned forward in anticipation, as if by their very movement they could inspire him to greatness. Margaret leaned
forward as well, willing the old bard to find his last rhyme.
There'd be hell to pay otherwise. He scratched his cheek.

Then he took to rubbing his chin. When he started to flex his fingers, Margaret knew the time for action had come.

"I am blest," she said suddenly. "See, Baldric, there it is. Well done."

"That wasn't what I wanted," he growled. "It doesn't rhyme."

"Oh, but it does. Try it, my friend, and see."

He scowled at her, then turned his attentions inward and muttered under his breath for several moments, seemingly trying on different words to judge their fit. Then he put back his shoulders and said, proudly,

And she said to herself, such largesse!

"Of fine minstrelsy," he added modestly.

"To be sure, my friend," she said, clapping politely. When the rest of her household didn't do the same, she swept them with a glare. They immediately took up the cause. No matter that he'd botched that last line. For the most part it had been a tolerable piece of work, the subject aside. As if she'd ever search over hill and dale for a lover!

Margaret helped Baldric down from his stool. "Sit you at the table, gentle sir, and sweets will be forthcoming immediately."

"Two of every kind," he stated, every inch the proud bard having just finished a rousing evening of entertainment for his lord.

"Of course," Margaret agreed.

She started back to the fire to George's side, when she noticed the three new men who had rotated in for their forty days' service. They were young men, freshly knighted and sent by their fathers to serve her, though no doubt under much duress. They were staring at her as if she were naked.

Margaret looked down at herself quickly. The surcoat and over tunic hid her mail shirt well enough. She was certainly well clad. Perhaps they had never seen a woman in mail before. Idiots, she scoffed silently. She was the only thing that kept their holdings secure. Let them try their hand at holding all Falconberg lands, in spite of everything.

Perhaps it was her person that they found laughable. What did it matter that she stood taller than most men in the keep? Her father had been very tall, as had been her brothers. It was a family trait she was proud of. She viciously suppressed the urge to roll her shoulders down and slump. She was a Falconberg and Falconbergs stood tall. Her father had said that so many times to her that she could hear his voice in her mind as clearly as if he'd been standing next to her. She was not ungainly. Her men were to be blamed for being shorter than she.

She turned her face toward the hearth and strode over to her captain. He looked at her gently and she could see understanding in his eyes.

"Cease, old fool," she said sharply.

"Margaret . . ."

"Enough," she said. "Use your wits for something more useful than idle thoughts."

"After what we've just heard, my wits aren't worth using." He shook his head. "He was just as unskilled in your sire's day. Worse, he had more wind for speaking."

"Saints, you chatter as incessantly as he does," Margaret groused. "If you cannot think of a way out of this tangle, be you silent and allow me to."

George sighed. "A pity we've no army at our call to put forth a show of force. Perhaps then Brackwald would think twice about coming against us."

Margaret shook her head. "And what would we do? Capture his holdings?"

George smiled. "Why would we want them? He's used his lands so ill, there's nothing left of them."

"Aye, there is truth," Margaret agreed. "'Tis a wonder he manages to feed his household. I daresay he doesn't do it very well."

"No doubt," George said, "else you could hold his larder for ransom."

Margaret almost smiled, but her straits were too dangerous for jesting. A pity there was nothing Ralf valued. She froze, then slowly looked at her captain.

"He has Edward," she breathed.

George blinked, then his mouth fell open. "Margaret, you cannot think—"

"Aye," she said, feeling the weight lift from her shoulders. " 'Tis perfect!"

"You've gone daft," George exclaimed. "You cannot ransom him."

"And why not? I saw him wandering over my land this morn. If he's fool enough to do so today, no doubt he'll be fool enough to do so in the future. I'll nab him while he's napping under a tree."

George shook his head. "He was returning from London. He likely won't leave Brackwald once he's there."

"Then I'll go into Brackwald and fetch him out."

"By the saints," George spluttered, "have you lost your wits?"

"I daresay I've finally found reason," she said, feeling a surge of good humor flow through her. "If I have something that Ralf very much wants, then I possess something with which to bargain. When I greet him at my gates in a month's time, 'twill be with my blade across his precious brother's neck. We'll see just how quickly Ralf vows to leave me in peace when that sight greets him."

George sighed deeply. He looked at her from under his bushy white eyebrows and frowned. He sighed again, very heavily.

Margaret waited. Of course, she would do what she pleased anyway, but having George's aid would be a boon.

He frowned again, gave forth another deep, long sigh, then looked at her stealthily, as if he searched for a faltering of her will.

She continued to wait, unmoving.

"We'll have to bribe his gate guards," he grumbled finally.

Margaret fought not to grin. "Easily done."

"And we'll need a cooperative servant or two. I've been inside Brackwald only once and that was years ago."

"I've gold enough for that."

"And disguises."

Margaret wanted to laugh out loud with relief. For the first time in months she felt as if she might manage to keep her home.

"Done," she said.

George shook his head. "This is madness, Margaret."

"You have a better idea?"

He pursed his lips. "Your father would have me flogged if he knew I had agreed to this scheme."

Obviously, he had no better idea. Margaret smiled happily.

"He would instead praise you for your bravery. He loved nothing more than a good abduction."

He grunted. "Then I suppose we now know where you come by your notions. You'd best be off to the table and shore up your strength. We've much to do in the next few days."

Margaret nodded triumphantly and took her place at the lord's table. Her heart was so light she was able to completely ignore the stares of her new knights. Let them think what they wanted. Her permanent garrison didn't pay her any heed. The others would learn to do the same quickly.

For once, being either stared at in horrified fascination or ignored did not trouble her. Freedom was within her grasp. If she could thwart Brackwald once and for all, her life would finally be peaceful. She could concentrate on the training of her men and the efficient running of her keep. Aye, she might even feel safe enough to sleep without her mail on. That would be a welcome pleasure.

As she sipped at her wine, she turned over in her mind her memories of Edward of Brackwald. Where had the man come by such strange clothing? And such a breathtaking pair of aqua eyes?

It did not matter. He would be the coin she used to buy her freedom. She didn't have any more use for him than that.

Three

❧❦❧

ALEX SAT ON A STONE BENCH AND, FOR THE FIRST TIME in his thirty-two years, felt like a complete pansy. He'd never found himself in that situation before and he realized that he didn't care for it one bit.

He had four brothers, the elder two of which had gone to great lengths to toughen him up for kindergarten and the ensuing school years. He'd also played football and he hadn't been a wimpy quarterback hiding behind his front line. No sir, he'd been a defensive tackle and he'd taken down men twice his size. He'd never once backed away from a fight on the field or in the boardroom. But now things were different.

"Can you not be persuaded to lift a sword?" Edward asked, looking just as uncomfortable as Alex felt. "A light one, perhaps?"

"It isn't that I *can't* lift one," Alex said defensively, "it's that I *won't*."

"Ah, I see," Edward said, looking very confused. "Some sort of holy vow?"

"Something like that."

Edward gave him another perplexed look, as if Alex and his motivations were just beyond the comprehension of any sensible man. And they probably were far beyond the experience of any man from the year 1194. Alex shook his head with a grimace. Well, at least Jamie had gotten the time period right on his map. Alex would have to congratulate him the next time they met. It would be a great precursor to familial murder and mayhem.

Edward was still regarding him quizzically. Alex didn't dare enlighten him. After all, how was it you told a medieval knight that you had methodically taken over and destroyed multimillion-dollar companies for a living? That you'd had very shady dealings with people who were less than solid citizens? Probably even less comprehensible would be choosing to leave it all behind to turn over a new, more wholesome leaf. No, it was better just to let Edward think what he wanted about Alex's vows of chivalry.

But still, there might be some way to salvage some of his reputation.

"Look," Alex said, "I've fought in battles before."

"As you say," Edward said doubtfully.

"Numerous ones," Alex added. "Just a few months ago my brother-in-law and I laid siege to a keep in Scotland. There was a whole lot of fighting and rescuing going on. I know *how* to fight; I just don't do it anymore."

"Then how do you defend yourself?"

Alex shrugged. "I do my best to stay out of trouble."

Edward shook his head. "I won't pretend to understand this, but I won't press you further. Indeed, I admire you for the firmness of your convictions."

Actually, Alex thought, *you think I'm a wuss.* And he was beginning to think the same thing. But once he picked up a sword, it would be just that much easier to use it.

And his first thrust would be right through Ralf of Brackwald's heart.

Alex's teeth ached from gritting them too hard, and his hands were in knots from having clenched them too tightly. He'd been at Brackwald for over a week, and during that week he'd seen more injustices than he had in seven years of corporate piracy. Hell, Ralf even made *him* look lily white.

"Then perhaps instead of training we might seek something to ease our thirst," Edward offered.

"That I can do," Alex said, grateful to be on his feet and moving. He'd been sitting on a bench against the inner bailey wall all morning, watching Brackwald's garrison train. The men were almost as vicious as Ralf himself. How could Edward stand to come back to this?

The stench of the great hall hit Alex full in the face the moment Edward opened the door. Not even Zachary's room smelled this bad.

A loud smack echoed in the room, followed by a weak whimper.

"I'll teach you to refuse me," a voice snarled.

Alex's eyes adjusted to the smoky interior, and he followed the sounds to find Ralf pounding on someone. Alex thought it might have been a boy until he saw Edward's brother haul the being up by long hair. Rage flashed through him.

I'll never harm another human being.

His own promise to himself mocked him. Harm? He didn't want to harm—he wanted to murder! What right had Ralf to raise a hand to anyone? And to beat a woman senseless?

Alex felt his blood pressure go up several notches. He wanted to rush across the room and stop what was happening. But he couldn't. He'd ruined his share of lives, too. And if he beat Ralf senseless, was he any better than the volatile lord of Brackwald?

He looked at Edward. Edward's face was expressionless. Alex wondered how many times Edward had witnessed the same thing before.

Edward turned to him. "Let us be off. You'll want to see the countryside."

Alex looked back at the far end of the hall, where Ralf was finishing his work. Then he turned away, despising himself for both his rage and his lack of action.

A half hour later he was riding with Edward away from Brackwald, away from hell. Slowly he felt the anger seep from him. It was for the best. He couldn't interfere anyway. Who knew what sorts of ramifications he would cause if he changed Ralf's ways, not to mention what might happen if he killed Ralf with his bare hands.

His fingers flexed of their own will. The latter was almost too satisfying a thought.

He stared up at the gray sky and let the drizzle wash away his turmoil. He'd wanted a change of scenery. He could have been in Barbados, naked, tanned, and rummed. Lolling about in the surf with half a dozen equally naked, tanned, and rummed women. But instead, where did he find himself?

Facing his own demons in medieval England.

In February, no less.

"We're near Falconberg land," Edward remarked. "Perhaps we might manage to keep our heads even if we filch something to fill our bellies. I fear we left the keep without doing so."

"We didn't leave soon enough," Alex muttered.

Edward reined in his horse and looked at Alex gravely. "I cannot act against him, you know."

Alex smiled grimly. "I never said you should."

"Nay, 'tis my own heart that condemns me," Edward said.

"You couldn't change him, Edward. You'd have to kill him to stop him, and then you'd be no better than he is."

Edward nodded silently, then looked off over the field. "He wants this land, my brother," he said quietly. "And he's willing to do anything to get it. Even marry Margaret."

Alex couldn't help his smile. "Is she that bad?"

Edward looked at him and smiled in return. "Many years have passed since I saw her last, but I remember her being very tall and very full of choler." His smile faded. "She has humiliated my brother. I fear if he actually succeeds in forcing her to the altar, he will repay her in full measure."

"She humiliated him? How? I'm sure I'll enjoy hearing all about it."

"Supper first, my friend, then the tale."

Edward found a site he thought sheltered enough, then went in search of game while Alex busied himself with a fire. Finding dry wood was no easy task, but Alex had been an Eagle Scout after all. At least some of his training could be put to good use.

As he waited for Edward to return, he decided it was past time he returned home. He certainly couldn't do any good here. If he spent too many more nights under Brackwald's roof, he was going to do something he would regret. Screwing up history was not something he wanted going on his record. The list was long enough as it was.

Edward returned before long with a pair of hares. Cooking them took longer than Alex would have liked. He'd run into a Falconberg knight and had vivid memories of a boot digging into his ribs.

"Are we on her land?" Alex asked around a mouthful of spitted hare.

"Aye, but do not fear. We'll send a maid with a few coins tomorrow to appease her."

"Not up to going yourself?"

"And possibly find myself facing the woman over lances?" Edward shook his head, wide-eyed. "I wouldn't think of it."

"All right, let's have the whole story. What'd she do to Ralf?"

Edward leaned back against a log. "She entered one of his little private tournaments."

"I thought the church had outlawed tournaments."

Edward smiled dryly. "This is my brother we're talking about, aye? Why would he trouble himself over the possibility of excommunication when there was gold to be made or sport to be enjoyed? The king is locked away safely in Leopold's keep and John was in the south eating barrels of peaches. Ralf did as he pleased."

"And Margaret got herself invited?"

"Oh, nay, there was no invitation issued to her. Many unknown knights entered, hoping to hold others for ransom and fatten their purses. It was easy enough for her to arrive unnoticed.''

"And then what happened?"

Edward grinned. "She unseated every man she rode against, then finished off her day with the lance by dumping Ralf himself into the mud.''

"I don't believe it," Alex said, intrigued in spite of himself. Now, there was a woman with industrial-sized *cajones.*

"Ah, but 'twas Margaret indeed who took the field that day.''

"What a woman," Alex said. "And just how was it she revealed herself?''

"She took off her helmet, of course, and stood over Ralf as he wallowed in the muck.''

"I'm sure he was thrilled," Alex said dryly.

"I think he would have done her in if there hadn't been so many witnesses, and if she hadn't already had her blade to his throat. Word spread, of course, to the prince, who abruptly ceased sending men to Falconberg to court her.''

Alex shook his head in wonder. "Why should he, when she could best them all in the lists? She must be built like a tank—ah, a very large knight." Alex winced mentally. It was bad enough he was butchering French. Slipping in little Americanisms wasn't helping.

"As to how she is built, I cannot say. 'Tis most difficult to discern a woman's figure when she is sporting chain mail. Not that I'd dare try." Edward shivered. "She'd cleave me in twain for daring the like, no doubt.''

"Then what makes you think Ralf will ever succeed in marrying her? It sounds as if she's already let him know what she thinks of him.''

Edward looked at him for several moments in silence. Then he shook his head, a puzzled frown on his face.

"Where exactly is Seattle, Alex? Have you no king?"

Well, this ought to take some explaining. Alex knew there was no way he could tell Edward all the truth, but maybe some of it would help.

"Seattle is a very long way from here, and no, we don't have a king. I've been living in Scotland for the past little while, though."

"Ah," Edward said, as if that had suddenly cleared up the mystery for him. "Then I marvel at the fineness of your garments. I've never been north myself, but I understand your countrymen are somewhat on the, um, free-spirited side. That must be why you don't understand Margaret's danger," Edward said, nodding. "You see, my friend, she has no choice. If the king wills her to marry Ralf, she must do so, else he will take away her lands."

"Doesn't Richard know what kind of man Ralf is?"

Edward shrugged. "He has been gone from our shores for many years. What happens in such a small shire is likely of little import to him. All that matters is how well he thinks Ralf can hold both Brackwald and Falconberg. If he thinks it can be managed, he will not hesitate to command the alliance."

"Doesn't Margaret have any other family?"

"Nay. All her brothers, save the eldest, went crusading. The eldest was gored while hunting, and her sire fell ill several years later. She's held the keep alone for the past year."

"How old is she?"

Edward shrugged again. "A score and five? Too old to be wed easily. She could only be desired for her lands. I know 'tis the only reason my brother considers her."

Poor Margaret. Alex didn't even know her, but he felt sorry for her. No woman deserved that. She might have a face like a sow and the cuddliness of a porcupine, but she was a woman, after all.

Edward sighed and threw his last bone into the fire. "Again, 'tis none of my affair. I've heard rumors that the king's ransom has been paid. He will likely return to England to see to his affairs here, and I mean to rejoin his company then." He looked at Alex. "Do you care to come? We could use another blade in the French wars—"

He stopped, then grimaced. "Forgive me. I forget myself and your vow."

"Never mind. I need to be getting home anyway. I think I'll start out tomorrow."

Edward nodded. "Fortunate are you to have only one more night to spend in that hellhole. I envy you."

Alex scattered the remains of the fire and watched as it died out. He couldn't blame Edward for his sentiments. He was very lucky that he had a home to go to where there was love and affection.

And it was well past time he started his own family. He nodded to himself as he swung up into the saddle. So he'd put away his sword for good. That didn't mean he couldn't lay a siege. Fiona MacAllister had no idea what she was in for. He was a much better prospect than Zachary. He could cook. He had his pilot's license and owned half of Jamie's Lear. He could fly her anywhere she wanted to go and have enough change left over to take her out to dinner. Maybe he'd go home and fly her to Barbados.

That was the *only* way they were going to get there. They certainly weren't going to be two-stepping it over any of those damn X's.

IT WAS EARLY evening before he and Edward returned to Brackwald. Alex left the dinner table as soon as he could and escaped to his room before he inflicted bodily harm on his host.

He knew he was fortunate to have a private chamber, and he had gone out of his way to thank Ralf for it. So what that the room was smaller than his bathroom at home; it had a door and a makeshift mattress. He couldn't have asked for more.

He lay down on the straw mattress and put his hands behind his head, staring up at the cracks in the wooden ceiling. What was going on above him was very distracting. By the grunts and moans, he had little trouble figuring it out. Man, what a life.

But what else was there to do? Speculate on how many

of their peasants would die of malnutrition this week? How much food they could wring out of their soil this month? Who would lay siege to their holdings this year? Alex let out a long sigh, immensely grateful he had been born in another century. At least all he had to worry about was his car getting dinged in the parking lot and whether or not his mutual funds were yielding what they should. How removed the majority of twentieth-century men were from the day-to-day struggle against death. Here it was inescapable. Alex could understand why Jamie had such a forceful personality. How could he not, when the Middle Ages had been the environment to shape his character? Even Elizabeth, who had only been in Jamie's time a few months, was more difficult to push around than she had been in her youth.

Alex pulled a scratchy sheet over the lower half of his body, feeling the faint hint of a draft. It was no wonder Margaret of Falconberg was such an Amazon. Was she truly as formidable as Edward's stories had made her sound? Alex sincerely hoped he never met up with her. The memory of almost being decapitated by one of her young knights was enough for him. Heaven help him if he ever ran into the old battle-ax herself.

He fell asleep, dreaming of Fiona MacAllister's lovely freckles.

MARGARET YANKED GEORGE back into the shadows behind her.

"You stay here," she commanded softly.

"By Saint Michael's knees, have you gone daft?" he returned in an angry whisper. "*You* stay here. I've been inside Brackwald."

"I move with more stealth."

"Barely."

She glared at her captain. By the saints, he was easily old enough to be her sire. As if he could move about without his bones creaking! "Now is not the time for insults." She threw her reins at him and started off, only to be jerked back by the collar of her tunic. She whirled around to face him, ready to give him full measure of her irritation. The look on his face stopped her words abruptly.

"Watch your back, my girl," he said, looking genuinely concerned. "The last of the Falconbergs wouldn't want to end up in Brackwald's dungeon. I'd likely kill myself trying to free you."

Margaret felt an uncomfortable unfolding in her chest. So George had unbent far enough to show her concern. That was hardly reason enough to weep. She took a step backward, away from him.

"I will return posthaste with young Edward and we will be on our way."

Without another look, she crept quietly along in the shadows. She was taking a very great chance moving about with her mail still on, but it was the only way. She would be as quiet as she could be, but if it came to a fight, she wanted to be protected.

Her plan of attack was simple: walk through the great hall as if she belonged there, on up the steps and down the hall to Edward's chamber. One of the stableboys had found her coin to his liking and had divulged everything from the layout of the chambers to the locations of the food stains on Ralf's favorite surcoat. She wondered if he might have given her such tidings even without payment. No one she had spoken with had seemed overly fond of their lord.

She slipped inside the great hall and paused, astonished. She had never seen a place in a more wretched condition. Margaret pitied the poor souls who had to endure living there. It would be a very cold day in hell before Ralf of Brackwald set foot inside her hall. She would never allow her people to live in this kind of filth.

Ralf certainly seemed to be free with his drink, judging by the number of drunken knights sprawled out on the floor and on benches. Margaret picked her way over them, working her way slowly toward the steps. Not a soul challenged her.

She made her way up the stone steps as quickly as she dared, then started down the corridor. She counted three doorways, then stopped before the fourth. Her palms were damp and she wiped them on her legs in annoyance. This deed was simple enough for a child. She was no child; this was too far beneath her to cause her any worry.

The room was unbolted. Margaret sent a prayer flying heavenward. A bolted room was not impossible to enter, just difficult. The less noise she made, the better.

She slipped into the chamber and shut the door softly behind her. The ceiling boards gaped so badly that candlelight from above spilled down into the room as if it had been sunlight. She had no problems making out the long, obviously masculine form stretched out carelessly on the pallet.

She drew her sword and approached the bed.

ALEX WOKE TO the feel of cold steel across his throat.

"Move and they'll be scrubbing your blood from these sheets for weeks," a husky voice hissed.

Alex didn't even attempt a nod.

The blade was pressed more firmly against his skin. "Do as I say or you'll be naught but food for the hounds. Understood?"

Alex inclined his head only enough to communicate his compliance. The blade was removed and, like lightning, he had a hold of the wrist holding the sword. He jumped from the bed and jerked his would-be murderer under a shaft of dim light.

"You!" Alex exclaimed. He immediately recognized the brown-eyed lad who had tried to kill him his first day in the Middle Ages.

The tip of a knife produced from heaven only knew where pressed against his bare belly. "I'm very skilled with this. Do as you're told and you'll come to no harm."

"After you promised to kill me before?" Alex asked, almost amused. The lad was maybe an inch shy of six feet but slender. No match for a man of six-foot-four and athletic-club prowess. He may have been determined never to pick up another sword, but that didn't preclude him from disarming someone else. Gently, of course.

The lad growled in frustration. "I am not in the habit of lying. If I say you will come to no harm, that is precisely what you will *not* come to!"

"All right already," Alex said. "You tell me what you're up to, and I'll think about going along for the ride."

The lad gasped. "As if you had a choice!"

"I do, my young friend. I assume you're here without Ralf knowing of it. All I have to do is set up a howl and you'll be spending your free evenings in the dungeon."

The knife drew blood. Alex winced at the sting of it.

"Your brother would be powerfully grieved to find you dead. If you force me to kill you, I'll certainly do it before you even let fly a squeak."

Alex's eyes widened in surprise. "I'm not Edward."

The lad snorted. "You are as poor a liar as your brother. Now, dress and do it silently. You waste my time and time is precious."

Alex released the lad's wrist and folded his arms over his chest. "Look, kid, I'm *not* Edward of Brackwald, and I'm not moving an inch until you tell me what you're up to."

"I'm going to hold you for a bloody ransom!" the lad exclaimed. "Does that ease your mind any?"

"I don't know," Alex said with a grin. "How well do you treat your captives?"

"Well enough. Find your clothes and don them. I'll not repeat myself again."

Alex hesitated only a moment before he complied. At the very least he would be dressed. There was far too much of him exposed for comfort. No sense in giving the boy any handy targets to cut off.

He had hardly pulled on his boots and leather jacket before he felt the point of a sword in his back. So much for escape. A false move and that sword would go right through his very expensive leather coat, between his ribs and into his heart. It'd been a while since he'd dealt with a hotheaded, blade-wielding brat.

"Downstairs. Carefully. Remember that I wouldn't think twice about killing you."

"You keep saying that," Alex said conversationally, "but I'm inclined to think you haven't the balls for it." He eased out the door calmly, sure he would regain control of the situation once he was out in the courtyard. So what if all those men in the hall had passed out from too much ale; the gate guards would still be at their posts. Wouldn't they?

He was ushered out of the great hall and toward the stables. Alex went willingly until they reached the stable entrance, then he turned.

"This is far enough. I think you're in way over your head here. Kidnapping is a punishable offense."

The lad ignored him. "George!" he whispered urgently. "Make haste!"

A voice behind him answered. "Margaret, you were to ply him with wine first!"

Alex's mouth hung open. "Margaret?"

"Silence, fool!" his captor exclaimed. "I'm fully prepared to turn you into a woman if need be."

He didn't doubt that. But the indignity of it all! Good grief, he was being kidnapped by a woman!

The sharp pain of a sword hilt against his temple caused him to stop thinking abruptly.

"Damn you," he gasped, feeling the world begin to fade rapidly. "At least make sure . . . you bring . . . my horse. The chestnut . . . gelding." Beast wouldn't appreciate being left in Ralf's stables. Alex groaned and threw his arms around Margaret of Falconberg to break his fall.

And with his last coherent thought, he realized that it really *was* hard to tell a woman's shape when she was wearing chain mail.

Four

❧❧❧

MARGARET STOOD AT THE FOOT OF THE BED AND LOOKED down at the man who lay in her father's chamber. He was as still as death. She chewed on her lower lip anxiously, then forced herself to stop. This was not the time nor the place to turn into a giddy maid.

She rounded the bed confidently, then put her finger to the man's neck. His pulse was steady and strong, like the rest of him. Her back still ached from trying to put him on his horse. She was sure it was his horse she had taken; the beast was just as arrogant and cheeky as his master. Even with George's help, getting the man back to Falconberg had been sheer misery.

The faint light of dawn forced its way through the cracks in her shutters, but it was too poor a light to aid her at present. She lifted the candle from the small table near the bed and moved it closer to her captive. Just the sight of his face made her stomach tighten painfully. She had the sinking feeling she had just made the greatest mistake of her life. Perhaps another woman would have been delirious over the beauty of the man's face, for 'twas indeed beautiful. Ruggedly so. And he certainly took pains with his appearance. His face was clean-shaven. To her horror, she found herself itching to run her fingers along that jaw and feel its strength.

She frowned, disgusted with herself. As if she had time to moon over a man!

Then again, why not? Just because she ran her keep with

an iron fist didn't mean she couldn't appreciate the sight of a fine-looking man as well as the next woman. And this was a man to be appreciated over and over again. She would indulge herself for a brief moment. She allowed herself few enough pleasures that this was surely permissible.

His face was beautifully sculpted with a fine, straight nose, prominent cheekbones, and a generous mouth. The night before she'd watched that mouth go from being taut with well-controlled fear to relaxed with laughter. The insolence of the man to laugh in her face when she had informed him he was her prisoner. She'd been half tempted to stick him just to show him she wasn't to be trifled with. But to mar that finely fashioned form? It had seemed almost a sacrilege.

And then there were his clothes to add further to the mystery. She held the candle over him. What strangely fashioned hose he wore. The cloth was like nothing she'd ever seen before. She reached out a hand to touch it. It was heavy blue cloth, but surprisingly soft. Indeed it was worn almost clear through to the skin at his knees. And even through the cloth she could feel the heat of his skin and the hardness of his muscles.

She pulled her hand back as if she'd been bitten. As if she should stand there and fondle the man!

She turned her attentions to his other garments. He wore a shirt made of much the same stuff as his hose, though it appeared to be crusted over with some kind of substance. She didn't want to investigate further. Perhaps he was clumsy when he ate. She couldn't reconcile that with his clean-shaven appearance, but men were strange creatures.

His cloak was passing odd. It was cut close to his body and hardly reached his hips. The garment seemed to be fashioned of very fine leather. Why had he not had it sewn to be of some use? What did it serve him if it did not cover his backside at least?

Margaret stepped away, her hand trembling. The truth was hard to accept, but she knew she could avoid it no longer. She put the candle back on the table and hugged herself, trying to stifle the tremors that were growing inside her. Damnation, but she'd made a disastrous tangle of things. And it all had to do with the man before her being so infinitely pleasing to the eye.

The Brackwalds being, of course, notoriously ugly.

Even if the man's insistence that he wasn't Edward hadn't haunted her, his comeliness would have.

Just who was it she had tied up in her father's chamber?

Her only consolation came from knowing the man was obviously someone of importance. If he'd been but a mere knight, he wouldn't have been sleeping in Ralf's finest chamber. Margaret swallowed, ignoring the dryness of her mouth. Hopefully he was someone Ralf would want returned. The saints preserve her if the man was one of John's cohorts. The prince would surely not look kindly on her having stolen one of his men to further her plans.

She left the chamber and walked wearily down the steps to the great hall. George would have to be told, but she didn't think she was up to it at the moment. What she wanted was a cup of ale. Solutions to her problems would have to come later.

SHE HADN'T GULPED down but two fortifying cups before she knew the time for solutions was at hand. She heard her handsome prisoner bellowing even before one of her serving maids came flying down the stairs into the great hall, as pale as a ghost.

"My lady," the girl said breathlessly, "there is a man in your late sire's chamber!"

"I heard him," Margaret said wearily. "As I'm sure the servants have been gossiping already about who he is, tell them he's a guest. He won't be here long."

The girl curtsied and fled. Margaret mounted the steps, feeling her mail weigh more heavily on her than usual. She hadn't reached the door before George was huffing down the passageway behind her.

"I'll subdue him," George panted. "He's a bit on the spirited side. I'm surprised, as I'd heard Edward was most mild mannered."

"It's not Edward of Brackwald," Margaret admitted reluctantly. "I made a mistake."

"*What?*" George shouted, aghast.

Margaret winced. Between George and the prisoner, she began to wonder if the walls would start to crumble.

"Enough!" she shouted, pounding on the door. She threw George a dark look. "How was I to know? He told me he wasn't Edward, but I assumed he was lying."

"Margaret, how could you have been so foolish?" George exclaimed.

"I didn't do it apurpose," she said stiffly. She ignored her captain and faced the door. "Prisoner?"

"What?" came the angry answer from within the chamber.

"Stand you away from the door."

"You tied me to the damned bedpost!" the man thundered. "How am I supposed to even *get* to the door?"

Margaret drew her sword and unlocked the door. She entered the chamber cautiously. The man was standing on his bound feet, hunched over and looking very uncomfortable. She had fettered his arms behind him and then secured another rope between his wrists and the bedpost. She surveyed her handiwork with an approving glance.

"Cut me loose!" the man demanded.

Margaret bristled at the arrogant tone of his voice. "When it pleases me," she said curtly, closing the door behind her.

He jerked on the ropes, and she backed up a pace reflexively. It was no wonder she'd had such a hard time getting him on his horse. He was huge. He was easily a hand taller than she and just that much broader. And he had a formidable temper. Anger was written in every line of his body, from his crushed-together ankles to his mussed hair. If he could have gotten his fingers around her throat, he would have no doubt enjoyed himself immensely.

Margaret gritted her teeth. Not only had she abducted the wrong man, she'd had the grave misfortune of abducting one who was infinitely more dangerous than she had expected. Saints, she had been lax!

"Are you going to cut me free, or stand there dithering?"

She stiffened in spite of herself. The insolent wretch. She put the tip of her sword into the wooden floor and folded her hands on the hilt.

"I do not dither. If I cut you loose, I will likely find myself murdered, or worse," she said coldly. "I am not a fool."

"Of course not. That's why you so carefully checked the identity of your kidnapee."

"Kidnapee?" she echoed. Where was this man from? Not only was his French poor, he seemed to have trouble remembering many of his words. That was surely the only explanation for the way he mixed together French and an accented dialect of the king's English.

"I'm talking about myself," he said impatiently.

"Ah," she nodded. "I see." What an odd way he had of speaking. Was he one of Richard's allies from the continent? The very thought chilled her to the marrow. The king would have her head for this!

"Margaret!"

She blinked at him. "What?"

"Cut me loose!"

She shook her head. "I don't dare."

She had to think. If he were one of Richard's allies, he would return to the king with the tale of her foolishness, augmented greatly no doubt. The saints only knew what would befall her then. Despite his captivity, Richard's arm was still very long.

She resheathed her sword, then paced to the window and back, ignoring her prisoner's repeated attempts to attract her attention. She could not set him free. The risk to herself was too great. The saints only knew how the king would have his envoy choose to punish her. She could be stripped of her lands. She knew she held them by only a tenuous grasp as it was. Worse, Richard could force her to wed with anyone he chose—as if he hadn't already attempted that! Only this time she knew he would brook no disobedience. By the saints, he could force her to wed with Brackwald and see that she did so. A kinder thing to do would be to see her hanged, but even that wasn't too pleasant an alternative.

She looked back at her captive. He was glaring furiously at her. She couldn't set him free. It was obvious she couldn't retain him in the keep forever. She sighed deeply. It was a drastic measure to take, but she saw clearly it was her only choice.

"I regret this," she began, "but I fear I must kill you."

The man didn't even blink. "Don't be an idiot," he said, through gritted teeth.

Margaret folded her arms over her chest and looked at him coolly. "I think it is the best choice."

He growled in frustration. "You said I would come to no harm. Don't compound your mistake by adding murder to it. Cut me loose, then I'll leave and we'll pretend this never happened."

"I've rethought the matter and changed my mind. The king would never forgive me for this."

"What does Richard have to do with this?"

Margaret winced. This man was on such familiar terms with the king that he called him by his Christian name? She groaned inwardly. Aye, he would have to die. Perhaps she could bury him where no one would find him. The king was very far away, and news traveled slowly. His Majesty would believe that his friend had merely had an unfortunate accident and been lost on the roads. Ruffians abounded, as did disgruntled Saxons who had lost their homes. Aye, there were many who could be blamed for such a tragedy.

"Margaret, what does Richard have to do with this?" the prisoner demanded.

"You would know that better than I," she said tartly.

"I would?" he asked, looking surprised. "What do I know of Richard?"

"You speak of him as if you were dear friends," she said, trying to be patient, but finding his pretend ignorance very tiresome. "Surely you see now why I have to do away with you. Should you return to the king with this tale, he would take away everything I hold dear. It would not surprise me to have him put my neck in a noose."

He looked even more surprised than before. "Why would he do that? You just made a mistake. Surely he would understand that."

"Cease with your ploys. You know him far better than I and you are well aware of what a monarch does to disobedient vassals. I will do you the courtesy of a last meal, then I'm afraid you will have to die."

"Damn it, I am *not* one of Richard's buddies!" he exclaimed. "Hell, I'm not even English!"

That caught her off guard. "You aren't?"

"No, I am not." He paused for a moment, then frowned. "I'm from Scotland." He looked at her as if he expected her to say something.

Margaret shrugged. "A barbarian from the north. Richard has spies everywhere."

"I'm not a spy. If you kill me, you'll kill an innocent man."

Margaret shook her head, amazed at his tenacity. She had to admire it, for she would have done the same in his place.

"Whatever else you are," she conceded, "you're a very good liar. I will bring you a meal in an hour's time. Enjoy it, for 'twill be your last."

"Unbelievable," he said, rolling his eyes. "Fine. Go ahead and kill me. My blood will be on your hands. Innocent blood," he said pointedly.

Margaret looked at him again, trying to judge. He was

lying, wasn't he? What man wouldn't lie to save his neck?
He cleared his throat pointedly and she looked up out
of habit.

"Aye?"

"I don't suppose you'd allow me to pass my last few
hours in freedom, would you? To be quite frank, I have a
few unmentionable needs to take care of."

She hesitated. Cutting him loose was out of the question,
at least his arms, anyway. But she could sympathize with
his desire to relieve himself. And it *was* the least she could
do for a condemned man. She pulled her knife free from
her belt. The man was perfectly still as she approached.
She paused a few paces away.

"A score of men wait without. Harm me and you'll die
without your meal."

His pale blue eyes hid no deceit. "I doubt you'll believe
this, either, but I've never laid a hand on a woman. To
hurt her," he added with a trace of a smile.

Margaret snorted. His meaning was entirely too clear.
She could hardly hold him responsible for his charm,
though. Only a fool would have been able to resist him.

"Perhaps I am a fool after all," she muttered under her
breath as she knelt before him and cut the bonds around
his ankles. He grunted and swayed the moment the blood
rushed back to his feet. She stood and put her hand out to
steady him. How solid he was to the touch! She jerked her
hand away, then fetched a chamber pot. She set it on the
floor next to him.

"There. That should serve you well enough."

"And how do you propose I use it? Are you going to
help me?"

To her horror, Margaret felt color flood to her cheeks.
She couldn't remember the last time she had blushed, but
she knew it hadn't been long enough in the past. And damn
the man if he wasn't wearing a mocking smile. She took
her knife and jammed it into the table next to him.

"Use that, knave," she said, spinning on her heel and
stalking to the door.

"Alex," he called after her.

She didn't want to turn around, but she did. "What did you say?"

"Alex. My name is Alex. And that knife isn't going to do me any good where it is."

"Then find a way to move it," she threw over her shoulder as she jerked open the door and bolted out into the passageway. The man was mad! How could he even for a moment think that she would be fool enough to cut him free?

She made her way quickly down to the kitchens. The sooner the man was fed, the sooner he would be dead and one less thing she had to worry about.

Five

❧❀❧

ALEX STARED DOWN AT THE CHAMBER POT LONGINGLY. Here was just one more reason he should have gone to Barbados. At least if he'd been captured, he would have been naked—which certainly would have solved his current problem.

The door opened slowly. Alex looked up, intending to give Margaret of Falconberg a very long human rights lecture. Only it wasn't Margaret. It was a grizzled old warrior whose crusty expression was enough to make Alex back up a pace. If he could have backed up a pace. He tried anyway and ended up sitting down on the bed with an ungraceful thump.

The man closed the door behind him softly, and Alex wondered if he would even get that last meal. He wasn't ready to meet his Maker yet. Fiona MacAllister needed him. That didn't begin to address what would happen if Zachary were left at home too long with all of Alex's toys. His brand new Range Rover would be trashed inside a week.

"Damnation," the man said, stroking his bewhiskered chin. "She's bloody right about it."

"I beg your pardon?" Alex said.

"You certainly aren't Edward of Brackwald."

"No, sir."

Alex didn't call too many people "sir." Some men just seemed to demand it. Like the man currently giving him the once-over. Alex felt like he was sixteen, being grilled on why he'd broken his curfew. He had the most ridiculous urge to give a list of plausible reasons as to why he found himself currently loitering in medieval England.

"Your name, young man?"

"Alexander," Alex replied promptly. "Sir," he added, suppressing the urge to salute as well. Not that he would have been able to. He cast another longing look at the chamber pot.

"Alexander of what? Who is your sire? Who's man are you?" The questions came at him like machine-gun fire. Military men hadn't changed, so it seemed.

"Ah," Alex stalled, wondering where to start, "it's a long story."

"And I have nothing but time." The man folded his arms over his chest and waited.

Well, this just wouldn't do. Alex knew he would have to make up something, obviously. What sort of reception would a Scot receive anyway? He racked his brains to try to remember just how relations had been during Richard's day. William Wallace hadn't come on the scene yet, so maybe the Brits just looked upon the Scots as their barbarian cousins in the north. It could be worse.

"My father," he said, deciding on mostly truth, "is of Seattle."

"Seattle?" The man shook his head. "That is not familiar."

And it won't be for some time, Alex added mentally. "It isn't in England."

"France? The continent?" The older man rubbed his chin thoughtfully. "Then why, by all the saints, is your French so poor? One would think you hadn't spent much time in Phillip's country."

"True," Alex agreed. "I haven't been to Seattle in many years. I lived for a time in New York, ah, York," he amended, "but mostly I made my home with my sister and her husband in Scotland." That was a little lie, but it was better than dropping a time-travel bombshell. "In a little village near the Benmore Forest. My brother-in-law is laird of the clan MacLeod.'' *Or will be in a hundred years or so*, he added silently.

The man chewed on that information for an eternal moment, then spat out another volley of questions.

''What are you doing in England? Why are you begarbed in such a fashion? Why were you at Brackwald?''

''I'd fallen off my horse when Edward found me. He offered me the hospitality of his brother's hall. Such as it is.''

''You were in Brackwald's finest chamber.''

''That isn't saying much.''

A flicker of amusement crossed the man's face, but it was gone as quickly as it had come.

''To where were you riding?''

Alex gave him a weak smile.

''I was out riding on my brother-in-law's land, and I took a wrong turn and wound up in England.''

''Indeed.''

''It's the truth,'' Alex said. ''I didn't mean to come here, and if you could see your way clear to cutting me loose, I'll get back on my horse and be off Falconberg soil in an hour.''

The man stared at him for another eternity, and Alex had no doubts his fate was being decided right then and there. The old soldier could have drawn his sword and cut him down where he sat.

Without warning, he motioned for Alex to stand. Alex did so, but he was less steady on his feet than he would have liked to be. He'd faced career death before, fending off angry CEOs, pit-bull attorneys and judges with expensive contempt-of-court rulings on the tips of their tongues. He'd also found himself along with Jamie in a Scottish dungeon with open wounds on his back and his sword out of reach, and yet he'd lived to tell. Only that had been back in the days when he'd still carried a sword.

Now he felt very vulnerable. He didn't want to die. He had the feeling, however, that no amount of fast talking was going to influence the battle-seasoned warrior coming toward him with a grim-as-death expression on his face.

"Turn around."

"Are you going to stab me in the back?" Alex said with as much bravado as he could muster.

The man laughed shortly. "Watching you sneak looks at that bloody pot is giving me the urge myself, lad."

Alex felt his wrists come free of their bonds, and he groaned in spite on himself as the blood rushed back to his hands. He turned around.

"Thank you. I think."

The man actually smiled. He turned and walked toward the door, then looked back at Alex.

"George, formerly of York, lately of Falconberg at your service," he said, inclining his head.

"York?" Alex choked.

" 'Tis a rather large place," George offered. "Perhaps that is why we've never met."

"Right," Alex said weakly. "I'm sure that's it."

"I'd make use of that pot, my lad, before the lady Margaret returns."

"Great," Alex muttered. "I'll get comfortable just in time for her to cut off my head."

Sir George actually smiled. "Like as not, you'll talk your way out of that."

And with that, he was gone. Alex sighed in relief. One confrontation successfully negotiated.

He turned his back to the door and had no sooner applied himself to the task at hand when the door behind him opened and a woman gasped.

"Merciful saints above, you're untied!"

"And very busy, thank you," Alex threw over his shoulder. "Do you mind?"

The whisper of a blade coming from a sheath was answer enough.

"Lady Falconberg," he said, through gritted teeth, "let me pee in peace, would you?"

There were several other gasps, and Alex felt himself

beginning to blush clear down to, well, down far enough. Wonderful. All he needed was an audience.

"Margaret, let the lad be," a well-worn voice said from the hallway. "I daresay he isn't going anywhere at the moment."

Thank heavens for Sir George and his understanding of the male persona. Alex finished, tucked himself away, did up the buttons of his jeans, and turned to face his audience.

There was Margaret, of course, and behind her a handful of servants. They were all staring at him with expressions varying from horror to intense interest. Margaret's fingers were twitching on her sword hilt. Alex almost commented on that when he saw that one of the less horrified-looking women was carrying what could have been mistaken for dinner. He gave her his most winsome smile.

"For me?" he asked hopefully.

The woman with the platter started forward, but Margaret stopped her by putting her sword out like a railroad crossing arm.

"Use your wits, Alice," Margaret said sharply. "There is a knife by his hand. Wish you to meet your end thusly?"

Well, that was irritating. Alex started to give Margaret a lecture on the finer points of his character, but he was cut off by a tremendous rumble in his stomach. No time for talk.

He yanked the dagger from the little bedside table and walked across the room. Ignoring Margaret's suddenly raised blade, he handed the dagger to her, hilt first.

"Now may I eat?" he asked politely.

Without waiting for an answer, he relieved Frances of the wooden board she carried and walked back to the bed. He set the board on the table and sat down. He didn't care who watched him. He didn't care what fate held in store for him. When it came to dinner, he never let anything distract him.

Lunch and dinner meetings had always been a total wash for him. How was he supposed to concentrate on piracy when smoked salmon fettuccine was demanding his full attention? Or when finely roasted fowl with little herbed veggies was sending little wafts of scent his nose's way? And at the moment he didn't care if Margaret had plans to use him to fertilize her garden. If she would just wait until he'd finished eating, he wouldn't argue with her.

"It looks like you have a better cook than Ralf," he said, looking over the roast chicken and planning his assault. "Vegetables, too. How nice."

He spared Margaret a glance and saw she was clutching her sword in one hand and what could have been used as an eating knife in the other. She didn't look as if she had any intentions of relaxing her death grip on either. Oh, well. When in Rome . . .

He tore off a hunk of chicken and popped it in his mouth. He closed his eyes and chewed. Ah, looks were certainly not deceiving. The chicken was delicious. Nicely seasoned. It didn't contain much dirt that he could discover. Alex sampled everything, closing his eyes periodically to more fully enjoy the experience. He did look up once, just to see if there might be some sort of liquid to wash everything down with. A rotund woman was standing by the door, holding a bottle by its neck. She had on a food-splattered apron, and Alex wondered if she might be the cook. Now, this was a woman whose acquaintance he needed to make immediately.

He rose, ignoring Margaret's renewed bristling, and walked slowly across the room to the bottle-toting woman. He gave her his most innocent smile. He had several smiles in his repertoire. His favorite was his pirate's smile, but he had the feeling he'd better save that for Margaret later, while trying to talk his way out of losing his head. For now, innocent and faintly desperate would have to do.

"May I, good woman?" he said, holding out his hand and endeavoring to look thirsty.

The woman blushed and handed the bottle over without hesitation.

"Are you responsible for this heavenly meal?" he asked politely.

"Aye, milord," the woman said, beaming her approval on him. She was obviously someone who took it personally when bodies consumed her offerings with relish.

"If I thought I could," Alex said, dropping his voice to a conspiratorial whisper, "I'd steal you away from Falconberg to come cook for me. You have a gift."

The woman blushed clear to the roots of her hair and turned toward the door.

"Out," she commanded her help. "He can't have had his fill yet. Down to the kitchens for something else!"

Margaret made a sound of intense disgust. Alex winked at her before he returned to his makeshift table, took a swig of wine, and applied himself to the rest of his dinner. He chewed and swallowed, methodically working his way down to bones and bare wooden plate.

When seconds came, he polished them off with just as much gusto. All right, so it wasn't the Four Seasons. It was better than anything he'd had so far in medieval England, and it was a far sight better than the unidentifiable gruel he'd subsisted on while haunting fifteenth-century Scotland with Jamie.

"Is it possible you've finished? Or should I search the larder for something else?"

Margaret was done watching him eat it seemed. He took one last healthy swig of wine, then put the bottle down and pushed his table away.

"Finished. And it was delicious. Thank you."

She dismissed his apology with a frown. "I've heard last meals always do taste better than others."

Alex leaned back against the wooden headboard and looked at his captor. Margaret was tall and she looked very annoyed, but those were the only things Edward had gotten right. Whoever had started the rumor that Margaret of Falconberg was ugly needed to have his eyes checked.

Alex started his perusal at her feet. Her boots were scuffed and worn. This was a woman who meant business.

The thought crossed his mind that, had things been different, they would have made a very dangerous team. He had the feeling Margaret could be just as ruthless as he was. She had the scuff marks to prove it.

Leather cross-garters held her mail securely against her legs. That had to be less than comfortable, but she didn't seem to be shifting around as if she found it so. Her surcoat came down to her knees. It and a tunic covered her body, and, of course, more mail. It was virtually impossible to tell her shape.

But he could certainly look all he wanted to at her face. The woman was nothing short of beautiful. Her hair was dark and pulled back off her face severely in a tight braid. It was long. He'd seen how far down her back it went. That had been a surprise. He would have expected her to have cut it off as it had to be a detriment in battle. He chewed on that very telling fact for a moment or two. For all her posturings as a warrior, Margaret still hadn't been able to give up that last concession to femininity. It was very interesting and he promised himself more thought on it later—when he'd managed to avoid the gallows.

He looked at her face again. What did she need with a lance when she could have knocked men over with her looks alone? He wondered if she had any idea just how appealing she was. Her eyes were dark, her lips full, her cheekbones beautifully sculpted. If she hadn't looked so incredibly irritated, he would have gotten to his feet, pulled her into his arms, and kissed her with every ounce of passion in his unprincipled pirate's soul.

"Are you quite finished?" she asked curtly.

Alex couldn't help but smile. "I could look all day, actually."

She bristled. Alex didn't think she could look any more offended, or ill-at-ease.

"If you had to defend this keep, you would also dress as I do," she bit out furiously.

Well, of course. Alex opened his mouth to say as much, but he wasn't fast enough.

"I will not be scorned by a prisoner!" she exclaimed. "I care nothing for what you think. Look your fill, fool, and mock if you will. I'll be the last thing you see before I send you off to hell."

She waved her sword menacingly at him. Alex stared at her, suspicions blooming and blossoming in his mind. Well, there was definitely more to Margaret than he had thought. He turned her words over in his mind. Quickly. She wasn't moving yet, but her fingers were twitching. So, she thought he was mocking her. Was that what she got from her own household? Why should she care?

Alex had the feeling that underneath all that mail and bluster was a very frightened, very lonely young woman. A young woman who very possibly needed help.

Damn. There went his chivalry again, rearing its ugly head.

A body cannot come home until his task in the past is finished.

Well, maybe this was why he'd found himself in medieval England. Maybe it was nothing more than a chance to help someone who just didn't have anyone else to turn to. He gave Margaret his best tell-me-all-your-secrets attorney smile and patted the bed next to him.

"Come and sit. Let's talk."

She gasped in outrage. "What kind of fool do you take me for?"

"Tie my hands if it makes you feel any better. I just want to find out what you're up against. Maybe I can help."

"How? By betraying me to Brackwald?"

"I already told you I have no ties to Brackwald. Edward found me after you'd just about slit my throat and helped me by taking me to his hall. I have as little use for his brother as you do."

She hesitated. Alex could see the wheels turning. And then her sword lowered until it rested point down on the floor.

Alex scooted back on the bed and sat cross-legged with

his hands resting in plain sight on his knees.

"I give you my word I won't move. At least pull up a chair. I'll bet you've been on your feet for hours."

"Since dawn yesterday," she said, then clamped her lips shut and glared at him.

Alex smiled to himself. This was one tough cookie.

"Have you eaten?" he asked.

"Supper, last eve," she muttered. She looked at him in irritation, as if she wanted to behead him for even dredging that much out of her.

Alex got off the bed slowly. He held up his hands and carefully walked toward the door.

"Don't finish me off yet," he said. "You'll enjoy it much more on a full stomach, I'm sure."

He opened the door, faintly surprised she let him do it, poked his head outside, and bellowed for her cook.

The good woman couldn't have been far because she appeared at the top of the steps almost immediately.

"Aye, milord?" she asked breathlessly.

"Perhaps a meal for Lady Falconberg?"

"Aye, milord," she said, curtsying and propelling her substantial self back down the stairs.

Well, he had the older set all sewn up. Now, if he could just work the same magic on the younger. At least Margaret was still in the same place. She could have been advancing on him with blade bared.

Alex set up a table, pulled a chair up to it, and returned to his seat on the bed.

"Please sit, Margaret," he said. "I give you my word I won't move."

"And what good is your word?"

"Well, it hasn't been much good before, but I've turned over a new leaf. Made a change," he clarified at her puzzled look. "I'm not a liar."

"I daresay most all men are liars," she muttered. She sounded fairly convinced of that, but she had loosened her grip on her sword. Alex took that as a good sign.

"Maybe the ones you've known before. But I'm different."

He didn't want to get his hopes up, but she looked for the briefest of moments like she would have really liked to believe him. He could have sworn she was on the verge of coming across the room and sitting when the door burst open and Cook trundled in with a small contingent of kitchen help.

A meal was laid quickly and after another curtsy and blush, Cook departed, her helpers trailing after her like obedient sheep.

Where he had failed, food succeeded. Margaret came and sat. She laid her blade across the table and kept her knife in her hand.

"I'm very handy with this," she said, waving her dagger at him.

"I'm sure you are and I'll bet you've worked hard to become so."

She threw him a suspicious look, as if she weren't sure what the underlying meaning of that was, then turned to her meal and started to eat.

She wasn't enjoying it. Alex never let anything get in the way of good food, but Margaret obviously didn't have his finely honed skill. She chewed, but it was methodically and without enthusiasm.

"Not good?" he asked.

Margaret looked down at the wooden trencher and her expression was one of faint surprise, as if she hadn't really seen what she was consuming.

" 'Tis edible."

Alex shook his head mentally. Poor kid. Maybe her face said twenty-five, but her eyes said fifty. Alex hardly dared speculate on the burdens she'd already been forced to bear in her short life. If what Edward had said was true, she'd been keeping a roof over her head and land-lusting men outside her gates for at least a year. Heaven only knew what kind of childhood she'd had. Had she ever just had time to play? Had she ever known the pleasure of beautiful clothes? Had anyone ever come to get to know her, just plain Margaret? What a waste!

Alex liked to think he wouldn't have been that stupid. If he'd been the baron's son next door, he would have dated her the moment he could, then showered her with every possible extravagance. He would have taken her traveling, shown her marvelous places, exposed her to exotic tastes and smells, heaped beautiful clothes and jewels on her until she was buried in them. He would have made her laugh. He would have stripped away her clothes until they were skin to skin, then he would have loved her, time and time again—

He rubbed his hands over his face and shook his head. Good grief, as if he really needed to get involved with anyone in the past! Especially a shieldmaiden who would just as soon skewer him as look at him twice.

He looked at her to find that she was watching him. Whatever she had seen in his face had obviously affected her, because she shoved her chair back and grabbed her sword.

"Fool," she snapped.

"Huh?" Alex said.

"I dress this way because I must," she hissed. "Who is it you think keeps this bloody roof over your head?"

"But—"

"Think you *you* could do the like?"

"Well—"

"And my father was very tall, too!"

"There's nothing wrong with—"

"I am not ungainly!"

And with that, she ran for the door, opened it, and slammed it home behind her.

The key turned in the lock. Alex shook his head. Even distracted she was thorough.

He got up and began to pace. What a telling conversation that had been—one-sided though it was. Did she honestly think he looked at her and found her unattractive?

And, more important, did it really matter to her what he thought?

Well, at least she hadn't done him in. Maybe the next time he got within shouting distance of her, he would tell her that he didn't think she was ungainly. Even with her mail, she was very graceful. And he liked tall. Kissing short women gave him a neck ache.

Kissing?

He groaned. He was losing it. Margaret was not a woman to be trifled with. He couldn't make love to her and then walk.

And he would have to walk. Once he figured out what he was supposed to do, he *would* have to leave. And since he couldn't stay, that meant he couldn't get involved. He would do his best to help her, then he would round up Beast and head back to Scotland. Hopefully too much time hadn't passed in his own day. He didn't want Zachary getting a jump on him in wooing the grocer's daughter.

Though somehow, after seeing Margaret of Falconberg up close and personal, wooing Fiona MacAllister just didn't seem all that exciting. She wouldn't have been caught dead in chain mail. He had his doubts she could hold down the store, much less a fort.

But that was okay. He didn't have a fort to hold down. Nope, the twentieth century was the place for him, and he'd get back to it just as soon as he'd done his medieval duty.

The last thing he needed was a twelfth-century shield-maiden to complicate his life—and what a complication Margaret would be.

Six

MARGARET DUG HER HEELS INTO HER STALLION'S SIDE and leaned forward, the lance balanced in her right hand. She struck the quintain directly in the center. She sat up a bit too quickly and lost her smug smile abruptly as the counterweight caught her full in the back. The blow sent her flying face-first off her horse. Fortunately it had not rained the night before, and she landed only in dirt, not mud.

She turned her head to the side and breathed heavily, ignoring the dust she managed to inhale. Dust and manure were good smells. At least they were honest smells. Not like the perfumed missive she'd received that morn. Damn Ralf of Brackwald to hell!

She felt herself being rolled over carefully. She lay on her back and stared up into her captain's angry blue eyes.

"Are you trying to kill yourself?" George bellowed. "Concentrate or cease!"

Margaret suppressed the urge to say something satisfyingly vulgar. Instead she accepted his hand up, collected her lance and her shield, and walked away. As she did so, she realized how out of character that was. She never left the field unvictorious.

It was a sure sign she was not herself.

What was even more disturbing was the reason why she was so distracted. She wanted to believe it was because a messenger had delivered threats from Brackwald earlier. Aye, that was surely the case. She was angry, and justifiably so, at Brackwald for ruining her morning and she'd gone to the lists determined to work out that anger. Of course it had nothing to do with her captive.

Nothing at all.

One of her knights came and took her shield and lance. Several others murmured encouraging words as she passed, but she didn't pay them heed. She spoke to her men, 'twas true, but only to train them. Chatting pleasantly was not something she permitted herself. Let them find their camaraderie amongst themselves. She was their liege-lady, not their drinking companion. She wanted their respect, not their friendship.

Come, sit. Let us talk.

Damn that Alex. As if she had time to sit and speak of nothing!

Just who was he, anyway? Alex of what? Who was his sire? He came from Scotland, but who were his people? For all she knew, he could be a bastard some stone mason had sired on a kitchen wench. But, saints, it had been a fine coupling if he was what they had produced.

She clapped a hand to her head. Merciful saints above, she was going daft! The man was pleasing to the eye, she would give him that, but did that mean she must needs moon over him like a love-struck calf?

Ah, but to sit and talk. What an astonishing notion. To lay aside her cares for even an hour, to have speech with someone who did not depend on her for protection and sustenance. To just be Margaret and not Lady Falconberg. What a heady pleasure that would be.

"My lady?"

She stopped at the steps leading up to the great hall, turned, and looked at Sir Henry, George's second in command. The young man was her finest knight. Even so, she had never been comfortable around him. They were of an age, and likely should have had something in common. Yet he would never meet her gaze.

Not like Alex.

Despite herself, she found herself standing taller. Alex

certainly hadn't looked at her as if she were little more than a man. Perhaps she wasn't as uncomely as she'd been led to believe.

"Aye," she said finally, realizing Sir Henry was staring through her.

"Brackwald's messenger waits without the gates still. Do we reply, or will you have him wait longer?"

Margaret considered. She could tell the man to come back on the morrow, but heaven only knew the havoc he might wreak in her countryside. On the other hand, she wasn't about to make a hasty reply until she'd learned the truth of the matter before her. Ralf had sent word, demanding the release of his "beloved Lord Alexander." Either Alex was a liar, or Ralf was laying hold of yet another tale to run to Prince John with. Margaret knew she could ill afford a false move now.

"Bring him inside and put him in the guard tower. See he's fed well, but keep him under guard. He will return to Brackwald whole. Is that understood?"

Sir Henry bowed and walked away, not having met her eyes even a single time. Was she that hard to look at?

Saints, what was happening to her? A se'nnight past she wouldn't have cared had someone not looked at her. Having Alex in her home had driven what few wits she still possessed straight from her.

She entered her hall and slowly walked past the hearths, considering Ralf's missive. Had Alex lied to her? Was he indeed a beloved friend of Ralf's?

It had been almost a se'nnight since she had fled his presence. She hadn't even had the courage to return to speak with him. Alex, however, had done nothing untoward to any of the servants she'd sent to bring him meals. Even George had braved the lion's den repeatedly, emerging to announce he found Alex to be a "fine young man with a brilliant head for strategy." That fine young man hadn't demanded to be released, though she had heard that he was becoming increasingly annoyed at being confined.

She couldn't blame him. She would have been driven mad by the first day.

She mounted the steps. After hesitating for only a moment at her father's chamber where Alex was, she continued on her way to hers. She stood at her table and looked down at the missive which lay there. Should she take it to him and confront him with it? And if she confronted him, could she bear to hear he had lied to her?

She stood and dithered for another quarter of an hour before she realized just what she was doing. By the saints, she had never dithered in her life! Snatching up the parchment, she strode purposefully from the room. She opened the door to her father's chamber and entered.

Alex was standing at the window. He turned around slowly, then leaned back against the stone.

"Are you hurt?"

Margaret looked at him blankly.

"The quintain," he said impatiently. "It bested you three times this morning."

Margaret realized with a start that her sire's chamber did indeed overlook the lists. Why she hadn't remembered that before, she surely didn't know.

Alex had been watching her. To her horror, she felt her cheeks begin to flame. He had to have been staring at her long enough to see her go flying face-first into the dust. Saints, what a fool she must look!

"I was distracted," she said stiffly.

He folded his arms over his chest and smiled.

"By anyone I know?" he asked.

"As if you would distract me," she said, trying to sound as haughty as she could. Somehow, it wasn't working very well, and her voice came out as more of a squeak.

"I wasn't suggesting myself," he said, his eyes twinkling. "But now that you bring me up—"

She drew her sword and brandished it. "You be silent!"

He only laughed. If she'd had the spine, she would have run him through. Somehow, she just couldn't bring herself to do it. It would ruin his clothes. Aye, that was a sensible enough reason for restraint.

"Does everyone in Scotland dress as you do?" she blurted out. His clothing was powerfully odd, especially his hose. His tunic, however, was clean. Perhaps one of the maids had seen to it.

"How nice of you to notice what I'm wearing." Along with his clean tunic, he was now wearing an infuriating grin.

"I didn't come to discuss your clothing!"

"Then what did you come here to discuss?"

"This," she said, shoving the missive at him. "Read it, then endeavor to convince me Ralf lies. I vow I think you're the liar here."

Alex gently pushed aside her blade and took the piece of parchment. He held it up to the light from the window and stared at it for several minutes. Finally he shook his head.

"Lousy penmanship."

Margaret wished he would stop using those foreign words. "Penmanship?" she echoed.

Alex smiled grimly. "The way he writes."

"I'm certain Ralf's scribe fashioned this. Ralf can barely sign his own name."

"Then his scribe is a lousy writer. I can't make out half of what he says."

Margaret looked at him closely. "Perhaps it is that you cannot read."

"I can read," Alex replied. "It's just this medieval Norman French that's throwing me."

"Medieval French?" Where by all the saints had this man learned to speak? Perhaps the Scots were more uncivilized than she'd thought.

"Just ignore me," he said with a sigh. "Come here and help me puzzle out some of these words. I am assuming you can read them well enough."

"Of course!"

"I meant no offense, Margaret." He stepped closer to

the window. "Please come over here. I promise not to bite."

Margaret made the grave mistake of looking at him. The sunlight fell down upon him softly, as if it were pleased to caress something so perfectly made. It seeped into his dark hair, warmed his strong features, rested on his muscled form. She noticed, with a start, that he was clean-shaven. She frowned. It had to be Cook's doing. The woman, who Margaret never dared cross, had obviously fallen completely under Alex's spell. Margaret could hardly blame her. How could a body look into those pale eyes and not feel a little faint? Were they blue? Nay, perhaps green. Margaret stared into them, fascinated by their color. Perhaps a bit of both blue and green.

Her gaze dropped to his mouth. Saints, what finely fashioned lips he had. She had the overwhelming urge to reach up and touch them. Were they as soft as they looked? She chewed on her own lip to distract herself. It only made matters worse. She'd kissed her father and brothers, but not on the mouth, and definitely not with what she was feeling at present. Teeth appeared between those tempting lips and Margaret realized with a start that Alex was laughing at her.

With a growl of mortified, hapless fury, she whirled away from him.

She didn't get far. The lout had the temerity to grab her by the wrist! She jerked back toward him, her knife already drawn in her free hand. The missive crumpled violently as Alex grasped both the parchment and her wrist with his other hand. He held her hand well away from his belly. A pity, as her fondest wish was to embed her blade there.

"I wasn't laughing at you," he said quietly.

She stared up at him, open-mouthed. "How did you—" She clamped her lips shut. As if she should allow him to know what she had been thinking! She glared at him. "I care not what you think."

I know," he said, his expression grave. "I know you don't care what I think, Margaret. But for the record, I was laughing at myself. Because I now realize how my food must feel when I'm looking at it.''

Suspicions as to what that might mean developed furiously in her mind, but she chose to ignore them. He hadn't been laughing at her. She would take that and call the battle a standoff.

"You are a very strange man, Alex."

"I know. Now, do I dare let you go?"

"As if you could keep me captive," she said haughtily. She ignored the fact that his hands were like vises around her wrists. She would be damned if she would admit she'd met her match in this man. If he just hadn't distracted her with those bloody lips of his, she would have had the jump on him and she wouldn't have found herself practically standing in his embrace against her will.

"You're right, Lady Shieldmaiden," he said humbly. "Would you be so good as to put away your blades and read this to me?"

She knew she should have been offended at his title for her, but somehow with the way he said it, it sounded almost like a compliment. She nodded. He released her wrists and she put away her sword and dagger. He stepped back into the alcove, and she followed him to the window. He smoothed out the parchment carefully and held it up to the light.

"The 'Lady Falconberg' part I understand," he said. "Now, what is this business here about grief and distress?"

Margaret had to agree with Alex about Ralf's scribe's penmanship. It was very poor.

"He says he is suffering terrible grief and great distress over the theft of his beloved friend Alexander of Seattle." She looked up at him. "Is that where you are from? In Scotland?"

"Actually it's not in Scotland. It's on another continent."

Well, he wasn't telling all the truth. And where Seattle actually was she couldn't have said. The man was obviously hiding something. Margaret frowned. A finely fashioned face had turned her reasoning to mush. She would have to be more careful.

"What are you doing in England?"

"I was out riding and took a wrong turn."

"You're lying."

He smiled. She flinched. She wished he would stop doing that. It was becoming increasing difficult to keep up her guard when he looked at her like that.

"I'm not lying," he said. "I really did take a wrong turn. I never meant to wind up here. But here I am, and I think I'm here to help you. So, finish this ridiculous letter, Margaret, and let's see what can be done."

She sighed and looked at the letter again. "He says if I do not deliver you within the se'nnight, he will have no choice but to take drastic measures to accomplish your recovery. He speaks of vengeance. I've no doubt he will also send a messenger to Prince John to snivel out his sorry tale."

Alex smiled. "He didn't say exactly that."

"Nay, but he meant exactly that, the miserable wretch. Now," she said, taking a pair of steps backward and putting on her most intimidating frown, "what say you of this foolishness? Are you indeed his beloved Alexander?"

"No, I'm not."

Margaret liked to believe she had skill in discerning a man's character. She could readily believe Alex was lying about where he came from, but she was equally ready to believe he wasn't lying about this.

"Then you truly have no ties to Brackwald."

He shook his head. "Edward just offered me help. I was planning to leave the day after you so kindly spirited me away. If I'd had to stay any longer in Ralf's hall, I would have killed him."

Margaret understood that completely. It also occurred to her that perhaps she shouldn't have stolen Alex so soon. He would have solved all her problems for her if she'd just left him at Brackwald another few days.

"He really is unbelievable," Alex said with a shake of his head. "Doesn't he think we'll talk? Or is he counting on you having thrown me in the dungeon, gagged and bound?"

"Likely so."

"Your reputation proceeds you, then."

Suddenly, and without warning, weariness descended. Margaret sat down. She shook her head at her own actions. She never sat. For as long as she could remember, she had been on her feet, in command of herself and her men. Perhaps this Alexander of Seattle was a demon made of flesh and was sapping her very will to go on. She watched him as he sat down on the stone bench that faced hers. The sun continued to fall on him, leaving her in the shadows. She smiled without humor.

"My reputation, I fear, will not save me this time."

She tried to keep up her show of spine, but, for the first time in years, she couldn't manage it. She put her head in her hands and sighed.

"By the very saints of heaven," she whispered, "I wish it would."

She felt a hand on her head. It surprised her so, she jerked back and narrowly missed smacking her head against the stone. She looked at Alex in shock. He held up his hands.

"I was just trying to help," he said.

"I need no aid of that sort," she replied, shaken. She couldn't remember the last time anyone had touched her. That Alex had dared the like did not surprise her. The man couldn't string two words together without throwing in something from a foreign tongue. Perhaps his manners were as haphazardly put together as his language.

"No one touches me," she managed, trying to regain her balance.

"That's too bad. You could stand some touching. But," he added, "maybe later."

Margaret let her hand fall away from her dagger hilt—only then realizing she had the blade halfway from its sheath. She pressed herself back against the wall and stared at the man facing her. She had no idea what to say. She didn't want his help. She certainly didn't need his help. But she was so very tired.

"What does Ralf mean by vengeance?" Alex asked.

Margaret forced herself to shake off the bleakness. "More of what he's done already. Murder my serfs, steal my cattle and sheep, humiliate my knights."

One of Alex's eyebrows went up. "Humiliate your knights? What has he done to them? They seem to be very skilled. Perhaps not as ruthless as Ralf's, but more than able to hold their own. Did he best them on the field?"

Margaret sighed deeply. "He ambushed several of them, sheared them like sheep, and sent them home naked."

"He didn't."

"Ah, but he did. I haven't had the heart to rotate them in for their forty days' service since."

"What a slimeball."

"Aye," she agreed. "A slimeball." Heaven only knew what that was, or what language it came from, but it seemed to fit Ralf very well.

"So, how did you retaliate?"

She shrugged. "What could I do? Murder his serfs? Risk my own men to take his? I did nothing. I cannot kill innocent people."

Alex smiled at her. Margaret could have sworn the sun began to shine more brightly as a result.

"I take it that's why I'm still alive?" he asked.

She met his pale aqua eyes unflinchingly. "Aye, my lord. That is why you are still alive."

"You're not as ruthless as I thought, Margaret."

She rubbed her hand over her face. "I used to be. As of late, I scarce recognize myself."

"Hmmm," he said.

"I haven't been sleeping well," she retorted.

"I see."

"I've been distracted!"

He only smiled.

"And not by you," she snarled.

"That's too bad. You've certainly been distracting me." He smiled at her again, a marauder's smile that sent heat flooding to her cheeks. She knew how his supper felt, because he was looking at her in that same devouring way.

"By the saints," she spluttered, "I am not a leg of mutton, for you to be regarding me thusly!"

"Oh, Margaret," he said, shaking his head with an amused smile, "you really are something else."

She glared at him. But she didn't rise to her feet and flee the chamber. She was weary. Aye, that was it. If she'd had the strength, she would have hied herself down to the lists immediately, just to escape Alexander of Seattle's questionable self. She surely had no desire whatsoever to remain and listen to his foolish words, nor to melt under his heated gaze.

But she had no strength, so she remained where she was.

"You're very beautiful," he said, still wearing that mercenary's smile.

"And you're a fool."

He shrugged. "Maybe so. But I'm not blind."

She had to leave before the last remaining shreds of reasoning she possessed slipped away from her. Saints, this was a danger she had never anticipated. No man had ever looked at her thusly. Or perhaps they had, and she hadn't been interested enough to notice. Obviously Alex was not a man who found himself ignored very often.

"If you've nothing better to speak than empty words," she said, grasping for something to say, "then I will leave you."

He stood up suddenly. "Let's go walk. I think better when I'm on my feet."

Before she could even open her mouth to agree, for she, too, thought better while moving, he had pulled her up and was towing her toward the door.

"Which way out?" he asked.

"Left. Down the stairs."

She found herself following him—likely because he had

hold of her hand and seemed determined not to let go. Margaret was overwhelmed enough by the sensation to let him lead her where he willed it. His hand was warm and secure around hers. As she walked next to him across the great hall, she felt for the first time in years that she might not be ungainly. Alex was at least a hand taller than she. It was an amazing thing to have to look up to meet his eyes.

He was also broader than she, even with her mail on. It was the most ridiculous thing she'd ever experienced, but she actually felt fragile. Protectable. By the saints, it was a pleasurable feeling! To feel as if she could actually lay aside the burden of being the defender, even just for a few moments.

"—outside the gates?"

She looked up at him. "Forgive me. You were saying?" What had he been saying? Had he been speaking this entire time?

There went that infuriating grin again. Margaret scowled up at him, but he only laughed.

"My, my, but we *are* distracted," he said.

"I have a stone in my boot."

"I'll help you take it out—"

" 'Tis none of your concern," she said, backing away from him. She didn't back far. He wouldn't let go of her hand.

He smiled. "I asked if we could walk outside the gates. Is your sword enough, or should I call for another guard for you?"

"I could have a sword fetched for you." Surely with arms like that, he could wield a sword with ease.

He shook his head. "No swords for me, Madam Shield-maiden."

"Then you cannot wield one?"

"Can, but won't. It's a long story. Now, shall we go?"

"I have time to hear the tale," she said, digging in her heels.

"You may have the time, but I don't have the desire.

Maybe I'll tell you over supper some night. Now, let's go.''

Stubborn man. Margaret vowed she would have the tale when she so pleased. Perhaps later. When she was less distracted.

She walked with Alex out through the gatehouse and across the drawbridge. She felt her men staring at her and knew she was blushing furiously, but she could do nothing about it. Alex didn't seem inclined to release her hand, nor was she inclined to pull it away. She liked very much how it felt there.

Alex stopped at the top of the road that wound down the hill. He looked out over her lands, then turned and smiled at her.

''Your land is beautiful.''

She had to agree. The keep was perched on a hill in the midst of other rolling hills, though the others were not so tall. The land was rich and lush. Her fields were productive. Her serfs were well-fed and, for the most part, contented. She worked hard to see them protected and treated fairly.

The late-winter sun came out from behind a cloud and shone down on the fields. Planting would begin soon enough. Spring was her favorite time of year. She loved to see things grow.

But all that would cease if Brackwald had anything to do with anything of hers. She sighed deeply. Her holdings would look as wretched as his did inside a pair of years. The man had no head for managing farmland. His peasants were half-starved and ill-treated. He used the soil 'til it could bear no more, then continued to plant. She shook her head. Nay, she could not allow Brackwald to have this beauty before her.

Alex let go of her hand, walked away a few paces, then returned. He stared out over her fields, rubbed his jaw with his hand, then took to pacing again.

He stopped suddenly, and turned to look at her.

''The king has seen your lands, hasn't he?''

She nodded.

"Hmmm." He walked away again, then came back. "How does he feel about Ralf?"

She shrugged. "I know not. Brackwald is loyal enough to him to have sent the king gold for his crusades, though unwilling to go himself. He seems very thick with the prince, but that is likely something he will have hidden from the king. Not that it matters. The gold means a great deal."

"You lost your brothers crusading, didn't you?"

She looked away. "Aye. I have no love of it. Holy wars I do not understand."

She felt Alex take her hand again. "I'm sorry, Margaret. It has to have been hard this past year, doing all this on your own."

She looked at him, wondering where he'd learned that. "Did Edward tell you as much?"

Alex nodded. "He said that your father had just recently passed away and that you've been keeping things going since then."

She felt a strange sense of relief that she had managed to fool the rest of England for so long. And along with that sense of relief was another, more foreign desire to inform Alex how long she'd been at the helm just to see how he would react. Would he be impressed? There was only one way to know.

"My father died ten years ago."

His jaw went slack. "You're kidding."

Margaret looked up at him and frowned. "Kidding?"

He looked stunned. "It means to jest. You can't be serious. You've kept this keep running for ten years? Alone?"

"Who else would do it?"

"Oh, Margaret, honey," he said, squeezing her hand. He looked at her and shook his head. "I'm so sorry," he said gently. "I can't imagine what you've gone through. It must have been very hard."

He sounded so sorry for her that she found herself feel-

ing the same way. By the saints, it *had* been difficult. She
had rarely let herself dwell on just how dangerous a thing
it was she did. If the crown had ever learned of her sub-
terfuge, she likely would have been hanged for it.

For the first time ever, she felt tears begin, tears of fear
and sorrow. Saints above, she hadn't cried when her family
had died. And she had certainly never wept from the burden she'd carried. But to do so now, some ten years later?
It was madness.

The next thing she knew, she had been gathered against
a solid chest and wrapped in Alex's strong arms. That she
could have borne. But when she felt his hand skimming
over her hair, reason fled and she wept in earnest. She
clung to him and bawled like a child. She wept for her
father, who had done the best he could with a girl-child
he hadn't known how to raise. She wept for her mother
who had died giving her life. She wept for brothers who
had teased her and loved her.

And she wept for herself. For the childhood she hadn't
had. For the husband she would never have. For the ex-
quisitely comforting embrace she enjoyed at present, but
which she knew she could not keep. Saints above, if she'd
had any idea her foolish plan to kidnap Edward of Brackwald would have gone this awry, she would have agreed
to wed Ralf months ago!

She pulled away. It fair killed her to do so, but she knew
she couldn't remain. She dragged her sleeve across her
face and turned away. There was no sense in humiliating
herself further by having Alex see her in this state.

"Forgive me," she said in a choked voice. "It has been
a most trying day."

She felt hands on her shoulders. Alex turned her back
around and, despite herself, she allowed it. She looked up
into his eyes and almost started to weep again. That
wouldn't do. She straightened her spine.

"Aye?" she asked, trying to sound curt.

He only smiled. He brushed away her remaining tears
with his thumbs.

"You've had to do it all by yourself for so long," he said gently. "Will you let me help? Just this once?"

"What can you do?" she whispered.

"I'll think of something." He took her hand. "For now, let's just send Ralf's messenger back to tell him that I'm here as your guest. Ralf will make of it what he will, but it will buy us some more time to think of a better plan."

"I suppose," she said slowly. "He will of course think I'm lying."

"Let him. He'll send someone else to investigate, and by then we'll have a better plan in place. Let's go back home and at least do this much. We'll worry about the rest later."

And Margaret, who never let herself be led, never followed orders, and certainly never intended that any man should control her life, found herself walking back to her keep with her hand in a stranger's, feeling more at peace than she had in years. No matter that his garments were the strangest she had ever seen. No matter that his speech was a convoluted tangle of foreign tongues. No matter that he was the most handsome man she had clapped eyes on in all her score and five years.

His shoulders were broad. Surely they could accept some of her burden for a few hours. But only for a few hours. It had been a most trying day and she wasn't at her best. Soon she would feel more herself and those broad shoulders wouldn't seem so appealing.

Alex smiled down at her.

Margaret flinched. She would also have to invent a way to become impervious to that smile.

She felt him lace his fingers with hers and sighed deep within her soul. This would be more difficult. No one had ever warned her what a devastating impact holding hands with a man could have on a woman's sensibility. She would have to give that more consideration later.

For now, all she could bring herself to do was smile back up at him.

By the saints, she was fast losing her wits!

And, more distressingly, she was enjoying it!

Seven

A WEEK LATER ALEX STOOD IN WILLIAM OF FALCON-berg's bedroom, cinching a leather belt around his waist. Margaret had given him her father's clothes without comment; he could only assume it didn't bother her. He had stashed his leather jacket in a trunk by the bed, hoping it would remain undisturbed. He was tempted to destroy it just to be safe, but it was his favorite coat—the only one he'd ever been able to keep from finding its way into his sister's closet. At least he'd managed to forget his wallet back in the twentieth century. Heaven only knew what the maids would think if they found that while cleaning.

He took one last look around, then left the room, pulling the door shut behind him. The plan was now in place and he hoped it worked out. Ralf had held true to form and sent another messenger to find out just what was going on. Margaret had sent the second man back with much the same story. Alex was hoping it would keep Ralf distracted long enough for Edward to sneak out of the keep.

Sir George had found a bribable guard at Brackwald who had delivered a request to Edward to meet Alex at a predetermined place for a little tête-à-tête. After giving it a great deal of thought, Alex had come to the conclusion that the only way to keep Ralf out of Margaret's hair was to convince Richard that wedding her to Ralf would ruin a very profitable estate. Richard, being Richard, would hopefully see the monetary impact on his tax-collection efforts and decide maybe Ralf wasn't such a great choice.

What Alex *hadn't* said to Margaret, however, was the other item of business on his agenda. Even though Ralf was slime, Edward was actually very nice. Much as his nineties guy mentality balked at the idea, he knew Margaret would need at least a husband's name to use as a front. And if she had to marry someone eventually, well, why not someone nice, like Edward?

But somehow now he just wasn't as enthusiastic about the idea as he had been the night before.

He walked down the hallway to the stairs before he could give that any more thought. He brushed the stone of the walls lightly with his fingers. It was a wonder he hadn't gotten claustrophobia before now. Modern man was very spoiled with their spacious hallways and graceful, straight stairs. Alex maneuvered himself down the tight, spiral staircase, uncomfortably aware that he was clearing the sides by only a couple of inches and that he was definitely having to duck not to hit his head.

That was another thing. Medieval man had been shorter, from what he had seen. It was no wonder Margaret was so self-conscious about her height. He considered her only a few inches above average but the rest of the household no doubt thought her a giant. Maybe she had Viking blood in her. He smiled at the thought. Somehow he had no trouble envisioning her at the helm of a Viking warship, bellowing for her comrades to pull harder at the oars so they could land and conquer that much more quickly.

He rounded the last corner and breathed a sigh of relief to be out in the great hall, away from those uncomfortably steep stairs. Man was not meant to tread those kinds of steps in hiking boots. Maybe Margaret's counterparts had smaller feet, too.

The hall was empty except for an old man dragging a stool toward the hearth. He didn't look like anyone from the kitchen, so Alex didn't spare him much thought. What he wanted was breakfast, and the sooner the better.

He walked across the back of the hall and stopped at an opening in the wall. It seemed to lead down a short passageway to another room. Alex closed his eyes and sniffed deeply. Yes, definitely the kitchen. He started down the passageway, already salivating at the smell. Maybe he could just pull up a stool to the worktable and sample a little bit of everything. He hesitated, wondering if he should have brought some sort of offering for Margaret's cook. A man couldn't go wrong with a bouquet of flowers.

Alex stumbled suddenly, courtesy of a shove in his back. He threw out his hand to catch himself against the wall.

"What the—" he began.

"Beg yer pardon, m'lord," a boy gasped out, slipping past him and bolting for the kitchen. "I must tell the others!"

"Tell them what?" Alex asked with a frown. He pushed himself away from the wall. Maybe the kid knew something—such as the fact that the last call for breakfast might just have been sounded. Alex was ready to start sprinting himself.

He entered the kitchen only to find everyone going the wrong way—away from the pots and kettles. Young boys and girls, kitchen help by the look of their food-smeared shirts, scurried past him. It was the sight of Margaret's cook coming toward him, however, that worried him the most.

"Good woman," he began with his best smile, "if you would be so kind—"

"No time, my lord," Cook said, shooing him out of her way.

"But—"

"Not now," she said, setting him aside bodily and hastening down the passageway. "The tapestries must be saved!"

"The tapestries?" Alex echoed. What possible tapestry mishap could be more important than fulfilling a culinary duty, especially when he was feeling so faint from hunger? He paused and sniffed carefully in the direction of the hall. The smell of smoke was no more pervasive than it had been when he'd been there a moment ago, and he certainly hadn't seen any wall hangings on fire.

Well, whatever Cook and her helpers had gone to check on couldn't possibly need more manpower than they could provide by themselves. Alex looked at the kitchen, then shrugged. If there wasn't anyone here to help him, he'd just help himself. He poked around the tables, then polished off a couple of apples, a hunk of bread, and cheese that was starting to go a little green around the edges. It was nothing he wouldn't have found in his own refrigerator, so he didn't think too much of it.

There was a kettle of porridge sitting off the fire looking somewhat abandoned, so Alex made himself at home in front of it. He helped himself to a couple of bowls, then poured himself a generous mug of ale. Once he'd quenched his thirst, he stood and stretched. At least he could now be chivalrous on a full stomach. And the sooner he did his good deed, the sooner he could get home. The sooner the better, as far as Fiona MacAllister was concerned.

Though, compared to Margaret, Fiona was starting to look much less interesting.

"Don't even go there," he warned himself.

The last thing he needed was to start looking at Margaret as anything but a rescue project. To help her was the reason he'd been plopped back in the Middle Ages; he wasn't here to date her.

He ambled out into the great hall and paused at the sight that greeted his eyes. Most of Margaret's household seemed to be gathered over by the hearth in the far wall, watching something. What were they up to? A morning battle ritual of some kind?

He'd had a look at the keep the night before—his first night of freedom—but things were much clearer in the light of day. Margaret's hall was comfortable and tidy, and the furnishings were well-made and seemingly well-cared-for. Alex looked at the wall hanging he currently stood near and ran his fingers over the stitches. Then he frowned.

The bottom of the piece was hanging in tatters. It was completely at odds with the rest of the hall, and he wondered if Margaret had a serious rat problem.

He strolled across the floor and stopped next to the lady in question.

"What's up?" he asked.

The group, as one, whirled on him, shushing him. Margaret clapped her hand over his mouth.

"Don't interrupt him," she whispered frantically. "He's well into today's offering."

Alex looked over her fingers at the old man standing atop his stool. He pulled Margaret's hand away.

"Who's that?" he whispered.

"Baldric, my sire's bard."

Alex looked at Baldric the Bard and found himself being regarded with a look that made him back up a pace. Alex smiled weakly and clamped his lips shut.

"Ahem," Baldric said, thrusting out his chin and causing his beard to bristle up like a cat's tail. "Where was I? Oh, no matter. I'll begin again."

Alex could have sworn he heard the audience groan under its breath, and he smiled. How bad could this guy be?

> *There once was an ogre from Kent,*
> *Who found that his waistcoat was rent.*
> *He searched high and low*
> *for a needle to sew,*
> *As he fancied himself a fine gent.*

Alex gaped. A *limerick*? He was listening to a *limerick* in 1194? He could hardly believe his ears. But no one around him seemed to find it out of the ordinary. They were all listening intently.

> *And a gent never shows his bare, ahem,*
> *For to do so would cause serious mayhem.*
> *Though his covering be sparse,*

> *he must cover his arse,*
> *Or offend those fair maids 'round about him.*

Alex laughed. He couldn't help himself. This wasn't exactly *Beowulf*. Maybe this explained why Margaret had been so anxious for Baldric to get it over with the first time.

Then he shut up abruptly at the glare he received from the *artiste*. Alex gulped.

"It's really good," he said quickly. "Best I've ever heard."

"Harumph," the Bard said, lifting his nose regally. He made no further comment, but plunged in again, his voice ringing out enthusiastically into the hall.

> *So our gent from Kent took up his steel,*
> *his great waistcoat rent for to heal.*
> *His thumb soon was sore*
> *and he cried out, "No more!*
> *'Tis sewn enough, I must have me a meal!"*
>
> *Though pleased he'd been ever so crafty,*
> *Small stitch'ry had left him quite dafty—*

"Hey," some brave soul blurted out, "that ain't a proper word!"

Baldric's fingers flexed and Alex wondered if that meant he was ready to do bodily harm to a certain mouthy onlooker.

"Well, it ain't!" the poor sap said, turning to look at the rest of the household.

"Of course it is," Margaret said firmly. "It's a *new* word, made up especially for us."

The man shook his head. "I don't think—"

A gloved hand was clamped over his mouth. Alex watched in astonishment as two knights lifted the man by his shoulders and feet and carried him out of the hall. Margaret looked at the rest of her household.

"A *new* word," she repeated.

They all nodded vigorously, then everyone turned back expectantly. Baldric took a moment to compose himself, then started up his last verse again.

> *Though pleased he'd been ever so crafty,*
> *Small stitch'ry had left him quite dafty.*
> *The rent though reduced*
> *had left some threads still loosed,*
> *and the result was forever quite drafty!*

There was dead silence. Alex looked around, but everyone seemed to be waiting—for what he had no idea. Feeling as though someone ought to do something, he started to clap.

"Sshh!" Margaret hissed, whirling on him. "He's not finished!"

"He sounds finished to me. Hey, Baldric, are you finished?" he called.

Baldric looked down his nose at Alex. "Of course I'm finished!"

"That's what I thought," Alex said, clapping pointedly.

The rest of Margaret's household clapped as well, though probably less enthusiastically than Baldric might have wished. Alex watched as Margaret helped the old man down from his stool, led him to the high table, and called for sweets from the kitchen. For a moment Alex entertained the idea that something sugary might have been hiding in an uninvestigated nook, then he caught sight of a plate full of sweet*meats* and abruptly lost his appetite. There wasn't much that could do that to him, but steamed brains was definitely high on the short list. He turned away before his wimpy twentieth-century stomach betrayed him.

Margaret was coming toward him, fastening her cloak at her throat. "Now that's seen to, we can be away."

"Baldric has an interesting sense of meter," Alex noted.

Margaret rolled her eyes. "It worsens with every poem he composes. But at least today he found the last rhyme.

'Tis usually that which eludes him.'' She looked vastly relieved. ''I must admit I wasn't up to helping him search for it this morn.''

''The subject matter was riveting. Does he usually go in for ogres?''

''That is one of his less offensive choices. Generally he gives his opinion on Brackwald and the smell of its inhabitants, or upon my finding a husband.''

Alex smiled. ''You must love that.''

''As I said, ogres are always among the less offensive subjects. Now,'' she said briskly, ''I've horses waiting for us in the courtyard. I'll introduce you to Sir Henry, then we'll be off.''

Alex bit his tongue. There was no way he could talk to Edward about wooing her if she were sitting right there. He would definitely lose appendages. He'd just break the news to her as he was leaving and deal with the inevitable eruption then.

Sir George was standing with another young knight.

''I don't believe we've met,'' Alex said, looking the kid over.

''Henry of Blythe,'' the young man said, with a small bow.

''Great. You know where this place is we're to meet Edward?''

''Aye, my lord, I do.''

''You'll come with me, then.'' Alex looked at Margaret. ''I'll need something for a bribe in case I run into one of Ralf's loyalists. Silence can be bought, I assume?''

''I'll bring coin along,'' she said.

Alex smiled and put his hand on her shoulder. ''Thank you for trusting me. Now, trust me some more and stay home.''

She blinked. ''I cannot.''

''Yes, you can.'' He held out his hand. ''Bribery?''

The volcano began to smolder. ''I said *I* will bring it along. Besides, you have not yet told me what it is you plan. You may discuss it with me as we ride.''

Alex smiled at George and Sir Henry. "Excuse us." He took Margaret's hand and tugged. He was faintly surprised to find that she allowed it. He stopped at the back of the hall, took one look at her frown, and decided more privacy was called for. She might have trusted him, but she obviously had no intentions of staying behind. Her free hand was on her sword hilt. Alex smiled. Did she realize it?

"You are laughing at me again," she said stiffly.

He shook his head. "Not the way you think. You're very cute."

"Cute?"

"Cute," he confirmed. "Charming. Intoxicating."

She stared at him, uncomprehending. Alex wanted to check his forehead. Was he feverish? Since when did a woman go from cute to intoxicating in such short order?

But that's what she was. He pulled her toward the stairs. He had to get out, quickly, before he became so intoxicated he did something stupid. He didn't want to speculate on what that might be, but he had the feeling it would include Margaret's lips under his repeatedly.

He pulled her up the stairs behind him, then kept her hand in his down the hallway to his room. He brought her inside and shut the door.

"You can't come," he said, turning to look at her. Her hand moved again to her sword. "I mean it."

"I will come," she stated. "And I mean it, too."

"It's going to be very boring. Edward and I are just going to discuss his slimeball brother."

"I won't be left behind," she insisted. " 'Tis my fate you speak of."

She had a point. Alex had known she would want to come, and he'd prepared himself with all sorts of excuses why she couldn't. He was reminded sharply of all the times his sister Elizabeth had wanted to tag along after her brothers. He'd had a whole list of tried-and-true "this is why you can't" lines he'd used on her for years. Somehow, he had the feeling they weren't going to fly with the woman in front of him. Not that they'd flown much better with

Elizabeth. Alex shook his head. He was doomed to be surrounded by strong-minded, stubborn women.

But what a way to go.

He put his hands on Margaret's shoulders. She moved away. He closed the distance with one large step and put his hands again on her mail-covered shoulders.

"Don't," he said, anticipating her next try at moving back from him. She stood still and frowned up at him. Her mail was cold under his fingers, even through the cloth. He had the most insane desire to pull it off her. A long shoulder rub would do her good.

"Margaret," he said, hauling himself back to reality, "I'm going to be gone less than a day. Edward needs to hear what Ralf's done from someone who isn't involved. Someone on the outside who has nothing to gain by reporting it." He smiled down at her. "See what I mean?"

She frowned at him. "And if you forget all the things I told you yestereve?"

"I won't forget."

"How do you know?"

"I never forget important details. I'll tell Edward everything you told me. Trust me."

She sighed. "I suppose this is the best way."

"It is."

"I am not happy about it."

He smoothed a few wisps of hair back from her face. "I didn't think you would be."

"I don't like being left behind."

He smiled, pained. "I know, Margaret. And I'm sorry."

She fumbled in the bag at her belt and pulled forth several coins. "This should serve you well enough. Ralf's men are greedy."

Alex took the coins she held out, feeling the chill of her hands as he did so. He took her hand and brought it to his mouth to blow on it. That was all he meant to do. Honestly. How his lips found their way to her palm in kissing formation, he couldn't have said. He looked at Margaret to find she was staring at him with her mouth open.

"What do you?" she breathed.

"Warm up to this," he said, slipping his hand under her hair to the back of her neck.

It was a bad idea. He knew it. Kissing her was one of the stupidest things he'd ever planned to do. It would confuse the issue. He was there to trot out his chivalry skills for a brief moment, do good, then hightail it back home and convince Fiona MacAllister that he was good husband material. The very *last* thing he needed to be doing was kissing a woman he was certain had never been kissed in her entire life.

Don't do it, Smith, an inner voice warned.

He tilted her face up with his thumb under her jaw. She was staring at him in complete confusion, mingled with trust and what could have been mistaken for the beginnings of a crush.

Alex understood completely.

He pressed his lips against hers.

He groaned in spite of himself. He kissed her again, just as lightly, just as innocently. It was an effort, especially since what he wanted to be doing was plundering her mouth with all the ruthlessness of a seasoned pirate. And once she was overcome enough to forget she was wearing a sword and knew how to use it, he wanted to strip everything off her, including her blades, carry her to the bed, and lose himself in her.

Intoxicating? The woman was more than intoxicating— she was life-threatening!

He tore his mouth away. "Wow," he gasped.

"Aye," she agreed, looking as stunned as he felt.

He kissed her again, a hard, brief kiss. "I'll be back. Stay here. Okay?"

"Okay," she repeated. She reached up and touched her mouth. "No one has ever dared the like," she whispered.

"Yeah, well, no one else had better dare the like or they'll be answering to me," he said with a growl. "Ggrrrr," he repeated, just on principle. The surge of proprietariness that rushed through him almost brought him to his knees.

Damn. As if he could do anything about it!

"I've got to go." He kissed her again and strode from the room, hoping she wouldn't follow.

He thumped down the steps, collected Henry from the hearth, and practically sprinted for the door.

"I'll be back," he threw over his shoulder at George.

"Godspeed, lad," George called.

Alex nodded and slammed the hall door shut behind him. The horses were ready, and it took hardly any time at all to be out of the gates. Alex didn't dare look behind him. Either he would see Margaret changing her mind and coming down the hall steps, or he would see her standing at the door, looking as overcome as he felt. He couldn't bear the thought of either.

What a mess!

ALEX SPENT THE rest of the afternoon pacing in the small clearing Henry had chosen for the meeting site. He thought moving would help him forget the feel of Margaret's lips under his.

Somehow, it only made it worse.

By the time the sun went down, Alex was beginning to wonder if something had happened to Edward. Had Ralf somehow gotten wind of the plans? Had he been a complete fool to trust Edward?

By the middle of the night he was ready to pack it in and go home. He had just risen to put out the fire when Edward walked into the clearing.

"Forgive me," he said, breathing hard. He cast himself down by the fire. "Saints, I thought Ralf would never slip into his cups! I half feared I wouldn't reach you until the sun was up."

Alex smiled grimly. "Your brother is not a convenient man."

"There's truth in that," Edward agreed. He smiled at Alex. "You're looking well. I was certain Margaret would have tucked you away safely in the compost heap by now.''

"Long story," Alex said, trying to smile but feeling it had come out very strained. He looked at the small man who was standing at the edge of the clearing. "Your scribe?"

"Aye. Charming, isn't he?"

The man bore a strong resemblance to a ferret. Alex frowned.

"He can be trusted?"

"He's one of my own men."

"If you say so. Since he's here, why don't we get started?"

Henry kept watch while Alex sat across the fire from Edward and outlined in detail everything he knew personally about Ralf's harassment. He looked at the scribe's notes, just to be sure. Alex had been accused in the past of being too suspicious, but the instinct hadn't failed him yet. Satisfied that the man was recording the details correctly, as satisfied as he could be while trying to read script that was practically illegible, he then turned to the facts surrounding what Ralf had done to Margaret according to her and George. Edward only shook his head, his expression of disgust deepening with the telling of each incident.

"And the last was the burning of one of her west fields, just shortly before I came," Alex finished.

The scribe looked up. "And what of her kidnapping of you, sir knight? Does that not say something about her character?"

Edward shot the man a cold look. "I think your task is done here, Haslett. The keep is only a few hours' ride. If you set out now, you'll be there in good time to break your fast. I can see myself home."

The scribe didn't need to hear that twice. He prepared to depart, reluctantly leaving Edward with his notes. Alex watched him go.

"You're certain about him?"

"He's that way with everyone. What he doesn't know

is that I can read as well as he can." Edward smiled. "I just keep him around because I'm lazy."

Alex leaned back against a felled log and smiled. "I'll take your word for it. How much longer are you going to be at Brackwald?"

"Longer than I'd like. I need coin to travel back to France, and Ralf is loth to part with any of his."

Alex tossed him Margaret's contribution. "Will that help?"

Edward smiled grimly. "It all helps, but I'll need more than this. I thank you for it just the same. Unfortunately, I'll need to prostrate myself a time or two more before Ralf's feet and vow eternal loyalty. He'll part with his gold in his own time."

"I'm sorry it can't be sooner."

"So am I."

"It will have to be soon, though, if Richard is to be told about what Ralf's up to." Alex looked at Edward. "I was thinking he probably wouldn't be too eager to marry Margaret off to Ralf when he finds out what kind of damage Ralf's been doing to her land."

"There is truth in that, my friend. Her land is very productive." He looked at Alex closely. "You seemed to have survived your stay well enough. No bruises from her having tossed you about."

Alex smiled. "No bruises."

Edward waited. "What? No more tale than that?" He laughed. "Come, Alex, and regale me with stories of your stay in the lioness' den."

Well, this was the opening he'd been waiting for. Now was the time to bait the hook and drop it into the stream.

So, why did he find himself all of a sudden very reluctant to say anything?

"She's not at all what you'd expect," Alex said unwillingly. "Not at all."

Edward looked at him expectantly.

"She's beautiful," Alex snarled. "All right? She's

beautiful and intelligent and desirable and a man would be a fool not to want her."

Edward's look of polite curiosity turned into something else entirely.

"Indeed," he said, sounding much too interested. "Tell me more."

Alex knew he had to do it. Hell, it was probably exactly what he had to do to get back home. He had no choice but to paint Margaret in the most appealing light possible, endow her with every virtue in existence, make her so irresistible that Edward would be frothing at the mouth to have her.

Damn it, anyway.

"Where should I start?" Alex growled. All right, so he would do it. But he would make Edward beg for every scrap of information.

"Start at her head and work your way down," Edward said, with a grin. "And travel slowly, my friend. Wouldn't want to miss any important landmarks."

Alex had the overwhelming urge to smash his fist into Edward's face.

"You'll have to uncover those landmarks yourself," Alex said curtly.

"Is she indeed beautiful?"

"Very."

"Not angry looking?"

"Oh, she can be angry looking," Alex said, "but that's just her fire. It's a fire that would warm the *right* man," he said pointedly, "long into his old age."

Edward lifted one eyebrow. "I'm not opposed to getting scorched now and then. Now, what lies underneath that mail?"

"I wouldn't know."

"Hmmm," Edward said, stroking his chin. "Even better, my friend. Perhaps I will be the one to tell you, once I've managed to remove it."

Alex took a deep breath. This was getting out of hand. Margaret wasn't his. She needed a man from her own time, someone who could help her hold her land, help her plant, help her do all those medieval things Alex was sure a summa cum laude in jurisprudence couldn't possibly figure out.

"You'll have to be careful," Alex said, trying to keep all emotion out of his voice. "She's used to being at the head of the garrison, you might say. If you can respect that, you'll make a good impression."

"I have a healthy respect for her skills with the lance," Edward said, still grinning stupidly.

"She doesn't seem to know much about the birds and the bees."

Edward looked at him blankly.

"Relations between a man and a woman," Alex said, between gritted teeth. "You know."

"Ah," Edward said, nodding. "I'll remember that."

"Woo her carefully."

"Trust me. I will."

The worst thing about it was, Alex knew Edward would. He wasn't Ralf. From what Alex had seen, Edward was a decent guy, trying to do the best he could in very trying circumstances. If Margaret could just overlook his face, she would probably find Edward to be a very nice, very considerate husband.

And all her fire would be completely wasted. Alex had the feeling Edward wouldn't have a clue what to do with it.

Unlike himself, for instance.

"Did you bring anything to drink?" Alex asked.

"A toast to my future nuptials?" Edward asked.

"What the hell. Why not?"

ALEX WOKE, SHAKEN. Literally. Someone was shaking him. He pushed the hand away.

"Leave me alone, Zach. Horrible nightmare. Need Twinkies."

He tried to roll over and bury his face, and his pounding head, in his pillow. Unfortunately, all he got was a mouthful of grass. So much for chalking it all up to a nightmare.

"My lord, please wake!"

Alex opened one eye. Great. Sir Henry was hovering over him, looking very anxious.

"My lord, we've been away the whole of the night. Lady Margaret will be frantic."

"Where's Edward?"

"Already departed for his home, my lord. He bid me tell you he will remember all your advice for him in regards to his wooing."

Alex groaned. He put his hands to his head and sat up gingerly. Man, when was the last time he'd had a hangover this bad? It was all Edward's fault. Alex wished several bad things to come the man's way. Hives on his wedding night. A healthy case of impotence. Boils.

"My lord, I beg you!"

"All right already," Alex said. He let Henry pull him to his feet and help him find his horse. After several embarrassingly unsuccessful attempts, he finally managed to heave himself up into the saddle. Keeping himself there all the way to Falconberg was touch-and-go, but he managed it.

His head cleared, eventually. He turned over in his mind the events of the past evening. Ralf had been exposed for the slimeball he was. Edward would hopefully soon find himself taking over his brother's estate. Margaret would be rid of her obnoxious neighbor. Even more important, she was now suitably suitored. He had arranged everything as best he could. His task in the past was now finished and he could go home.

So, why wasn't he jumping for joy?

He certainly should be. The twentieth century was the place for him. It would definitely be the *safest* place for him once Margaret learned what he'd done about setting her up with Edward. She'd be hopping mad. Alex had no intentions of hanging around within swinging distance when she found out. Yes, reading about it while warming his toes next to a toasty fire with a Ding-Dong or two at his elbow was his safest bet. Talk about *The Taming of the Shrew*! Margaret would make Kate look like Donna Reed.

He tried not to think how much he would have liked to have been her Petruchio.

Eight

❧❧

MARGARET CLIMBED THE LAST OF THE STEPS TO THE BAT-
tlements. She couldn't remember how many times she'd
made the climb since dawn. Easily a score. The sun was
slipping down toward the horizon as she walked out onto
the parapet. He'd been away for over a day. She was almost frantic.

She'd tried to leave the keep. George had blocked her
way, blade bared. If she hadn't been so distracted, she
would have bested him. As it was, she had found herself
disarmed within five strokes.

So she'd taken to pacing.

"Riders, my lady," said a guardsman to her left.

Shielding her eyes against the sun, she could make out
two riders coming slowly toward the gates. She turned and
ran for the steps.

She descended them faster than she ever had before.
Twice she slipped, twice her heart caught in her throat.
She gained the great hall and ran across it to the door. She
threw it open and ran down the steps. The portcullis was
just being raised.

It was him. Margaret stood in the courtyard, feeling
wave after wave of relief wash over her. He was home.
Unharmed.

He slid off his horse and landed unsteadily. Margaret
ran across the courtyard and threw herself at him.

"Oof," he said, staggering backward.

"Oh," she said, ashamed.

He didn't release her. Indeed, he gathered her even more closely to himself.

"It's okay," he whispered. "I'm okay, Margaret."

"I wasn't worried for you," she choked out, burying her face in his throat.

His chuckle rumbled deep in his chest. "It was concern over my horse, I know. He's just fine, too."

Margaret felt his strong arm around her, his other hand brushing lightly over her hair. She was sure she'd died and gone to heaven.

"Do you want to hear about Edward?"

She shook her head.

"Do you want to hear about anything?"

She shook her head again.

"Shall we just stand here awhile?"

She nodded.

He didn't move, except to tighten his arm around her. For the first time in years, she wished she weren't wearing her mail. She pulled back far enough to look in his bloodshot eyes.

"I could take it off," she offered.

He looked momentarily puzzled. Then one corner of his mouth tipped up in a half smile.

"That's very tempting."

"Wait here. I'll be right back."

"Whoa," he said, tightening his arm around her and stopping her escape. He bent his head to her ear. "I'll come inside with you. Your entire household is watching me maul you out here."

Margaret looked around to find that was indeed the case. Her entire garrison, most of the kitchen help and, most notably, Sir George, were all staring at her as if she'd sprouted wings. Margaret drew herself up.

"He has brought promising tidings," she said haughtily.

They might have believed her had Alex not laughed. She glared at him, but he merely grinned and took her hand.

Her dignity was in tatters about her, so she let him lead

her into the house. Cook followed hard on her heels, already bellowing orders for a meal to be prepared for Sir Alexander's pleasure.

"What are the chances of a bath?" Alex asked.

"A bath?" Margaret echoed, horrified. "Whatever for?"

"I'm pretty grimy. And I need to shave."

"Cook could heat water and you could bathe in the kitchen," she said doubtfully. "If you like." Secretly she thought it a very poor idea. The maids would never recover from the sight of him naked.

Just the thought of *that* made her blush all over again. She left him downstairs and fled up to her chamber. A bath? Saints, what an idea. Well, he certainly smelled better than any other man of her acquaintance. Perhaps there was something to it.

She opened her chamber door, then froze. What if she smelled poorly? She couldn't remember the time she'd had a bath in a tub. It wasn't healthful to do so.

She contemplated her alternatives. Death by the ague wasn't a pleasant prospect, but neither was offending Alex with a poor smell.

She gathered her courage in hand. If he could bathe, so could she.

AN HOUR LATER she descended to the great hall. If she'd had a gown, she would have worn it. The best she could do was her youngest brother's finest tunic and least patched hose. She felt vulnerable without her mail. She'd even left her sword above. Her knife, however, was tucked safely in her boot.

She had ceased to wonder about her actions. She knew she was being a fool. Alex was merely a man. He surely wasn't worth losing her wits over.

Now, if she'd just held that thought a little longer while she still had wits left to use.

Perhaps this strange malady that possessed her was like a fever. She would suffer for a few days, then it would pass and she would be back to herself. She would be sensible and wear her mail. She wouldn't risk life and limb to immerse herself in a tub of lukewarm water merely to avoid offending his nose. And she would put her hair in a plait again. Of course, she had left it loose simply because it would dry faster thusly. She had no desire to please Alex with the one womanly attribute she still possessed.

She lingered in the shadows of the stairwell as long as she could. Would her people laugh at her?

Would Alex?

He was standing by the hearth on the far side of the hall, deep in discussion with George. Margaret stepped out from the shadows and started across what had suddenly become a vast expanse of floor.

George caught sight of her. His mouth dropped open. Margaret couldn't decide if he were pleased or horrified. A heavy silence descended abruptly. Margaret snuck a look or two at the rest of the bodies sitting at her long tables. Every one of them was looking at her with that same open-mouthed expression. Margaret concentrated on putting one foot before the other.

And then Alex turned.

There was no open-mouthed look of astonishment from him. He blinked a time or two, then a look descended upon his face, a look that Margaret had never before seen, but it turned her blood to liquid fire in her veins. Her malady had suddenly sprouted a fever. She thought she might just burn to cinders on the spot. Her pace faltered, and she stopped.

Alex strode over to her. He stopped a hand's breath from her and stared down at her with that same devouring look.

"It's no wonder you wear mail," he said, in a low, husky voice. "No one would get anything done around here otherwise."

Margaret took a step back. What did he mean? She gestured behind her to the stairs. "Should I put it back on—"

"No."

He said the word with great conviction. Margaret felt some of her apprehension melt.

"Then you are saying this is a good thing?"

He grinned that wolf's grin of his. "I'm saying, don't ever go out in the lists like this. Your knights will kill themselves because they'll be so distracted looking at you. And they better not be looking at you," he growled suddenly, turning a glare on the men who were seated at the long tables.

The men immediately looked away.

Alex smiled down at her. "You are . . . well . . ."

Margaret steeled herself for the worst. "Aye?" she asked grimly.

"Intoxicating."

"Oh," she said. Then she frowned. Intoxicating? Perhaps he meant that he was feeling as if he'd slipped into his cups. With the foreign words he continued to use, one just never knew.

"If you are feeling so faint, perhaps food will clear your head," she said, gesturing to the high table. "I think your mind has been weakened from the lack of it on your journey."

"I don't think that's my problem," he said with a smile, but he followed her to the table just the same.

Margaret sat down next to him and squirmed until a blessed meal arrived, distracting Alex. Once his gaze was off her and onto Cook's fanciest meat pie, Margaret finally felt her blush begin to fade. Saints, but the man could keep her off balance.

She prodded him about his meeting with Edward, but it was hard to compete for his attentions against Cook's flaky crust. Between grunts and two-word answers, she gathered that Edward had been talked to, would soon find his way to the king, and her life would be quite a bit less troubled than it had been in the past.

"And you're certain Edward will do this thing?" she asked.

"Hmmm," he said, chewing contentedly on a roasted turnip.

"At least Edward has more sense than his brother."

"Um-hum."

"Will he be a better neighbor if the king forces Ralf to hand over his lands?"

Alex frowned and swallowed. "Edward is nice enough, I suppose."

"You don't care for him?"

Alex frowned again. "What I think doesn't matter. I think you'll like him fairly well."

Margaret shrugged. "I won't see much of him. Hopefully."

"You'll probably see more of him than you think," he said, with something of a growl. He dragged a hand through his hair. "At least your troubles from Ralf are over. I've done what I needed to do."

"Done what you needed to do?" she asked.

He nodded, then reached for his wine and gulped it down.

Margaret felt a coldness steal over her. She had the awful feeling his next words would be *and now I'll be taking my leave of you.* She looked away while she could still breathe normally.

She tortured her fingernails. She fingered her eating dagger and chopped her soggy trencher into little bits of bread. That took a goodly while, but even so, she was staring at a disorderly pile of crumbs far too soon for her taste.

Alex hadn't moved. Margaret finally gathered her courage and looked at him.

He was looking at her as he'd looked at his supper a handful of moments before. Then, seemingly reluctantly, he began to smile. Her first instinct was to assume he was smiling because he found something amusing about her appearance, or her person. With an effort, she held back her suspicions until she knew just why he was gazing at her thusly.

"Why are you looking at me thusly?" she asked. She

was very proud of herself. No hint in those words of what she was trying so very hard not to think.

"Because I just can't help myself."

She frowned. "I'm not sure if that is a good thing or a bad."

"I'm certain it's bad," he said, still smiling that little smile. "Very bad."

"Then stop yourself."

"I can't."

"Use more effort."

"I don't want to."

Margaret frowned at him again. "You suffer from a serious lack of self-control. If you do not wish to look at me, then do not."

His smile deepened. "Have you ever been near something that was so breathtaking that you couldn't keep your eyes off it? A painting? A work of art? Something so perfectly formed, so arrestingly beautiful that your eyes seemed to possess a will of their own?"

You? she wanted to say. Aye, she could understand well enough what he meant. She nodded her head. There had certainly been times she hadn't wanted to mark the man sitting next to her, hadn't wanted to think about him, had regretted the moment she'd first clapped eyes on him. But to not look at him? She was powerless to stop herself.

"Let's go for a walk."

He was on his feet and pulling her to hers before she had a chance to voice her opinion. And then she found she had no desire to gainsay him. If she just hadn't found the sensation of his hand on hers so pleasant, she would have been far more able to assert herself. By the saints, he was working a terrible magic on her. In the space of less than a fortnight she'd gone from a formidable warrior to a giddy maid. But now she was beginning to understand just exactly why the serving wenches giggled when Sir Henry grinned at them. Margaret had never understood it. Sir Henry was a fair-looking man, but he didn't heat her blood.

Not as Alex did.

She put her hand to her forehead as she followed Alex up the steps. She wasn't feverish. But she felt feverish.

"Cloaks?" he asked.

She didn't think she would need one, but she fetched a pair anyway. She knew she should have been demanding to know where they were going. Instead, she found herself standing in the passageway, trembling as Alex fumbled with the clasp of the brooch that held her cloak together under her chin. She looked up at his beautiful face, so close to hers, and felt her heart beat harder in her chest. She had the most insane desire to go back into his arms, to have him run his hands through her hair again, to feel protected by his strong arms around her.

She looked at his mouth. She knew exactly how his lips felt now. *Wow* was the word he'd used. Scottish dialect, obviously. It was certainly descriptive enough.

Margaret saw fingers come to rest against his lips and realized, with a start, that those fingers were hers. She blushed and jerked her hand away.

Alex caught it, then brought her fingers back to his lips. "You're killing me," he said, with a faint smile.

Margaret looked down immediately, half expecting to see that one of her weapons had left its sheath and was poking him somewhere. But she wasn't wearing any weapons except her knife, which was still safely tucked in her boot. Saints, there wasn't even any mail to pinch him, should he have come close enough for that to be possible.

Strong fingers were under her chin, lifting her face up. "I meant that you were driving me crazy."

"Crazy?"

A small huff of laughter was his answer. "I can't think straight anymore. All I think about is you."

"Truly?" she asked surprised. "Then perhaps we are suffering from the same malady." She pulled back. "Saints, Alex, what if the entire keep comes down with this?"

He laughed again, a more hearty one this time. "Heaven

help them.'' He put his hand behind her head, took a step closer, and kissed her full on the mouth. ''Come on. Let's go upstairs. The cold air will do us good.''

And with that, he took her hand and pulled her down the passageway. Margaret felt her lips with her free hand. He'd kissed her again, without so much as a by-your-leave. Saints, but she liked that about him.

She followed him, then he surprised her by stopping at her favorite place on the parapet. The moon was full, the sky cloudless. As far as the eye could see was Falconberg soil. Margaret looked over it and, for the first time in months, felt some sense of relief at the sight. Alex had bought her time, perhaps even her freedom.

''Thank you for your aid,'' she said, looking up at him.

He put his arm around her shoulders. ''It was truly my pleasure. It was worth the trip.''

''Trip?''

''Journey. It was worth journeying here, even if all I could do was help you get Ralf off your back.''

The men on the battlements paid them no heed after the first incredulous glance. Alex led her over to the east wall, the one from which she could just make out Brackwald's keep on a clear day. Alex leaned back against the wall and opened his arms. She went into them willingly and sighed in pleasure as he wrapped his arms around her.

''Do I smell better?'' he asked.

''I didn't care before,'' she murmured.

His lips on hers startled her.

''Sshh,'' he murmured, ''don't go.''

''I didn't intend to.''

For some reason, that comment made him chuckle. Margaret thought to ask him just what he found so amusing, then discarded the idea. If she spoke, she'd have to pull her lips away from his, and no power on earth could persuade her to do that.

''Put your arms around me,'' he said, between kisses.

She tried to put her arms around his waist but his back

was pressed up against the wall and he didn't seem to want
to move.

"Alex—"

"Up around my neck. Under my cloak so your hands
don't get cold."

She felt that such an embrace left her pressed rather too
intimately close, but Alex seemed to find it to his liking.
Indeed, he tightened his arm around her back and pulled
her even more tightly against him. Actually, having the
length of his hard body pressed against hers gave her the
oddest feeling in the pit of her stomach. She had the most
insane desire to laugh. Before she could open her mouth
to comment on that, she felt Alex's hand at the back of
her head. She groaned as his hand tangled in her hair.

His only answer was to use that hand to pull her head
back to his. Margaret immediately realized she was his
prisoner. His hand had taken her head captive and his arm
around her waist held her virtually immobile against him.
His mouth was taking possession of hers with purely barbaric arrogance.

Again and again he brushed his lips against hers, sometimes lingering, sometimes only teasing her. She was torn
between smiling and frowning at his play. By the saints,
this was serious business, and he seemed not to have the
proper respect for the way her knees were beginning to
buckle.

Then he began to kiss her differently. Why were his lips
parting? No longer did both his lips meet hers in such
perfect symmetry. Nay, he had parted his lips and was
kissing her as if he intended to ingest whatever part of her
face he first came in contact with. She avoided his lips and
looked up at him. Forcing herself to ignore his handsome-
ness, which nearly stole her breath, and his height, which
made her feel decidedly fragile, she frowned.

"What are you doing?"

"Trying to kiss you properly. You're supposed to open
your mouth."

"Oh," she said blankly. "Why?"

"You'll see."

She nodded wisely, pretending to know exactly what he was talking about. She opened her mouth.

"Bettah?" she asked, trying to keep it open.

The sweetness of his smile made her want to weep. He slid his hand along her neck and shut her mouth by means of his thumb under her chin.

"Not yet. I'll tell you when."

"I see," she said, feeling a bit foolish. "Well, I wasn't quite sure."

"I know. That's why I told you."

She nodded and closed her eyes, tilting her face up. "Put your hand under my hair again, Alex."

Margaret sighed in pleasure as his fingers delved into her hair until the palm of his hand was cradling her head. Such delicious captivity. His mouth began again to work its strange dance, opening against hers and pulling on her lips. She pulled away far enough to breathe a question.

"Open?"

"Just follow me," he whispered. She leaned against him again, wondering at the hoarseness of his voice. Too much ale, she decided finally. It was hard on the throat.

He pressed his lips against hers and opened his mouth. She followed his lead, unsure why he found this so pleasurable but willing to give it a try. After all, she'd never kissed a man before Alex. He likely had more things to teach her before he was through.

She shrieked as she felt his tongue slide between her lips. It was instinctive to wrench away from him. It was only as she felt her foot slip off the edge of the walkway that she remembered where she was. In a heartbeat, she was being jerked back against Alex's chest and felt the heaving of his body as he sucked in air.

"You startled me," she said weakly.

"Damn it, that was close!" he exclaimed. "Don't do that again!"

He tightened his arms around her until she squeaked involuntarily.

"By the saints," she managed, "what were you trying to do?"

He blew out his breath and gave her a lopsided grin. "Where I come from, we call that French kissing."

"Ah." She nodded. "I see. Are you going to French kiss me again?"

"Not on a four-foot-wide walkway. Let's go downstairs."

Margaret picked her way along the walkway behind him, noting the dampness of his palm. She understood completely as she felt as if she'd spent the entire evening parrying fiercely. Not even the chill air cooled her flushed skin.

Once they reached the corridor leading to the chambers, Alex paused and looked carefully down the passageway. She stood on her toes and peeked over his shoulder.

"What do you seek?" she whispered.

"I don't want anyone seeing me kiss you senseless in this hallway."

"But—"

He backed her into the shadows and his mouth swooped down on hers like a vulture swooping down on its hapless prey. Margaret wound her arms around his neck and held on for dear life. He pinned her against the wall with his unyieldingly hard frame and tilted her face up with his hands.

Then he opened her mouth. She wasn't prepared for the rush of heat that washed over her. Alex might have had the finest of table manners, but he was no acquiescent lord when it came to this kissing of his. He plundered her mouth with a sweet ruthlessness that left her trembling. The pleasure was so sweet, she prayed he would never stop kissing her.

Which is exactly what he did. He tore his mouth away and leaned his forehead against hers.

"We have to stop," he panted, "while I still can."

"I don't want you to," she said, trying to capture his lips again with hers.

He put his hands on her shoulders and pushed back, holding her away. "Margaret, we have to stop now. We're not going to end up making love tonight."

"Is that more kissing?"

"Not even," he said hoarsely. He pulled her down the passageway and deposited her in front of her chamber. "Go to bed."

"Nay."

He tipped her face up with his finger. "Yes."

"I would have one last kiss."

"No."

"Yea."

He sighed and then pushed her inside the room and shut the door behind him. With a groan, he pulled her tight against him and kissed her.

Margaret thought she was prepared for his assault, but found herself again on unfamiliar ground. He was painfully tender, but no less knee-weakening. By the time he lifted his head and gazed down at her with stormy blue-green eyes, she was dazed and convinced she'd never recover.

"Go to bed," he commanded.

She nodded, mute.

He took her face in his hands. "You are the most beautiful, passionate woman I've ever known. Don't let anyone ever convince you otherwise."

Before she could find her wits to speak, he was gone. She walked to her bed and sat down, stunned. Never had it occurred to her that such feelings were possible. Her body was raging with fever and her mind was aswirl with dizziness.

Was this love? The kind of love that Baldric spun tales about, the kind that drove men to take up the sword in their lady's defense, the kind that left maids languishing at their tapestry frames dreaming of their champions?

She lay back slowly and closed her eyes. A pity Alex was not lord of Brackwald. She would wed him and be glad of it. And then her dreams would be happy ones indeed.

She blinked. Could she wed with him just the same? Surely he had land in Seattle. Though she'd never asked him the particulars, she was certain he must be a lord of some sort, in spite of his lack of spurs and sword. But would he be willing to trade his own fief to become lord of hers?

Or did he indeed feel that he'd done what he'd come to do and now he would be taking his leave?

She turned over with a groan and buried her face in her quilt. It would only trouble her to think on it more. If the opportunity presented itself, she would speak to him of it on the morrow. For now, all she wanted was to content herself with the memory of his kiss.

She drifted off to sleep with a smile and a very flushed face.

Nine

❦

"AND ONCE HE ROUNDS UP ENOUGH GOLD, HE'LL BE OFF to find Richard and settle things." Alex looked at George. "Think you can keep Ralf at bay until then?"

George rubbed his face wearily. "We've managed it so far. A month or two more won't matter."

Alex looked at Margaret's captain and wondered if he himself looked so bleary-eyed. Maybe it had been a while since George had pulled an all-nighter. Alex could sympathize as he was still feeling the effects of his night out with the boys. Edward of Brackwald was hazardous to his health.

And to his peace of mind.

"I sense there is much more to it," George said, with a suddenly piercing glance.

Alex squirmed. He was thirty-two, for heaven's sake, too old to be squirming. "Geez, George, where'd you learn to do this?" he asked with a half laugh.

The crust softened enough to permit a very small smile. "I have three sons, my lord."

"That answers a few questions."

George waited. He seemed to have an unlimited supply of patience.

Alex sighed. "All right," he said, surrendering. He looked around him to make certain they weren't being eavesdropped on. "Edward is going to ask the king for Margaret's hand. I gave him advice on how to woo her. I think he'll make a good husband for her. He's not much to look at, but he'll treat her well.''

"And what is wrong with you that you cannot stay and wed her?"

"Me?" Alex choked.

"Aye, you. You're a strong man with the will to rule her and the head to govern Falconberg."

"I can't stay."

"Why not?"

"It's a long story."

"And I've an abundance of time this morn."

"It's better not to know."

George leaned back in his chair and stared at Alex for several minutes in silence. "Are you an angel or a demon?" he asked finally.

Alex laughed uncomfortably. "What makes you ask?"

"There is something about you," George said, stroking his chin. "Something passing strange."

Alex smiled. "I come from a strange time—I mean, place," he corrected. He rolled his eyes mentally. That was a Freudian slip if ever there were one. "*Place*," he reemphasized. "I'm not an outlaw, I'm not a criminal, I'm not running from justice. I was out riding on my brother-in-law's estate and I took a wrong turn. I think I was meant to be here in England to help Margaret. Now that she's helped, I can't stay any longer. I have to go home."

"Hmmm," George said, continuing to stroke his chin.

"Yeah, hmmm."

"You aren't wed, are you?"

"No, and I won't be unless I get home and put my little brother in the dungeon. He's really interfering with my matrimonial plans. I hate to think of what he's done to my Range Rov—"

Alex looked up and forgot what he was going to say. Margaret was just coming into the hall from the stairwell. She looked like she hadn't slept a wink. Her hair was again loose. And she still wasn't wearing her mail.

These were all very bad signs.

"How can you leave her?" George whispered. "By the saints, my lord, she is a prize worth fighting for!"

"Tell me about it," Alex said, his heart sinking. Good grief, he should have hightailed it out of there before she got up. Cowardly, yes, but easier than seeing her again.

She saw him and her face lit up. Alex felt slimier than he ever had in seven years of swimming with the sharks. What had he been thinking to kiss her the night before? He should have delivered his message and then gone to his room.

It had been pure selfishness on his part. He'd wanted her and he'd taken as much as he dared. And, if he were to be totally honest with himself, he had wanted to leave an indelible mark on her—one Edward of Brackwald didn't stand a chance in hell of erasing.

Alex would have rubbed his hands over his face and groaned, but he couldn't bring himself to tear his eyes away from the woman coming toward him. She was striking when she was angry—but when she smiled? She was beautiful enough to make him hurt just looking at her.

And his time in the Middle Ages could now be counted by minutes. Damn it anyway.

He had to go. He'd done his bit, completed his task, and now he had to go home. George would help Margaret hold down the fort until Richard could come to her aid.

Until Richard and *Edward* could come to her aid, Alex corrected himself with a scowl. The thought of Edward coming within ten feet of Margaret made Alex want to hit somebody. Especially after last night. He wanted to laugh joyously at how innocently she had let her jaw hang open, inquiring if that was okay. His heart hammered suddenly against his chest when he thought of how close she had come to falling off the walkway. He shifted positions in the chair as he remembered how the briefest of forays into her mouth had sent his blood pressure soaring. It had taken all his willpower not to send them both tumbling onto her bed. He could just imagine how cross-eyed making love to her would leave him. Her responses would be completely genuine, completely without calculation, completely innocent. What would she do when he brought her pleasure? Probably yell loud enough to bring the roof down on their heads. He had the feeling he would be doing the same thing.

"Good morrow to you, Alex," she said, coming to a stop next to his chair.

George cleared his throat pointedly.

Alex stood up, hoping he didn't look as miserable as he felt.

"Margaret, I need to speak with you privately for a moment."

He winced at the sweet, innocent joy that flashed in her eyes. At that moment he'd never in his life felt more like a snake. And he had no one to blame but himself. He never should have kissed her. It would serve him right to find himself impotent when it came time to bed the grocer's daughter.

At the moment impotence seemed the lesser of two disappointments. Compared to Margaret, Fiona MacAllister held no appeal for him at all.

George threw him a dark frown as Alex ushered Margaret from the table and up the stairs. Alex couldn't blame him. Margaret would either weep or demolish all her men one-by-one in the lists. Alex didn't want to know which it would be.

Alex stopped at Margaret's father's chamber, the one he had occupied during his stay. She entered, then stood in the middle of the room, looking at him hesitantly.

"Aye?" she asked.

Alex closed his eyes briefly and prayed for strength. Hell! Why hadn't he managed to keep his mouth to himself?

"Alex?"

Her husky voice made him break out in a cold sweat. How could fate do this to him? Why couldn't he have found her in the twentieth century? Why couldn't she have been a savvy lawyer who was just waiting for the right man to come along and offer to father her children and divide fifty percent of the care and feeding of those children with her?

Her dark eyes were full of confusion and apprehension. He couldn't bear to see them full of hurt, hurt that he would put there. He walked over to the window and stared out over the cloud-darkened landscape.

"Margaret, you won't understand this, but I have to go."

"To see Edward again?"

He shook his head. "No." He took another deep breath. "I have to go home." He heard her swift intake of breath. "It was really a mistake that I even wound up here. I probably should have gone back right away, but I thought a few weeks in England would be interesting." He turned to face her. The devastated look on her face hit him like a sledgehammer in the gut. He leaned back against the window, pressing his palms against the wall for support. "Honey," he began softly, "I *can't* stay."

"You're wed," she whispered, her words cutting through the still air and dropping to the floor like shards of glass. "*Dieu*, what a fool I am."

"No, I'm not married," he corrected her quickly. "And if I had my choice of women, I would choose you."

"Liar," she said, her voice breaking.

"Margaret, listen to me," he said, holding out his hands. "Seattle is not only across a very vast ocean, it's in a completely different century. Don't you see? I have family I left behind, family that will be worried about me. My brother-in-law will probably foul up a dozen centuries trying to find me. I have to go back."

"You're a liar," she said, tears welling up in her eyes.

"No, I'm not."

"Then you're daft," she said shrilly. "Daft and cruel. Why did you stay at all if you planned to leave?"

It took him only two steps to cross the room to her. He wrapped his fingers around her upper arms and pulled her to him.

"Don't you think this pains me as well?" he asked hoarsely. "I never meant to come here. I never expected to meet a woman who makes every other woman I've ever met pale to insignificance. Don't you think the sound of your voice will haunt me when I'm home? Don't you think I'll lie awake at night and grieve because my arms ache to be around you?"

"You lying whoreson!" she cried. She jerked away from him and fled from the room. Alex heard the sound of her chamber door being slammed and bolted and knew there was no point in going after her. She wouldn't open up to him. Even if she did, what good would it do? She might understand the concept of time travel, but she would never believe it.

He dragged his hand through his hair and let out his breath slowly, blowing it through pursed lips. What a mess he had made of things. At least he had warned Edward what things would be like at Falconberg. With any luck, Margaret would rebound right into his arms.

The thought made him sick.

With stiff, mechanical motions he stripped off William of Falconberg's clothes and donned his jeans and denim shirt. He retrieved his leather jacket from the bottom of the trunk. There was nothing else to be done.

George was waiting for him in the great hall. Alex almost wished the older man would demand some sort of satisfaction. A good beating would be nothing less than he deserved. At least the pain of a bruised body might have dulled the agony of mind and spirit he endured presently.

"I think you've broken her heart," George said bluntly. "Something I thought no one could ever do."

"I never meant to."

"Can't you love her?"

Alex squirmed uncomfortably. What did it matter if he could? He couldn't stay. That was the cold, hard fact. "It doesn't matter if I could."

"Damn you, Alexander, why must you be so stubborn?"

Anger was good. Alex wished he could muster up a bit of his own. It might make him feel better. "If there were any way I could remain, believe me I would. Margaret is a woman without peer."

"You couldn't take her with you?" George asked, his ears perking up.

Alex had already considered that alternative and dismissed it. "If I did, she could never come home again. I don't think she'd like that."

George sighed, then looked heavenward. "I imagine she wouldn't." He looked at Alex gravely. "Well, then, I see there's nothing else to be done. I'm grateful for your aid. Margaret will be, too. In time."

Alex nodded and stepped away. He didn't even allow himself the luxury of another look around the hall. He had to go home. Maybe Zachary had wrecked the Range Rover. That would give him an excuse to beat someone senseless.

Alex saddled Beast with shaking hands. He rode through the gatehouse and across the drawbridge. The view before him began to blur. He dragged his sleeve across his eyes and swore most foully in Gaelic. It didn't help.

But smashing his fist into Jamie's face several times certainly would. Alex decided that was the first thing he would do once he got home. He couldn't remember the last time he had been so miserable.

It started to rain. Alex wasn't surprised. It was a perfect accompaniment to the misery in his heart. He hadn't meant to hurt her.

"And just what did you think you were going to do?" he asked himself out loud. He had no answer for it. He'd been a total jerk. It didn't matter that she was irresistible. He'd known he would have to leave and she would have to stay. He should have kept his hands and his damn mouth to himself.

If she just hadn't been so intoxicating . . .

It took him at least an hour to get to the faery ring. The rain continued to mist around him. Not a nice downpour that would have been over in a few minutes. This was rain that soaked him to the skin, plastered his hair to his face, felt like it was determined to get right down to his bones. It would have served him right to die of pneumonia.

The ring wasn't blooming, though the green shoots left no doubt as to where it lay. Alex wondered if that might stop him from getting home, then shrugged his doubt aside. It wasn't flora and fauna that made the difference. There was a gate here. It could be the dead of winter and he'd still get home. The ring hadn't been blooming in the twentieth century, either.

He urged Beast forward until they were standing in the midst of the ring. "Well, here goes nothing," he muttered under his breath.

They waited.

Beast tossed his head.

Alex looked up at the sky. It was still full of clouds, and the mist continued to swirl around him.

Was she still in her bedroom or had she headed for the lists to wreak havoc on her guardsmen? Would she fall straight into Edward's arms when he came to claim her?

"Okay," Alex said, with a sharp shake of his head, "this isn't helping. I've got to concentrate on something else."

He turned his mind to Jamie's keep and conjured up the most accurate mental picture he could. He made sure to include Jamie's Jag in the front and his own Range Rover. No sense in plopping himself forward to Jamie's fourteenth-century keep.

Alex felt unease nag at him, but he shoved it away. He'd done this before, when he and Jamie had gone back to tidy up the past. All you did was think very hard about where you wanted to go and *poof!* you were there. At least that was how it had worked before.

Beast pranced nervously, disrupting Alex's concentration. Alex dismounted and soothed his horse with long strokes along his neck.

"Hush now, monster," he said softly. "We're almost

home, then I'll have Zach give you a nice rubdown. Think about those tasty oats at home, Beast, and that fresh hay. No more of this medieval fodder for you, my friend.'' Alex continued to whisper, bringing image after image to his mind and concentrating with all his strength. His head began to ache with the effort, but he didn't give up. Just a few more minutes and he'd be home.

And Margaret would be left behind him eight centuries in time. He would never see her again. He would never watch her reach unconsciously for her knife when he'd said something to irritate her. He would never see her emotions pass over her face with perfect clarity.

He would never in his lifetime find anyone to compare to her.

''Hell,'' he groaned. ''This is definitely not working.'' He threw his arm over his stallion's neck. ''Let's try a few key phrases, Beast.'' Alex planted his feet apart and looked up at the sky.

''Beam me up, Scotty.''

Nothing.

''Take me home, country road.''

Alex wanted to laugh, but this wasn't funny. It hadn't taken any key phrases to get home with Jamie.

''I want hamburgers. I want Twinkies. Geez, I'll even take a Lilt at this point.'' Lilt seemed to be the Brits' equivalent of Sprite. Maybe not his favorite, but pop was pop when you were stuck in medieval England.

He *wasn't* stuck. He'd do this on his own or die trying.

Unfortunately, nothing seemed to be happening.

''Damn you, Jamie!'' he shouted. ''I finished my job, now get me the hell out of here!''

Silence. He contemplated a trip to Jamie's ancestral home in Scotland but immediately discounted the idea. He'd traveled back through the centuries under the boughs of that magical wood near the keep but only with Jamie. There was no guarantee it would work. Especially not in February. If the cold didn't get him, the snow would. Or the Scots. Alex could speak Gaelic as well as the next Celt, but would they leave him alive long enough to realize that? A bloodcurdling scream tore through the stillness of the morning, abruptly stopping Alex's intention to drop to his knees and weep. He yanked on the reins and pulled his horse into the shadows. The screaming continued, more than one voice. Leaving Beast tethered, he crept back through the woods.

Hoarse shouts mingled in the air with the strangled cries of what sounded like a man and a woman. The metallic taste of fear came immediately to Alex's mouth. What in the hell was happening down there? There was a road leading through the forest, but the trees were too thick to see who was on it or what they were doing to their victims. Alex knew he would probably be outnumbered and probably arrive too late, but he couldn't just walk away. Whatever the reason for the fight, the opponents were surely mismatched. Alex heard the ring of steel and the stomping of hooves. Mounted knights were involved, that much he could tell.

A small body crashed through the undergrowth and into Alex's arms before he saw it coming. The child began to scream, and Alex hastily clamped a hand over its mouth. His mouth. It was a small boy, probably no more than two or three. His eyes were wide with terror and he had soiled himself repeatedly. Alex's heart broke.

"Hush, little guy," he whispered urgently. "I won't hurt you." He gathered the child close and wrapped his coat around him, still keeping the boy's mouth covered. He rocked the child slowly, trying to cover the boy's ears and his mouth at the same time. Alex hardly needed to see who had been slain to know it was the child's parents. He felt an overwhelming urge to retch.

He stiffened as he heard the jingle of horses approach. He ventured a look through the trees and saw three knights on horseback gathered not thirty feet away.

"Ye fool, ye lost the child!"

"I weren't the one supposed to kill the child! That was

yer task, ye bloody idiot. If ye'd not been so busy with rapine, ye'd have seen it accomplished!''

The third man spoke. "Bah, bloody peasants. Who gives a rat's arse about 'em? The boy'll be dead by morning. If the cold don't get him, the wild beasties will.''

"Aye," agreed the first. "We must away 'afore Falconberg's scouts spot us. 'Twas risky to chase 'em this far onto 'er land.''

"Brackwald demanded it," the second knight growled. "We did naught but what 'e told us to do. I'm for returnin' and collecting me gold.''

"Aye," the third agreed. "But 'tis a pity we didn't see Falconberg. I'd like to ride that hag a time or two.''

The other two guffawed and tried to top the first's boasts. Alex gritted his teeth and forced himself to remain immobile when what he wanted to be doing was beating the bloody hell out of each of the three.

And then he realized what had seemed so strange.

The knights were wearing Margaret's colors.

But they weren't her knights.

The child in his arms continued to tremble, and Alex began to rock him again, praying the motion would give him a bit of comfort. He waited until he could no longer hear the knights, then remained motionless for another quarter of an hour. All he needed was to be ambushed by three men in chain mail.

He had to see if anyone was left alive. He rose to his feet and started through the woods toward where he'd heard the sounds coming from. Then it occurred to him that this was perhaps not exactly a sight fit for the child in his arms. He paused and listened. There was no sound, not even the sound of birds. The odds of anyone having survived were very slim indeed. Maybe the best thing he could do was head back to Falconberg and have Margaret send her men back to take a look around.

Alex made his way back to Beast and swung up into the saddle. He turned his mount toward Falconberg. At least the boy in his arms had had the good sense to run.

Did the peasants train their children to do just that? The poor kid. Orphaned and terrorized. What kind of world was this anyway?

It was a world he was now stuck in.

At least he had something to concentrate on besides his own crushing panic. He released the boy's mouth and wrapped him more securely in his coat. The child was weeping silently, and Alex's heart wrenched at the sight. He gently brushed the dark, curly hair back from the boy's face.

"It's okay, little fella," he said softly. "We'll get you home and into a nice hot bath. You'll like Meg. I think she'll like you, too. What's your name? No, never mind. We'll figure that out later." Alex ignored the horrific stench that hit him square in the nose. Just a few more minutes and then the boy would be clean and dry. With any luck at all, the lad would be young enough that the horror would fade quickly.

The gate guards were surprised to see him. The drawbridge was let down immediately, and he heard his presence being announced all the way up to the keep. Great. Margaret would probably bar the door before he got there.

George was waiting for him on the steps. Alex dismounted with the boy still in his arms. A stableboy took Beast away. George looked at Alex with a relieved smile.

"Changed your mind, did you?"

"No, I didn't," Alex said. Even saying it numbed him to the core. "I couldn't leave."

"Ah," George said with a nod, "you couldn't leave her."

"I didn't say that. I couldn't get home. It was physically impossible. Don't ask me to explain because you wouldn't believe me if I did. For now, I just need a place to stay until I figure out what to do. Will Margaret let me stay?"

"I don't know. She hasn't come out of her chamber yet."

"Good grief, George!" Alex exclaimed. "Have you checked to see if she's all right?"

"So young and arrogant you are, lad," George grumbled. "Think you she would weep so much over you?"

"I would weep that much over her."

"Then stay, and solve the problem for the both of you!"

Alex sighed. "I can't, George. I need to get this little guy settled, then decide what to do."

George grunted, then looked at the smelly bundle in Alex's arms. "Who've you got there?"

"I'm not sure. Let me get him cleaned up, then we need to talk. There are very strange things going on."

George nodded and led the way into the house. Alex carried the boy upstairs to William's room. He held the boy close and continued to rock him as a tub was brought up and buckets of water emptied into it. Cook came in on the heels of the last bucket of water with a tray full of food. Margaret came in right behind her.

Alex couldn't help but look at her. She looked as bad as he felt.

"I never gave you leave to enter my house again," she said hoarsely.

Alex stood near the tub with the child in his arms and hardly knew where to start. He wanted to apologize for hurting her. He wanted to clutch her to him and tell her how damned scared he was because he thought he might never get home. He wanted to promise her he'd stay until he was certain she was safe. Seeing firsthand the outcome of Ralf's cruelty had left him more unnerved than he'd imagined it might.

But what he really wanted to do was grab on to her and never let her go. Ever.

Unfortunately, it was the one thing he couldn't do.

So instead, he stood there motionless, holding onto a small boy who clutched his coat with both tiny hands. All he could do was stare at her, mute.

"Who is this?" Margaret asked.

Alex swallowed, hard. "A child of one of your servants, I assume. Brackwald's knights killed his parents."

"Merciful saints above," she breathed. "Are you certain?"

"Very."

"And you rescued him? Without a sword?"

He shook his head. "He was being chased. I just happened to be in the right place to catch him and hide him."

She nodded absently. "Those who live on the borders teach their little ones to run at the first sign of trouble. Are his parents still alive?"

"I didn't look. If they weren't, I didn't want him to have to see it. If you want to send someone, I can tell them where to go. Do you want to bathe him?"

Margaret jerked backward, looking as if he'd asked her to put her hand in a snake pit. "I know nothing of children," she gasped. "I cannot tend him."

"Great," Alex muttered. He knelt down beside the tub and tested the water. Satisfied, he stripped off his coat and the child's filthy rags, rolled up his sleeves and put the toddler into the water.

"I thought you were going home."

Alex couldn't look at her. He could hardly bear to say the words. "I tried. I couldn't."

"Perhaps it was that you didn't want to."

Alex met her gaze and winced at the faint flicker of hope he saw in her eyes. "I don't want to go, but I can't stay," he said softly. "I have to go home. If I can get there."

He watched her digest that, then continued to look at her as the transformation took place before his very eyes. She stiffened her spine and the light went out of her eyes. Her hair might have still been loose and her mail still reposing in her bedroom, but Margaret the Shieldmaiden was definitely back in charge. *All men are liars.* Hadn't she said that to him when he first met her? So he hadn't outright lied to her. He'd never said he would stay. But he'd certainly kissed her as if he meant to hang around. It amounted to about the same level of deception. He sighed. So much for having won her trust.

"The child will sleep here," she announced.

"That's very kind of you."

She paused. "You may stay to watch over him. For however long you will."

"Of course. Also very kind."

"I am doing it for the child. No one else."

Alex understood that message loud and clear. "I know. I don't blame you for being angry with me."

"I wouldn't waste my anger on you," she said quietly, then left the room.

Ouch. Alex knew he deserved that, but it stung just the same. But it was much less than he should have had coming to him. He had been a complete idiot. He never should have gotten involved with her personally. It would have saved them both a good deal of grief.

And he also would have missed out on the French kiss of a lifetime.

Alex looked down at the boy who was watching him now with wide, tear-filled eyes.

"She's a hell of a woman," he said.

The boy only blinked.

Alex smiled. "I've never met anyone like her, little guy, and I've met more women than you've ever seen. And that's the problem. Who could I possibly ever run into in my time who would compare to her?"

The boy said nothing.

"My thoughts exactly," Alex agreed. "But the thing is, I just can't have her. We're worlds apart, literally." He smoothed the boy's hair back from his face. "My work here is done, anyway. I'm sure it was just a fluke that the circle didn't work. I guess my hanging around longer certainly worked out well for . . ."

Alex paused and looked at the toddler sitting in very murky bathwater.

"For you," he finished.

Well, that answered a few questions. Maybe rescuing this little guy was the last of the things he had to do in the Middle Ages. Alex felt an overwhelming sense of relief. That had to be it. He'd saved Margaret and now he'd saved one of her people. Whew.

Alex smiled. "All right, buddy, let's get you out of that tub. I think it's time you had a little nap. I'll hang around for a couple of days and make sure you're settled. A good night's sleep will help. Things will look better in the morning. My mom always said that was true." He rinsed the child off, then dried him with a soft cloth. "I guess you don't have to go to the bathroom, so I'll just tuck you in." He dug around in William's trunk until he found a soft undertunic. It was hopelessly large, but looked kind of cute on the dark-haired, pale-eyed lad. Alex gathered him close again. "What's your name, little one?"

"Amery."

Alex pulled back in surprise. "Amery?"

Amery put his thumb in his mouth and began to suck.

"Well, Amery, I'm Alex. Nice to meet you. Don't worry about Meg. She'll take care of you." He scooped Amery up and carried him to the bed. The child cried out the moment Alex put him down. This might prove more difficult than he'd anticipated. He tucked Amery in, then sat with him until the boy fell asleep.

Then he leaned back against the chair and closed his own eyes.

What a hellish day it had been.

He had the feeling the next few just weren't going to get any better.

TWO DAYS LATER he stood in much the same place, looking at the little boy sleeping in his bed. Fatherly feelings welled up in him. It was well past time he settled down and started a family. Maybe if he concentrated on that thought while in the faery ring, he'd actually make it home this time. Yes, he'd just hurry right home and apply himself to the task of finding a wife.

He studiously ignored the fact that the perfect choice was sleeping down the hallway from him.

He walked out into the passageway and into Margaret.

Literally. He reached out to steady her and caught an armful of mail. Alex met her eyes and groaned silently. Where in the twentieth century would he ever find anyone who could hold a candle to her?

She jerked her arm away. "Pay more heed to where you are going," she said curtly.

"Margaret, I have to go."

"Then go."

Don't you care? was on the tip of his tongue, but he didn't say it. What difference did it make? He couldn't stay and he couldn't take her with him. Was this his just desserts for a poor career choice?

"I wish I could stay. . . ."

"You can't wield a sword," she said. "Of what use are you to me?"

Never mind trying to convince her that indeed he *could* wield a sword and that he'd learned his technique from one of the most ruthless Scottish lairds of the fourteenth century. He simply nodded.

"You're right. And anyway, I need to go."

"Then *go*," she said, pointing to the stairs. "And be quick about it."

He wanted to kiss her. He would have if she hadn't had her knife halfway out of its sheath. So instead, he gave her a look he hoped said everything he'd never be able to say, then he turned and walked carefully down the steps.

George was standing near the door. "Off again?"

"I think it will work this time," Alex said, hoping he sounded more confident than he felt.

"I wish I had the entire tale."

"Trust me. You wouldn't want it."

And with that, Alex pulled the hall door shut behind him. He retrieved Beast from the stables and headed across the drawbridge as the sun started to rise. He was tired. He was even too tired to enjoy thoughts of wringing Jamie's neck, which was the very first thing he would do when he got home. The least his brother-in-law could have done was to put a warning label on that map. *Warning: Time-*

traveling in medieval England only leads to intense heartbreak. Proceed at your own risk.

Alex pointed his horse west and tried to think of home. All he could think about was Margaret.

Ten

MARGARET STOOD ON THE BATTLEMENTS. IT WAS THE place she always came to think. Staring out over her land usually gave her much needed perspective when the events in her life seemed too overwhelming. This eve standing on the wall gave her no relief. She could not stand on the east wall without remembering how Alex had kissed her there. Sleeping or awake, the feel of his mouth was branded on hers.

At least he was finally gone. She'd watched him ride off from her current position on the battlements. She hadn't wanted to do it, but she'd forced herself. Seeing him leave would be the only thing that would convince her he'd made his final choice.

And that choice was not her.

"Fool," she whispered.

She turned away from the east and walked the perimeter to the west wall. She stared out over her baileys, looking at the glow from small fires here and there. The smith's hammer no longer rang out. Her men no longer trained in the outer bailey. True, it was well past time to cease working, but the keep seemed somehow deserted. Or maybe 'twas she who was deserted.

She had lost three of her brothers with one missive sent from the king's scribe, yet it had not pained her this much. She'd buried her eldest brother, then her father a pair of months later, and she'd never felt this alone. She'd known what her task was and what she would have to do to see it accomplished. Never once had she allowed herself the luxury of sitting and thinking about how her life might have been had she not been mistress of Falconberg.

Alex was to blame for having shown her how life could be. And blame him she would. If he had never come along, she never would have relaxed her guard. She never would have sat with a man simply to speak of nothing of consequence. She never would have known how it was for a man to look at her and see just Margaret. Saints above, how she wished she had never kissed him! Her mouth would never forget how it felt to be under his.

"My lady?"

Margaret turned to see her page Timothy standing hesitantly next to her.

"Aye, lad?"

"The child screams for Lord Alex. I was sent to fetch you."

"Saints, what know I of children?" Margaret asked.

Young Timothy only shrugged, looking as helpless as she felt.

"Very well," she said with a deep sigh, "I will do what I can."

It turned out that very little was what she succeeded in doing. The child, Amery, as she learned was his name, wanted Alex, and there was no convincing him that he could not have what he asked for. Margaret tried to reason with him, but her words fell on deaf ears. He seemed incapable of sitting still and listening to her. The child screamed and wept and generally behaved very poorly. Margaret was hardly surprised. Alex had already ruined her life. It seemed that he'd left behind a gift that would soon ruin her ears.

"Saints!" she exclaimed, after what seemed hours of listening to the young boy carry on. "I cannot believe this is one of my people! Surely children here are raised not to be so fractious."

"Actually," George said, from where he stood near the

doorway, shielding his ears with his hands, "he's one of Brackwald's peasants."

"That does not surprise me," Margaret grumbled. Then she jerked her gaze to her captain. "What mean you by that?"

"The peasants who were slain were his, not ours."

"I thought Brackwald had attacked our people."

"Nay. He attacked his own, wearing your colors."

"The whoreson," Margaret breathed. "By the saints, the wretch will stop at nothing." She looked down at Amery, who, blessedly, had ceased to howl. He was staring up at her, as if he expected to be packed off at any moment back to Brackwald. "Do you understand me?" she asked. She had no idea what intelligence a child this young possessed. He seemed to have little vocabulary outside of "Aweks" and "Whaa."

In answer, the child held out its arms, as if it wished to be picked up.

Margaret frowned. "I've no time to humor you, Amery. You will stay here, but you will behave without me tending to you." She wagged her finger at him for emphasis. To her horror, the boy latched onto her finger and used it as a means to hoist himself up onto her lap. "Wait, by the saints," she spluttered.

The boy arranged himself on her lap, took hold of her long braid in one hand, stuck his thumb in his mouth and stared up at her.

Margaret looked at George for aid. He only held up his hands and backed out of the chamber.

"Wait!" she called. "Help!"

The passageway became, quite conveniently, empty. Margaret vowed heads would roll as soon as she'd managed to extricate herself from this predicament.

Amery snuggled closer, then closed his eyes and let loose a little sigh. Well, perhaps the lad had worn himself out. Margaret leaned back against her chair and put her arm around the boy's back. No sense in not giving him something to lean against. For all she knew, if she didn't he would fall to the floor, and then she would have his screaming to contend with again. Aye, and there was no sense not to secure his feet as well. With both arms around him, he surely wouldn't take a tumble. She nodded to herself over that and leaned her pounding head back against the chair.

Saints, what a day. She sincerely hoped it would be the last such day she would pass in her lifetime.

She felt herself begin to relax, though she fought it for quite some time. The last thing she wanted was to relax her guard enough for thoughts of Alex to creep back into her mind.

Somehow, she was overtaken by them just the same. What could it hurt to dream of him one last time? A few last thoughts, then she would put him from her mind forever.

She fell asleep with tears running down her cheeks.

ALEX WOKE, STIFF and sore. He looked up at the sky. No jets flying overhead. Of course Jamie lived so far north a jet was fairly rare. And the estate was so large, you could go for days without even hearing a car.

Neither of those things made Alex feel any better—mainly because he suspected he wasn't on Jamie's land.

He sat up, shivering. Wherever he was in time, it was obviously still February because there was frost on the leaves he'd used to cover himself with the night before. Damn it anyway, what was the deal? He'd spent the bloody night in that faery ring, thinking himself into a migraine, trying to get himself home.

It obviously wasn't working.

He'd started to panic around three A.M. An Eagle Scout could still tell time even by medieval stars. It was about four A.M. that he realized he just wasn't going anywhere. He'd tried to sleep then, hoping he would dream himself home. It didn't look like that had worked, either.

Alex dropped his face into his hands and groaned. He was stuck. There was just no other conclusion to come to.

He'd used every ounce of lawyer's logic the night before
to solve his dilemma. He'd considered the sun's position,
the weather, the innermost desires of his heart. He'd factored in Jamie's nonpresence, what he'd accomplished in
medieval England, the fact that he needed Twinkies to survive. He'd contemplated his own checkered past, the res-
titution he'd tried to make, the change of heart he'd had.
He'd given thought to Elizabeth's experiences with Jamie's forest, how she hadn't wanted to leave the first time,
how she and Jamie had traveled forward in time seemingly
because they wanted to stay together. Alex had examined
his own heart.

And he'd done his damnedest to ignore the effect Margaret of Falconberg had had on him.

It wouldn't work with her. It *couldn't* work. He would
screw up history if he stayed. She needed a medieval guy.
He could certainly negotiate the inner workings of the
modern automobile, but that didn't exactly qualify him to
start fixing things around the castle.

But what other choice did he have?

He shook his head sharply. No. He would not allow that
damned faery ring to control his destiny. He could get
home if he really wanted to. The gate in Jamie's forest
was always open. He'd used it twice and had had no trouble. It would work for him again if he wanted it to.

But did he?

He moved backward to lean against a tree where he
could examine his choices more comfortably. The way he
saw it, he could either chance a trip to Scotland or remain
where he was and work things out with Margaret.

*You never know when you'll have to go back to the
Middle Ages and rescue me from too much beer and
wenching.*

His own words came back to him, words he'd said to
Jamie after hearing Jamie's own time-traveling tale.

He'd just been kidding!

Did he want to be rescued? To go back to what? His
car? His bank account? Fiona MacAllister? As if she were

even an option! For all he knew, Zachary had hoodwinked her into believing he was a tidy, responsible citizen with prospects. What he had waiting for him in the twentieth century were just things, material things he could live without.

There was his family, though. Alex smiled wistfully. He would miss Christmas reunions in Seattle with kids and sleeping bags strewn from one end of the house to the other. He would miss his brothers and Elizabeth. He would miss flying home to sit in his parents' kitchen and chat with his mom over brownies and play a little one-on-one with his dad in the driveway. It would be hard not to pick up the phone and hear them on the other end.

But lots of people took jobs in faraway lands with bad phone service and rotten mail delivery. Staying wouldn't be much different than that. And much as he loved his family, they couldn't replace the chance to have a family of his own.

With Margaret.

He turned over in his mind what it would mean to stay. There were the obvious things, of course, like day-to-day living. He'd always liked camping. He could do it for the rest of his life and probably be very content. That was about the level of civilization he was dealing with. He had some rudimentary medical skills, thanks to his dad's insistence. He was full of common sense. He could make a few improvements to Margaret's castle without completely throwing England's progression to the industrial age off.

But that wasn't what would make staying worth it.

Margaret was the prize.

Alex rubbed his hands over his face. How could he even contemplate walking away from her? How could he have actually imagined he would have succeeded? He would have spent every minute of every day of the rest of his life kicking himself for having been too cowardly to grab the best thing that had ever walked into his life. The century was irrelevant. Everything else was unimportant. There was nothing in this century or any of the others that could possibly hold a candle to her.

Why had he been stupid enough to try to believe otherwise?

He rolled to his feet and stretched. He would go back to Falconberg and fix what he'd broken. Margaret would be furious with him, but he would prove himself to her. Maybe he wouldn't be of any use to her as a swordsman, but he could certainly give her surgeon tips on germ control. Maybe he could help out in the kitchen. Maybe he could marry her and be her baron consort.

He straightened with his saddle in his hands. Could he marry her? Or would the king laugh at the idea and give her to Edward anyway?

"When hell freezes over," he muttered as he swung the saddle onto Beast's back. He would lie like a rug if he had to to convince Richard he was good husband material. Yes, there were many things he'd do before he let Edward get his paws on *his* future wife.

Assuming, of course, he could keep her from decapitating him long enough to convince her she should marry him. For all he knew, she might actually come to want him again. He smiled, feeling better than he had in hours. His fate was in his hands again.

He did, of course, studiously avoid the thought that scared the hell out of him: He would live and die in medieval England and no one would be the wiser.

Alex swung up into the saddle and turned Beast back to Margaret's hall. Maybe he could get himself inserted into the history books. At least his sister would stumble across him while doing research. His family would know he'd been well and happy. He couldn't ask for more than that.

His good mood lasted until he could see Falconberg in the distance, then his bravado began to dissipate. His arrival had all the earmarks of a doozy of a humiliating moment. Margaret would throw up her hands over it, probably after suggesting he take up residence in her dungeon. Margaret he thought he could handle. It was George that made him nervous. He had the distinct feeling he wouldn't get away with any more hedging. Sir George of York would have the whole story, or Alex knew he probably *would* become very familiar with Margaret's dungeon. Damned faery ring. It had caused him a severe amount of stress.

He reached the castle almost too soon for comfort. The drawbridge was half up, but it lowered as he approached. Well, so far, so good. The guards saluted him as he rode by. Men trained in the lists instead of gathering together to capture him. That was a good sign.

George was standing in the doorway to the great hall. Alex dismounted, and a teenager immediately appeared to take his horse. Alex looked at George and smiled weakly.

"Mornin'," he said, trying to sound casual.

George very slowly and very deliberately folded his arms over his chest. Alex had seen that move before on his father. George really meant business this time.

"My lord," he said slowly, "I pray you, come to a decision and carry it out! This is a most distressing habit you have begun."

Alex sighed. "I'm here for good this time, George."

"I fear I require the entire tale," George stated.

"I think—"

"The *entire* tale this time, my lord."

"Maybe I should talk to Margaret first. I owe her that much."

George's look darkened. "The sun will not set on this day ere you have given me what I demand."

"Yes, sir."

George grunted. "Young Amery will be happy to see you. He was less than pleased to have you leave."

"Well, I don't know that I should get invol—" He shut his mouth abruptly at the look on George's face. "I'd be happy to see the little tyke. Where is he?"

"One of Cook's maids has the keeping of him. A young girl with an endless supply of energy."

Alex smiled. "I'll just bet." No sooner had he said that than he heard a high-pitched, childlike scream of joy. He turned and saw Amery trundling across the inner bailey as fast as his little legs would carry him, followed by a girl of about twelve who looked completely exhausted. Alex scooped Amery up and winced at the choke hold the little boy put on him.

"Aweks, Aweks, Aweks!" Amery cried, over and over again.

It was enough to make a grown man get misty-eyed. Alex buried his face in Amery's freshly washed hair and breathed deeply. This was a good thing. Living in the Middle Ages would be a good thing. He could adopt Amery.

And why not? It wouldn't mess with history's time line. If Alex hadn't been there to rescue him, Amery would have died. He could adopt the boy, marry Margaret and live happily ever after.

Well, he would worry about it later. Now what he had to worry about was convincing Margaret to let him stay. And he had to convince himself that keeping his hands and his mouth away from her until he could convince her to trust him again was a good idea.

"Where's Margaret?" Alex asked George, rubbing Amery's back soothingly.

"Off stirring up mischief."

Alex's hand froze of its own volition. "By herself?"

"Nay. She took a handful of the more reckless lads."

"Good grief, George, why didn't you stop her?"

One of George's eyebrows went up. "Such concern you show, my lord."

"Look, I never said I didn't care about her. I just said I couldn't stay and marry her."

"Yet, here you are."

Alex growled in frustration. "She could get herself killed!"

"She's quite skilled at seeing to herself."

"Well, I don't think she's quite herself lately," Alex muttered. "Do you have any idea where she would have gone?"

"Aye. She will have gone to ride the borders. She hasn't

been gone long. We'll find her.'' He nodded to the men who were saddling up near the stables. ''I thought you might care to go have a look, so I had the lads prepared once we saw you were coming back home.''

Alex looked at the young girl who stood nearby looking like she could really use a nap. ''What's your name?''

''Frances, my lord,'' she said, bobbing.

''You're back on duty, Frances. Amery, I have to go, but I promise you I'll come right back.'' How much English Amery understood, Alex couldn't have said, but it was for darn sure he understood the tone in Alex's voice because he began to howl. Alex kissed Amery on the cheek, then extricated himself from the boy's clutching grasp. Frances took the screaming bundle; fortunately she seemed to be stronger than she looked. Alex swung up into the saddle. ''I'll be back,'' he said, coming close to a shout to be heard over Amery's bellowing. ''Amery, I'll be back!''

Well, logic wasn't doing any good. Alex turned Beast toward the gate and urged him forward. The sooner he made sure Margaret wasn't in over her head, the better he would like it.

Eleven

❧❧

IT WAS A PERFECT DAY FOR FOUL DEEDS. NOT ONLY WAS it cold as hell outside, it was drizzling. Alex hadn't ridden a mile before his jeans were soaked and his hair was plastered to his head. His leather coat was some protection, but what he wouldn't have given for a nice four-wheel drive with a good heater and functioning windshield wipers. Beast was anything but pleased with the weather and wasn't shy about letting Alex know as much. He had his hands full trying to control the spirited gelding. Just when Alex thought he couldn't become any more uncomfortable, a wind picked up out of the north. The arctic breezes left him feeling as though he wore nothing at all. He longed for a hot shower as he had never longed for anything else in his life.

Before long they were greeted by the sound of raucous laughter and coarse jests.

Alex threw George a look. "Wonderful."

"You have no sword, my lord—"

"I won't need one," Alex said as he thundered around a grouping of poorly made huts. He ducked as he saw a man lift a crossbow and point it at him. Margaret's knight behind him cried out in pain. Alex would have turned to offer aid, but he was too preoccupied with the horror before him.

Margaret's six knights were dead, along with a dozen of her peasants. Blood was everywhere; on the buildings, seeping into the mud, on discarded weapons. Horrible as that was, that wasn't what sent him into an almost mindless panic.

Margaret was currently trying to keep half a dozen men at bay while another half dozen looked on and laughed uproariously, shouting suggestions to her on how to defend herself.

Arrows started flying, and Alex's only thought was to get to the ground and take Margaret there with him. If he could just get to her, he thought he might be able to get her out of there.

"Margaret!"

She whirled around to look at him. Alex's warning shout died in his throat. The largest and ugliest of Brackwald's knights grabbed her from behind and laid his sword across her throat.

The sounds of battle raged around him, but all Alex could do was stare at Margaret held captive by that hulking man and know that he was part of the reason she found herself there.

"Damn it!" he exclaimed, his eyes locked with hers. "George!" he shouted.

"Aye?" George called back.

"I need help!"

"I'm a bit pressed at the moment," George said tightly. "See to it yourself, won't you? I'll save one of these for questioning. Bloody whoresons, who wants to live?"

Alex swallowed and looked back at Brackwald's soldier. The man pressed his blade more firmly against Margaret's throat and grinned.

"Looks like I have something you want," he said, spitting a huge glob of mucus at Alex.

Alex didn't flinch as it hit him on the neck. "I'd let her go, if I were you," he warned.

Geez, even saying it sounded stupid. As if he had anything to back that up with! A battle of impressive proportions raged around him, and he could only stand there, weaponless, and try to reason with a man who didn't exactly radiate excessive intelligence. If he didn't do some

.

pretty fine talking, Margaret would be dead and he would be responsible. The slightest turn of the blade and her throat would be slit.

She was as still as a statue. She wasn't weeping or pleading for mercy. For all her expression revealed, she might have been strolling in the lists, looking over her men.

Then again, there was the look in her eye. He flattered himself that she looked a bit relieved to see him. But it didn't take a brain surgeon to determine that even though she might be somewhat happy to see a friendly face, she was also convinced he couldn't do a damn thing to save her.

It took him about a split second to make up his mind. He could bide his time and hope George and the six knights they'd brought along could finish all of Brackwald's boys, then still have enough energy to deal with Margaret's captor. Or he could deal with her captor himself, which meant breaking the vow he'd made to himself to never again harm another human being.

His vow, or Margaret's life.

The choice was very easy to make.

He shrugged out of his leather coat and looked at the man.

"Fight me for her."

Margaret closed her eyes and a shudder went through her.

"Hey," Alex said crossly, "I can do this."

Margaret opened her eyes and looked at him. She said nothing out loud, but her eyes said *I certainly hope so*. Alex scowled at her, then turned his attentions back to the man who held her captive. He ignored the sickening fear that made his arms and legs feel like they were going to sleep.

"I think I'll be keepin' her," the man said, still grinning. He gave Margaret a squeeze.

"Why don't you take me instead," Alex offered. "I'm worth more to you than she is."

The man spat again. "Who're you?"

"Alexander of Seattle, friend to the king, beloved of Lord Brackwald. If it's gold you're after, I'm your man. I'll bring you far more than she will."

"How much?" the man asked calculatingly.

"More than she will. Trust me."

Out of the corner of his eye he caught sight of Margaret's right fingers inching something out of her sleeve. Probably a knife. Well, in the time it would take her to move her body and skewer her captor's family jewels, her captor would have dragged his blade across her throat. If only someone would shove the tip of the blade forward so Margaret could wrench away. No, that would take more luck than anyone in the group had at the moment. Alex knew it was up to him to work this out.

"Of course, I'm only worth something to the man who can take me." He shrugged. "I suppose that man won't be you."

The unkempt knight's reaction was so quick, Alex hardly had time to react. Fortunately Margaret was quicker witted than he was, and she managed to avoid the man's blade as he shoved her and sent her sprawling.

Then Alex realized he had much more pressing problems to deal with—such as a medieval knight covered in mail, brandishing a sword and planning on having him for dessert. And there he stood in jeans, a denim shirt, and hiking boots. No sword, just his good looks and wits.

Heaven help him.

"A sword?" Alex asked hopefully.

"Can ye wield one?" the grinning giant of a man asked.

Alex checked out the surrounding terrain with as much peripheral vision as he could spare. "Maybe," he said slowly, "if I could figure out which end to pick it up by—"

Brackwald's knight lunged. Alex ducked and rolled. He came up with a sword in his hands. The hilt was slippery with someone's blood; Alex was only grateful it wasn't his. Yet.

It had been a while since anyone had tried to kill him,

and he immediately realized how out of practice he was. Parrying for exercise was not quite the same thing as fighting for your life, even if your sparring partner was James MacLeod.

He winced the first time the tip of the man's sword glanced off his shoulder. Warmth immediately saturated his shirt. Great. All he needed was a body covered with wounds sewn up by a medieval healer. Another cut on his forearm was all it took for him to decide he'd had enough.

Damn, but he was out of shape. And he was unprotected. What he wouldn't have given for a good mail shirt. Though he'd fought half naked against medieval clansmen, he'd also been fresh from his days of piracy and several weeks of MacLeod Swordfighting 201.

"I should have paid more attention in class," he muttered as he wrenched his back spinning out of the way of a thrusting blade.

He didn't spin fast enough. He'd escaped the man's forehand, but the backhand was there faster than he'd anticipated. He held the blade away with his own borrowed sword, but his elbows were bending in ways they weren't designed to. Alex felt cold, hard fear in a way he hadn't ever experienced in his life.

I am going to die in medieval England. His mind screamed for him to find a way of escape, but he knew there was none. Another few seconds and his arms would give way and that blade would come ripping through his side. The man bearing down on him was grinning madly.

And then, quite suddenly, a look of astonishment came over the man's face.

The pressure against Alex's sword eased and the man began to lean to one side. He kept leaning until he met the ground. Alex looked down in surprise. A knife was protruding from his back.

Margaret didn't waste any time with pleasantries. She jerked her knife free of the man's back, then grabbed Alex and spun him away from her.

"Back to back," she barked. "Do the best you can."

"The best I can?" Alex spluttered. "He didn't have me. I was on the verge of—"

Margaret's elbow connected with his kidney and Alex shut his mouth abruptly. He held up his sword, grateful he was still alive to do it, and looked around him for another foe.

But the battle was over. George was herding a pair of bound Brackwald knights to horses.

"Wounded first, burying last," Margaret said, stepping away.

Alex almost lost his balance. Margaret turned him around and put her hand on his shoulder. Her fingers came away bloody. Alex started to pull on his sleeve, but she stopped him. She cut off both his sleeves and bound them over the worst of the cuts. Alex put his hand on her arm.

"Thank you."

She pulled away.

Alex caught her by the arm and tried to turn her back to him. She turned and the look she gave him almost brought him to his knees, it was so cold. As if he meant nothing to her.

And it was then he realized just exactly how much she meant to him.

Why had he ever tried to go home? He'd been kidding himself. He'd never in all his days met a woman like Margaret of Falconberg. He would have spent the rest of the twentieth century and a healthy chunk of the twenty-first looking for someone like her and he never would have been satisfied.

And now he had chosen to stay in medieval England.

With this woman.

Who couldn't stand the sight of him.

Well, this was the first hurdle to be overcome. Maybe if he could get his arms around her and keep them there long enough, she actually might forgive him for leaving her. And while he had her in his arms, he would tell her all the details he'd left out and maybe that would soften her heart. And once she'd forgiven him, he would give serious thought to figuring out how to have a future with her, because he damn well couldn't imagine a future without her.

Well, there was no time like the present to start.

"I think I'm going to faint," he said, putting his hand to his brow. If it could work for Scarlett O'Hara, it could work for him.

"By the bloody saints," Margaret muttered.

Alex swooned.

Her arms were around him. This was a good sign.

"Must you be such a weak-kneed woman?" she demanded.

Alex gritted his teeth. He bit his tongue while he was at it. She had her arms around him, and he didn't care how that was accomplished.

"Get me home," he said weakly. "But don't forget my coat."

Margaret cursed, but reached down and picked up his coat just the same. She pulled his arm over her shoulder and grasped him firmly around the waist. She was muttering under her breath and sounding very disgusted, but she was holding him. Alex vowed right then that he'd be out in the lists just as soon as he stopped bleeding. He'd already broken his vow never to pick up another sword. There was no sense in not going the rest of the way.

Margaret led him to Beast. "Can you ride?"

"Not without help." He looked at her and tried to look faint. It wasn't much of an effort. In fact, he was starting to feel a little light-headed.

"Oh, but you're a useless piece of baggage!" she exclaimed as she held his stirrup. Alex managed to get his foot up and Margaret shoved him up into the saddle. She swung up behind him without effort. She wrapped her arms around him and took the reins away.

Alex closed his eyes. All right, so getting to this point had been humiliating. The end certainly justified the means.

"Alex!"

He jerked awake and realized he'd almost fallen off his horse.

"We must needs make haste," she said, kicking Beast into a gallop. "Stay in the saddle, won't you?"

"I think you'll have to hold me there—"

She swore in frustration.

Every yard was another agony and by the time they reached the castle, Alex didn't care if Margaret's arms were around him or not. What he wanted was a shot of Demerol and a soft bed.

Margaret got him up the stairs. Alex wasn't quite sure how she managed it, but she was obviously stronger than she looked. The mist in his head cleared long enough for him to find himself being dumped rather gently, all things considered, into a chair. He leaned his head back and watched Margaret throw his coat on the bed, then lean over and shrug out of her mail. The sleeve of her padded undershirt was stained with blood.

"You're hurt," he said, struggling to sit upright. "Let me look at it."

"And what would you know of healing?"

"My father is a healer. I learned a lot from him."

She shot him a look of pure frost. "Which is the lie, how your sire earns his bread or your claim to spurs? Both cannot be true."

Well, it just wasn't his day.

"In Seattle a healer is a very important, usually very wealthy man." He looked at her unflinchingly. "And that's the truth."

"And your claim to knighthood?"

"I never claimed anything. It just seemed best to let people assume what they wanted to."

She could have wilted an entire field with that look.

"All right," he said with a sigh. "I lied."

She pursed her lips. "I should have known."

"Look," he said, trying to get to his feet, "I promise I'll tell you all the truth and anything else you want to know just as soon as we get ourselves sewn up." He found himself back on the chair suddenly, thanks to her hand in the middle of his chest. "At least trust me to know what to do with a cut."

"I'll wait for my own surgeon," she said, turning away from him.

"Make way," a rusty voice said imperiously from the hallway. "I've come to heal."

Margaret looked at him with raised eyebrows. "And so he appears. A true healer."

A filthy old man with a bag of leeches and an armful of pouches containing heaven-only-knew-what entered the room as if he were the king.

"All stand aside," he said, as if he spoke to a room full of people instead of just two. "I'm here to heal the lady Margaret."

"I don't think so," Alex said.

"And what would you know of it, sir knight?" the man asked, coughing and spewing spittle all over the room. "Not much, I'll wager." The man reached into his bag and pulled out a slimy leech. "Your arm, Lady Falconberg."

Margaret might have had nerves of steel, but slugs obviously made her queasy. Alex watched her turn several shades of green before her color settled into a nice, pasty white. She sat down on the bed with a thump.

"Ah, my good man," Alex said, diverting said healer's attention, "these wounds here are too trivial for one of your great skill. I'm certain there are others below with more need of you than us."

The old man turned a bloodshot eye on him. "And who'll tend you both? You, sir knight, look to have little enough blood to spare, but a good draining would likely serve you well."

"I'm handy with a needle," Alex said quickly. "I can tend the lady Margaret."

The old man looked at him skeptically. "What know you of healing?"

"A small amount," Alex said. "And should I have a

question, be assured I will send for you posthaste.''

"Aye, Master Jacob," Margaret said faintly. " 'Tis but a scratch I have. My men are in greater need than I."

Master Jacob grunted. "Very well then. I'll come back later to bleed you both."

"Over my dead body," Alex muttered as the man left the room. He looked at Margaret. "Can you sew?"

"I'd rather you bled to death," she said curtly.

Alex started to say something but found himself distracted by the small body that screeched as it burst into the room and toddled over to him as fast as the little legs would go. Alex scooped Amery up and held him close.

"It's all right, Amery," he said soothingly. "See? Meg and I are both fine. A little dirty, but unhurt."

Amery buried his face in Alex's bloody neck and sobbed. Alex held him close with one arm and beckoned to Frances, who was standing near the door. "I need a needle, thread, and lots of hot water."

"I do not sew well," Margaret muttered.

"You're going to learn how," Alex said. "Frances, see if Cook has those things, won't you? And a couple of candles." He looked at Margaret. "Just think about how much fun you'll have causing me all that pain. And do you have any strong drink?"

She nodded. "In my trunk."

"Good. I want you good and drunk before I start working on your arm."

She looked up at him suspiciously. "Why?" she demanded.

He looked at her. There was dirt and blood on her face, streaked by dried sweat. Alex was certain he'd never before laid eyes on a more beautiful sight. She was relatively unhurt, and she'd live many more years full of giving him grief. He smiled.

"Because I don't want you to feel any pain," he said. "Go fetch it. Amery and I'll be waiting for you here."

She left the room without further comment. Alex put both his arms around Amery and hugged him gently.

"I'm okay, son," he whispered. "Amery, relax."

Within moments Cook had arrived and was seeing the chamber prepared for healing activities. Alex sat and watched as candles were lit and buckets of water were brought in for washing. Frances appeared momentarily, her eyes wide with fear. Alex beckoned to her.

"Take Amery, would you? Amery, Frances is going to take you downstairs and get you something to eat. Bread? Butter? Jam?"

None of those things seemed to make any impression, which meant that Amery was screaming his head off as Frances carried him off. Alex waved reassuringly, then leaned back against the chair and just concentrated on breathing. His shirt was trashed, but at least he'd managed to save his coat. Things could have beeen worse.

Margaret entered the chamber, carrying two bottles of something Alex hoped was drinkable. She'd removed her sleeve and tied a bandage of sorts around her arm.

"Let me look," he said, waving her closer.

" 'Tis nothing."

"Then you won't mind if I look."

She set the bottles down on the table next to Cook's needle and thread, sighed heavily, and then unwrapped her arm. Alex looked at the cut. It wasn't deep, but an emergency room certainly would have sewn it up.

"As you can see," Margaret said, " 'tis nothing to trouble yourself over. Now, can you sew yourself up, or must I call for Master Jacob?"

"I'd like you to do it."

"I know nothing of healing matters."

"I'll teach you what you need to know."

"I have no desire—"

"Please," he asked, feeling very light-headed all of the sudden. "I don't trust anyone else, Margaret. Just do this one thing for me."

She scowled. "I don't know why I should."

"Because you want to know all the truth I have to tell

you, and you won't get it if you leave me in the care of that leech. How about that for logic?''

She picked up the needle. ''All right. What will you have done?''

Alex looked at the needle and grimaced at its thickness. He'd had more than his share of sutures, but those very small, very sterile little needles were a far sight less intimidating than the thick piece of steel he was looking at.

''Wash your hands first,'' he said, gritting his teeth as he sat up and tried to strip off what was left of his shirt. ''Then hold the needle in the flame of the candle. It will burn off all the germs.''

''Germs?''

''I'll explain later, okay? Please just do it.''

She looked like she wasn't going to until he pulled away one of her makeshift tourniquets. Alex didn't let himself think much about what he needed to do. He uncorked a bottle of whatever spirits she'd brought and poured it over his arm.

''Yeouch!'' he bellowed. ''Ouch, damn it,'' he said, blowing on his shoulder as best he could. ''Damn it to hell!''

Blowing was not a good idea. He began to see stars.

''Just sew,'' he gasped. ''Start at one end and finish at the other. Do the best you can. If I don't make it through, just pour whatever that stuff is on the other cuts and sew them too. Got it?''

She was as white as a sheet. Her lips were bloodless and compressed in a very tight line, but she nodded just the same.

Alex leaned back against the chair and tried to concentrate on just staying conscious.

All in all, it was a very unpleasant experience. Margaret was not a seamstress, neither was she good at judging depths. Alex began to wonder if she intended to sew his bones together along with everything else. George appeared out of nowhere to hold a candle over him so Margaret could see better. George dripped wax on his bare chest twice which made him flinch which made Margaret jerk the needle.

He prayed for unconsciousness, but it never came.

By the time Margaret had finished, her hands were trembling uncontrollably. Alex took them and brought them to his lips.

"Thank you," he whispered. "You did a good job."

Tears were streaming down her face. "Don't ask me to do it again," she said, sniffling loudly.

"Better you than Master Jacob. Why don't you head off to bed? You could probably use some sleep."

"You're the one who needs sleep," Margaret said. "And food. I'll have some brought immediately."

Well, at least she wasn't planning on tossing him into the dungeon. Alex leaned his head back against the chair and closed his eyes.

This was a hell of a welcome-home party.

$Twelve$

MARGARET WOKE. EVERY BIT OF HER BODY TINGLED. AH, so she'd had a bit of a fever. And from such a paltry wound. She shook her head, and her flesh sent up renewed protests. She'd become soft. There would be no more of that. She would rouse, dress, arm, and put herself back in her normal mode of doing things. No matter that Alex was dwelling beneath her roof again.

Assuming he hadn't left while she'd slept.

She threw back her covers and crawled from her bed, though less agilely than she would have liked. She had a modest wash, then dressed. By the time she managed to don her mail, she was sweating profusely. She shuffled to the seat in the alcove and sat, panting. By the saints, she needed to train harder.

Once she'd caught her breath, she shuffled back across her chamber and opened the door. The sound of screeching was so loud, she wondered how she'd missed hearing it.

A score of dreadful possibilities assaulted her poor brain before she had even set foot to the stairs. Perhaps Baldric had taken to unraveling himself instead of the tapestries. Or perhaps something had happened to Alex. . . .

"As if it matters to me," she said, through gritted teeth. She thumped down the steps and skidded out into the great hall. She came to a sliding stop and her mood darkened considerably. Aye, Alex was behind this, to be sure. The wailing was coming from that wee Amery he'd brought home with no thought for the child's future or welfare.

Said child was currently fighting his keeper with tiny fists and prodigious wails.

"Amery, lord Alex is sleeping," Frances said, sounding as if her wits, and her patience, were stretched to their very breaking point.

Margaret could sympathize. And then Frances caught sight of her and looked as if she'd been given reprieve from the gallows.

"See you, Amery, there is the lady Margaret!"

"But I . . ." Margaret spluttered.

She held out her hands to ward Frances off only to find a small, squirming bundle foisted upon herself. She held him out at arm's length and spluttered again, but her protests resounded off Frances's retreating back.

Margaret looked at Amery. He returned her look. Silently. Well, at least that was progress. She held him firmly about his slight chest and marveled anew that something so small could produce such a volume of noise.

"Magwet," he said. Then he smiled at her.

"Indeed," Margaret said, at a complete loss. "I do not recall giving you leave to use my name, young Amery."

"Magwet," he said again. And he stretched out his scrawny arms toward her. "Pwetty Magwet."

"Indeed," she repeated.

Well, no sense in leaving the lad dangling out there so uncomfortably. She brought him close and settled him on her mail-covered hip as if she'd been doing it the whole of her life.

Amery reached around her with one hand and brought her heavy braid forward over her shoulder. Then he clutched it in one of his pudgy fists and smiled up at her.

"Pwetty hai-uh," he announced. Then without further comment, he popped his thumb into his mouth and concentrated on seemingly sucking the flesh from the bone. He looked up at her and the soft skin around his eyes crinkled as he smiled at her. Then he turned his attentions back to her hair that he held so tightly.

"Harumph," Margaret said, undone. She'd never suspected children to be so unsettling. To be sure, they were disruptive to a household. If young Amery wasn't bellowing his head off for Alex, he was eluding Frances and bellowing seemingly for the sheer sport of it. Hard on the ears indeed.

Yet it was this other habit the child had of crawling into her arms and latching onto her hair that left her feeling completely unbalanced. Who would have thought the sweet, innocent touch of a trusting child could stir up such tender emotions in her breast?

"Damn that Alex," Margaret muttered under her breath. If it wasn't Alex touching her hair, it was his small shadow. How was she to keep her wits about her in the face of this dual assault?

Amery's thumb came free of his mouth with a distinct popping sound. "Damn Aweks," he repeated cheerfully.

"Oh, nay," Margaret breathed, "you shouldn't say such."

"Damn Aweks now?" Amery asked hopefully.

What a thought. Margaret was so tempted to smile that she almost succumbed.

But only because Amery was such an angelic, cherubic child. It had nothing to do with Alex.

"His damning couldn't happen with enough swiftness to suit me," she confided. "What say you we break our fast, then seek him out?" *And you can bellow so loudly in his ear that the maids will be scraping his remains from the ceiling for a se'nnight.*

It was such an appealing thought, Margaret almost forewent the pleasure of a hot meal. Unfortunately, her belly seemed not to concur. Watching Alex leap from his skin would have to wait.

AFTER A HEARTY meal of porridge and cleaning up Amery's meal from off the front of the oversized tunic he seemed to have borrowed from her late brother's trunk, Margaret led her small charge up the stairs to the sleeping chambers. Climbing steps with a small child was a tedious process, but it gave her ample time to savor Alex's startled awakening, so she didn't begrudge Amery his independent ascent.

She paused at Alex's chamber door and put her ear to the wood. Ah, no sound. She pushed open the door and gestured for Amery to enter.

"A loud awakening call is best," she offered as Amery bounded into the chamber.

She pulled the door almost closed, leaving herself just enough of an opening to hear clearly Alex's surprise over his rude awakening.

"Aweks? Aweks?" There was a long pause, then a wail. "Aweks!"

The terror in Amery's voice brought Margaret into the room as if she'd been flung there. She was at the bedside instantly and she stretched her hand out, fully expecting to feel cold flesh.

He was burning up.

"Oh, merciful saints above," she breathed.

And still Amery continued to scream Alex's name.

"Amery!" Margaret exclaimed. "Be you silent!" She pulled the boy off the bed and held him to her, turning his face so she could look at him. "He sleeps, lad, nothing more! Here, feel you how his flesh is hot?" She knelt by the bed and let Amery touch Alex's hand. "See? Now, stay you here and keep hold of his hand. I will fetch help and soon he'll awaken."

Or so she hoped.

She fled to the doorway. "George!" she screamed. "Cook! Help me!"

A score of people were soon crowding inside the room. She shoved all but Cook and George out. Cook was not a healer, but she was a far sight less congested than Master Jacob. Margaret never had believed in bleeding either and shunned leeches whenever possible. She stood behind Cook, wringing her hands as her rotund servant checked Alex's wounds. Then Cook stood and announced her opinion.

"He must be bathed with cool water until the fever breaks. Open the stitches in the shoulder. Draw the pus from the wound with hot cloths until it bleeds freely. Then it must be resewn and watched carefully. He must eat. I will prepare broth and send up water."

"And keep young Amery downstairs," George added. "Seeing him failing thusly will only upset the lad."

"He's not going to die," Margaret said, whirling on him. "Damnation, he is a strong man!"

"And he spent much of that strength watching over you," George retorted.

"Me?" she asked, taken aback. "When?"

"The whole of the day yesterday and far into the night. After you sewed his wounds and sent him away, he returned to assure himself you would come to no harm."

"I did not ask that of him," she said, surprised Alex would have done as much for her. She also marveled that she'd slept so deeply that she hadn't noticed him. Perhaps her paltry wound had taken more out of her than she'd thought.

"Alex watched over you freely and now pays the cost," George said grimly. "Perhaps that should prove his trustworthiness."

"I never doubted his honor," Margaret returned hotly. " 'Tis his honesty I question."

George paused until Cook had retreated from the room. "Margaret," he said softly, "he had his reasons for wishing to return home. There are also things he may not be allowed to tell us. But if you ask my opinion, I'll wager he cares a great deal for you. A man does not put his life in jeopardy as he did for a woman he feels nothing for."

Margaret pursed her lips and turned away. "You're a bloody romantic," she grumbled.

George reached out and tugged roughly on her bound hair, a gesture he had made hundreds of times while she was growing up, but one he had not attempted in at least ten years.

"Tend him well," he said gruffly. "He deserves to

live." He walked to the door, then paused and turned. "A messenger's arrived from Brackwald come to demand Alex's release."

"Oh, by the saints," she groused, "what else would it be?"

"What will you have done with him?"

"How belligerent is he?"

"Very."

"Toss him in the dungeon."

"Done." And with that, he left the room.

Margaret turned her attentions to Alex. She hastily lit a fire in the hearth, though it was more for her than Alex. Though Alex burned with fever, her hands were like ice.

Cook bustled in with servants trailing behind her, bearing basins of water and clean cloths. Cook held a clean knife, needle, and thread. She looked down at Margaret sympathetically.

"Would you rather I did it, my lady?"

"Nay, Cook, I do not fear the deed." She took the knife and slit the stitches in Alex's shoulder. That made him thrash about again, dislodging the sheet that had covered him from the waist down. The view of his body drew murmurs of approval from Cook's help. Margaret sent them scurrying with a deep frown. She turned back to Alex and smoothed his hair back from his fevered brow.

"Alex, 'tis Meg," she said, feeling slightly embarrassed at using the name, with Cook standing right there. "Hush and let me do this thing. It will make your fever come down."

"Meg?" he said thickly, struggling to open his eyes.

She leaned down and pressed her cheek against his. "Aye, 'tis me. Hush now and rest. You have a fever. Let me tend it for you."

"Don't . . . leave," he whispered hoarsely.

"I won't," she promised softly.

"No . . . wife . . . ."

"No wife," she agreed. "Now will you go to sleep?"

She doubted he'd heard the last. Already he had slipped

back into the fever. Margaret dipped a cloth in the hot water and put it to the shoulder wound. Alex flinched, but she didn't pull away. Again and again she drew forth the infection until the wound bled cleanly. She looked up and received a nod of approval from Cook.

Sewing his shoulder was no less miserable this time than it had been before. He was fairly still, but he moaned each time the needle pierced his flesh. By the time she had closed the wound, she was weeping.

"There, there now," Cook said, taking the needle from her and cradling Margaret's head against her ample middle. "No need for tears, my lady. A fine job you've done, to be sure. Now, see if he'll sip a bit of this warm broth, then you'll bathe him with cool cloths. I daresay you'll be up the night doing the same, but I'll see that someone comes to give you a rest."

"Nay," Margaret said quickly, pulling away, "I'll do it alone."

"Then I'll send up something to strengthen you a bit later and more broth for the young lord. Take this cup and see if he won't drink a bit of this."

The broth smelled delicious. Margaret waved it in front of his nose, then put her hand behind his head and lifted it.

"Alex, drink some of this," she coaxed. " 'Tis something Cook made especially for you, and you know how it displeases her when you do not eat." She flashed Cook a smile, uncomfortably conscious that she had never had much speech with her servants, then turned back to Alex. "Alex, honey," she said, using that strange term he had called her, "drink this. Please, Alex. Open your mouth." She opened her mouth, as if somehow that would convince him he should do the same.

Miracle of all miracles, he obeyed her. She only managed to make him ingest two mouthfuls, but that was something.

"Well done, my lady," Cook said, pleased. "Now, cool him down and perhaps he'll have another drink later. I'll be downstairs if you need me. I fear young Amery may be a problem," she trailed off with a frown.

"Send him up in an hour or so. I daresay he won't sleep at all if he's not allowed to sleep in Alex's chamber."

"That young one's already impossible," Cook grumbled as she left the chamber.

"As is his benefactor," Margaret muttered to herself.

She reached for a basin of cool water and wrung out a cloth in it. The actual fashion in which she would have to touch Alex to bathe him had never occurred to her. At least he was asleep. Having those pale blue-green eyes open and looking at her while she was at her task would have been simply too much to bear.

She started with his right arm, draping it over her knees and smoothing the cool cloth over his skin. He sighed immediately, and she jerked her gaze to his face, sure he would be giving her that mischievous grin. Nay, he was quite asleep and the frown had almost faded from his brow.

She marveled not only at the muscles, but the lack of scars, though what scars he did have surely came from swordplay. She shook her head. He claimed not to be a knight, but bore the marks of it just the same. Where was Seattle and what odd things went on there? It was hard to imagine a place where healers held places of honor and knights did not.

Well, she would just have the entire tale when he awoke. It was far past time to know it.

She even washed his hand, remembering how his fingers felt in her hair and against her face. The strength of that hand could have easily broken her jaw, yet he had never touched her ungently. Though she had the distinct feeling there were times he would have liked to throttle her.

Feeling decidedly bold, she started to work on his chest. After all, 'twas simply more of his skin, was it not?

She realized her mistake the moment his muscles jumped under the cloth. Nay, she knew what it felt to be crushed up against this broad expanse and feel those steel-banded arms encircling her. Aye, offering to bathe him had been a very foolish thing to do.

The door burst open, making her jump in surprise. Amery ran across the chamber, obviously prepared to cast himself upon Alex. Margaret caught him around the waist.

"Be still, little one," she said softly. "He is sleeping."

Amery looked up at her with a heartbreaking troubled look. "Die?"

"Oh, Amery," she said softly, feeling her heart melt at all the love that was behind that question, "nay, lad, he will not. But we must let him rest."

Amery looked at her doubtfully.

"It may be several more days that he sleeps. That is why we will stay near him and tend him. See you the fire over there?" she asked, pointing to the hearth. After he nodded, she took his small hand. "That is where you will sleep while Alex is resting. Frances will make you a pallet on the floor so you may rise and see him when you wish it. Perhaps tomorrow you will help me tend him, aye?"

Amery nodded solemnly.

"There's a good lad. Run off and play with Frances now. Alex needs to sleep."

She watched Amery scamper off, then turned her attentions back to the man who lay as still as death on her father's bed. She hoped she'd spoken truly and that Alex merely needed sleep.

He had to wake, she thought with a scowl. She had several questions to put to him, and she had no intention of him going to his grave before she had her answers!

Thirteen

❧❦❧

FAINT LIGHT FORCED ITS WAY THROUGH THE SHUTTERS covering the window. Margaret blinked. Perhaps the rain had stopped. Rain didn't trouble her as a rule, but four days of the bloody stuff, unrelenting and unceasing, was enough to drive a woman of the strongest mettle daft.

She stretched, groaning as she did so. Every muscle in her body screamed from the abuse she'd put herself through over the past several interminable, exhausting, terrifying days. She'd passed most of her time wondering if Alex would live or die.

"Margaret."

She jumped at the sound of that hoarse voice. Immediately she dropped to her knees by his bedside. She put her hand to his head.

"The fever is still abated," she said, relieved.

"How long have I been out?" he croaked.

"Five days."

He groaned. "Do I have all my appendages?"

"Aye. All of you is still intact."

He opened his eyes and looked at her. "Have you been here the entire time?"

She pursed her lips. She could lie, of course, but no doubt some fool would tell him the truth of the matter. But the last thing she wanted was for Alex to think she'd remained by his side willingly. No matter that she'd spent much of her time on her knees praying he would live. That didn't mean she'd forgiven him for hurting her.

He reached for her hand. "I think you must have been here," he whispered. "I did nothing but dream of you."

Saints, but the man was easier to manage when he was senseless and drooling. She frowned at him.

"You didn't have to," he said. "Care for me, that is."

"Nay, I did not," she said. What she should have been doing was escaping his grasp on her hand and fleeing for safer ground. Somehow, though, she just couldn't make herself move.

"Then why did you?"

She mustered up her remaining wits to search for an appropriate answer. Coming up with nothing, she merely scowled at him.

Alex smiled. "Could this mean you're having kind feelings toward me?"

"My arm was too sore to allow me to train. I sat in this chamber because the, um"—she cast about for something plausible—"the sun is brighter here, and I thought it would serve me to bask in it."

"With the shutters closed."

Margaret was on her feet before the thought took shape in her mind.

Alex kept hold of her hand, and she had to admit he was strong even in his sickness. When she tried to pull it from him, he clasped it with both hands. She contemplated the merits of dragging him out of bed and across the floor to prove her point, then realized such a movement would dislodge his coverings, and the saints knew she'd seen more of his naked self than was good for her peace of mind.

So she remained standing, immobile, and instead delivered to Alex her most formidable glare.

And he only gave her a contrite look.

"I'm a very sick man, Margaret," he said humbly. "The radiance of your presence is the only thing that will cure me. Don't take it away."

"You've been spending too much time listening to Baldric spin his foolishness."

"He wasn't in here while I was sleeping, was he?"

"Aye, he favored me with a verse or two."

Alex groaned. "I knew it. I was having nightmares in iambic pentameter—not that he'd know what that was if it bit him on the butt."

"Alex!"

"You have to admit he's not very consistent."

Margaret agreed, but she'd be damned if she'd say as much. "He has a unique sense of rhythm and rhyme. Generally it is most acceptable. Over the years he has simply developed his own style and forms."

" 'There was a young maiden from Falconberg, which lies to the west of Brackwald where dwells the foul-smelling, horrid-looking' . . . though I have to agree with his assessment of Ralf. I seem to remember something about trolls and ogres. Or did I dream that?"

"Nay," she said, trying to tug her hand from his. "He favored me with a rousing rendition of 'The Ogre and the Troll.' "

"A little poem about romance among the short and ugly?"

"Short, ugly, and green, actually."

He laughed, but the laughter made him start to cough and that seemingly pulled on his shoulder. He released her and doubled up in pain. Margaret took him gingerly by the arms and held him down.

"You must be still," she commanded. "The fever has been fiercely upon you."

"Thanks," he gasped, "I can feel that."

She resumed her seat in her chair. "Perhaps you should sleep more."

He shook his head. "We need to talk."

"Of what?"

"Us."

"Us?"

"Yes, us. You and me. Where we're going."

"We are going nowhere."

He took a deep breath and then let it out slowly. "I have things to tell you."

Margaret found herself on her feet with her arms wrapped around herself. She had intended to fold her arms over her chest in a pose designed to intimidate. Instead she found herself hugging herself as if she prepared for a blow. So, now she would have the truth. Perhaps it was just as well. It couldn't be any worse than what she'd imagined.

"You *are* wed," she said flatly, then she could have chewed off her own tongue. As if she should care about his marital state!

"No, I'm not. Once and for all, Margaret, I am not married. I have never been married."

"But you will marry," she said darkly.

He smiled and she had to turn away before the beauty of it hurt her more.

"Definitely. The sooner the better."

She stared past him, out the window. "And what other truths do you have for me?"

"If you could find me something to eat, I'll tell you whatever you want to know."

"And why couldn't you have done so before?"

"When you know everything, you'll understand. I promise you."

Margaret turned and walked away. The promises of a man. Ah, what a fool she was to even think to believe in them!

But she fetched him food anyway.

And she waited while he ate. And she wondered what he would tell her. At least he was concentrating completely on his food. Alex was, at the very least, consistent when it came to ingesting his meals with singleness of purpose. And at least he'd managed to dress the lower half of himself in her sire's clothes. Margaret took a small quilt from off the bed and draped it around his shoulders. It would be much easier to concentrate on sorting truth from lies if she weren't distracted by sight of his bare flesh.

And once the small table had been cleared away, Alex

rose and held out his hand for her. She looked up at him narrowly.

"You're too ill to go walking abroad."

"Let's go sit in the alcove. Where the sun is," he said with a faint smile.

"Of course," she said, as if she'd been planning to do it all along. She had, after all, claimed she had been in his chamber for that purpose only. No sense in becoming as much a liar as he was.

She sat down across from him, but soon found herself distracted by the play of light on his features. The fever had taken its toll. He was pale, and there was darkness under his eyes. His cheeks were stubbled and his hair mussed. But his eyes were still that pale bluish green that her own witless eyes seemed to find so attractive. It was surely the only reason she couldn't seem to tear her gaze from his. Aye, to be sure, his eyes had been the start of all her grief.

"I am going to tell you the truth."

"As you should have from the beginning."

"I don't know that you would have believed me."

"And I will now?"

"I think now you're less likely to use me to fertilize your garden."

"We shall see."

He smiled briefly. "I'm sure we will." He rubbed his chin, then took a deep breath. "Okay, here goes." He paused—too dramatically for Margaret's taste, but she held her tongue. "I'm not from England."

She snorted. As if she couldn't have divined that.

"I'm not from Scotland, either."

She frowned. "Then you did lie."

"No, I told you I was most recently from Scotland, which is true. Three weeks ago I was staying with my brother-in-law, James MacLeod, who lives in the Scottish Highlands. I went out for a ride about a half mile from his house, wandered into the middle of a damned faery ring, and the next thing I knew, you were shooting at me."

"A warning shot," she muttered. "I should have kept to my mark."

"I appreciate your forbearance."

"I'm quite certain you do. Now, how is it you were at one moment in the Highlands and the next you found yourself here? This I do not understand."

Alex drew in a great breath. Margaret watched him hold it, then let it out slowly. Perhaps he intended to spin a tale as fanciful as one of Baldric's.

"The truth," she reminded him.

"The truth," he agreed. "I think that faery ring is some sort of gate. Like your barbican. You're in the inner bailey one moment, you walk through the tunnel and the next you're outside the walls."

"And?"

He shrugged. "That's it. One minute I was in Scotland, the next I was in England."

She grunted. It was all she could manage. The man looked perfectly sane, yet here he spouted complete nonsense.

"And there's more."

"Somehow, I suspected as much."

"When I was in Scotland, I was in the year 1998. One thousand nine hundred and ninety-eight."

"I can count, thank you very much," she said, but her disappointment increased with everything he said. Saints, but the man *was* daft.

Alex blinked. "Then you believe me?"

"Of course not! What kind of fool do you take me for?"

He began to frown, as if she had done him a great injury. "It's the truth. Can't you tell? I don't even talk like you do."

She shrugged. "Perhaps you are a mason's bastard and have no learning."

"Do I look like a mason's bastard?" he demanded.

Actually, he looked like an outraged nobleman who had just had his parentage disparaged, but she wouldn't admit that even under pain of death. So she shrugged as carefully as she could.

"What else am I to think?"

"I'm telling you the *truth!*" he exclaimed. "I'm from the future."

"And I am simply to believe you?" she asked, feeling increasingly annoyed. "That you are from—from what did you say?"

"The future. 1998. I was born in 1966 in a land called America. You Brits don't even know the place exists yet."

"Then how can you be from it?"

"Because I just am!"

"But it doesn't exist!"

"It *does* exist," he said hotly, "you just don't know about it!"

"Fanciful imaginings."

He started to wheeze.

Margaret frowned. "Perhaps the fever has addled your wits. Aye," she said, nodding to herself, "that must be it. You should return to your bed."

He was already on his feet, and none too steady thereon. He stumbled to her father's trunk and pulled forth his strange garments. He returned to the alcove, shoved them into her hands, and collapsed on the bench opposite her.

"There," he panted. "Have a look at those."

They were indeed strangely made. The blue cloth of his hose was heavy, yet supple. She fingered a small silver disk, then realized there were several more descending from the first. Silver surrounding bronze and somehow welded to the cloth. She frowned. What purpose could those possibly serve? She shot Alex a dark look.

"Buttons," he supplied before she could open her mouth to berate him. He reached over and held up the cloth facing the devices he called buttons. "Buttonholes. The buttons go through them to hold up your clothes."

Margaret took hold of one of the buttons and after several fumbling attempts managed to slide it through the buttonhole. She blinked in surprise. Saints, what a fine idea.

But this proved nothing of his story.

"This proves nothing," she said, in case he misinterpreted her fascination with his clothing. "There are many strange things wrought in other places."

"And other times."

She waved away his words. "Cease with that babble," she commanded. "Now, tell me what it is you do in this America where you live. Is it in the Holy Land?"

He looked at her in disbelief. "You really don't believe me."

"Of course not. I am no fool. I have more learning than either my father or my brothers had, for my grandfather willed it so. I have never seen buttons or buttonholes or heard tell of anyone stepping through a blade of grass to another land that is not his own."

Never mind the tales Baldric had made up of faeries and ogres and beasties. Those were a bard's foolishness. Margaret had two very good eyes, and she had never once seen anything remotely resembling a sprite. Alex perhaps had taken a blow to his head. Either that or he was as daft as Baldric. Infinitely more pleasing to the eye, but daft just the same.

Regret swept over her. A pity. Alex was, despite his flaws of not being a knight and not possessing all his wits, a very fine looking man. And she certainly had found it pleasant to kiss him. Now what was she to do with him? Lock him in her dungeon?

"All right," Alex said, folding his arms over his chest, "we're getting nowhere with this. Why don't you ask me the questions and I'll give you the answers."

"Will they be different than the ones you've just given me?"

"They'll be the truth," he said curtly. "Ask what you want to."

Well, there was no sense in not trying a final time to

wring some sense from him. "Very well. Did you live in Scotland?"

"Yes."

"And in York before that?"

"New York. It's in America."

"Which must be on the continent."

"Right. It's on *a* continent."

Margaret felt a curious lightening of her heart. "We begin to make sense of this," she said, relaxing. "Your French is poor, and your English strangely spoken. Perhaps this comes from traveling?"

"Close enough."

"Are you a healer's son?"

"Yes."

"How did you earn your bread?"

He smiled and Margaret almost flinched at the sight. It wasn't a very pleasant smile. She had the feeling it was the kind of smile he gave his supper before devouring it.

"I was a pirate."

She blinked. "A pirate?"

"A mercenary," he snarled.

"Ah," she said slowly. "This answers several puzzling questions."

"I didn't start out as one," he added quickly, as if it were something she should know. "I started out doing good."

"And then?"

"And then I found I earned more by laying sieges, taking over property, grinding into the dust anyone who got in my way."

"Hmmm," she said, looking at him with new respect. "Indeed."

"Indeed," he growled.

"And yet you seem so pleasant on the surface." Well, this certainly shed a different light on the man.

He laughed suddenly, though it wasn't a humorous one. "I'm rotten to the core, Margaret."

"Are you?" she mused. "Surely a man who can touch

a woman as you—'' She shut her mouth with a snap. Saints, she was a babbling fool!

Alex was smiling at her in that devouring way he had. Pirate? Whatever the word meant, it surely fit him. The man was born to plunder.

''Where is your sword?'' she asked, grasping onto something more comfortable to speak about. ''And your gear?''

''I don't have either—sword or gear. I gave it up.''

''Why? Were you so poor a pirate?''

''I was a very good pirate,'' he countered. ''I was disgustingly rich and unrepentantly ruthless.''

''Hmmm,'' she said, impressed in spite of herself. ''And you had many victims?''

''The list is incredibly long.''

''And you stopped because . . . ?''

He shrugged. ''I decided I'd done enough damage. I hung up my sword for good.''

''As penance,'' she stated.

''Yes.''

Well, this she could understand. She didn't necessarily agree with him, for a man had to earn his way somehow, but she could understand.

And, despite herself, she found that once again she was looking at him with new eyes. If he could be believed, he had made great sums wreaking havoc, yet he had walked away from it all because he had simply chosen to do so. Such strength of will was something she couldn't help but admire. Surely there had been times he had been tempted to heft a sword, yet he had not done so, simply because he had said he would not.

Until five days ago.

She realized then what it had cost him to rescue her.

''Ah,'' she said softly. She looked at him and felt her heart soften. ''And yet the other day . . .''

''It was either you or my vow,'' he said. He lifted one shoulder in a half shrug. ''It wasn't a hard choice to make.''

Her heart softened the more. Saints, never in her life had she met such a man.

Daft and befuddled though he might be.

"And I would do it again."

She met his eyes.

"Again and again," he added. "If it meant I could keep you safe."

She refrained from pointing out to him that she could keep herself safe. For the first time in ten years she had met someone who didn't have to rely on her for protection. Indeed, she might even be able to turn to him.

"And I will do it again," he said. "For the rest of my life."

Margaret blinked. She shook her head as well, certain she had heard him wrong.

He said no more, only leaned back against the wall and watched her with those pale eyes of his.

"What mean you by that?" she managed in a strangled voice.

"What I mean is that I'm not leaving." He said the words very deliberately. "Until you tell me to go."

If that wasn't a promise, she'd never heard one. "Never?" she asked, wishing the word hadn't come out in such a choked tone of voice.

"Never."

Margaret couldn't breathe. There was no deceit in his gaze, no shifting of his eyes, no squirming of his body. He meant what he said. She wasn't sure if she should throw herself into his arms or bolt the other way.

"Though I'll admit," he said with a half smile, "it's a fairly rusty sword I'm laying at your feet."

"Indeed," she whispered.

He smiled. "Indeed." He shrugged and the moment passed. "So, now you know everything about my past," and he paused and shook his head as if to clear it—no doubt to rid himself of those foolish notions he had of a homeland that didn't yet exist, "where should we go from here? I can hire on as a stablehand."

Margaret held on to the stone of the bench beneath her for support. "Ah, perhaps you should spend a few hours in the lists."

"Probably."

"And a few hours in the chapel praying you haven't lost all your skill."

"I fight well enough," he assured her. "Now, what of us? Where do we go?"

She was tempted to say "to Brackwald to rid ourselves of its lord," but perhaps Alex should heft a sword for a day or two before they ventured—

Margaret froze.

Brackwald's messenger.

"Oh, by the saints!" she exclaimed, jumping to her feet. She glared down at Alex. "This is all your fault!"

"Huh?"

"Brackwald's messenger. I tossed him into the dungeon!"

"And the problem is?"

"I left him there over a se'nnight ago!"

Alex stood and swayed. "Then I guess that's where we're going first."

"You're going nowhere." She steered him over to the bed and sent him toppling into it with one firm shove.

"Margaret!"

Margaret felt her head clear the moment she stepped out into the passageway. There was just something about that man that muddled her thinking each time she was around him.

Well, at least she hadn't been taken in by his fanciful imaginings. She knew he wasn't wed and she knew he'd been a mercenary. The last was the easier of the two to deal with—she'd just have George aid him in regaining his skill.

As for the former, perhaps she'd confine Alex to the garden and herself to the lists. If she could keep herself away from him, she might have hope of retaining her wits.

He had taken up his sword again in her defense.

And would continue to do so.

Saints, but it was almost enough to make her forgive him.

$\mathcal{F}ourteen$

❧❀❧

ALEX CLAWED HIS WAY TO THE EDGE OF THE BED. HAD he ever in any state of dementia thought that courting a shieldmaiden would be fun? Fiona MacAllister wouldn't have tossed him onto the bed like a rag doll. All right, so Margaret had heaved more than tossed. The point was, she'd muscled him out of her way so she could go do her own rescuing. He wasn't having the chance to show her he would be a good addition to her keep. And he wouldn't have the chance until he'd made it off the bed—and the chances of that looked mighty slim at the moment.

He crawled to his feet, then waited several minutes until his head cleared enough for him to cross the room. Opening the door was a new challenge, one that took him several more minutes to recover from. While the room spun madly around him, he leaned against the doorway and contemplated the morning's events.

So she didn't believe him. He supposed he shouldn't have been overly surprised. It was way beyond her scope of experience, and he probably sounded like he'd completely lost his marbles. Well, maybe he'd be able to convince her of it eventually.

He had a lifetime to try.

He gingerly eased away from the doorframe. Getting down the hallway wasn't so bad until he got to the top of the stairs. He looked into the gaping darkness that contained Margaret's circular staircase and wondered at the advisability of what he currently contemplated. He didn't want to miss out on getting a firsthand account from the prisoner, but getting there was going to be a problem. He leaned against the wall and waited until his body recovered from being forced to move from the bed. Once he thought he could walk without blacking out, he gingerly inched toward the stairs.

It was slow going. Luckily the stairwell was small enough that he could prop himself up with a hand on either side. He did it more than once, trying not to torment himself with visions of an antebellum mansion's sweeping staircase and delightful banister. Rocks were good, solid building materials. He liked rock. It was a good thing, because he was going to be living with it for a very long time.

Alex stumbled out into the great hall and fell to his knees in the rushes. He remained hunched over until the stars whirling around his head faded and he was certain he would retain breakfast where it currently resided. Through the haze that had become his brain, he found the nearest wall. He used it to get to his feet, then leaned back against the tapestry-covered stone and sucked in great gulps of air. He didn't want to think about the magnitude of the infection his body had been fighting off for the past five days. He felt very lucky to be alive.

"Ahem!"

Alex rubbed his eyes, then looked down. His vision cleared just in time to see Margaret's minstrel give him a dirty look.

"Ahem!" Baldric repeated. "Move out of my way, whelp."

"I don't know if I can—"

Alex found himself moved bodily. It wasn't that hard, given his condition.

"Well, if you're that serious about it," he muttered. He watched as Baldric bent down, picked up the end of a thread and very calmly and deliberately began to unravel the tapestry. "Hey," Alex said weakly, "you can't do that."

Baldric wound the string into a ball. He stared off into space for a moment or two, then shook his head and unraveled some more, muttering under his breath.

"Baldric, buddy, you're ruining the tapestry."

Baldric shot him a steely glance from under bushy eyebrows. "It helps me finish my work."

"By unwinding someone elses?"

Baldric smiled suddenly. "Aye, lad. You're the first to see the logic in it." He patted Alex on the arm, then turned back to the wall and unraveled with renewed enthusiasm.

Alex bent to catch Baldric's eye, then had to grab on to the wall hanging to keep from pitching forward into the muck. "I have an idea. Why don't you let me be your audience. You know, sort of a focus group of one."

Baldric looked at him, then shook his head and returned to his work of destruction.

"Sometimes talking things out is all you need," Alex tried. He had to do something soon, otherwise it would be *adios* to another few inches of art before Margaret could come back up to the hall. Besides it would give him a perfect excuse not to have to move anymore. Getting to the dungeon was completely out of the question. At the moment Alex knew he'd be lucky to make it to a chair.

Baldric scowled at him. "I can't say my verse properly unless the lady Margaret's here." He hefted his little ball of thread, looked at it critically, then obviously decided it was just too skimpy. He attacked the tapestry again, unwinding industriously.

"She's down in the cellar, interrogating a prisoner," Alex said, beginning to wonder if just picking Baldric up and moving him out of harm's way was the thing to do. Too much more of this and Margaret would be looking at bare walls. Alex now understood where all the piles of thread had come from.

"Prisoner?" Baldric said, his ears perking up. He looked at Alex. "Is she torturing him?"

Alex shrugged. "Could be."

Baldric stroked his chin thoughtfully. "This is meet food for a fine verse or two."

"It certainly is. How 'bout we mosey on over to the fireplace?" Alex gingerly removed the ball of thread from Baldric's bony fingers and managed to surreptitiously put his hand under the bard's elbow. "Which hearth do you prefer?"

Baldric nodded to the one across from the kitchen entrance, motioning with a kingly gesture to his stool. Alex fetched it and another and managed to get himself and the seats to the fire before he had to sit and put his head between his knees to keep from passing out.

"Think you she'll use hot irons?" Baldric asked.

"Maybe," Alex wheezed, unable even to see the floor between his feet for the stars.

"Those wee pinchers that grasp little skins?"

Alex couldn't help but notice the thinly suppressed enthusiasm in Baldric's voice. "I guess if she has them on hand, she'll probably use them."

Baldric fell silent, no doubt considering the poetic possibilities of the devices he'd stumbled upon.

"Anything else down there, think you?" Baldric asked.

Perhaps the well had run dry already. Alex carefully looked up.

"Well, she might have leg irons," he offered.

Baldric turned his nose up.

"The rack?" Alex suggested.

"The rack?" Baldric turned that one over in his head for a moment or two. "It sounds most interesting, but I fear I am unfamiliar with it. How does it work?"

Alex braced himself with his hands on his knees so he wouldn't pitch forward onto Baldric's toes. "Well, you stretch the prisoner out flat and tie his hands and feet to long, thin barrels that you turn with a crank. The more you turn, the more the prisoner gets stretched until, well, you can imagine how it goes from there."

"Well," Baldric said, looking very impressed, "it sounds a marvelous invention indeed."

"Does Margaret have one?"

"I think not," Baldric admitted reluctantly. "But it would make for a fine tale, don't you think?"

"What the hell—use it anyway."

Baldric started to pace. Alex propped his elbows on his knees, then his chin on his fists. Satisfied he was properly balanced, he relaxed and closed his eyes. He could hear Baldric muttering under his breath, pausing, then resuming his pacing again. Alex opened one eye to scan his surroundings, hoping to see that Margaret had finished with her business and could rescue him before he passed out. Servants hovered at the edge of the hall, eyeing Baldric warily. Maybe they were ready to jump to the rescue of Margaret's wall hangings. Heaven help the rest of England if Baldric ever decided to become a traveling unraveling minstrel.

"Finished!" Baldric said triumphantly.

Alex opened both eyes. "And so quickly, too. I'm impressed."

"'Tis a prisoner from Brackwald," Baldric replied. "I've much to say on the matter."

"I'll bet you do. And I'm sure everyone else will want to hear it. Shall we get them to gather 'round?"

Baldric gave a regal wave of dismissal. "Gather them if you will. I've no time for seeing to such trivialities."

Alex managed to lift his chin off his fists. "Hey," he called weakly, "everyone come over here. We've got some great stuff about torture coming up."

There was a sudden flurry of activity. Watching people run made Alex dizzy, so he turned back to Baldric. The bard was arranging his stool to his liking, then clambering up on top of it.

"Don't you want to wait for Margaret?" Alex asked.

Baldric gave a disdainful huff. "She should know I'm ready to delight her with another of my choice verses."

"Now, Baldric, buddy," Alex said, "you know she's down in the cellar torturing the prisoner. How is she going to know you're ready to perform?"

Baldric scowled. "She should just know. She was always about to listen to my verses when she was younger."

Alex tried another tack. "She's providing you with subject matter. Give her a couple of minutes to get up here. She'll probably need a rest after wielding all those implements of pain and suffering."

Baldric looked down his nose and pursed his lips, but seemed to give in readily enough. With great ceremony, he licked four fingers of one hand and slicked down the ten or so hairs remaining on the top of his head. He straightened his robes of barddom and folded his hands very sedately in front of him in the classic opera singer pose. Alex shook his head and blinked several times, but Baldric's pose didn't change.

"That's an interesting look for you," Alex offered.

"A traveling minstrel showed it to me a few years ago," Baldric whispered out of the corner of his mouth.

"Fascinating." And it was. Who knew what sorts of people were roaming through medieval England? Alex didn't want to speculate.

"He taught me several new rhyme forms as well. I try to work them in as I may, though the weak-stomached ones here don't appreciate them overmuch." Baldric looked at him solemnly. "Too modern, you know."

"I'll just bet," Alex said, barely avoiding choking on his reply. "It's a rough crowd here."

Baldric bestowed a sunny smile on him. A not-quite-as-toothful-as-it-might-have-been-twenty-years-ago smile, but a sunny one nonetheless.

"You've quite a head for thinking, lad." He turned and looked over the hall. "Ah, here comes the lady Margaret now. I will begin."

And without further ado, he did just that.

'Twas a marvelous morn for a racking!
And the prisoner had to agree
that not an iron or pincher was lacking
from the choices our maid eyed with glee.

> *She posed a short question or two,*
> *her keen eye missing nary a flinch.*
> *He answered her not a thing true,*
> *so said she, "Let's try a pinch!"*

Alex laughed. Baldric frowned down at him, and Alex quickly wiped off his smile.

"Sorry to ruin the mood."

"Harumph," Baldric said. He reassumed even more firmly his operatic pose and cleared his throat purposefully.

Alex couldn't see anything but the front row of spectators. He watched them shift as Baldric continued on. The small lake of legs parted and Margaret came to stand at the forefront. Alex looked up at her and smiled. She frowned at him, then looked at her bard.

> *The irons were hot in the fire,*
> *the prisoner was trembling with fear.*
> *So sure was she he was a liar,*
> *she gave him a pinch on the ear!*
>
> *He yelped and he pleaded for mercy,*
> *but she only reached for a tong.*
> *He begged her to cease for sure was he,*
> *that he wouldn't last all that long.*

"By the saints!" a man choked.

Alex looked up to see a filthy, disheveled man standing next to Margaret. He was currently inhaling a bowl of something steaming. He was looking at Baldric with what seemed to Alex to be a distinct lack of patience. After having shared a tender moment with Baldric at the tapestry, Alex felt intensely indignant that someone so obviously uncultured would dare pass an opinion on Baldric's best effort of the day. Alex also sincerely hoped he hadn't looked that appalled when he'd first heard the bard's poetry.

Alex's next thought was that he really should get up and

tell the guy not to stand so close to Margaret. If he'd thought he could get to his feet and stay there with any success, he would have. The porridge piled high on that spoon was added incentive.

Baldric was rubbing his chin. Alex looked from the bard to Margaret, who was biting her lip. Maybe the rhyme was beginning to unravel.

"I'm liking the torture," Alex said. "Nice and gruesome, Baldric."

Baldric stopped rubbing and recaptured his bardly look.

> *The hot irons were liberally applied,*
> *the lout's screams were throaty and full.*
> *And our lady never she shied*
> *from using that poker so dull.*

Baldric paused and looked faintly perplexed, as if he just wasn't sure that last rhyme had worked. Then he shrugged and forged ahead.

> *Broken and battered and frail,*
> *the prisoner relented and 'fessed,*
> *Meg tossed her fell irons in a pail,*
> *and came up for cider well pressed.*

Alex looked at the man next to Margaret. He was shaking his head, yet still managing to spoon in porridge at an alarming rate. Alex scowled at the man, partly because he wasn't showing very good concert etiquette and partly because it seemed very unfair that he himself should still be hungry while someone so rude was eating well. Alex put his hand over his belly and prayed Baldric would wind things up quickly before serious rumbling ensued.

> *The prisoner was left in the dungeon,*
> *to rot and soon go on off to hell,*
> *as befits all foul folk from that noisesome*

> *keep at Brackwald—and indeed you can*
> *smell the reek from here. . . .*

Baldric paused and stared off into the distance, no doubt trying to get a better look at those cue cards his muse was holding up.

"Dungeon?" Alex asked, hoping to head off another round of tapestry unraveling. "Is that really what you want?"

Baldric shook his head, then took to scratching his bearded chin. "Perhaps 'pit.' But that rhymes with sh—"

"Aye, well to be sure it does," Margaret interrupted. "Perhaps 'hole' would work, aye?"

Baldric paused and seemed to consider that. Then he nodded and began again.

> *The prisoner was left in the hole,*
> *to rot and soon go on off to hell,*
> *as befitted his dark, noisesome soul,*

He paused and a look of panic descended on his features.

"How about 'And all ended astonishingly well'?" Alex asked.

Baldric paused, frowned, and then muttered under his breath for several moments. Alex looked around and saw that the entire household was holding its breath. Well, all except that jerk scraping his bowl with his spoon. Even wooden spoons and bowls made a great deal of noise when scraped, especially when you were listening to them on an only partially full stomach.

> *The prisoner was left in the hole,*
> *to rot and soon go on off to hell,*
> *as befitted his dark, noisesome soul,*
> *And hell welcomed him with its fanciest bell!*

Baldric looked exceptionally pleased with himself.

"Well done!" Alex exclaimed, clapping to cover up

what surely would have been something less than complimentary from the porridge eater. The man was holding on
to his bowl, looking very condescending. All right, so the
last wasn't all that great. There had definitely been some
good things about torture. Alex was very tempted to suggest Margaret take Baldric's advice and use a few pinchers
on the man standing next to her.

Baldric clambered down off his stool and patted Alex
on the head. "Any time you need aid with your prose, lad,
I've an ear you can bend. Verse isn't for the faint of heart,
no indeed! Sweets, m'lady! I've a need for several
sweets!"

Margaret took Baldric by the arm and led him over to
the high table. Alex got to his feet through sheer willpower
alone, then looked at the well-fed lout standing in front of
him.

"And you would be?" he demanded.

"No one interested in making your acquaintance," the
man said stiffly. He turned and looked for Margaret.
"Lady Falconberg, we must make our plans."

"Hey," Alex said, reaching out to grab the other's arm
and missing by quite a distance. He felt himself falling.
"Oh, no—"

Miraculously he found himself holding on to Margaret
instead of the floor. He smiled weakly.

"Thanks."

"You were to remain abed," she said, frowning.

"I'm feeling much better. Besides, you might need my
help."

The filthy one snorted. "And what help could you possibly offer, bard?"

"I beg your pardon?" Alex said, blinking.

"And I pity you if that is your master," the other added.
"Saints above, but his verse is foul!"

Alex kept an arm slung around Margaret's shoulders for
support as he leaned over and gave the well-fed snob a
healthy shove.

"His prose is just fine, and who the hell asked you?"

The man regained his balance and reached for a non-existent sword. "I'll see you repaid for that insult!"

"If I survive your smell long enough to cross swords with you!"

"Enough!" Margaret exclaimed. "Alex, this is Sir Walter of Brackwald—"

"What's he doing out of the dungeon?"

"—a comrade-in-arms of Edward's," Margaret finished, frowning at him. "Sir Walter, this is Alexander of Seattle."

Sir Walter frowned. "*You're* Lord Alexander? From Edward's description, I expected someone more"—he paused and looked Alex over critically—"um, fearsome."

"I've had a fever," Alex growled.

"It would have killed a weaker man," Margaret added. "Now, let us retire to my father's solar and speak in private."

Alex didn't miss Walter's pointed look at his arm slung around Margaret's shoulders. He merely gave the other man an unpleasant smile and let Margaret help him up the stairs. Impressing Walter would have to come later. Showing Margaret he was a man who could stand on his own two feet would also come later—when he thought he could stay there for an extended period of time without help. He would eat, then hopefully regain a more intimidating air.

He made it to the solar and into a chair without any mishap. He spent the next little while concentrating merely on breathing and trying not to pass out. It was touch and go. A second breakfast arrived in short order, and Alex made quick work of finishing it. Once he felt slightly more human, he leaned back and tried to pick up the thread of conversation that he'd lost somewhere between the porridge and the green-tinged cheese.

And it was then that he knew he really didn't care for the way Walter of Brackwald was eyeing Margaret.

He felt every proprietary cell in his body stand up and demand to be counted. He did so, and then decided he had enough of them to let Sir Walter know in no uncertain terms just which way the wind was blowing.

He took a deep breath, ready to plunge into the verbal fray. He opened his mouth to demand Sir Walter back off, then felt his world begin to spin again.

Fifteen

❧❧❧

MARGARET HEARD ALEX'S GASP FOR AIR AND LOOKED AT him in time to watch him turn a pasty white and pitch forward.

"Alex!" she exclaimed, jumping forward to catch him before he hit the floor.

He caught himself with his hands and gingerly righted himself. "I'm fine," he wheezed. "Really."

Margaret frowned at him. "You have risen too soon. Perhaps another few days in your sickbed would serve you."

"I'm perfectly fine," he insisted, clutching the arms of his chair for support. "Let's get on with this."

He obviously had no intentions of returning to his bed. Though she was tempted to haul him there herself, she refrained. She had no liking for Sir Walter or the sorry tale he had told her. Perhaps Alex would have the same opinion of the man's story, if he could remain upright long enough for the retelling of it. It would be interesting to know what Alex thought of the man. She turned to Sir Walter.

"Perhaps you would be good enough to repeat what you told me below."

Sir Walter shrugged. "As you will." He looked at Alex. "I traveled to Brackwald a se'nnight ago to find Edward in his brother's dungeon."

"What?" Alex exclaimed. "How did that happen?"

"Ralf has accused him of treachery. It would seem that

Edward had imagined up an entire list of grievances against Lord Ralf and forced his scribe to put them to paper. Lord Ralf fully believes that Edward intended to send the lies to the king.''

"Well, isn't that interesting," Alex murmured.

"Lord Ralf believes that the lady Margaret and his brother are conspiring against him to thwart his coming nuptials''—he nodded at Margaret—''and cause him to lose Falconberg lands.''

Alex's expression was completely unreadable. Margaret had no idea what he was thinking, but she sincerely hoped he was thinking something. The saints pity her if his brain was too ravaged by fever to make sense of Sir Walter's words. She sensed the man was not what he professed to be, but it would take more than her word to convince others of that.

"Help me understand this," Alex began slowly. "You and Edward are comrades, right?"

"Aye."

"Good friends?"

"Nigh onto brothers."

"So, of course you don't believe what Ralf is saying about him." It wasn't a question.

"Of course not," Sir Walter said blandly. "Edward is not capable of betrayal."

But you are, Margaret thought instantly. She glanced briefly at Alex only to find him looking at her. His face was impassive, but she could see in his eyes that he shared her sentiments. He turned back to Walter.

"Then if you don't think him capable of betrayal, why did you leave him in Brackwald's dungeon?"

"I didn't want to," Sir Walter said. "Edward said to leave him there until I could fetch you to aid him."

"How flattering," Alex said with a smile. "I'll admit he was very impressed with my swordplay."

"Indeed, he was."

Margaret forced herself not to flinch at that blatant lie. The night she and Alex had discussed what he would say to Edward, he'd told her that Edward thought him completely incapable of lifting a sword, much less wielding it with any skill. Was Sir Walter truly so foolish as to let something so obvious slip out?

"Well, this is a little more complicated than I'd thought originally," Alex said with a yawn. "As you can see, I'm not back to fighting shape yet. I would need another couple of months to regain my strength." He smiled, but it wasn't a very pleasant smile. "We had a little skirmish with ruffians a few days back. I imagine Margaret and I are lucky to be alive."

"We live in perilous times," Walter agreed.

"Do you think you can keep Edward alive for a few more weeks?"

Walter nodded slowly. "Perhaps we can feign negotiations for your release from Falconberg. That could take up a goodly amount of time, yet leave Lord Ralf with something to gnaw on."

"Excellent idea." Alex put his hands on his knees as if he intended to rise, then paused and looked faintly puzzled. "There is something I don't understand, though."

Margaret looked at Walter. He didn't seem troubled, but she noticed that he had begun to sweat. Perhaps he was merely suffering the aftereffects of a se'nnight in her dungeon.

"How is it," Alex asked, "that you and Edward are such good friends, yet he is the one in the dungeon and you are not? It would seem to me that Ralf would have thrown you both in."

Walter shrugged. "I told Ralf that Edward and I no longer saw eye-to-eye. 'Tis a strategy we've used often enough with him. Happily he believed it as readily this time as he has in the past."

"Interesting. One other question, though. If I am unsuccessful in freeing Edward from the dungeon, what will Ralf do with him?"

"Likely put him to death."

"That seems a little drastic," Alex said.

"The king is far away. He will learn eventually of Edward's unfortunate hunting accident and the tale will be finished."

Margaret felt a chill go down her spine. "Hunting accident?"

Walter looked at her without flinching. "Aye. It happens quite regularly in these parts."

Margaret felt the chamber begin to spin. Indeed, she thought she just might lose her meal. Aye, she knew much of hunting accidents, for hadn't her eldest brother died of one?

It had been an accident, hadn't it?

She suddenly found her hand in the grip of a large, warm hand. Alex wasn't looking at her, but he was squeezing her hand hard enough to make her flinch. She leaned back against her chair and let out her breath slowly. She wouldn't give Walter the satisfaction of knowing how deeply his words had upset her.

"This has been a most interesting morning," Alex said, "but I believe our lady Margaret should have a rest. Wounds from our skirmish, you know."

"Tragic," Walter said with a nod. "Now, perhaps we might discuss how Edward's release will be accomplished?"

"Oh, why don't you give me your thoughts on it," Alex deferred. "I'm sure you've given this a great deal of thought out of anxiety for Edward's welfare."

Margaret studied Walter as he outlined to Alex his plan for distracting Ralf with some imagined attack on his border while Alex entered Brackwald and fetched Edward from the dungeon. He seemed concerned about Edward and anxious enough to have Alex's help, but somehow none of it rang true.

He finished with his words and looked at her with a smile. That made her uncomfortable all over again. It was a look akin to the looks Alex gave her from time to time, but such a look from Walter made her blood run chill.

"Well, I'll give that some thought," Alex said, rising.

He leaned heavily against the chair. "I'm sure we can work out the details over the course of the next few weeks." He smiled. "Wouldn't want anything to go wrong."

"Of course not," Walter said, rising also. "Perhaps the lady Margaret and I can discuss it while you rest. You seem quite overcome."

"Actually, as I said before, the lady Margaret needs rest as well. We'll have Sir George show you the way out." Alex walked to the solar door, giving Walter no choice but to follow. "Give me a fortnight to regain some of my strength, then we'll begin our negotiations. Perhaps you'd like a visit to Margaret's kitchens before you return home."

"But we should plan," Walter protested.

"Oh, we will," Alex said, opening the door. "Margaret and I will speak together privately, then inform you of our decision."

"But—"

"If you'll excuse us?"

Alex's tone was so dismissive, Margaret felt the urge to leave.

"Aweks!"

Margaret caught sight of Amery the moment before he flung himself through the door and wrapped himself around Alex's leg.

"Bloody babe!" Walter exclaimed. "Saints, I almost tripped over him." He pointed furiously at Frances who stood hovering at the doorway. "You, there, get this wretch away from me!"

Alex scooped Amery up, then pulled Frances into the chamber. "Sir Walter, it's been a pleasure. We'll talk soon."

And with that, he pushed Walter out into the passageway and closed the door behind him. Frances was trembling so badly, her teeth were chattering. Margaret watched Alex put his arm around the young girl and pull her close just as tenderly as he had Amery.

"He g-gives me a f-fright," Frances said.

"He gives all of us a fright," Alex said with a sigh. "Frances," he said, stroking her hair gently, "you're not to go anywhere near him, understood? You and Amery will sleep with the lady Margaret until Sir Walter is gone. And when you're tending Amery, you'll stay in the kitchens near Cook at all times."

"Cook is very handy with a knife," Frances offered.

Margaret met Alex's gaze and found a sudden spark of humor there.

"How could we expect anything else? Go curl up in one of those blankets while Margaret and I talk. Come on, Meg. I've used up all my standing energy for the day."

Frances didn't have to hear that twice. She was bundled up in a blanket and curled up in a chair before Margaret could find her own seat. Alex drew up his chair and sat next to her. Amery turned, looked her over, then held out his arms imperiously.

"Ah," Margaret said, stalling.

"Magwet," Amery demanded.

Margaret frowned at Alex as she took Amery onto her lap and arranged his small frame comfortably. "You've spoiled the lad."

"Me? I've been asleep for the past five days. He was perfectly behaved before that."

Margaret frowned some more. " 'Twas only a treat or two from the kitchen. Cook is notoriously stingy with the children. I had to remedy that."

"Of course."

Alex leaned his head back against the chair. Once Margaret was certain Amery was well settled, she turned a critical eye on his rescuer.

Alex was pale and his breathing was labored. She didn't want to feel concern for him, but she could hardly help herself. How could she feel anything else? The man was obviously daft, obviously still weakened from the fever, and she had the feeling that he was Ralf's next target for murder. How could she not be concerned?

"I think you have overdone this day," she stated. "You should be abed."

He didn't open his eyes, but he lifted one eyebrow and smiled faintly. "Think so?"

"Aye, I do."

"Are you going to watch over me some more?"

"I should," she said grimly. "The saints only know what Sir Walter would do if he found you unattended. Likely plunge his dagger through your heart."

Alex rolled his eyes. "He's some piece of work. Did you hear that bit about Edward wanting me to rescue him because I'm such a fine swordsman? Walter should have checked his facts more carefully. You know Edward thinks I can't tell one end of a sword from the other."

Margaret frowned thoughtfully. "I must admit I wondered the same thing about you."

"Your confidence in me is staggering."

Margaret shrugged. "What was I to think?"

He waved away her words. "Nothing other than what you thought. I didn't give you anything useful to judge me by." He opened his eyes and looked at her solemnly. "Have I apologized for not telling you the entire truth from the beginning?"

"Nay, you have not."

"Then I apologize. I should have trusted you. I shouldn't have let you think I was a knight. I should have told you where and when Seattle was. Not," he added, "that you would have believed me then."

"And I certainly don't believe you now," she reminded him. "But it is a weakness of yours I will tolerate. I certainly cannot send you out into the world unprotected. At the very least I will stay near you to do that."

"Protect *me*?" he choked. "I don't need you to protect me!"

Margaret wanted to point out to him that he could barely remain upright in his chair, but she resisted the impulse. No doubt his manly pride was suffering and that would lead him to more bellowing if she didn't concede the battle now.

"Of course not," she said mildly. "Now, what think you of Sir Walter? For all we know, he was sent here with the express purpose of luring you to Brackwald."

"Ralf must not be too happy with me."

"I daresay he cares nothing for being duped, and he no doubt feels you have done just that."

"Probably. I just can't believe he thinks I'm stupid enough to come."

Margaret shrugged. "Perhaps he thinks Walter will convince you he truly intends to betray Brackwald." She shook her head and wished Ralf of Brackwald were safely wed—to someone besides herself. "I daresay he only understands treachery and assumes that's all others understand as well."

Alex looked at her seriously. "You really don't think he had anything to do with your brother's death, do you?"

"Don't you?" she asked, feeling the truth of it cut through her again. "One more soul in the way of his desire for my land."

"I'm sorry, Margaret."

Margaret tightened her arms around Amery.

"We'll win, Margaret. I'll make sure of it."

She laughed, but it was without humor. "Win what? Your life? My freedom? I surely don't know how."

"We'll go to the king and tell him of Ralf's schemes."

Margaret sighed. "Richard is captive in Austria and couldn't help us even if he wanted to, which I daresay he wouldn't. Neither he nor his father were that fond of my sire."

"Richard isn't in Austria."

She blinked. "How do you know?"

"It's old history." He smiled faintly. "1998, remember? I know what's going to happen."

Margaret could hardly believe her ears. Indeed, his words shocked her so, she clapped her hands over Amery's ears to spare him.

"You're mad," she blurted out.

"No, I'm not. Look, it's what, almost the end of February? Richard will be in Nottingham near the end of March. That gives me a month to get in shape and for us to come up with a good plan to get his help."

Margaret felt quite sure her eyes were fair to falling from her head. "Richard is in *Austria*," she repeated. "Captive. Waiting, no doubt eternally, for his ransom to be paid."

Alex waved his hand dismissively. "That's being taken care of by his continental enemies. The entire ransom will never be paid and Leopold will just be glad to be out of the whole mess, but Richard won't care because he's free. He's coming back to England to kick John's butt, whip his barons into shape and be recrowned in London. I think that happens in April. Then he's going to head back to France, and he'll never set foot on English soil again. We have to get to Nottingham in March or you'll miss your chance to get Ralf put out of the picture entirely."

Margaret could only stare at him, her mouth open. She could feel it hanging almost to her chest. Here he spoke of events that were to come as easily as if he were the master of them.

Alex smiled. "I always did like English history. There's some wild stuff coming up in the next few years. It's a great time to be alive."

Amery pushed her hands away. Margaret was half tempted to use them to cover her own ears.

"How," she said, and her voice sounded to her ears as if someone had their hands around her throat, "how, by all the blessed saints, do you know this?"

Alex frowned at her. "We discussed it this morning, remember? The faery ring?"

"You learned all this in a *faery ring*?" she demanded.

"No, I learned all this in the twentieth century, which is eight centuries further into the future than the twelfth. Where I come from, your future has already happened."

Margaret shook her head. "Impossible."

He sighed, as regretfully as if he'd been trying to teach her something very simple that she hadn't been able to master even after repeated attempts.

"Just trust me on this, okay? We have a month to get ready to meet Richard. Let's keep our ears open for his arrival and then you'll see I'm telling the truth."

Well, there was some logic to that. She would go along with him, then try not to gloat when she proved him wrong.

"Ralf is our only problem," he continued. "We'll have to stall him until we can get him to meet us in Nottingham."

"And how do you propose to get him there?"

"We'll tell him we're going to the king to rat on him."

"Rat?"

"Tattle. Fink. We'll make sure Ralf knows we're off to find the king and tell him in the most glorious of detail just what Ralf has been up to. And we'll tell him that we're making a substantial contribution to Richard's coffers all in the name of aiding the king in his French wars."

"Well, bribery is something Ralf understands."

"I thought so, too. We'll go just the two of us. George can pop over to Brackwald and get Edward out of the pit, then meet us wherever the king happens to be holding court."

"Indeed," she said, suddenly finding that she almost hoped Alex spoke truly. It would be a fine thing indeed to have Ralf lose all hope of having her land. "Perhaps Ralf will demand that the matter be settled on the field. I can see to that."

"Wait a minute. What do you mean, 'settled on the field'?"

"Ralf may wish to have the matter settled over lances. 'Tis often done."

Alex frowned. "I hadn't thought of that."

"Not to worry. I can take him."

"You?" Alex jerked upright, then put his hand to his

head and winced. "You're not facing anyone over lances," he said through gritted teeth.

"Of course I am."

"No," Alex said, leaning his head gingerly against the back of the chair. "I'll do it."

"You will not."

He glared at her weakly. "I said I'll do it and do it I will."

Margaret pursed her lips, but said nothing. The man was obviously still suffering under fevered delusions if he thought he would be holding a lance any time soon.

"And you'll promise me you'll stay off the field, or I'll leave you here."

"Ha," she said, then snorted at his efforts to sit up and look intimidating. "How can you hold a lance when you can't hold yourself upright?"

"I have a month. I'll be in shape by then."

"If that means you will have your fighting form back, I have my doubts."

"I *will* do it."

Margaret had her doubts, but she decided arguing with him was useless. He could believe what he wanted. It wouldn't hurt him to train a bit, but it would be strictly for his own pleasure. Ralf would be vanquished, but not by Alex. She would see to it herself.

She escorted Frances and Amery to the door, then returned and helped an unprotesting Alex back to bed. He groaned when his head flopped against the pillow, then his entire body went completely limp. Margaret quickly put her fingers against his throat. His pulse was steady and strong. Perhaps sleep was all he needed.

She left his chamber and made her way down to the great hall. First she would assure herself that Sir Walter had indeed taken his leave of them, then she would spend the afternoon in the lists. If Alex spoke truly, and she hoped he did, she had precious little time to hone her skills before going to the king. It would be her best chance to humiliate Ralf a final time and hopefully win her freedom.

I won't go until you tell me to leave.

Alex's words from the morning came back to her, and she pondered them as she made her way to the kitchens. Those certainly sounded like the words a man would use if he intended to remain by her side.

But as what?

She shook aside her idle thought before it could distract her more. He'd apologized for not being truthful with her, and she realized that she'd forgiven him. Mostly. It was very hard to stay angry with a man who wasn't in possession of all his wits and fully believed he'd used a faery ring to step from one world to another. Maybe his sanity would return in time.

Hopefully she wouldn't lose hers in the meantime.

Faery rings. It was Baldric the Bard fodder!

$\mathcal{S}ixteen$

❧❦❧

ALEX SAT DOWN HEAVILY ON THE STONE BENCH AND leaned back against the wall. He didn't want to admit that his chest was heaving, but he had no choice. Even after a week he could hardly keep going for more than a half an hour or so without a rest. Good grief, he felt as winded as if he'd just run a marathon. He groaned. Maybe if he'd actually run one he might be in better shape now. Too bad no one had had the decency to warn him that he would find himself in medieval England contemplating the possibility of facing a medieval lord over lances. He might have been prepared otherwise.

"My lord?" a young voice warbled. "If I can serve you?"

Alex opened his eyes and saw his newly made squire standing there at attention. "A new body would be nice."

"My lord?"

"Never mind, Joel. What I could use is a cup of ale. Is that a squire's task?"

"Gladly, my lord!" Joel exclaimed and scampered off enthusiastically.

Alex smiled to himself at the sight. All right, so Joel was an orphaned kitchen lad who couldn't tell one end of a sword from the next. He was handy with a paring knife and very chipper. A guy couldn't ask for more than that from his squire. Joel couldn't have been a day over twelve, but he seemed more than ready to take on a man's task.

Margaret had offered Joel to him a week ago and done

it as stiffly as if she had expected him to laugh at her for it. Alex was more than aware of the reluctance of her peers to send her any kin of theirs. Considering the knightly training Joel *wouldn't* receive as Alex's squire, Alex felt like he was getting the better end of the deal.

"Your ale, my lord!"

Alex accepted the cup gratefully and gulped it down. It was cold and rainy out, but that hadn't done much to quench his thirst. It had to be the unfamiliar weight of the chain mail. The only stroke of fortune was realizing Margaret's eldest brother had been every bit as tall as he was. The downside was now that the mail fit, he had to wear it. He spared one last fleeting thought to the happy possibilities of Barbados' native dress, then handed the cup back to Joel.

"Will you have your sword again, my lord? I have it here."

Joel struggled to hand Alex the long sword. Alex took it with a sigh. He wasn't quite ready to dive back into the lists yet, but Joel was looking at him with serious hero worship. He couldn't disappoint the kid.

He took the sword and hoped the late lord of Falconberg didn't mind the loan. Margaret's father had seen his share of battles, if the scratches and dings on the blade were any indication. Alex wondered how many men William had killed, if he'd found it difficult to do so, and if he wished he'd died in battle instead of at home of grief.

"Ah, my lord, here is Sir George to train with you!" Joel sounded overjoyed at the prospect.

Alex looked at Margaret's captain and knew his days of avoiding the man were up. He'd been putting George off for a week now, saying he'd be much better prepared to tell his story when he was in better shape.

Sir George came to a halt before him and placed his sword point-down into the ground. He leaned on the hilt and looked at Alex sternly.

"I believe you've a tale to tell me," George said.

"Okay," Alex agreed, hauling himself slowly to his

feet. "You can have it, if you're sure you want it."

"Aye, I want it."

"We might want some privacy."

"The lists are conveniently empty, as you can see."

Alex saw the last of the men heading off to the great hall. Damn, no chance of an extension on account of crowds. "Yes, well, I can see that. Thank you."

Alex followed Sir George out into the lists and steeled himself for an hour or so of intense torment. And that didn't even begin to describe how uncomfortable he would be answering the man's questions. George was pretty old by medieval standards, but he was definitely in shape. There would be no mercy from this direction.

"Where were you born?"

The question, and the flashing blade, were unexpectedly quick to come at him. Alex parried off the stroke and offered the best answer he could.

"Seattle."

"That is unfamiliar to me."

"I'm sure it is. It's on a different continent."

The blade continued its relentless assault. "Not, I take it, the same continent on which rests Rouen and the Acquitaine?"

"Right," Alex said, blocking a wicked thrust. "A different one."

George withdrew his sword so quickly, Alex almost went sprawling face-first into the March mud. "Then why don't we know of it?"

"It hasn't been discovered yet." Alex winced as he said it, remembering how the same conversation with Margaret had gone.

"Then how is it you know of it?"

"Because," Alex said, taking a deep breath, "I'm from a different century."

George blinked slowly.

"The twentieth," Alex added.

He watched George digest that, then count surreptitiously on his fingers. He looked up at Alex and blinked some more. "Well," he said finally. "This is news."

Alex could only nod.

"A new continent as well?"

Alex nodded again. "And it's a big one."

"Show me."

"Show you?"

"Draw me a map."

Alex could hardly believe George was still with him. Then again, maybe it wasn't so hard to believe. George had been around awhile and had probably seen quite a few unbelievable things.

"Okay, a map," Alex agreed. He looked around to make sure the coast was clear, then chose the firmest bit of mud he could find.

"This is England," he said, drawing the outline with his sword. "Here's the continent with France and Normandy. It extends east and becomes Russia. Well, it used to be Russia. Where I come from it's now an entirely new map of -ia states, but we won't worry about that right now."

George grunted, but continued to listen closely to the unfolding geography lesson.

"Here's Africa and the Middle East. You know all about Jerusalem and Egypt, right?"

George nodded.

"Okay, here's what's new. That other continent is called the Americas, North and South." Alex drew it with sweeping stokes, hoping he was getting the Atlantic Ocean as big as it needed to be. He passed on trying to outline Greenland. "This is New York on this side," he gouged a little hole, "and on the opposite side is Seattle." He left his sword spearing the Space Needle, then looked up at Margaret's captain. "That's where I'm from, originally."

"Hmmm," George said, staring thoughtfully at the map. "And then you moved to this New York?"

Alex smudged the map lines with his boot, obliterating all traces of what he'd shown Margaret's captain. "Yes. Then I gave up my work in New York and came to live with my sister and her husband in Scotland.''

"And then you found yourself in England . . .''

"After I'd been out riding one morning,'' Alex finished. "I wandered through some sort of gate on my brother-in-law's land. One minute I was in Scotland and the next I was in England.''

George stroked his chin thoughtfully. "Passing strange.''

"That's not the half of it.''

"I'll have the rest now.''

Alex took a deep breath. Maybe this would work better with George than it had with Margaret.

"I was in Scotland in the year 1998. When I found myself in England, the year was 1194.''

"1998,'' George repeated.

"I swear it's the truth.''

George considered. Alex could see him turning the thought over in his mind and weighing the possibilities of it. He looked at Alex closely, then considered some more. Alex hoped he looked honest and briefly toyed with the idea of trying to find a facial expression that would convey that, but he had the feeling it wouldn't help his case any. George would either believe him or he wouldn't.

George frowned. "Then this is why you were so anxious to be gone.''

Alex nodded carefully. "I needed to get home.''

"To the year 1998.''

"Yes.''

"But you weren't able to open this gate.''

"No.''

"Why did you not just break it open? Was it locked?''

Alex sighed. "It wasn't a gate like the gate in the bailey wall. It was''—he took a deep breath—''a faery ring.''

A corner of George's mouth twitched. "A faery ring?''

"If you can believe it.''

George chuckled, though he looked to have tried to muffle it well enough. "Forgive me, Alex, but you're beginning to sound a bit like our good bard with his elves and trolls hiding under flowers and such.''

''You think I don't know this? A faery ring, for pity's sake! Why couldn't I have vanished in something dignified, like a stone circle?''

George did laugh then. ''I've no idea, lad. I daresay Fate has her own manner of jesting, far beyond our pitiful minds to understand.''

''And I hadn't even been heading for England,'' Alex added with a scowl. ''I'd been planning on Barbados.''

''Barbados?''

''It's an island in a very sunny part of the world. Everyone lies on the beach and drinks rum. I have a feeling the women don't wear much. I think it probably doesn't rain much, either.''

George squinted up at the gray sky, then looked at Alex. ''I'm sorry you missed that gate,'' he said sympathetically.

''You and me both.''

''Is it anywhere close where we both might venture through it?''

''Unfortunately that gate's on my brother-in-law's land.''

''Well, Scotland is reportedly a very odd place.''

''I'm living proof of it.''

George shook his head slowly. '' 'Tis a most fantastical tale.''

Alex waited.

George shook his head once again, then smiled faintly. ''I always wondered how long the world would last. Already the land holds so many souls.''

The plague would unfortunately take care of that, but Alex refrained from saying as much.

''I would like to hear how the world had changed, if you would indulge me.''

Alex blinked. ''You believe me?''

''Shouldn't I?''

Alex laughed shortly. ''Margaret thinks I've lost my mind.''

George shrugged. "She is her father's daughter and believes what she can touch."

"And you don't?"

"Alex, lad," George said, putting his hand on Alex's shoulder, "I'm old. I've outlived my wife and four of my children. I've seen three kings come into power, and lived through famine and war. At this point in my life, I am not above believing almost anything is possible."

"Well," Alex said, surprised at how relieved he was to finally be taken seriously, "thank you."

"No need, lad." He stepped back and resheathed his sword. "What say you we seek out a meal. We'll work again this afternoon and perhaps you'll indulge more of my curiosity."

Alex hesitated, but before he could express his concern, George had spoken.

"I'm old," he said again. " 'Tis merely an old man's curiosity." He smiled. "I have no more use for the tidings than that."

Alex nodded and resheathed his own sword. What could it hurt to give George a rundown on a few things? It would be a pleasure to actually talk about home for a change.

"I'll take your blade for you, my lord!"

Alex caught Joel just before Joel plowed into him in his enthusiasm.

"Hold on there, kid. It's not going anywhere."

"But I'm eager to serve, my lord!"

"And you're doing a great job. Here, take the helmet, too. I'll be going back out later, so keep them in the great hall, okay?"

"Okay, my lord," Joel said, nodding vigorously. " 'Twill be an honor!"

Alex entered the hall with George in time to find the last of the household gathered around the hearth for Baldric's daily offering. Alex approached on one side and paused to see what the subject would be.

*From Brackwald there arises such a smell
that not an ogre or beastie can bear,*

*The land 'round about is so full of cesspool water
and table scraps
that all creatures must hold small bunches of herbs
to their noses to ward off the ill affects
of breathing in the putrid stench which is enough to
make any creature
swoon directly. . . .*

Oh, this was going to be something else. A juicy free-form introduction on Baldric's favorite subject. The audience was listening raptly as the bard grew more enthusiastic, and more rambling. Alex shook his head and felt a fondness for the old man who lived to comment on Ralf and his surrounding environs. There was just never a dull moment in this place.

Alex searched the crowd until he found Margaret. She was sitting on a stool with Amery in her lap. Amery was leaning back against her shoulder, watching Baldric with wide eyes, giving his thumb a thorough workout. His other hand clutched Margaret's braid as if it were a life preserver. Margaret had her arms around him and her jaw resting against the top of his head. Frances stood next to Margaret, leaning against her slightly.

Protectiveness surged through Alex so strongly, it almost brought him to his knees. That small group of souls was what he'd been looking for the whole of his life. To think he might have turned his back on them—to think he had *tried* to turn his back on them and go home.

No, this was home, with its unraveled wall hangings and wacky entertainment and its well-pressed rushes under his feet. And his family. There across from him.

He almost turned around and walked back out into the lists to practice some more swordplay. This was worth fighting to protect.

It was worth fighting to keep.

And keep it he would, if he had to promise Richard the Lionheart the moon to get it. There had to be a way to save Margaret from Ralf and win her for himself. Money talked, even in the twelfth century, and Alex would find a way to use it to his advantage.

Margaret shifted, then caught sight of him. The smallest hint of a smile touched her lips.

Had he ever thought he could leave her? He'd been insane.

He smiled back at her and wondered if what he felt was obvious. He'd told her before that he wouldn't leave. That was a promise he fully intended to keep.

> *The stench wafted high to the heavens,*
> *So the ogre wrinkled up his pug nose,*
> *and pulled forth from his pocket a cloth*
> *that smelled ever so strongly of rose.*
>
> *Then the faeries and ogres did plan*
> *to rid the fair isle of the stink.*
> *"Send Ralf off to war with no armor,*
> *For he is a no good rat fink!"*

There was a sudden murmur of agreement after that last verse, and Alex had to turn away before he lost it. Someday he was going to have to sit down with Baldric and find out just what he'd learned from that traveling minstrel who'd taught him the new rhyme forms. The man had obviously taught him a few new words while he was at it.

He walked back out to the lists, Joel bouncing along at his heels like a happy puppy. Sending Ralf off to war wasn't such a bad idea. It would certainly solve a few of his own problems.

He nodded to himself. It was a good solution and he'd have to thank Baldric for the idea. Richard could certainly use a few new men for his French campaign, couldn't he? Ralf was a perfect choice.

Alex just hoped he could avoid being another good choice. He wouldn't have considered dodging the draft in 1998, but "army enlistment" took on a whole new meaning in 1194.

He looked at his squire standing a few paces away, poised and ready to serve. "Find me a partner, would you, Joel? I've got work to do."

Three weeks was not a very long time. He sincerely hoped he'd manage it.

He didn't want to think about what might happen if he couldn't.

Seventeen

MARGARET STOOD IN THE ALCOVE OF HER BEDCHAMBER and stared down at the lists below her. To be sure she had dozens of other things she could have been doing, but somehow here was where she found herself. She'd stopped trying to deny that she stood there because it gave her the chance to watch Alex. She could have done it just as easily while standing in the lists. But here he didn't know she watched him.

He currently ran the perimeter of the lists as intently as a woman chasing an escaped fowl might have. *Jogging* he called it, and he claimed it was very good for the stamina. Margaret had tried it one morn while Alex had been partaking of a meal and found it not at all to her liking. She felt as if her back had been permanently thrust up into her head.

Alex obviously found the practice beneficial, for he did it a handful of times each day, running until he was fair dropping with exhaustion. Margaret wasn't about to bid him cease. Watching him move with his lanky, smooth stride was a pleasure she wouldn't soon deny herself.

Of course, of late it had become more difficult to watch him for the crowd. He'd begun jogging alone, but had since acquired a following of impressive proportions. There was Joel, of course, trailing at his master's heels like an obedient puppy. Sir Henry had been one of the first to join Alex on his exercise. Margaret half suspected he and Alex pushed each other far past when they should have quit out of stubbornness not to be the first to cry peace. She could understand that and was secretly pleased to note Alex was never the first to give in.

The rest of her men joined him at least once a day and seemed none the worse for the new form of training. Perhaps it was how warriors trained in Scotland. After all, 'twas rumored to be a fairly desolate expanse with long distances to travel between settlements. Perhaps they ran to harden themselves to the labor.

Or perhaps he'd learned it in 1998, that unfathomable place he'd claimed to come from.

"Impossible," she said with a snort. "Fanciful imaginings."

The body of the group stopped, leaving only Alex and Sir Henry still at it. Margaret watched them circle the lists half a dozen more times before Henry stumbled, then ceased and hunched over with his hands on his thighs. Margaret fancied she could hear him panting from where she stood. Alex ran lightly over to where Joel had collapsed against the wall, collected his squire and headed for the well.

Margaret walked away from the window. Now would begin another rigorous session of swordplay. After that would come a meal, a small rest, then the afternoon at the quintain. Margaret couldn't fault Alex's drive to succeed. In less than a month he had gone from barely able to walk down the stairs without a rest to a warrior whose determination and endurance rivaled her own. His skill had come as well. He had a gift for it. Some men didn't, and it took them years to perfect their art. Alex wielded her father's sword as if it had been made for his hand alone. He was fearless at the joust and merciless with the blade.

She had to admit, grudgingly, that he was almost her equal.

Though she'd never say as much to him.

By the time she'd broken her fast, convinced Amery the lists were not the place for him, and then listened to a short verse from her bard, the men were already again at their play. Margaret crossed the field to where Alex and George went at each other with all the seriousness of sworn enemies. Margaret folded her arms over her chest and observed them critically.

It was almost too beautiful to watch. Alex moved with lethal grace, his sword flashing in the pale spring sunlight. Margaret watched his eyes inside his helm, saw the calculation in them, knew that he watched for the first sign of weakness. When it came, he moved in without mercy, parrying and thrusting, driving George backward. Then came the moment of glory when George's sword went flying end over end up into the air, and Alex threw his head back and shouted with laughter.

Margaret thought she might swoon on the spot.

It was all she could do not to stride over to him and kiss him full on the mouth. She remembered very well just how it felt, and the urge to do so was almost overwhelming. She'd almost made up her mind to indulge herself when Sir George ripped off his helm.

"They do *not*," he gasped.

"Oh, but they do," Alex said, taking off his own helm.

"But such staggering sums!"

"Obscene, isn't it?"

"By the saints," George said, shaking his head. "This I can hardly believe."

Margaret cleared her throat. The pair of them turned to look at her, shifting as guiltily as two lads caught with their hands in Cook's stew pot.

"Margaret," Alex said, squirming.

"Who are they and what do they do?" she demanded.

"Ah . . . well . . ." Alex stalled.

"We were discussing the customs of the people where he, ah—" Sir George looked at Alex with a pathetically helpless expression.

"Where I was born," Alex finished. "They have very odd customs there."

"In Seattle," she said, the very word feeling strange on her tongue.

"Right," Alex said. "Seattle."

Margaret scowled. Amazing how she could feel such lust for the man one moment, then want to wallop him strongly on the head the next. She could only grunt in response.

"The lads," Sir George ventured, "make vast sums playing games, if you can fathom that."

"Games?" she echoed.

"Aye, games peculiar to the region of Seattle and its surroundings," George said, warming to the topic. "With balls of different colors and shapes. Most interesting."

Well, they'd both lost all sense. There was no other explanation for it. Alex had pulled George into the realm of his folly, and the both of them were wallowing in it.

Margaret rolled her eyes and walked away. Men. Games. Somehow, the two seemed to go hand in hand.

She left them babbling with renewed vigor, with Alex expounding on some ridiculous ceremony entitled the NBA playoffs. The saints only knew what sorts of sacrifices the ritual entailed. No doubt many small animals lost their lives in the process.

Margaret looked over her lists to identify a partner on whom she could vent the sudden frustration that coursed through her. What cared she if Alex chose to delude George with his witless fantasies? She had no desire to learn more of Seattle, or to listen to his mindless chatter about games that men supposedly played. What she wished he would be talking about was how Ralf could be bested. And what of his claim that Richard would come north? The month of March was drawing to a close. If Richard were to visit Nottingham, he would be doing it soon. Yet, she had heard nothing but rumors.

There was a part of her that sincerely hoped Alex was telling the truth. Pleading her case before the king himself would surely solve her troubles.

Well, there was no sense in worrying about it at the moment. She needed to train in the event that she found herself with a lance in her hand and Ralf at the other end of the field.

"Sir Henry," she called, motioning the knight over to her. "Indulge me."

Henry waved off his current partner and walked toward her. Immediately several other men abandoned their play and came over to watch. Margaret ignored them. She was accustomed to this kind of attention. Perhaps men wouldn't look at her because she was a woman; they certainly would look at her to see her swordplay.

And so she gave them something to watch. Henry was not her equal, something she had no qualms about proving to those who observed her. She toyed with him at first, letting him wear himself out with his swinging. When she saw that his cuts were slipping just the slightest bit, his strikes just beginning to miss their mark, she began to do more than just deflect his blows.

She consciously strove to put aside what she knew of Henry's habits. She made herself forget what hand he favored and what side he feinted to when pressed. She took each of his moves and looked at them afresh, searching them out for signs of weakness.

Margaret pressed him on the left, just to see what he would do. There was no sign of hesitancy, so she eased off her attack, then suddenly lunged for his right. He stumbled away, landing heavily on one leg. The crowd murmured, but she paid them no heed. She wouldn't accept any praise until she'd bested Henry thoroughly.

She worked his right side strongly, then held off, toying with him on the left until he caught back his wind. Then she concentrated on his left, deciding that victory might be sweeter this time if she just wore him down until he could take no more.

It took a very long time. Henry was a very fine knight and had been well trained by Sir George and her own father and eldest brother. But he was, when all was said and done, simply not her equal.

He stumbled backward suddenly and went down hard

into the muck. Margaret followed him, unwilling to show him the slightest mercy. It would ruin her reputation, of course.

"Peace," Henry gasped, lying motionless in the mud. "I yield."

Margaret pulled off her helmet and shoved back the mail coif. "Well done, Sir Henry. Indeed, you have almost winded me. 'Tis a feat to be proud of."

She held out her hand to help him to his feet. Ruthless though she might have been, she wasn't above the occasional bout of chivalry.

She received praise from the men around her, and she accepted it with a regal nod. No sense in letting it show that even now such words were pleasing to her ear. Praise from herself was, of course, enough to satisfy her, but 'twas nevertheless sweet indeed to be recognized as a formidable warrior by men who judged each other by exactly such a measure.

The substantial group broke up, and there was much ribbing of Sir Henry by his fellows. Margaret didn't follow them from the field, and she certainly didn't participate in their jesting. This was something she had always remained above and would continue to remain above. The crowd dispersed and soon she was alone on the field.

Except for Alex.

He was staring at her with a slight smile playing around his mouth. It set her to bristling immediately.

"What?" she demanded.

He shook his head with a smile. "Nothing. I'm just impressed."

"As you should be."

He laughed. "Margaret, I have never in my life met a woman quite like you."

"Harumph," she said, unsure of his meaning. "Then I pity you," she added.

"You should," he said with a deep smile. "My life has been incredibly dull up to this point."

Margaret watched him watch her and felt more uneasy

than she had in days. "Why do you stare at me thusly?" she demanded. She waved her sword at him. "Cease with it, for I like it not."

"Then how would you like to go take a walk on the roof? The clouds seem to be breaking up. It might be a nice view."

She felt her eyes narrow. "A walk on the roof? I know what that entails with you, Alexander of Seattle." And the mere thought of it was enough to make her blush. Aye, she knew well enough indeed what liberties he would take if he managed to get her up off the ground and into his arms.

And damn her traitorous self if it didn't find the idea almost irresistible.

"My lady, my lady! My lady Margaret!"

Margaret tore her eyes away from Alex to see Timothy sprinting across the field, waving a slip of parchment over his head. He stumbled to a halt before her and shoved the parchment at her.

" 'Twas a messenger come from Lord Odo of Tickhill. He will hold a tourney within the se'nnight!"

Margaret looked at Alex quickly. "These are promising tidings."

"And 'tis rumored the king himself will attend!" Timothy added.

Alex only smiled. "Told you so."

Margaret scowled. "Tickhill is a fair piece north of Nottingham. Why would Richard, assuming he has returned to England, travel there if his goal is Nottingham?"

Alex shrugged. "Maybe he needs to enjoy himself for a couple of days, visit his subjects, break a few lances. Let's get busy with that note for Ralf. We'll see who gets to Tickhill first."

Margaret handed the parchment to Alex to read. "Well done, Timothy. I'll have another missive to be sent within the hour."

Timothy raced off and Margaret turned to Alex.

"You seem to have predicted this well enough."

Alex shoved the note back at her. "I'd better go practice at the quintain for a few hours, then work on some live opponents. If Ralf wants to settle this in front of the king, we'll do it on the field."

"You?" Margaret gasped.

"Of course, me," he said, looking at her as if he dared her to disagree.

And so she did, for she was certainly in the right. "*I'll* be the one to fight him."

"No, you won't."

"Aye, but I will."

"This is man's business, Margaret. I'll take care of it."

"You're not even a knight!"

"And you are?"

She gritted her teeth, but had no rejoinder for that. "My father was a knight," she said finally.

"I know, but that doesn't really mean anything for you, does it? Besides, there's more to being a good warrior than a set of spurs, which you also know very well."

She couldn't deny either. She chewed on her lip and searched for another way to prove to him that he was completely unprepared to face Ralf over lances, especially when it was her life and land at stake.

"You aren't ready," she stated firmly.

"I'm ready enough."

"It's my land!"

"And Ralf and I both want it," he said, "but Ralf isn't going to get it."

Margaret started to reply, then realized what he'd said. And she felt a coldness come over her, as if wind had come from the north suddenly and blown through her bailey. She could hardly believe her ears.

"You want my land?" she asked, stunned.

He shook his head. "Not in the way you think."

"Then you want . . ."

"You," he said, sounding rather exasperated. "All right? I want you, and if that means I have to have your land to have you, then that's what I'll have. And I'll be damned if Ralf is going to take you away from me when there's a chance I can stop him.''

"You want me,'' she repeated, as close to speechless as she'd ever felt herself.

"I only care about your land because it's yours. And it's going to stay yours if Ralf has to be finished for it to happen.''

He wanted her. He only cared for her land in that it was hers. She could hardly take it in. The feeling that rushed through her was intensely pleasurable. She didn't want to enjoy it, but somehow she just couldn't stop herself. He'd vowed he would stay with her, but this was more than simply remaining. For better or worse, he wanted her, and the very thought of it made her giddy. She looked at him and felt a fondness well up in her, a fondness she was sure nothing could dissipate.

"Go get me a lance, Margaret. I've got a lot of work to do this afternoon.''

Margaret felt the glow dim just the slightest bit, but she ignored it. Perhaps he was also so caught up in the emotions of the moment that he wasn't thinking clearly. Surely he meant to go on more about how much he wanted her.

"Go on,'' he said, making shooing motions with his hand. "I need that lance now, not yesterday.''

Ah, the glow was definitely dimming. Margaret frowned at him.

"Lance?'' she repeated.

"Yes,'' he said, looking more annoyed than amorous, "it's still what I need. I needed it five minutes ago.''

"I can fight for myself—''

"No.''

"I'm more than skilled—''

"Forget it. Go get me a lance.''

The glow was gone now. Margaret looked at the frighteningly handsome man before her and wondered what temporary madness had caused her to think having him want her was a good thing.

"I will *not* go fetch you a lance.''

"Yes, you will, then you'll go back inside and stop distracting me. I can't work when you're around."

She would have had a scathing retort for that if he hadn't reached out and run his hand over her head and down her braid.

"A beautiful distraction," he said shortly, "but a distraction nonetheless."

Damn the man if he didn't say the damnedest things at the worst possible time. She shoved aside those hints of pleasure that crept back up upon her.

"You'll not move me from my purpose with those sweet—" She cleared her throat and grasped for her wits, "I mean those ridiculous words. You'll have no need of a lance because I plan to do this deed myself. I have bested Ralf in the past. I will best him again and put an end to this foolishness."

"No, you won't," Alex repeated, looking more stubborn than anyone she'd ever seen.

She had to admire the trait because she considered it one of her best, but the display of it in him did little to aid her at present. She pointed her sword at him.

"I will fight him."

He drew his own sword. "No, I will."

"We will see who has the pleasure," she said, sending him her most intimidating frown and plopping her helm back atop her head. She took up a fighting stance. "I'll best you here and show you facing Ralf would be pointless."

"Pointless?" Alex gasped. "Why thank you so very much for the vote of confidence!"

"Vote of what—"

The answer didn't come, but Alex's assault did. Margaret fell back instinctively. It was her favorite ploy, one she'd used again and again. It was the perfect way to have a man show her what his intentions were. She'd bested more than one hotheaded lout thusly. They generally revealed all of themselves within minutes and then 'twas but a small matter to take advantage of the weaknesses they'd shown.

Without warning, Alex regained control of himself. He circled her, testing her own limitations. She could feel him doing it, and it was almost infuriating enough to cause her to lose her temper. To find her own ploy used against her was almost more than she could take.

And then he began to taunt her. She saw the idea pop into his head for it showed readily enough in his blasted eyes. Soon a small smile graced his mouth. Margaret was tempted to wipe it off, but she knew he would be expecting the like, so she refrained from giving in.

He slashed at her viciously, likely seeking to take her off guard. She slammed her sword against his, feeling the meeting of blades ring completely through her body. She held him off, her blade locked with his. His smile deepened.

"Not bad for a woman."

"For a *woman*?" she gasped. "You arrogant cur!"

"Arrogant and good. Admit it."

"I'll admit nothing," she said, giving him a mighty shove backward.

Distressingly, it hardly moved him, and she was forced to fall back to evade him.

And it was then that she realized just how he intended truly to best her. He didn't come at her hacking like an uncivilized barbarian. Here was no brutal mercenary who ran roughshod over his enemy and crushed with sheer power instead of finesse. Here was a man who wielded his blade with skill and grace, who used his wits to anticipate her moves, to draw her out, to make her reveal more of her strategies than she ever intended.

It was then that a warmth that had nothing to do with exertion began to spread through her.

Every time their blades met, she felt a jolt go through her that had nothing to do with metal upon metal. Each time he either eluded her thrusts or slipped just a bit under her guard, she felt a dizzy pleasure deepen inside her.

She had misjudged the man.

He was her equal—in wit and cleverness.

And he wanted her.

By the saints, it was almost enough to bring her to her knees.

Their blades came together with a mighty crash. Before she knew what he planned, he had grasped her sword arm. He tossed aside his blade, then removed hers from her unresisting fingers. He ripped off his helm and shoved back the mail coif. Margaret found herself doing the same with identical urgency.

His pale eyes were flashing with an almost savage intensity. Margaret felt her knees become unsteady beneath her. Alex reached out and hauled her against him. Margaret clutched his mail-covered shoulders to keep herself from falling to the earth.

"Alex—"

"I want no one but you," he growled, then he captured her mouth with his own.

Nay, she thought, but the thought was gone before it could have made it to her lips.

She wasn't ready to trust him with her fate, and she surely wasn't ready to believe his foolish tales of faery rings, but saints above, she was more than ready for this!

He ravaged her mouth mercilessly, leaving her no choice but to cling to him or risk falling to the ground. Her head spun. Her body trembled. She felt as if she'd been set afire. Then he lifted his head and looked down at her fiercely.

"I will fight him."

She was too befuddled to spar with him further. She would argue later, when she could breathe again.

But there were other things besides breathing she needed to see to immediately.

"The missive to Tickhill," she reminded him.

"Later," he said, kissing her again.

"Edward," she managed when he lifted his head to drag in a huge breath.

"He'll keep," Alex said, "but I won't. Come back here."

Well, those were only the start of the details she would have to see to soon enough. They would have to make preparations for the journey to Lord Odo. George would have to set in motion his plan to liberate Edward from Brackwald's dungeon. Having Edward at Tickhill to bear witness would surely convince the king of Ralf's treachery.

She would also have to choose men to stay behind and watch the keep, as well as see to keepers for Amery and Baldric. Amery was too young to travel with them. Heaven help Lord Odo's wall hangings if Baldric came along to the tourney.

Alex's hand tightened in her hair, and he tilted her head to more fully invade her mouth.

"Pay attention to *me*," he commanded, just before he mounted a renewed assault.

Margaret put her concerns and her doubts aside. They were all things that could keep a moment or two longer. She'd been hungering for Alex for days. Not even the king would distract her from having her fill of him.

Merciful saints above, but the man could kiss!

Eighteen

❧❧❧

HIS BUNS HAD DISAPPEARED. WELL, MAYBE THEY WERE still there, but they had lingered through On Fire, slipped slowly and with a great amount of tingling through Numb, and now had come to rest very softly on Not There At All. Alex didn't dare rub to see if his suspicions were true. He'd probably lose his grip on the reins and plunge head-first from his horse into the rutted trail. The only appealing part of that scenario was then he wouldn't care anymore about his missing backside because his face would be broken and setting up a howl in a different region of his anatomy.

He was just seriously considering the merits of a free fall when Margaret reined in.

"Stop, Beast," Alex begged as his horse clomped to an ungraceful halt next to hers. "Oh, I wish your name was Range Rover," he moaned.

"Just over that rise," Margaret said, pointing ahead. "We've made good time, in spite of everything."

Everything included Amery, Frances, Joel, and Baldric. Alex had wanted to leave them at home, but the protests had been deafening. Baldric had turned out to be a terrific horseman, and Frances and Amery seemed to have no trouble clinging to various bits of the same saddle as they bumped along at Margaret's furious pace. Joel was strapped to the back of a horse along with all of Alex and Margaret's gear. Margaret had graciously offered her lance and a shield as extras, should Alex have need of them.

Alex had been immediately suspicious. Though she had promised to sit meekly in the stands, he had the feeling he shouldn't believe her.

They were surrounded by as many of Margaret's knights as they'd thought feasible. Alex was sure Ralf wouldn't stay home when he heard they intended to rat on him to the king. Alex also suspected Ralf wasn't above a little petty thievery on his way south. He could only hope they wouldn't be ambushed as they traveled. Margaret had set a grueling pace, and Alex imagined Ralf wouldn't catch them anyway.

Next to him Margaret pulled the mail coif up around her face, then looked at him and smiled grimly. "You must take the lead now, much as it galls me to let you do so."

"If you ever compliment me, I'll probably fall over dead from shock," he said dryly. "So don't ever do it. Really. I don't think I could take it."

She scowled at him. "I cannot ride in as Margaret, else they will stick me in some pitiful solar with all Tickhill's ladies and I will go mad."

"Then just how," he asked carefully, "is it you intend to reveal who you are? Will you pose as my squire?"

She shrugged. "I'll mill about the lists."

"Absolutely not. You promised you'd watch from the stands. In a dress, so I know you aren't up to something." He reached over and pulled back the coif. "You swore, Margaret, on your father's sword."

"The promise was exacted from me when I wasn't feeling completely myself."

He knew that well enough. It had taken a good hour of kissing to even get her to agree to his conditions. But agree she had, and he wasn't about to let her weasel out of it. He fully intended to take care of Ralf himself.

He pulled her braid from her cloak and let it flip down her back. "A promise is a promise."

"Oh, damn you," she said, but only sighed. "As you will, Alex."

Red flags went up all over the place. She'd given in way

too easily, and he had the feeling she had something
sneaky planned. Well, he'd just have to deal with it when
the time came. Now what he had to worry about was getting himself into the joust when he had no spurs, no
money, and a borrowed sword.

It didn't look pretty from where he sat.

"Let us be off, then," she said. "I may as well resign
myself to several days of misery. Odo's wife is particularly
unpleasant."

"Then let's try to make it as quick a stay as possible."

It took another hour to reach the castle at Tickhill. The
keep was bigger than Margaret's and boasted both an inner
and an outer bailey. Even from a distance, he could see
that the castle was crawling with busy little workers. Alex
felt himself relax, only then realizing just how tense he
had been. If the flurry of activity was any indication, Lord
Odo had indeed succeeded in getting Richard to take a
little jaunt north.

And why not? Richard had just exercised his kingly
powers by crushing a minor rebellion at Nottingham. He
was probably in a fabulous mood and thought a little sport
over the weekend to be a perfect way to wrap up his north-
ern victories. Margaret had said Lord Odo was a staunch
supporter of the king. What with all the trouble John had
been stirring up, Richard probably wouldn't have passed
up a chance to renew a few old ties while he was in the
area.

As happy as Alex was for the king's recent liberation,
he was happier for himself that Richard had taken the time
to come to Tickhill. He would have chased the Lionheart
all the way back to London if he'd had to, but he and his
backside hadn't exactly been looking forward to that trip.

The courtyard was a veritable hive of activity. They negotiated their way through scurrying workers and came to
a halt in front of the great hall. Alex dismounted, groaning
as he did so. He'd be lucky even to get to the tournament
field after this kind of traveling punishment. Well, at least
there was enough confusion in the area that he might ac-

tually be able to get himself entered into the tournament. Hopefully Lord Odo would be so busy worrying about the king that he wouldn't overly scrutinize his tournament entrants. Alex suspected his lack of spurs might be a very big problem.

Margaret tugged on his arm. "Look over there."

Alex followed the nod of her head. Leaning against one of the outbuildings was none other than Sir Walter. Walter lifted his hand in a mocking salute.

"Great," Alex muttered. "Somehow I doubt Walter is traveling with Edward. Ralf is probably inside already, griping to anyone who'll listen."

"No doubt," she agreed. "Perhaps we'd best repair the damage while we can."

Alex answered Walter's wave with a warning look, then followed Margaret into the hall.

"Her knights murdered my people!" Ralf was bellowing. He paced angrily in front of the hearth. "Destruction of crops, looting, slaughter of animals! The woman will stop at—" He caught sight of Margaret and shut his mouth with a snap. "The bold wench," he snarled.

Margaret strode across the rushes. Alex had to trot to keep up with her. She stopped in front of a man who reclined in a chair next to the fire. His clothes were definitely nicer than Ralf's, and there was a noticeable lack of food spills on his tunic. Alex immediately had warm feelings for Odo of Tickhill.

"My lord Tickhill," Margaret said, inclining her head. "My gratitude for the invitation to your tourney."

Ralf choked. "You can't mean to let her—"

Margaret turned a very cool look on her neighbor. "Sir Alexander will ride for me, of course. Why would you think otherwise, my lord?"

Ralf spluttered with rage. "Look how she's dressed." He whirled on Tickhill. "Look at her! Dressed like a man in full battle gear!"

"One never knows what mishaps might befall a body while traveling—or at home," Margaret said pointedly. "I think it most prudent to protect myself this way.''

Lord Odo laughed. Alex looked at the man to find him smiling fondly at Margaret. "Well done, my girl. You put him in his place.''

"She did no such thing!" Ralf thundered. He advanced on Margaret, his face a very unattractive shade of red. "You manly bitch—''

Alex found, quite suddenly, that his fist had made contact with Ralf's nose. There was a very satisfying crunch, and the rather fragrant lord of Brackwald landed in an undignified heap before the hearth.

"You can have more if you like,'' Alex offered politely. "Maybe we should go outside so we don't disturb Lord Tickhill's peace and quiet.''

Ralf lurched to his feet, holding his nose. "I'll see you repaid, Seattle,'' he snarled, the blood dripping through his fingers. "See if I don't!''

"Let's plan on it, shall we?" Alex said. "I'll see you on the field.''

"Done.'' Ralf threw him a murderous glance then stormed from the great hall.

"Well, well,'' Lord Odo chuckled, "I see you've found a champion, my girl. Who is this brave soul?''

"Alexander of Seattle,'' Margaret said grudgingly. "He's decided to be my keeper.''

"There's a brave lad,'' Lord Odo said. "You've taken on quite a task, friend. I told her father when she was born that she'd be twice the trouble of any of his lads. Saints, at the moment of her birth you could hear her wailing from the lists!''

Alex was ready to hear more, but he was even more ready to hear it sitting down. He took in his surroundings as he looked surreptitiously for another chair. There was polishing and sweeping and straightening going on all around the hall, but Lord Odo seemed oblivious to it. He was sprawled comfortably in his chair, an island of calm in the midst of a raging sea of preparations. Alex sincerely hoped Tickhill was as relaxed about his tourney rules as he was about the impending arrival of royalty.

"I'd love to hear the whole story," Alex said, wondering if he dared borrow a chair or two from the high table.

Odo waved a hand and seats were immediately brought. Margaret sat down with a scowl. Alex settled into his chair with a heartfelt sigh.

"Oh, that's very nice," he said, certain he'd never felt anything so good.

"Don't think I know where Seattle is," Odo said, handing Alex a cup of wine. "On the continent?"

"That's right."

"On the coast," Margaret put in, "where they speak French very poorly and train their men to be overbearing louts."

Alex frowned at her. "I just defended your honor, thank you very much."

"I could have done it my—"

"Aye, no doubt," Odo interrupted, handing Margaret a cup. "Thank the lad, Margaret, and be done with it. Now, what is this foolishness Brackwald came and spewed at my feet?"

While Margaret recounted in glorious detail all Ralf's crimes, Alex took the opportunity to savor a very pleasant wine. He suspected he wouldn't have much chance to relax for the next few days, thanks to Richard's visit and Ralf's upcoming humiliation in the lists, so he knew he'd best rest up while he could.

Without warning, the front door burst open and a woman came flying inside trailed by half a dozen other frazzled-looking women. The first word that came to Alex's mind was *Chihuahua.* Alex watched in amazement as the woman trotted over to Odo's chair and began yipping at him. Literally.

"You're drinking the fine wine!" she screeched. "We've too few eggs, the eels won't be trapped, the oxen have escaped their pens, the wheat is full of sand, and I cannot find any fool willing to take his life in his hands to change the rushes!"

Odo drank deeply of his wine.

"I threatened the servants with the whip, yet no one wants to catch their death!"

"Leave the rushes, Lydia," Odo said, rolling the wine on his tongue and closing his eyes to savor it.

"Leave them? *Leave them?* This is the king, you fool!"

"Aye, and he'll come long enough to deplete my larder and my coffers, then be on his merry way. The bottom of his boots can bear the filth of my floors for a pair of days."

Lydia the Chihuahua threw up her hands, gave a little yelp when she saw Margaret, then turned and scurried off to the kitchens, howling her orders as she went.

"My wife," Odo announced. "She feels we are not prepared for His Royal Self. I, on the other hand, am determined to drink all my best wine before it is no more." He smiled pleasantly. "Perhaps you two will join me?"

Margaret shook her head. "I've no need of cloudy thinking on the morrow. 'Tis a most important day—"

"—to watch me best Ralf," Alex finished for her. "Isn't that what you were going to say?"

Margaret glared at him. Alex tapped the hilt of his sword—her father's sword—meaningfully. After all, she had put her hands there and promised to behave.

"Damn you," she muttered.

Odo laughed heartily. "By the saints, I wish William were alive to see this. Margaret, I believe you've met your match in this lad."

"We'll see," she said with a scowl.

"Right," Alex agreed. "We'll see you sitting in the stands in a dress, watching me unhorse Ralf."

Odo only laughed again. Margaret rose and inclined her head to him. "If my lord will excuse me, I should see to the stowing of our gear and the settling of my household."

Odo stopped laughing abruptly. "Did you bring that bard of yours?"

She smiled sweetly. "Oh, aye. And I'm sure he has much to say about the journey here."

"The saints preserve me," Odo said with a shiver. "Just

keep him away from the hangings. Lydia will have me strung up if he ruins her needlework!''

Margaret threw Alex a last dark look, then left the great hall. Alex smiled at his host.

"She's an amazing woman."

"That she is, lad. It looks as if you may just have tamed her.''

Alex almost choked on his wine. "Well, that remains to be seen."

"A pity you'll never have her. Richard won't settle her with a mere knight.''

Alex sighed as his conscience stuck him sharply in his rapidly recovering buns. "It's worse than that."

"Worse?"

"I'm not even a knight."

"But your sword and mail . . . surely you won them honorably.''

Alex smiled grimly. "I borrowed them from Margaret's father and brother.''

Odo looked him over carefully. Alex wished his dad could have come along for the ride. He would have gotten along very well with Odo and Sir George and their assessing glances.

"You use your fists well enough. Are you telling me you cannot wield a sword?''

"Oh, I can wield one well enough. I learned how at the hands of a ruthless Scottish laird. And I fought my share of battles for him.''

"Ah," Odo said, "a mercenary, then."

"Yes." There was some truth in that, at least. All those years of piracy had to count for something.

"Could you take Ralf?"

"I'm hoping so." Alex took a deep breath. "If you wouldn't mind if I entered your joust.''

Odo shook his head with a smile. "Not at all, lad. I've never been picky about who comes to play. The Lionheart's crusade robbed us of many young men, so it isn't as if there are all that many left for sport. If you can wield a lance, you're more than welcome to enter.''

"You don't think the king will mind?''

Odo shrugged. "I daresay you would find him over-looking much if you were to divide your spoils liberally with his purse.''

"Enough that he'll overlook my lack of spurs in regards to Margaret?''

"That I could not guarantee.''

"Then how is he on bribery?''

Odo held up his hands with a laugh. "I'm not the one to ask. I don't want him thinking I have anything left to put in his coffers. He had no trouble selling titles before he left for the Holy Land. 'Twas rumored he would have sold London itself if he had found a buyer. You might find him feeling the same now.''

"Then I'll just have to beat everyone.''

"He won't sell Falconberg cheaply. 'Tis good land.''

"I know,'' Alex said. "All the more reason not to let Ralf anywhere near it.''

Odo smiled. "You sound like you wish it was yours.''

"I do, but only if Margaret came as the prize.''

Odo leaned forward and refilled Alex's cup. "You're passionate, I'll give you that. I don't know that it'll be enough, though.''

"It will have to be.''

Odo raised his own goblet. "Then here's to good fortune for you, Alexander. I daresay you'll need it.''

AND THAT WAS the unsettling start to the rest of a miserable day. The most of Margaret Alex saw was at dinner, and Ralf was behaving so badly he spent more time holding her down than talking to her.

His final view of her was a glimpse as she made her way to the women's solar. She looked like she was headed for the gallows, and he had to sympathize with her. Judging by what he'd seen of Odo's household ladies, it wouldn't be a pleasant night.

His bed consisted of a spot on a floor that would have

been condemned by any rational health department. Maybe he was fortunate he'd never spent the night at Tickhill during the normal course of life when things were less tidy than they were presently. He prayed he wouldn't die from the filth before he could do Ralf in on the field.

The king was set to arrive the next day, then the tournament would begin the following. Alex closed his eyes and forced himself to relax. He needed sleep. His entire future depended on the outcome of that tournament—his future *and* Margaret's.

He wouldn't fail.

He couldn't.

Nineteen

MARGARET MADE HER WAY DOWN THE STAIRS, CURSING her skirts as they threatened to wind about her legs and send her tumbling down to the great hall. What fool had decided men could wear hose while women were consigned to skirts? It had to have been a man. No woman would have decreed such a ridiculous thing.

She'd prepared as best she could the evening before. It hadn't been hard to accomplish given the distraction the king had been to the household. He and his lady mother and their entourage had arrived late in the afternoon, sending the household into complete confusion. During the substantial diversion provided by the ceremonial welcoming of the king, Margaret had found it a fairly easy thing to sneak her gear out to the stables and bury it under a pile of hay in Beast's stall. She hadn't dared put it in with her own mount. Alex might have looked, and that she couldn't have had. No matter what sort of promise he'd extracted from her—which had been under duress, after all—she fully intended to see Ralf bested by her own lance.

There were few souls remaining at the table. Obviously the king and Lord Odo had already repaired to the lists, accompanied by the scores of Richard's devoted nobles who had arrived to celebrate the king's liberation. Margaret sat down at the board, amazed not only by the quantity of food still left upon it, but also by the quantity of disarray left behind. She couldn't help but be grateful the king would likely never think Falconberg worth visiting. Saints, but it would take her a solid fortnight to return order to her household after but one of his meals!

But the clutter was not hers to worry about, so she concentrated on providing herself with sustenance. There was ample left behind, and she broke her fast heartily. She wouldn't find herself weak when the moment of truth came.

She was just leaving the hall when she caught sight of Baldric leaning indifferently against one of Lady Lydia's tapestries. She approached him straightway.

"Good morrow to you, gentle sir," she said, standing in front of him and crossing her arms over her chest. "I would think you would be in the lists, gathering stories for your verses."

His arms were behind him. Margaret had no doubts he was thoroughly fingering Lady Lydia's needlework.

"Um," Baldric said, looking anywhere but at her, " 'tis a bit chilly out yet for these old bones."

Old bones indeed, she thought with a snort. What he was doing was deciding if the tapestries were worth his time. She recognized the look.

"I feel certain it has warmed up considerably by now," Margaret said, taking him by the arm and tugging. "There will be brash deeds wrought today, Baldric. You wouldn't want to miss out on the start of them."

"But—"

This was something else she'd prepared for. "I've something you can use to warm your hands." She looked about her. There was no one of importance to see what she'd filched from Lydia's solar. "Look," she said, drawing forth a piece of linen with a half-finished stitchery upon it. She held it up so he couldn't help but see how intricate the work was. Never mind that it had been tossed aside carelessly as something not fit for the hall. Baldric would no doubt find it as valuable as a chest of gold.

His eyes focused immediately upon it and his fingers twitched as he reached out to grasp it.

Margaret held it away. "I would exact a promise first."

He regarded her narrowly. "Aye?"

"You must sit at the back of the stands and see that my headcovering stays atop a pole I will place there."

"And where will you be?" he demanded.

"Where do you think?" she asked, exasperated. "Must you know the details?"

Baldric eyed the cloth longingly. "Perhaps not."

" 'Tis enough that you watch the pole and see it stays upright." She held the cloth closer. "Agreed?"

He could not have looked more intensely covetous. "Agreed," he said with a nod, then stretched out his greedy hands. "Ooh," he said, running his fingers over the stitchery. "Very nice."

"The pole," she reminded him. "The wimple and other foolish head coverings."

"Oh, aye," he said, but his mind was no longer on her.

Margaret towed him out to the lists and saw him settled in the stands. She placed him in the back where he was sure to be behind the majority of the company.

She looked for Alex. He was deep in discussion with Lord Odo, no doubt working out his strategy for entering himself in the lists. Margaret stood out in the open and waited until he had seen her. He did, eventually, and she could see by his stance that he relaxed when he noted that she was dressed in womanly garb. He waved.

"Men are fools," she said as she smiled brightly and waved back.

He turned back to Lord Odo, and Margaret bolted from the stands. Already she could hear women begin to come from the hall. She rounded the corner of the hall and almost plowed into none other but the Dowager Queen Eleanor.

"Eek!" screeched Lady Lydia. " 'Tis that creature, come to ruin my morning already!"

Margaret threw herself to her knees before the queen. "I beg your pardon, Your Grace."

Thin, though surprisingly strong fingers grasped her by

the chin and forced her face up. She looked at Eleanor and prayed she wouldn't be tossed in the dungeon for her mistake. The saints only knew that would throw a kink in her day.

"Your name, child," the queen demanded.

"Margaret of Falconberg," Margaret managed.

"Your Grace," Lydia yipped, "be not troubled. She is nothing—"

Eleanor held up her hand. Margaret caught an eyeful of the look of pure loathing Lydia sent her and gulped. She met Eleanor's eyes. The queen merely studied her in silence for a moment or two during which time Margaret died several deaths of unease. *Please don't stop me*, she pleaded silently. She *had* to be in the lists that day.

"A very beautiful girl," Eleanor announced suddenly.

And with that, she released Margaret's chin, stepped around her, and continued on her way. Margaret bowed her head and fought the urge not to break down and sob in relief. So strong was the impulse that she hardly noted the unpleasant things Lydia's ladies said about her in the queen's wake.

Once she'd regained her breath, she jumped to her feet and ran for the stables. There were no souls left save one lone stableboy who stood near the doors, obviously keeping watch. Margaret tossed him a coin.

"Alert me if anyone comes," she commanded.

"But, m'lady—" the lad protested.

She sighed and handed him another coin. "And remain silent, do you understand? I've begged for enough trouble as it is."

The lad shrugged and clutched the coins in his fist. Margaret ran for Beast's stall and hurriedly stripped out of her dress and donned her mail. It would have been easier with a squire, but she'd done it so long without one that she managed it in little time. She retrieved her shield, a pair of lances and her pole, then left the stall. Her head coverings she held tucked against her side. She saddled her own mount, then led him from the stables.

The stableboy's eyes bulged when he saw her, but she held a finger to her lips.

"Remember," she said. "You don't want to become acquainted with my sword, do you?"

He shook his head vigorously. Margaret suppressed her smile and continued on her way to the lists.

Frances and Amery had joined Baldric in the stands. Margaret handed the bard her pole and her headpieces.

"But, my lady!" Frances said, aghast.

"Sshh," Margaret hissed. "You'll ruin the ruse. Tend to Amery and help Baldric keep the pole upright. 'Tis most important."

"As you will," Frances said doubtfully.

Margaret retrieved her mount and her gear and made her way to the far end of the field, keeping her hood close around her face. No sense in being recognized right off.

She folded her arms over her chest and resigned herself to waiting. The moment to challenge Ralf would come soon enough, and then she would be done with him once and for all.

And then, of course, she would have to deal with Alex's inevitable fury, but that would come later. She could ill afford to think of it now. It would only distract her from her purpose.

ALEX RESTED HIS forehead against Beast's neck and sucked in great gulps of air. Oh, man, somebody should have warned him what he was getting in to. A month of training was not enough to prepare a guy for a full morning in the lists.

"My lord," Joel said, tugging frantically on his sleeve. "You've yet another challenger."

"Another one?" Alex wheezed. "Where are these guys coming from?"

"From the land round about, I think," Joel answered, still tugging. "My lord, he calls for you now."

"It's a brutal time we live in, Joel," Alex said, wiping his face with his surcoat. "Just brutal."

"As you say, my lord," Joel said, holding the stirrup. "You'll ride now?"

"Do I have a choice?" He mounted, then stared at his opponent. Well, the guy was small and looked nervous. Maybe this was his first day jousting. Considering it was also Alex's first day, he could well understand the boy's apprehension.

Then again, he was sitting on a hefty stack of ransom IOUs, and the kid knew it.

"Okay, let's get this over with," he said, urging Beast forward.

It took one pass. He caught the boy full in the chest and sent him flying back off his horse. He didn't get up. Alex wheeled around and rode back down the opposite side of the jousting rail.

"Are you breathing?" he called down.

The boy waved a gloved hand weakly in answer, and Alex sighed in relief. Victory was one thing; mortal injury was another.

Unless it came to Brackwald. He, of course, was still sitting on the sidelines, waiting it seemed for Alex to decimate the rest of the field. Alex had sat out a few rounds, but it hadn't taken long for the rest of the entrants to decide he was the man to beat. The first time his name had been called without a "Sir" attached, he'd watched the king sit up as if to protest. Alex had kept his fingers crossed and ridden anyway, before His Majesty could give it too much more thought. He'd had his first winnings deposited immediately with the king's treasurer. As Lord Odo had predicted, it had appeased the royal sensibilities.

Out of the corner of his eye Alex saw Ralf come onto the field.

"I challenge him," Alex called, then frowned. He was just sure he'd heard an echo.

He looked down the field to see another knight sitting there astride his horse, his lance in his hand. Alex whipped his head around to the stands. He could see Baldric on his feet, no doubt making copious mental notes of the scene for future reference. The top of Margaret's hat was barely visible, but still there. All right, who was this jerk and why did he pick now to mess things up?

"Alexander of Seattle was the first to make the challenge," a man declared from the king's pavilion. Alex wasn't sure what to call the guy. Color commentator just didn't seem to fit. He smiled in spite of himself, imagining how a twentieth-century sportscaster would have been detailing the day's events.

"Let's have a little background on the unpopular Lord of Brackwald," Alex said to himself. "Abusive, devious, and pungent. I don't think he stands a chance in hell of coming away with the prize, do you, Bob?"

"Nay, 'twas I who called first!" the other knight said frantically. " 'Twas I!"

"Give it a rest, kid," Alex said, taking his place at one end of the jousting rail. "Let's go, Brackwald. This is what you wanted!"

Ralf wasted no time. Alex found his wooden shield soon skewered with a very long, very sharp lance.

"Hey, these are supposed to be blunted!" Alex yelled at him as they passed each other on their way back to their squires.

Ralf only bared his teeth.

"Well, hell," Alex said, taking another lance from Joel and pulling Beast up at the end of the rail. "Looks like the man means business."

Ralf's next thrust went completely through Alex's shield. He found himself staring at a very sharp point only inches from his face. Alex wrenched the lance from the wood only to have the shield crack all the way down the middle.

Alex rode back to Joel, then held up the shield so the herald could see.

Richard held up his hand. "Another shield for the man."

Great. What Alex would rather have heard was that Ralf was going to be fined for using the wrong kind of lance.

Well, it looked like it was all up to him. No help from the royal corner.

"You're going to be coughing up some serious concessions for this one, Richard, my friend," Alex muttered under his breath as Joel struggled to lift up another shield to him.

Alex's last pass was successful. He knew he'd struck Ralf dead on the chest and heard the man's curses as he went flying off the back of his horse. It was only then that Alex realized how close the tip of Ralf's lance had come to impaling his wrist through the shield. He worked the lance free, rode back to the king's pavilion, and threw it at the herald. Then he turned back to see what was left of Margaret's enemy. No, his own enemy, the man who stood in the way of him getting what he wanted.

Ralf had lurched to his feet and was waving him on. "Come, Seattle, and let us finish this," he called hoarsely. "To the death!"

"Nay!" the knight from the far end of the field shouted. "Nay, not to the death!"

"You'll have your chance at the victor," the herald called. "Accept you this challenge, Seattle?"

Alex looked at the king, expecting him to at least say something *now*. Fighting to the death wasn't in the rules of late twelfth-century jousting, was it? But the king only leaned back in his chair and watched impassively.

"Great," Alex muttered. He dismounted, drew his sword, and shooed Beast away. "It could have been Barbados," he said with a sigh.

But then it would have no doubt been Margaret in his place, and who knows what would have happened. And Margaret deserved to remain the prize, not the corpse.

"All right Brackwald, you pansy, let's see what you've got," Alex said, limbering up his sword arm. "More dirty tricks?"

Ralf made everyone else there look like squires. Alex realized this immediately, and it was not a happy discovery. He'd known Brackwald was ruthless, but he'd suspected it was just because of his rotten personality. That the man should be so skilled as well just didn't seem fair.

"Given yourself over to the dark side of the Force?" Alex asked.

"I know not what that is, but if it means hell, aye I have," Ralf volunteered, delivering a wicked thrust along with those words.

Alex spun out of the way and countered with a backhand any tennis pro would have been proud of. "I don't think even hell would want you. You smell pretty bad."

And such bad teeth. A dentist's dream mouth. Too bad there wasn't a way to send Ralf to the twentieth century on the condition that he only stayed long enough to have the appropriate dental work done. Without anesthetic.

The unfortunate thing was, Ralf probably would have bounced right back from it. Whatever else his faults, the guy sure had stamina. Of course, he also hadn't spent the entire morning facing challengers one right after the other. Alex felt his sword begin to grow heavy in his hand. He gritted his teeth and reached down deep inside himself for enough energy to end this thing—and end it soon. He didn't have reserves enough for a drawn-out battle.

And then he suddenly realized that Ralf's guard had slipped. Alex watched as his blade slipped under Ralf's and drove straight into Brackwald's substantial shoulder.

"Arrgh," Ralf said, through gritted teeth. He stumbled back, clutching his sword arm.

Alex forced him back, never letting up on his strokes until Ralf went down heavily. Alex kicked away Brackwald's sword, then stepped on the man's hand before Ralf could reach for the dagger in his belt. Alex put his sword to Ralf's throat and smiled coldly.

"Will you die?"

Ralf's eyes were full of hate. "You haven't the ballocks to slay me."

"Haven't I? Funny, I seem to remember having them on me earlier."

"Then do it," Ralf sneered. "Finish me off."

Alex lifted his sword, then stopped as he realized what he was about to commit.

Murder in 1194.

He found, suddenly, that he just couldn't make himself move. He was about to take a life in 1194. Who knew what that might mean to the future? Never mind that he'd decided to stay and work things out with Margaret. The truth was, this wasn't his century, and he had no business murdering someone who belonged in this time period. No matter how much he wanted to bring his sword down and sever Ralf's head from his neck, he just couldn't do it.

"Coward," Ralf snarled.

"Shut up," Alex said absently. He looked at the king. "My liege, I claim Ralf of Brackwald to be vanquished. What says Your Grace?"

"Done," Richard said, his voice carrying clearly over the field.

Alex hauled Ralf to his feet by the arm connected to his injured shoulder. While Ralf was still howling, Alex caught him firmly under the jaw. Brackwald's head snapped back, and he collapsed in a heap at Alex's feet.

"Hope you're still alive now," Alex said grimly. He stepped back as a pair of Ralf's men came and collected the inert body of their lord. "His gear is mine," Alex called after them, "as well as coin, but I haven't decided how much yet."

It was only then that he allowed himself to feel any kind of relief. Ralf was taken care of. Maybe Richard would have kind feelings for him since he'd refrained from killing one of his vassals. And maybe those kind feelings would go so far as to convince Richard that Falconberg really should be put up for sale for whatever price Alex could come up with.

"Young knight," the herald called to the kid sitting at the far end of the field, "take your pleasure of Alexander of Seattle in lieu of Lord Brackwald."

"Nay," the knight said, shaking his head, "there is no need—"

"You lost your sport," the herald insisted. "Three passes with the lance, then five strikes with the sword to discover the victor."

Alex didn't protest. He'd denied the boy a chance at Brackwald. Offering a piece of himself was the least he could do. First he would disable the brat as quickly as possible and then find some deserted corner of Odo's hall to curl up in and have a very long nap. After he'd groveled at the king's feet for an extended period of time first, of course.

"Come on, kid," Alex called, "let's get it over with." He mounted and had Joel fetch him another lance from his pile of spoils.

Alex looked at the tall knight facing him and paused. There was something vaguely familiar about the stature of the boy. Then he shrugged aside his feelings. He'd seen more knights that morning than he would have liked. Maybe the kid had been loitering along the side of the field.

The herald called the start.

But that horse . . . Alex whipped his head around to look in the stands. Baldric was on his feet holding on to a pole.

A pole which was topped by a wimple and a cute little white cap.

Alex jerked his attention back to the knight thundering toward him.

"Damn you, Margaret—"

He would have said more, but her lance had caught him square in the sternum. For the first time that day, he found himself flat on his back, fully winded. He laid there for as little time as he could manage, then heaved himself to his feet and stalked across the field. Margaret, and now he could definitely see that it was she, was still atop her mount.

"Get down here!" he shouted at her.

"I will not."

He gritted his teeth. "Get down here and fight like a man."

"I bested you with the lance," she said—rather bravely, all things considered.

"Yeah, well, there's still the sword to go and mine has business with yours."

"I think I'd rather—"

"Coward," he taunted.

Good grief, but she was predictable. Alex would have laughed if he hadn't been so, well, so . . . he had no idea what he was, but he was certain he was feeling an equal measure of fury and lust.

Margaret snarled a curse at him as she jumped down from her horse. "You robbed me of my chance to best him before the king," she snapped. "I've been waiting for this for years!" She lashed out at him with her sword.

"Well, you're so very welcome for defending your honor," Alex retorted, deflecting her stroke. "You *promised* me you would stay in the stands!"

"My headcovering was there. It was enough."

"Don't even try to justify this," he warned. "You agreed to let me do it."

She seemingly had no answer for that.

"I'm stunned by the faith you've showed in me," he continued angrily.

"I *do* have faith in you," she threw back.

"You didn't show it."

"It's *my* life!"

And he'd worked his butt off to protect that life for her. Well, the time had obviously come to show her that he was fully capable of wearing the pants in the family. It was one thing to know that she knew he could and to still let her walk all over him. It was another thing entirely when she obviously thought he was completely unequal to the task of standing up and protecting her. And if he had to prove it to her on the field, then so be it.

"I am man, hear me roar," he said distinctly.

"What?"

"Prepare to be bested, you troublesome wench," he said in his best growl.

She gasped in outrage. Alex found himself with a fresh batch of energy. His manly pride had been insulted and dismissed one too many times. Never mind that he would rather stand at the head of the garrison as an equal partner with Margaret. The fact that she didn't think he could do it alone was enough to make him determined to prove it to her.

He fought her for a few minutes with a look of intense concentration on his face. Then he let his lips curve into the faintest of mocking smiles. It had always been the one thing guaranteed to send Jamie into a rage. It seemingly had the same affect on Margaret.

Alex let her wear herself out, and he continued to smile.

And when he'd had enough, he went on the offensive, forcing her back, using her own moves against her until he could see she was winded. Then with one movement— and he had to admit to himself that it was artistically done—he sent her sword flying. He watched it flip end over end through the air and was rather impressed with the speed and trajectory. Then he watched it come down.

It was then that a feeling of horror began to spread through him.

The blade was headed for the king's pavilion.

It ripped through the awning and thunked into the wood of the floor with all the force of a missile.

Right between Richard the Lionheart's knees.

Luckily for the king, he hadn't been sitting with his legs crossed.

"*Merde,*" Margaret breathed.

"You can say that again, toots," Alex said, grabbing her by the arm. He hauled himself and his errant would-be bride across the field and threw them both to their knees in front of the pavilion. He didn't dare say anything. He only hoped Richard's reaction wouldn't be to call for a pair of matching nooses.

"Alexander of Seattle," the herald called.

Alex looked up carefully at the herald. He stole a look

at the king. He was still staring, open-mouthed, at that quivering blade.

"Yes?" Alex ventured.

The herald pointed to the far end of the field. "There is yet another challenger."

Alex looked to his left and felt his eyes widen before he could stop them. Holy cow, that guy was big. His horse was huge. He was swathed all in black. Even from that distance, Alex could see he looked very fresh and well rested.

"Well, hell." As if almost severing the royal family jewels hadn't been enough. Now this?

His day had just taken a decided turn for the worse.

Twenty

❦

MARGARET KNEW SHE WAS DOOMED.

She knelt before the king's pavilion with Alex's fingers biting into her arm and stared at the horrifying sight that greeted her eyes from the far end of the field. The knight was enormous, she could see that from where she was. Alex was exceptionally tall, but she could tell that this man was equally that tall, only he seemed twice as broad.

As she watched the man come to the end of the jousting rail and take up a lance, she again considered her situation.

The king was still gaping at her sword thrust into the wood between his knees and seemingly had forgotten her for the moment. Even though she knew it wouldn't last for long, she was grateful for the momentary reprieve from his scrutiny.

Alex still had ahold of her as if he meant to do her bodily harm. Though he too had his attentions elsewhere, she knew that the lull in his irritation wouldn't last long, either.

And then there was a huge man swathed in black at the far end of the field pointing toward Alex with his lance, indicating that he had business with him. The unknown knight was freshly rested, and his demeanor suggested that mercy and patience were not among his attributes. Alex was weary after a full morning of war play. That could mean only one thing.

The man she loved was about to die.

Margaret looked at Alex's clenched jaw and found she

couldn't deny the feelings she had for him. Daft and be-fuddled he might be when it came to his past and his homeland, he was still the victor of her heart. She loved his pale eyes. She loved the beauty of his face. She even loved his unconventional training habits. And, saints pre-serve her, she loved him for taking up a sword and de-fending her honor.

She knew at that moment that she would do anything to keep from losing him.

"I'll go in your stead," she blurted out.

Alex turned a dark look on her. "You will not."

"Aye, I will. A lance!" she called.

He struggled to his feet. "I don't need you to fight my battles for me."

She jumped to her feet. "Why not? You fight mine for me."

He scowled. "And that's just how it should be."

She couldn't deny the excellent logic of that, but he looked so tired. Without thinking, she reached up and ca-ressed his cheek.

"Had I known this was the trial you would face after me, I wouldn't have forced you to fight me."

He blinked. "Really?"

"Well," she said, realizing that wasn't exactly the truth, "perhaps not. But," she added, "I likely wouldn't have dragged the affair out as long."

"You dragged—" he spluttered. "You did not—"

The black knight was banging impatiently on his shield with his lance. Margaret threw him a scowl, then turned back in time to have Alex grip her the more.

"Do me a favor and go sit in the stands," he said. "I'd like to think you're safe while I'm out there getting the hell beaten out of me."

He released her. Without giving her actions any more thought than necessary, Margaret grasped him by the shoulders and kissed him hard on the mouth.

"Win," she said simply.

Before she could back away, Alex had her captive by

means of his hand behind her head. He hauled her against him and ravaged her mouth. Margaret could do no more than to clutch him and pray her knees didn't buckle. He was very sweaty and he smelled passing unpleasant, but she didn't care. The fierce need she saw in his eyes when he lifted his head mirrored the emotion that ran through her so perfectly, all she could do was stare at him, mute.

"Go sit. Do not move."

She nodded. She was more than willing to seek out a seat before she collapsed in a heap on the field.

Alex made the king a low bow. "With your permission, Majesty?"

Richard waved him away and Alex turned and walked back to his mount. Margaret watched him go, feeling her knees very unsteady beneath her.

It was then that she realized the entire gallery was staring at her. The king was looking at her with a most calculating expression on his face. Margaret didn't dare speculate, but she was sure it meant trouble. She made him a deep curtsy, then fled for the stands before he could say anything. She made it as far as the railing before she could go no further. Drawing in a shaky breath, she turned and leaned back against the wood. She prayed, eyes open, that Alex would survive the day.

It didn't look to be a very promising prospect.

The two warriors came together with a clash. Alex teetered in his saddle, but did not fall. The second pass was just as close. Margaret clutched her hands together and wished for a melee. At least then they could have ridden in teams and she would have been able to aid Alex.

The third pass sent her love flying off his horse. Happily enough, though, the other knight had been caught by Alex's lance as well and had landed equally as ignominiously in the dust.

Alex had barely managed to sit up before the other man had leaped over the jousting rail and advanced. Margaret took a few paces away from the stands. Proprieties be damned. She wouldn't let Alex die.

The man came at Alex with blade bared.

"Get to your feet, you fool!" Margaret shouted. "Hurry!"

Alex managed to get up and have his sword out just in time to avoid losing his head.

"Yikes," he said, jumping away from the black knight's returning swing.

The black knight did a little hitch. Margaret watched him adjust the mail covering his legs. Perhaps some vermin of some kind had invaded his hose.

Alex looked tired. Margaret reached for her sword, just in case he would need aid, then realized her blade was still impaled in the king's pavilion. She drew her dagger and took another few paces out onto the field. The black knight was fighting very well, though for some reason he looked less than comfortable in his mail. Margaret watched as he took a pace back and held up his hand to call for a halt to the contest.

"What a bloody bother these things are," he said, drawing off his helm and tossing it aside. He was wearing a coif, but he had it on rather askew. Margaret watched as he pulled that off as well, then shook out a mane of dark hair. Despite herself, she found the sight of the man to be quite arresting.

As did Alex, obviously, by the way the point of his sword made abrupt contact with the dirt.

"Jamie?" Alex gasped.

The black knight grinned and made Alex a small bow. "In chain mail, no less," he said proudly. "Though you likely wouldn't believe what a time I had finding a suit of it to fit. By Saint Michael's knees, there are no metal workers of substance in the twentieth century! But I told Beth there was no sense in coming to fetch you if I didn't have the proper gear to bring along—"

Alex ripped off his helm, tossed aside his sword, and jumped forward to embrace the man who had seemingly had his demise on his mind but a few moments before.

"I can't believe it!" Alex exclaimed, pounding the man

enthusiastically on the back. "You finally found me!"

The black knight returned the pounding with a few stiff blows of his own. "Aye, well, we tried a gate or two before we stumbled upon your little ball of foil near the ring in the grass—"

Margaret watched as Alex suddenly stopped pounding. He pulled away and frowned at the other man.

"You had to find me _now_? Your timing stinks!"

"Well, our journey through the Future gate took more time than I'd expec—"

Margaret watched in astonishment as Alex's expression changed from annoyed to bloody furious. With a mighty shove, he felled the black knight, then leaped upon him with his hands about the other's throat.

"Damn you, James MacLeod!" Alex shouted.

James MacLeod? Alex's brother-in-law? Margaret took a brief moment to consider what this might mean, then she realized Alex was about to strangle the other man. That wouldn't do. She had questions to put to this Lord MacLeod, questions that would certainly tell the tale about Alex's sanity.

"Cease!" she called out. "Alex, cease you with this idiocy!"

"Damn you, Jamie," Alex was saying. "Why didn't you tell me about those damn X's?"

"I didn't think . . . you'd see the . . . map," Jamie wheezed, obviously struggling to take in air.

"You could have put some sort of warning label on it!"

" 'Tis still in the . . . _oof_ . . . experimental stage—"

Lord MacLeod began to turn a very unwholesome shade of purple. Margaret couldn't for the life of her fathom what had her love in such a temper, but 'twas more than obvious his brother-in-law was the cause of it. No sense, though, in not rescuing the man before Alex finished him off. After all, she did have her questions to ask. She strode out onto the field.

"Experimental? Damn you, Jamie, how could you leave something that dangerous just lying around?" Alex demanded, wrenching his brother-in-law about by the neck. "You've been weekending in Barbados, haven't you? I wind up in rainy old medieval England, and you've been sunning yourself on the beach. You've got a damned tan still!"

"Holidays are . . . *arrgh* . . . good for a body," Jamie managed, trying to fend Alex off.

"Holidays—"

Margaret grasped Alex by the back of his surcoat and pulled firmly. "Alex, let him up."

"Don't stop me now," Alex growled. "I've been fantasizing about this moment for several weeks."

Margaret could feel the eyes of the entire population of Tickhill upon them. Indeed, she was just certain the royal gaze was burning a hole in her back.

"Finish him later," she suggested. "When you have less of an audience. Besides, I have a question or two for this man, and you'll not do him in before I've had a go at him."

Alex took in a deep breath, then let it out slowly. He reluctantly released his victim and heaved himself to his feet. Lord MacLeod sat up with a grunt, rubbing his offended neck.

"My thanks, mistress," he said, shooting her a brief smile. He scowled at Alex. "I should think you'd be happy to see us. By the saints, Alex, we brought munchies!"

Alex swore with great enthusiasm. "Your timing couldn't be worse, damn it. I'm on the verge of getting married here!"

Jamie's mouth fell open. "You are?"

"You are?" Margaret echoed. She found her hand captured by Alex's.

"I am," he said, giving her a look that dared her to contradict him.

Based on that look, she decided that remaining silent would be in her best interest.

Alex glared at Jamie. "Let's just hope you haven't ruined my reputation with the king."

Jamie continued to gape at him.

"Don't get up," Alex said shortly. "We'll catch up later. Come on, Meg. We don't want to keep the king waiting any longer. Let's hope he still thinks I'm knight material after this fiasco here."

Margaret found herself being towed back toward the king's pavilion. She looked over her shoulder and found Jamie getting slowly to his feet, still staring after her and Alex with an expression of astonishment on his face. Margaret would have chided Alex for not being more hospitable to a man who had obviously come a great distance to see him, but Alex's mien warned her that chiding would not be well received.

Alex came to an abrupt halt. "Oh," he said.

Margaret followed his gaze and saw that Edward of Brackwald stood before the king, leaning heavily on Sir George.

"Well," Alex said, sounding somewhat unsure, "I suppose this is good."

" 'Tis a stroke of marvelous fortune," Margaret said, taking him by the arm and pulling him this time. "He'll tell the king of Ralf's treachery."

"Yeah, well, that may not be all."

She spared him a brief glance. "What mean you?"

He looked very uncomfortable. "I think Edward thinks he'd be a good husband for you."

It was her turn to come to an immediate halt. "And from whence might he have procured such a ridiculous notion? He knows I've no use for Ralf or any of his kin."

"Well," Alex mumbled, "I might have given him the idea."

"You *what!*"

He shrugged helplessly. "It was when I thought I'd be going home. I didn't want you stuck with Ralf."

"I can choose my own husband, thank you!"

"I realize that now, and believe me I want to be first on the list—"

"Damn," she groused. "Come along then, you blath-

ering fool. You may as well disabuse Edward of that foolishness now."

She dragged Alex to the pavilion, then cast herself down
on her knees next to Edward. He smiled carefully at her.

"Lady Margaret."

She tried not to breathe too deeply of the air about him.
Ralf's pit was obviously even less cared for than his hall.

"I'll not wed with you," she whispered sharply. "Best
forget the idea now."

He blinked. "But I thought—"

"Aye, there's always danger in that," she said. "Alex
does it often and look what trouble it lands him into."

"Ahem."

Margaret clamped her lips shut at the clearing of the
royal throat. She didn't dare look up at her king.

"Sire," Alex began.

"Rise, Alexander of Seattle," the king commanded.

Alex did. Margaret stole a glance at the king, and her
heart sank. His Majesty had something planned, and it
could only be something foul. He wore that look.

"We would know the name of this other knight," the
king said, pointing an imperious finger back toward the
lists, "and why you both chose to brawl in such a manner."

"He is my brother-in-law, Your Majesty, Laird James
MacLeod of Scotland," Alex said humbly. "It was a little
family squabble. I apologize deeply for carrying it out on
the field where it didn't belong."

Richard grunted. Margaret secretly thought the king had
no room to criticize. The saints only knew he'd done his
share of brawling with his family members, both on and
off the field. She watched him carefully for his reaction
and saw the royal wheels begin to turn. He couldn't help
but see the possibilities in two such tall, strapping men.
She said the briefest, most heartfelt prayer of her life that
Alex wouldn't find himself being invited to join Richard's
company. There was no telling where he'd end up if that
happened.

Richard motioned for Margaret to rise. She jumped to her feet.

"Aye, my liege?" she said promptly, hoping to distract him from possible thoughts of recruitment for his army.

Richard put his hands on her sword that still rested in the floor between his knees and frowned at her. "You've disobeyed us repeatedly. You should have been wed several years past, to the man of your father's choosing."

Was it her fault her father had been soft-hearted enough to indulge her in her refusal to marry as a child? And to be sure it wasn't her fault that her father had been dead these past ten years and quite unable to look for a suitable match for her. Neither of those, however, were details she dared share with the king. Best he not know the full extent of her disobedience.

She felt Alex stir beside her, and she quickly elbowed him in the ribs. The last thing she needed was him blurting out some item of interest better left unsaid.

"And since your sire is not alive to see to it," Richard continued, "the task of finding you a husband falls to us."

"I beg pardon, Sire," Margaret ventured, "but I do not think any of the men Your Grace could suggest will hold Falconberg as well as I can—"

She gasped at Alex's elbow in her ribs.

"What she means, Your Grace," Alex began, "is—

"—what I mean," Margaret continued, shooting Alex a glare, "is that I am certain Your Grace places the same value on his holdings that I do. I know that Your Grace would not want my lands to fall into ruin, or be ravaged."

Richard stroked his chin and regarded her with only thinly veiled impatience. Well, at least he hadn't gainsaid her yet. And her head was still atop her neck. Margaret was almost giddy with relief. Perhaps Edward could be questioned and Ralf could be shown to be the ravager he was.

"A blessing it is, then," Richard continued, "that we have found a man who can hold your lands and still have enough stamina left to rule you."

"Not Ralf—" Margaret began.

Richard waved his hand dismissively. "We had considered him, true, but he hasn't shown well today."

"I'm sure French soil would suit him better," Alex muttered under his breath.

Margaret wanted to agree, but didn't dare.

"And given what his brother has said about his actions the past few months, we can see he would be a poor choice."

The saints be praised for that, she thought.

Richard looked at Alex. Margaret almost flinched at the calculation there.

"How much have you collected today?"

Alex blinked. "I beg your pardon, Sire?"

"How much?" Richard asked impatiently. "For your ransoms?"

"Ah, I'm really not sure—"

"Goods which could be ransomed for five hundred marks, Sire," Richard's herald announced. "And that doesn't count the ransom due him from Lord Brackwald."

"The earldom of Falconberg shall be sold for five hundred marks," Richard announced.

Margaret blinked.

"See to the collecting of it for the new earl of Falconberg," Richard said to the man who'd spoken before.

"He's not even a knight," Edward blurted out from her other side.

Richard's look should have cut him down where he knelt. Amazingly enough, Edward remained upright.

"Do you question our decision, Sir Edward?" the king demanded, tapping the hilt of Margaret's sword meaningfully.

"Nay, Sire, 'tis—"

"Aye?"

Edward swallowed audibly. "Nay, Sire. 'Tis a most wise choice."

"Our thoughts exactly." The king turned back to Alex. "Prepare yourself this eve, for you will be knighted on the morrow and thereafter give us your fealty. The wedding will take place straightway thereafter.'' Richard leveled a stare at Margaret. ''You will go with the countess's ladies and see yourself prepared for the morrow as well.''

Margaret could only gape at him.

''We assure you that you wouldn't wish to face *us* over blades.''

That was truth indeed, especially considering the royal mood.

She found her hand again captured by Alex's.

''Your Grace is most kind,'' he said, squeezing her hand tightly, ''and we are most grateful for your forbearance and longsuffering.''

''Our army could yet use soldiers,'' Richard said, eyeing both Alex and his brother-in-law with something akin to regret.

''My lord Ralf seems anxious to serve,'' Alex offered.

Margaret admired his cheek. Saints, that would be the place for Ralf—trudging about in one of Richard's armies.

''So he does. But what of our newly made earl of Falconberg?''

Alex took a deep breath. ''I daresay the king could yet use gold for his wars.''

Richard pursed his lips. '' 'Twill be a heavy price, for our coffers are light.''

''It will be my pleasure to see to their filling. I'm certain I could do so with more success if I remained at Falconberg.''

Richard conceded the point with a grunt. ''Tickhill, see that the lady Margaret is suitably garbed and prepared for the ceremony. Come, Mother, and let us return to the hall for sustenance.'' He rose and immediately there was a flurry of activity from the courtiers surrounding him as they leaped to their feet to bow and scrape before him. Richard sidestepped Margaret's sword, cast her a final pointed look, then escorted Eleanor from the field.

Margaret didn't dare breathe until the king and the rest of the gallery had disappeared around the corner of the hall. It was only then that she found it in her to draw breath. By the saints, that had been close! To think that with a mere voicing of a few words, the king could have saddled her with Ralf for the rest of her life.

Lord Odo pulled Margaret's sword out of its resting place in the floor, then leaped over the railing with all the exuberance of a squire. He clapped Alex heartily on the shoulders.

"By the saints, lad, you did it! Well done!"

Alex was laughing. Margaret looked up and was surprised at the genuine pleasure she saw on his face. Alex turned her to him, then kissed her full on the mouth. She looked at him, stunned, when he pulled away.

"The earl of Falconberg," she whispered. "Not even my father held so lofty a title."

His smile was almost too beautiful to see. "It doesn't matter," he said, reaching out to touch her face. "What matters is your land is still yours and it will remain yours for the rest of your life."

She shook her head slowly. "Nay, 'tis yours."

"No, Margaret, it's yours and you are mine." He smiled and the sight of *that* smile made her want to fan herself. "I have to say, though, I think I've gotten the better prize."

He would have kissed her again, and indeed he seemed poised to do so, but Lord Odo whisked her away.

"Come, my dear," he said, handing her the sword, "let's see what use Lydia's seamstresses can be put to. She has reams of fabric she hoards like fine wine. She'll part with the finest for your gown—I'll see to it myself!"

Margaret managed one last look over her shoulder as she sheathed her sword. Edward was shaking Alex's hand, looking disappointed, but alive. Alex was still grinning madly. James MacLeod had joined the group and was still wearing that expression of astonishment. At least his face had returned to a healthy color. Margaret was itching to question him, but Lord Odo had a grip on her she had the feeling she'd never break, and she didn't have the heart to turn her blade on him. With any luck, Alex would leave enough of his brother-in-law for her to interrogate at her leisure.

Then she came to an abrupt halt.

One of the most beautiful women she'd ever seen had just come running through the gallery. She shoved a young child into James MacLeod's arms and then threw herself at Alex, clutching him as if she feared she'd never see him again. Alex laughed and returned her embrace.

"Come, my dear," Lord Odo said, tugging gently. "You've a wedding to prepare for."

Margaret was stunned enough to allow him to continue pulling her toward the hall. A wedding? With what she'd just witnessed, she wondered if there would be one.

Merciful saints above, who *was* that woman?

$\mathcal{T}$ wenty-one

❧❀❧

ALEX FELT GIDDY WITH RELIEF. THERE WAS NO OTHER way to describe it. It was better than passing the bar. It was better than any corporate takeover. It was, without a doubt, the best he had ever felt in his life. He hugged the sister he hadn't seen in weeks, then swung her around, laughing.

"Can you believe this?" he asked her. "We did it! We saved her land!"

"So I hear," Elizabeth said, putting her hand to her head and smiling weakly. "I take it congratulations are in order."

"If you only knew," he said, with feeling.

He had no idea where to begin in telling Jamie and Elizabeth everything that had gone on over the past few weeks. And that didn't begin to address sorting out his feelings about their arrival. Of all the times to have shown up!

Though he had to admit that, now that he'd gotten his desire to strangle Jamie out of his system, he was actually very glad to see them both.

At least he thought he was glad.

He shook aside thoughts that were better left for a less jubilatory time. He would think about just what his family's arrival meant to him and his future after his honeymoon. He didn't dare think about it now.

A very foul smell wafted past him. He blinked and noticed that Edward had come to stand next to him.

"Congratulations," Edward said, smiling gamely. "On both your title and your bride."

"Sorry about that," Alex said, not feeling sorry in the least.

Edward waved away the apology. " 'Tis obvious she fancies you. And I daresay you'll hold Falconberg very well for her."

"With any luck, you'll be in charge at Brackwald and then our border troubles will be over."

"Aye, with any luck," Edward agreed. "I'm to meet with the king after supper. Apparently, he knew nothing of Ralf's deeds."

"Well, you're living proof your brother isn't a sterling citizen. Glad to see you out and about again."

"I have Sir George to thank for that," Edward said. He nodded at Margaret's captain, then stepped back. "I should perhaps seek out cleaner clothes. I doubt His Majesty will be eager to smell me in my current condition."

Alex couldn't help but agree, but he refrained from doing so out loud. He waited until Edward had walked away before he turned to George.

"Well," he asked with a grin, "what do you think?"

George smiled just as widely. "I couldn't be more pleased."

"Neither could I." Alex laughed again for the sheer pleasure of it. "I can hardly believe it."

George elbowed him surreptitiously. "An introduction, my lord."

Well, George was obviously frothing at the mouth for a few more future details. He was staring at Jamie and Elizabeth with the same kind of awe someone else might have a full-fledged alien. Alex wasted no time in introducing Margaret's captain to his family.

"A pleasure," George said, his eyes quite a bit wider than normal.

"George knows everything," Alex explained. "And he believes me. Unlike Margaret, who thinks I've lost my marbles. And it wasn't like I sprang it on her first thing.

Good grief, she'd known me almost a month before I told her!''

"Okay," Elizabeth said, taking her son back into her arms, "it's time for the whole story. From the beginning."

"I heard you brought munchies?" Alex asked hopefully.

"Part of the time-travel survival kit," Elizabeth said with a dry smile. "Let's find somewhere private, and we'll break out the stash. Maybe after you take care of your fan club," she added, nodding her head toward the stands.

Alex looked over to the stands to find that there were indeed several souls waiting for him. Baldric stood there, looking as if he were just itching to start spouting verse—already his fingers were flexing purposefully. Frances stood there with a squirming Amery in her arms, and Joel was clutching as much of Alex's gear as he could get his arms around. Alex felt his chest tighten. What a crew it was. And to think he'd just won the right to provide for them. It made the victory all that much sweeter.

Alex made the introductions, then convinced George to take the little group back to the hall so he could debrief his family in private. It was a short trip to where Jamie and Elizabeth had left their mounts and their gear. In short order Jamie had removed his mail, they were sitting under a tree, and Alex was savoring his first Twinkie in over two months.

"This day just cannot improve," he said, licking his fingers thoroughly.

"Yeah, yeah, so now you've had your sugar hit," Elizabeth said, tossing a twig at him. "I want details. And don't think you're going to get away with that little stunt of almost strangling my husband."

"Indeed," Jamie said, rubbing his neck pointedly. "I believe I'll need the satisfaction of a lengthy wrestle to satisfy me on that score."

"The story first," Elizabeth said to Jamie. "I want him in one piece until he gets it all out."

Alex couldn't stop smiling. His family and Margaret all

in the same day. It was almost too good to be true.

"Well," he said, leaning back against the tree, "it all started with Beast having a cold and sneezing all over me."

"Oh, that was an auspicious start," Elizabeth said with a laugh.

"I should have known something was up. Anyway, I went upstairs to get cleaned up, then had to answer the phone because Zach is incapable of doing anything but decimating the fridge. It was then I found the map." He looked at Jamie. "I assumed you were just doodling, because I was just certain it couldn't mean what I thought it might mean."

"Your first mistake," Jamie noted.

"Fortunately it doesn't look like a mistake from where I'm standing now. Anyway, I decided a little change of scenery was in order so I thought I'd just head to Barbados—"

"Told you that's where he'd try," Elizabeth said, poking Jamie in the ribs.

"—but somehow I wound up too far north," Alex finished.

"You can't lay the blame for that at my feet," Jamie protested. "I was very clear about the location of the gates."

"How was I supposed to know you weren't making it all up!" Alex exclaimed.

Jamie pursed his lips. "Time traveling is not fodder for jests."

"Thank you. I know that now."

"Why didn't you wait for me?" Jamie asked. "I could have told you the truth of the matter."

"You weren't around. By the way, how is Barbados this time of year?"

Jamie looked at his wife and winced at the glare she was giving him. "Ah, well, perhaps not as pleasant a vacation spot as one might wish. But that's a tale fit for another day."

"Don't even think I'll feel sorry for you. At least you were looking at the sun."

Jamie made a noise or two of supreme discomfort, then waved Alex on. "You might pity me once you hear the details, but I assure you that you do not want to hear them now. Nor do I wish to relate them with your sister sitting here ready to chastise me yet again for but wishing to hoist a petard or two. Tell us instead of your adventures."

Jamie looked so desperate to distract Elizabeth, Alex couldn't help but feel sorry for him. He made himself more comfortable against the tree, then began at the beginning, starting with Margaret's boot in his side and then his kidnapping from Brackwald. Then he outlined his plan to set up Edward as Lord of Falconberg and his subsequent attempts to return to the future.

" 'Take me home, country road'?" Elizabeth asked.

"I was desperate," Alex grumbled. "By the way, just how is it you get back and forth?"

Jamie shrugged. "We just do. Though I can't say we have much control over our arrival and departure times."

"So Air MacLeod isn't a perfected means of travel yet?" Alex asked.

"Don't get him started," Elizabeth said darkly. "Just take my word on this: It doesn't remain unperfected from a lack of trying."

Alex suspected he would be wise not to ask for the details at the moment. Jamie's expression was turning philosophical in direct proportion to the deepening of Elizabeth's frown. Better to head off that argument while he could.

"Anyway," he continued, "after my last unsuccessful attempt in the faery ring, I found Amery running away from marauding knights, rescued Margaret from a few thugs, and decided that since I was here for good, I should make the best of things." Then he shook his head. "No, that wasn't how it was. I decided to stay." He smiled at his sister. "Margaret's what I've been looking for my whole life. I couldn't leave her."

"And yet you had to best her with the sword to convince her to marry you," Jamie observed.

"She doesn't persuade very easily."

"You could have tried wooing her," Jamie said. "To be sure, I have a very long list of appropriate strategies I could have given you."

"I don't think they would have worked on her."

Jamie shook his head in disagreement. "You'd be surprised what a fistful of wildflowers will fetch you."

"Trust me. She was more interested in my swordplay than my romantic ideas. I'm just hoping I can get her to the altar before she bolts."

Jamie exchanged a glance with Elizabeth, but was silent. Alex watched his sister fuss with young Ian's tunic, and wondered why the sudden silence.

"What's the problem?" he asked.

Elizabeth shrugged. "We just assumed you'd want to come home with us."

Alex sighed and dragged his hand through his hair. "If you'd come two months ago I would have gone without hesitation. It's too late now. I've made a life here, and it's a life I wouldn't trade. Besides," he said cheerfully, "you guys can come and visit. It'll just be like I took a job in a rain forest or something. No letters but a good care package every Christmas."

Elizabeth bit her lip and Jamie frowned. They again looked at each other, then both remained stubbornly silent. Alex rolled his eyes.

"All right, I give," he said with a sigh. "Why all the secret looks? Something I should know?"

"I don't know that we can get back here again," Jamie said. "It isn't exactly like filing a flight plan at the airport, Alex."

"Hey, how hard can it be to find medieval England?"

Jamie shook his head. "It isn't the place that presents the problem, Alex, 'tis the date."

"You found me easily enough."

"Ha," Elizabeth said. "Third time's a charm, buster.

The first time we landed here in the middle of John's Magna Carta troubles and we left right away.''

"And the second, we found ourselves in the company of Robin of Locksley," Jamie continued. "Though I must admit, that was a pleasant venture. I had come more fully prepared in English garb, and to be sure their style of fighting in the forest was more to my liking than this jousting business.''

Alex blinked in surprise. "Then how did you find me this time?''

"We happened upon your Margaret's keep, inquired as to the date and other particulars and learned that you had departed for Tickhill to try to speak with the king." Jamie shrugged. "We were fortunate. But there is no guarantee we will be so fortunate in the future.''

"All right," Alex said, sitting up and frowning, "just how much experimenting have you done?''

Elizabeth snorted. "More than he dares admit.''

"And you've never once controlled the destination time?''

Jamie shook his head. "We find ourselves arriving at a time where there is a task for us to accomplish.''

"And bringing me Twinkies wouldn't qualify?''

Jamie smiled grimly. "I think not.''

Well, it certainly put a different light on things. Alex realized then that he'd always entertained in the back of his mind the hope that somehow Jamie and Elizabeth would show up now and then just to keep him abreast of familial happenings and current events. That had just become a nonreality. This was very possibly the last time he would see his sister, his brother-in-law, and his nephew. It also meant that he would never again see any of the other members of his family. Never again would he have the dubious pleasure of walking by Zach's room and trying to identify the toxic smells coming from under the doorway.

"You love her enough to stay?" Elizabeth asked.

Alex dragged himself back from his less than cheerful

thoughts and managed a smile. "You of all people shouldn't have to ask that."

And with that, his decision was remade. Though he realized there had never been any real danger of him choosing anything else. He'd decided once before, but that had been when he'd been fairly sure he had no other choice of action. Now the choice had been given to him, but he found his decision to be the same one.

"Yes, I love her very much," he said. "I think you'll like her, too."

"Don't know that I'd want to face her over lances," Jamie said seriously. "At least not without a wee bit more practice at it. She certainly took you out with no trouble."

"I was distracted," Alex countered. "She was supposed to be sitting in the stands, not gallivanting around the lists."

"And who made the decision about where she should keep herself?"

Alex frowned at his brother-in-law. "I did. It wasn't where she wanted to be, but I put my foot down. You know, the 'begin as you mean to go on' kind of thing."

Jamie shook his head with a laugh. "Oh, brother, you've much to learn about women."

"I know plenty about them, believe me," Alex grumbled. "And considering how much I know about this particular woman, I think I would be wise to go check on her. She'll be stuck up in that solar with all those women, and heaven only knows what she'll do."

"Cabin fever?" Elizabeth asked.

"An intense aversion to Lord Odo's wife, actually. She's probably up there debating about whether or not she should hack them to bits and then escape." He deposited his Twinkie wrapper back in Elizabeth's saddlebag and rose. "I'd better go rescue her before she does something drastic." He looked at Elizabeth. "Want to tag along?"

"I wouldn't miss it," she said. She gave her son a hug and a kiss and passed him over to his father. "You'll watch Ian?"

"Aye," Jamie said, taking Ian and settling him comfortably on the ground. "We'll practice our swordplay, or some other such manly pursuit."

Elizabeth rolled her eyes as she rose to her feet. "Jamie, he's not even walking yet. Why don't you concentrate on keeping him from eating the native flora and fauna and leave the swordplay for later."

" 'Tis never too soon to begin—"

Alex found himself being pulled away by his sister. "I don't want to hear any more," she whispered. "Hurry, before I get another lecture on why it's a good thing that Ian has more wooden swords than stuffed bears."

"Come, Ian," Jamie said from behind him, "let us search in Papa's saddlebag and see what sort of weaponry he has brought for you. Och, but 'tis a fine day for lessons in parrying!"

Alex took one last look behind him to see Jamie rooting in his bag for the goods, then turned himself back around so his sister didn't give him whiplash from how hard she was pulling him away.

"I've told him no steel until Ian's at least six," Elizabeth said grimly, "but you can just imagine what he says to that."

Alex put his arm around her shoulders. "Oh, Beth, I've missed you guys."

"What you've missed is watching me never get my way with that man. Didn't I put my foot down about time traveling? Didn't I?" she demanded.

"Repeatedly," Alex agreed.

"Did it do me any good? Well, did it?"

"Oh, Beth," he said with a laugh, "you knew you'd never get your way on that from the start. And you can't tell me you don't enjoy it just a little bit."

She pursed her lips. "Everyone always wants him, Alex. The men want him for their armies, and the women want him—well, they just plain want him. I'm beating them off with a stick."

"You could think of it as great first-hand research."

"What I'd really like to be researching is the effects of a weekend in that overstuffed floral-print chair I just bought for Jamie's study, accompanied by a batch of Joshua's brownies and a good book."

"Don't look for sympathy here, sister," Alex said, shaking his head. "You've still got a tan. I'm starting to mold between my toes."

She looked up at him. "You can't tell me you haven't been having a good time, either. You don't look too miserable."

Alex smiled. "It's been wonderful. Now, if I only had the Range Rover to travel with, things would be perfect. Not that there's probably anything left of it," he said. "Can I hope Zach hasn't decided to do the noble thing and drive it every day so it doesn't die from lack of use?"

"I hid the keys," Elizabeth said. "He was starting to drool over it pretty heavily."

"I'm touched by his concern for my welfare."

"That's Zach," she agreed.

Alex fell silent as they approached the hall door, then took a deep breath. "Well, here goes nothing. I hope she hasn't changed her mind."

Elizabeth slugged him in the arm. "Of course she hasn't changed her mind. Doesn't she realize the catch she's getting? Hundreds of twentieth-century women will go into mourning when they hear about you getting married."

"Margaret's a tough sell."

"Look, she's probably sitting up there right now, staring off into the distance, daydreaming about you even as we speak."

Plotting the demise of Lydia of Tickhill and her ladies was probably more accurate, but Alex didn't try to convince his sister of it. He was too busy with his own plotting of how he would get her to the altar.

He sincerely hoped it wouldn't be at the point of his sword.

Twenty-two

MARGARET FINGERED THE HILT OF HER SWORD AND WON-
dered how Lord Odo would feel if she slaughtered all his
lady wife's women. Of course Lady Lydia wasn't in at-
tendance. She'd made it clear she had no desire to be in
the same solar with a woman in chain mail. Margaret had
no idea where the queen mother was, and it was probably
just as well. The saints only knew what Eleanor would
have to say about the entire affair with Ralf and Alex,
though Margaret tended to think the former queen of England would have agreed with her tactics.

Margaret straightened and looked over the heads of the
women circling her like vultures. She would ignore them.
No matter that they looked her over as if she were a leg
of mutton to be dressed for a meal. Or perhaps they considered her an entire sheep—a very large sheep. She felt
twice as tall and twice as wide as any of the women in
the same chamber.

It was excruciating.

Of course, she had no desire to be dressed as they were,
what with all their finely made gowns, their velvets and
silks. She had no wish to have her head covered by those
ridiculous wimples. Dainty slippers made for a very uncomfortable crossing of the lists. One healthy step in horse
dung and a girl's feet would smell for the rest of the day.
Besides, a sword would look passing foolish belted around
such gowns as the ones she saw before her.

And how would she ride astride her mount with those

skirts to contend with? How would she fight if she were forever tripping over hems and such? Was she to trade in her weapons for a handful of keys? Perhaps the women before considered such keys to be a symbol of power, but Margaret knew better. Power was cold steel in the hand and the skill to use it.

All in all, she thought she just might have chosen the better part.

But that didn't aid her in ignoring the looks of disdain and the blatantly spoken insults.

She again fingered the hilt of her sword. It gave her no relief, so she walked to the alcove and stared out the window. That was somewhat better. At least she didn't have to watch the harpies behind her as they discussed her flaws.

"Is she a maid?" one asked politely.

"Impossible to say," another said with a laugh.

"One could tell by lifting her skirts, but what man would brave her sword to do so?" another cackled.

"If she had skirts to lift!" another exclaimed, laughing heartily. "For all we know, she isn't a woman at all!"

Margaret tried desperately not to listen, but the chamber was far too small for that. She stared out the window with renewed determination. They could say what they wanted. Let them try to do the things she did each day. Why, if a man came at them with a sword drawn, they'd likely swoon at his feet.

"I say he flees, despite the king's command."

"I would, were I he," another said. "With his comely aspect and strong arm, he could have his pick of brides."

"Aye, what a face he has! Saints, just the sight of it is enough to have me on my back."

In a swoon, Margaret thought glumly. Aye, Alex's visage was enough to weaken any woman's knees.

And she was to be his.

The thought should have had her delirious with joy. Instead, she thought she would never again have the stomach for eating anything. No matter that he'd said he wanted her for himself before they'd even come to Tickhill. For a moment she wished she'd been nothing more than a peasant girl and he a mason's bastard. At least then she would have been sure that he wed with her out of love.

She wrapped her arms around herself. She realized as she did so that it had become a gesture she made with frightening regularity. It also didn't escape her why she felt the need to do so.

To protect her heart.

"Oh, oh!" one of the witless wenches squeaked. "He comes! Listen, can you not hear him arguing from here? What a melodious voice he has!"

"And such a fascinating accent he has! So foreign."

Margaret scowled. She'd heard Alex's accent far too much to find it fascinating. Annoying was more to her thinking. She turned to face the doorway and fixed a scowl firmly to her face. What cared she that he had come? Perhaps he only came to see what selection of ladies Odo could provide, now that he was soon to have a title and could likely have his pick of the lot. Margaret was half tempted to tell them he was naught but a healer's son. It would serve the wretch right if she did so and ruined his chances to further himself with these spiteful cats.

"Don't tell me no!" Alex was bellowing. "If I want to see Margaret of Falconberg, then I'll see her!"

Well, Alex had certainly taken on the tone of an outraged nobleman. Margaret was almost on the verge of feeling a bit of pleasure that he was demanding to see her, then she caught sight of the looks of disbelief on the wenches' faces.

"Surely he's here to tell her he'll have none of her," one of them whispered.

"Aye, and wishes to have this over with as soon as possible," another added. "How do I look? Wimple straight and covering all it should?"

Margaret watched them fuss over themselves and felt her heart sink within her. They had the right of it: Alex was surely coming to tell her he wanted nothing of her.

Why would he, when he could have his pick of any maid in England?

It mattered not to her. Margaret shrugged aside her hurt and stared at the doorway, willing Alex to come through it. He would find himself scorned before he could do the like to her.

"My lord, you cannot enter there," a man was saying.

"I want to see my future wife."

"But my lord, this is not the place for it! These are the women's chambers."

"Then I should have no problem finding her here. Out of my way, flunky boy."

Alex himself came to rest in the doorway, his eyes searching the chamber. Margaret watched him as he caught sight of her, then wondered at the expression that crossed his face. Relief? Happiness?

Two very large, burly guards appeared on either side of him. Alex ignored them.

"Margaret—"

The guards wrestled him away from the doorway.

"Margaret, I need to talk to you!" he bellowed as he was dragged backward. There was a great amount of scuffling, grunting and swearing. When she heard the ring of steel, she drew her sword.

Half the assembled ladies swooned.

Margaret ignored them and strode to the door.

Then she came to an abrupt halt. That woman was there, the woman who had wept over Alex. Was this then his wife? Nay, he'd said he had no wife. That much at least she believed. Was she then his lover?

The fighting continued in the hall, but Margaret spun away, fighting back the sudden sting of tears. What cared she that Alex had likely told the truth, but not all of it? Margaret stepped over wenches who seemingly recovered quickly from their swoons—likely because there was no one there to catch them—and continued to the alcove.

"Do you know Lord Alex?" one of the women breathed.

"Aye, know you aught of him? We would hear it all!"

Ha, Margaret thought with satisfaction. *Learn that he already has a lover and will have naught to do with you.*

"I know a great deal about him," the woman said. "But if you'll excuse me—"

"Nay, tell us all you know!"

"Aye, we must hear it all, every wit. How can he be won?"

"Does he care for fair hair, or dark?"

"I really need to speak with the lady Margaret," the woman said, sounding rather uneager to answer their questions. "If you don't mind—"

"Her?" one of the others gasped. "Why by the saints would you have speech with her?"

"Aye, a great cow of a thing is she," another said with a laugh. "Have a care, lest she trample you by mistake!"

Margaret put her shoulders back and turned around. She didn't want to. She wanted to break down and weep. But she was a Falconberg and Falconbergs stood tall. She faced those who mocked her and dared them to do it to her face.

Which they did, of course.

Margaret forced herself to look at the woman who stood across the chamber, silently listening. Saints, but she was so fair it was enough to make Margaret despair. How could she ever hold Alex when this was what he could choose from? She even spoke with his odd accent. Saints, but she could never compare with this creature. Such a face Margaret had never before seen on a maid. Indeed, Margaret could hardly bear to look at her.

"I'm Elizabeth."

Margaret couldn't manage words. She nodded glumly.

"Alex hasn't had time to tell me much about you. My husband was too busy justifying his mapmaking skills for that."

"Husband?" Margaret echoed. "Who? Alex?"

Elizabeth looked shocked, then she laughed. "Why, no. Jamie's my husband."

"Jamie? But I thought—"

"Alex is my brother."

"Ah," Margaret said. She found she could say nothing else without breaking out in a sweat from relief. She looked at Elizabeth and wondered why she hadn't seen it before. She and Alex shared the same eyes. "I should have seen," Margaret admitted. "I daresay my mind isn't at its best today."

"Lord Alex is your brother?" a shrill voice demanded.

"In truth?" another asked.

"Oh, oh!" another squeaked. "Here he comes!"

Margaret looked to the doorway in time to see her betrothed clutching the doorframe, his fists bloodied and his hair very mussed. He resheathed his sword and strode into the chamber. Every woman there caught her breath, save Elizabeth of course. Margaret couldn't help herself from joining the others in a gasp. There was something about the man that turned her bones to mush whether she willed it or no.

Lydia's ladies recovered well enough and were soon buzzing about him like so many flies having found a particularly fragrant pile of dung. Margaret watched him try to escape them, but he was obviously unaccustomed to these sorts. After a few failed attempts at earning his freedom from their circle, he merely stood in their midst, folded his arms over his chest, and frowned down at them.

"I sew very well, see?" one of the witless maids burst out.

"Nay, my seams are finer," another said, elbowing the first aside and shoving the hem of her sleeve into Alex's face. "A wife should be able to mend her husband's clothes."

And thus began a very tedious argument amongst the wenches as to who could sew the straightest seam, who possessed the most keys and who could put a whip to the servants with the most skill. Alex grew increasingly restless and looked at her numerous times for help. Margaret only shrugged. Let him release himself from this tangle.

He finally cleared his throat with great force. "I'm here

to see the lady Margaret," he announced. "Your skills are fascinating, I'm sure, but if you'll excuse me—"

"Her?" one of them laughed. "Why, I daresay she doesn't know one end of a needle from another!"

Alex's hand went to his shoulder in a protective motion. Margaret frowned at him. So she hadn't sewn a fine seam on that wound. It was closed, wasn't it?

Alex looked at the ladies. "If you'll forgive me—"

"Why, she's not even a woman!" a particularly venomous wench spat. "Look at her in man's clothing."

Margaret had heard this all before, so the insults shouldn't have troubled her. She found, though, that hearing them again while Alex was there to learn them all was a new experience in humiliation. She felt her shoulders slump despite her best efforts to keep them back. She couldn't even look Alex in the eye. All she would likely see was agreement anyway.

"Huge—"

"Manly—"

"Overly tall—"

And then Alex laughed. Margaret was shocked enough at the sound to look up. He was looking at the women about him as if they'd lost their wits. He shook his head with another grin.

"I like tall women," he stated.

The women around him were speechless.

"Besides," he said, pushing out of their circle, "I want a woman who can hold down my fort, not just jingle the keys on her waist. And seamstresses can be hired."

With that, Margaret found herself hauled into his arms. She stared up into his pale eyes and saw nothing but love and acceptance there.

"By the way, I like how you look in hose," he added, before he captured her mouth in a searing kiss.

Margaret wasn't sure if the noise was blood thundering in her ears or the thumps from Tickhill's dozen ladies all falling to the floor in a dead faint. She found, quite suddenly, that she didn't care which it was. Alex had made the women look like fools, and he had made her look desirable. She wrapped her arms around him and kissed him back with all the gratitude in her poor heart.

And then, as suddenly as he'd come to her, he was jerked away. Margaret had her sword halfway from its sheath, ready to do injury to Lydia's women, only to find it was Lord Odo's men who had entered the chamber and pulled Alex away.

"My lord," one of the guardsmen said, scowling at Alex over his bloody nose, "I'd suggest you give us no more trouble here today."

The other guardsman Alex had done damage to was scowling just as fiercely from the other side of the chamber, surrounded by half a dozen equally annoyed-looking men-at-arms. Margaret watched Alex consider the odds, then concede the battle. He looked back at her.

"Be there tomorrow," he said.

"Um," she began.

"Do not make me come get you," he said, biting off every word. "You won't like it if I have to."

Half Tickhill's ladies swooned yet again. Margaret felt like doing the same. What fool would have denied this man anything that he wanted?

"As you will, my lord," she managed.

He grunted, then turned and strode from the chamber, guardsmen trotting off dutifully behind him.

"Well," Elizabeth said brightly, "that settles that. I think I'll be needing a few seamstresses."

The women shifted uncomfortably. Margaret watched as Elizabeth silently looked them over. Saints, but the woman had a stare that rivaled the wind from the north for coolness. Soon came offers for the services of seamstresses and aid in procuring material. Margaret was, quite frankly, amazed. Perhaps the women feared Alex would come after *them* and it would go very ill for them. Either that or they feared Elizabeth might do the like. Margaret would have picked up a needle herself to have avoided having that chilly stare turned her way.

"Let's go walk in the garden," Elizabeth said, drawing her arm through Margaret's. "I hate being cooped up inside."

And before Margaret could say her yea or nay, she found herself walking through the castle and escaping the great hall. Once outside, she took a deep breath and realized how glad she was to be outside.

"My thanks," she said, giving Elizabeth a cautious smile. "I fear I'm not at my best while trapped indoors in such a small chamber."

"Especially considering the occupants," Elizabeth agreed. "I thought you were remarkably polite."

"Polite? I said not a word to them."

"You could have been carving them to bits," Elizabeth pointed out, with a grin. "I'm impressed with your restraint. Alex was just sure we'd find bloodshed."

"He can thank himself there was none. I cannot say what I would have done if he hadn't come."

Elizabeth only smiled. "I think he probably knew that. Here, let's see if we can find some sort of garden where we can sit. I don't suppose we should head outside the gates, though I could certainly use a good walk to clear my head. I hate bitchy women, don't you?"

Elizabeth was so forthright, all Margaret could do was blink in surprise. Indeed, it made her wonder if she shouldn't perhaps travel to Scotland one day. The women there were certainly made of different stuff than the maids in England.

"Are all the maids in Scotland so plainspoken?" Margaret asked.

Elizabeth smiled. "I suppose they are."

Margaret considered. "I think I should have been born there," she mused. "Perhaps I would have been more accepted."

"You do seem to be a little ahead of your time."

"True," Margaret agreed with a sigh. "And most disconcerting it is, too."

Elizabeth laughed, but it was a gentle laugh. Margaret

felt surprisingly cheered by it. Obviously she had missed out on much in not having a sister. Perhaps this marriage to Alexander of Seattle would be more tolerable than she thought.

"You joust very well," Elizabeth said as they sat in the midst of Lydia's herbs. "You must have worked hard to perfect your skill."

Margaret nodded. "I had to. My father passed on almost ten years ago and left me to hold his lands."

"Goodness," Elizabeth said, looking genuinely startled. "And you did this all on your own since then?"

Margaret nodded.

"Why don't you tell me about it?"

Almost before she knew it, Margaret found herself spilling out her heart to Alex's sister. She relived the fear of losing her family and knowing she could count on no one but herself. She told Elizabeth of the long years of keeping up the pretense that her father still lived.

But when she came to Alex's arrival into her life, she found she could no longer speak so freely. Love him though she might, wish to wed him though she did, there was still the matter of his state of mind. Elizabeth would likely not wish to hear bluntly that her brother was daft. To be sure, it would be better to put her questions about Alex's madness to James MacLeod, but perhaps she could test the waters a bit with Alex's sister to see how such questions would be received.

"Alex and I have had interesting words about his homeland," Margaret began, hoping she sounded as if his answers had distressed her not at all.

"Alex did mention that he told you where he was from," Elizabeth said.

"Aye," Margaret nodded, "he said he had been recently sojourning in Scotland." She chose her next words carefully. "He said he was originally from Seattle, which is on a continent." She studied Elizabeth carefully to see how she was accepting this.

"I see," Elizabeth said, just as carefully. "And that's it?"

Margaret sighed. Perhaps it was best Elizabeth hear it as soon as possible. She would learn the truth of it eventually.

"I fear he's daft," Margaret admitted reluctantly.

"Daft?"

"If not daft, at least quite befuddled. It grieves me to say as much," Margaret added quickly, "for I know you must love him dearly. But he spouted such nonsense to me when I put my questions to him that I knew I was right to fear for his sanity."

"What exactly did he say?"

Margaret shrugged. "Much I did not pay attention to. But he showed me his buttons and buttonholes and endeavored to convince me that he had stepped through a blade of grass from Scotland to England. And much other that made no sense at all."

Elizabeth only smiled faintly. "And you don't think that's possible?"

Margaret frowned at her. "How could it be? A man cannot travel over hundreds of leagues in the space of a heartbeat. I can only assume he's taken a strong blow to the head at some time in the past."

"You know, Margaret, if I were in your shoes, I'd have a hard time believing it myself."

"There's more," Margaret admitted, "though I half fear to mention it, lest you think me witless as well."

"I promise I won't."

Margaret sighed. "He spoke of coming from a different century." She looked at his sister and smiled grimly. "Fanciful imaginings, I know, and it grieves me to say as much. He is a fine man, surely, but I cannot understand why he believes as he does. Though I will be the first to admit that he knew much of Richard's movements before anyone else did." She listened to herself speak and began to wonder if perhaps she wasn't the one who had gone slightly daft. "I know there is a reason for it, but damn me if I cannot latch on to one."

Elizabeth plucked a bit of herb and twisted it for several moments in silence. Margaret found herself regretting her words. What sister would wish to hear of her brother's failings, especially when they were of this nature? And then Elizabeth looked up.

"Don't you think it's possible?" she asked. "That a man could come from a different century to this one?"

"Nay," Margaret said promptly, "I do not."

"Have you never believed in fanciful things?" Elizabeth asked.

"Never," Margaret said, shoving aside her speculations on faeries and ogres. "Never once."

Elizabeth only looked at her with a small smile. It was almost a sad smile, as if she knew something Margaret didn't. Margaret felt a sudden compulsion to explain herself further. She held up her blade.

"This I understand," she said, clutching the hilt. "This I can see with my eyes and feel with my hands. I can lift its weight. I know the course of its arc and how it sounds when it moves through the air. It never changes. And it will never leave me."

She listened to the last words come out of her mouth and had no idea where they'd come from. And she had even less idea whence her tears had sprung, but they came hard on the heels of her words.

"Oh, Margaret," Elizabeth said, taking her hands, "I'm so sorry."

"I fear he'll leave me," Margaret wept. "I shouldn't care."

"But you do."

"I'll be damned for it," she sobbed, "but I do."

"Alex loves you," Elizabeth said, her voice a soothing whisper. "He told me he did."

"He'll likely try to go home again," Margaret managed. "He said he wouldn't, but now that you're here ... it won't matter that we're wed."

"He's not going anywhere. We already asked him if he wanted to come back with us and he said no. I'll miss him, but I think he'll be far happier here with you."

"His heart will change—as will his mind."

Elizabeth shook her head. "I imagine you know by now that Alex is very stubborn."

"Indeed," Margaret said, dragging her sleeve across her eyes. "And most annoyingly so."

"If he says he's staying, then he'll stay. He won't go back on his promises."

Margaret thought on that a goodly while. If he said he wanted her, that he wouldn't leave her, then perhaps he meant it. Her sire and brothers had never truly vowed the like.

But she had surely never felt the love for them that she felt for this daft man from Seattle.

"Trust him," Elizabeth said. "He's waited his whole life to find you. He's not going anywhere."

Margaret nodded. Time would tell. It seemed as if Elizabeth had no intentions of spiriting her brother away. Perhaps he would stay after all. But there was still that other matter to be resolved. Margaret looked at her love's sister.

"You don't believe his foolishness, do you?"

"About the future?"

"Aye, that nonsense. And the gate in the grass."

Elizabeth twirled the herb stalk, then smiled. "I think," she said slowly, "there is much more to life than what we can see with our eyes and touch with our hands." She tossed the herb aside. "Stories about faeries had to come from somewhere, don't you think?"

"Harumph," Margaret said, unwilling to take a stand either way. "I'll give that some thought."

Elizabeth only smiled and stood. "Let's go see about your wedding dress, shall we?"

"Aye," Margaret said with a sigh as she pushed herself to her feet. "If I can bear their spitefulness."

"I'll handle them. You just worry about relaxing and standing still so they can fit you. Did I tell you how much

Alex loves you? You should see his face when he talks about you. I've never seen him like this before.''

Margaret knew Elizabeth was trying to soothe her and she appreciated it greatly. It was good to have her courage bolstered against the time she would have to endure Lydia's spiteful cats and their seamstresses.

By the time they reached the castle, Margaret was starting to believe Elizabeth's words. Alex had looked happy to have his title, hadn't he? And she most certainly came along with Falconberg, didn't she? And hadn't he said he cared nothing for her land, only her person?

She found herself fanning her cheeks. Saints above, she was to be wed with the man on the morrow. That would entail kissing and a good deal more, she knew that much.

"Margaret? You look a little flushed.''

" 'Tis nothing,'' Margaret croaked. "Exertion from the day, I'm sure.''

Elizabeth looked at her knowingly, then laughed. "I'll just bet. Come on. I think your dress should be green. It's Alex's favorite color.''

And it would look well with red, which was the color her face was going to be for the rest of her life. Margaret followed Alex's sister into the keep and prayed she would survive the next pair of days.

Marriage.

Saints, but it made a difficult day warring seem like a morning spent lolling about in the garden!

Twenty-three

ELIZABETH MACLEOD STOOD IN LORD TICKHILL'S CHAPEL and wondered if her brother might have been better off if she'd stuck with a safe career like food preparation or road construction—something that would have kept her away from research books on medieval Scotland. She couldn't deny that it had worked out well enough for her, since it had been that book on the Clan MacLeod to plop her back in medieval Scotland and into the arms of her husband. But she'd never intended that her own jaunt through the ages would so affect another member of her family.

Though it wasn't as if she could take all the blame for Alex's time traveling. Elizabeth looked up at her husband. Here was the man to blame, she thought with a scowl. He'd been the one to take Alex on a little jaunt through time to right a wrong; her brother had been doomed from then on.

Of course, so had she. She'd tried to put her foot down about Jamie doing any more wrong righting, but when he'd stalked into their bedroom one night wearing an eyepatch and carrying a cutlass, she'd known she was in trouble. His announcement that he'd found a spot of ground on his land that smelled suspiciously like rum had somehow led them back to Renaissance Barbados and a few adventures she'd been happy to return from.

She should have known Jamie's poking around on his land would land Alex in another century. But how could she begrudge him this? She'd never seen her brother more in his element.

He knelt before the altar, dressed in chain mail which was covered by a surcoat she'd stayed up most of the night to see finished for him. What little light came from the two windows of the nave fell down on him almost like a spotlight. He looked as if he belonged in this stark place with its stone floors and tallow candles. Elizabeth had watched him put in his time in the corporate world wearing silk suits and expensive Italian loafers, but somehow hammered metal rings and scuffed boots were far more appropriate. If anyone loved a challenge it was Alex, and he'd certainly found it here.

It had been a fairly overwhelming morning. The chapel at Tickhill wasn't very big, and it had definitely been a squeeze to fit everyone in who wanted to be in the same space as Richard of England. Elizabeth stood crammed against the wall, a choice spot reserved for members of the immediate family. She had spared a fleeting thought to twentieth-century standards of bathing before resigning herself to a few uncomfortable hours of not being able to breathe.

And then had come Alex's knighting ceremony. The king had come to the front of the chapel, dressed to impress in his royal robes with his crown gleaming on his head. Alex had knelt before him in freshly polished chain mail, his dark head bowed humbly. Elizabeth had been half tempted to pinch herself to make certain the sight before her was real. The king had raised his own sword, given Alex a sturdy blow to the side of the head, and informed him that was the last assault he ever had to endure without retaliation. Then he had handed Alex William of Falconberg's sword and instructed him to use it in defense of the realm, the widows and orphans and all those who could not defend themselves.

Jamie had then come forward and, with great deliberation, tied Alex's spurs to his heels. Elizabeth had exchanged a quick look and a smile with her brother and had known exactly what he'd been thinking. This was certainly not anything they had ever fantasized about over coffee back home in the neighborhood deli. Alex's dreams had included his own Lear and a nice country home, and hers had encompassed a successful career as a writer. Somehow, spurs and hobnobbing with medieval royalty hadn't been on the list.

Elizabeth dragged herself back to the present to find that Jamie had returned to her side. She watched as her brother, still kneeling on that cold stone floor, placed his hands in the hands of a medieval legend and pledged his life to him.

"I, Alexander of Falconberg, do swear . . ."

"Saints, Elizabeth," Jamie whispered into her ear, "if your sire could but see this!"

She nodded, smiling. Her dad was forever giving Jamie a bad time about his own claims to nobility. That his son should now have the same claim would have pushed him right over the edge. An earl in his own right and soon to be married to the daughter of a medieval baron. Elizabeth shook her head with another smile. She very much doubted this would have entered her parents' minds as they sent Alex toddling off to kindergarten all those years ago.

She looked across the nave and saw Margaret standing half in sunlight, half in shadows. She couldn't deny that Margaret was perfect for him. And it was perfectly clear that she loved him desperately. Elizabeth couldn't wish for more for her brother. If this was what Fate had in store for him, she certainly wouldn't stand in the way.

The priest replaced the king at the altar, and Margaret was summoned forward. Alex was immediately on his feet, holding out his hand. Elizabeth smiled as she watched Margaret approach. She looked wonderful and desperately happy, though Elizabeth could tell she was trying hard not to show it.

Green had been the right choice for her gown. That was another of Elizabeth's all-night projects. After a couple hours' sleep, she had risen to see Margaret dressed, though her real mission had been to make sure Margaret showed up at the chapel. She'd thought her brother was being a bit extreme with his renewed threats, but Margaret had seemed somewhat cheered by them.

Alex's voice was deep and steady as he repeated his vows. Margaret's was less steady, but she didn't hesitate. And then the priest blessed them and began Mass.

Elizabeth remembered vividly her own marriage to the man with his arms around her in his medieval chapel. But she'd only been surrounded by the members of Jamie's household. Leave it to Alex to find a way to get married with the ultimate in nobility present. Jamie had the right idea: Her dad would just croak when he heard about it.

Once Mass was finished, the king led the way from the chapel. Alex and Margaret had the place of honor behind the members of his household. Elizabeth caught her brother's eye and smiled through her tears at him. He looked happier than she'd ever seen him before and that was enough for her. Margaret, however, looked as if she were being led off to the chopping block. Elizabeth had tried to reassure her that consummating her marriage would be a good thing, but Margaret had remained unconvinced. Alex would have his work cut out for him.

"He looks powerfully happy," Jamie murmured in her ear. "Wouldn't you say?"

She turned in his arms and rested her cheek against his chest. "He does. And I'm happy for him."

"And a wee bit sad, no doubt."

Elizabeth lifted her head and smiled at him. "I'll miss him. But I think he belongs here."

"Aye, this is a good place for him, Beth. He's well suited to this labor. And he now has a fine mate."

She nodded in agreement.

"As do you," Jamie prompted.

"As if I needed reminding of that," she said, leaning up to kiss him softly. "I've never once regretted my choice."

"Nor have I. What say you we find ourselves a meal, then see if Alex's young Frances won't look after Ian a bit longer? I've a mind to seek out a bit of privacy to show you just how pleased I am that I had the good sense to wed you."

"Works for me," she said with a smile.

ALEX SAT NEXT to Margaret at Odo's table, which had now become the king's table, and couldn't stop smiling. He was married to the woman of his dreams, he'd managed to save her land, and he was looking forward to a large chest of Brackwald's gold to come his way very soon. Maybe all those years of corporate piracy hadn't been wasted after all. He'd tripled Ralf's ransom just by reminding Richard of all the damage Ralf had done to Margaret's property and her people. There was the pleasure of seeing Ralf turn purple with rage, of course, but Alex also knew he now had the means to make whatever additions to Margaret's garrison she might want, as well as fix that leak in her roof that turned the solar into a wading pool when it rained.

He sat back and stared out over the great hall, still feeling a bit stunned by the events of the morning. As if marriage to a woman eight hundred years older than he wasn't enough to send his head spinning. He'd pledged fealty to Richard of England. Somehow, it was the very last thing he'd ever thought he would do.

He looked at the woman of his dreams and smiled at her. She was fingering her dagger hilt as she surveyed the occupants of the great hall. Well, at least she wasn't looking at him as if she'd like to carve him up.

"It looks like Odo managed to dig out another bottle of good wine," he said, hoping to distract her from whatever mayhem she contemplated. "Want a sip?"

She nodded and accepted the cup. "Many thanks, husband."

Alex laughed at the grimness with which she used the term. "You're very welcome, wife."

Her face was becoming a very attractive shade of red.

"I had to try it and see how it felt on the tongue," she admitted.

"What, the wine or calling me husband?"

"The latter."

"And how was it?"

She actually seemed to be taking time to analyze it. After due consideration she looked at him with a small smile.

"Pleasing," she conceded. "Though you may well imagine I never thought to hear myself say those words."

He tried not to choke. "I'm flattered."

"As well you should be."

"Oh, Margaret," he said, leaning over to kiss her firmly on the mouth, "I really do love you."

"Do you?" she asked, seemingly surprised.

"Of course I do. Didn't you know?"

She shrugged. "I thought you might. You look at me very intently quite often. Then again, you look at your supper in much the same way, so I wasn't all that certain."

He smiled dryly. "It's not the same thing at all. I like food. I love you."

He waited. And when she said nothing in return, he elbowed her.

She frowned at him. "What?"

That was the thing about Margaret: Fishing for compliments never did any good.

Alex sighed. "I just told you I loved you. Some sort of sentiment in return would be well received at this point."

She looked at him thoughtfully and that, for some strange reason, scared the hell out of him. He didn't expect anything less than an honest answer, but he wasn't sure all of a sudden that he wanted to know the truth.

She turned in her chair so she could look at him even more closely, and Alex had the insane desire to squirm. Great. He'd just risked life and limb to have this woman and she wasn't sure how she felt about him.

Though she had shown up in the chapel. That was a good sign. She hadn't hesitated while repeating her vows, though she had stumbled a bit over that "obey thee in all matters" part. The priest obviously hadn't heard her mutter "when it suits me" under her breath, but Alex had. He'd squeezed her hand and winked. The day she actually obeyed him in anything would be the day they were firing up snowmobiles in hell.

"Well," she began, "I had tender feelings for you from the beginning, I think."

Tender feelings were good.

"Though those were certainly trampled upon when you left without a backward glance."

"I glanced backward a lot," he countered.

"You didn't. I watched you from the battlements."

Alex raised an eyebrow over that. So, she'd been watching him. Her eyesight must have been failing her or she would have seen him almost clotheslined by a stray branch as he twisted in the saddle for one last glimpse of her keep.

"I think, though, that my heart was truly softened when I learned what it had cost you to pick up a sword in my defense. Not that you were all that successful with it."

He smiled. "It's the thought that counts."

She pursed her lips. "Perhaps." She looked up at the ceiling for a moment or two. "I fought it fiercely after that, but 'twas sadly enough a battle I could not win." She looked at him and smiled. "Aye, I believe I love you well enough."

An "I love you" with both hands on the table and daggerless. Alex wondered if it would be rude to haul her upstairs while she was having such warm feelings for him.

Well, there was certainly no time like the present. Alex pushed back his chair—and heard a muffled *oof*. He paused, half crouched, and looked behind him. One of the king's pages was there, clutching his middle.

"Oh, sorry," Alex said, sitting back down. "Didn't see you."

"My lord," the boy wheezed, "the king sends a message to you."

Great. Maybe Richard wanted to head up the bedding ceremony. Alex wondered if telling the king there was no way in hell he was going to see Margaret naked would be a violation of his recently pledged oath of fealty.

"Yes?" Alex asked carefully.

"He invites you, the lady Margaret, and the Scot who is your brother-in-law and his wife to his crowning in London." The page, who had no doubt seen a great many things, looked as stunned as Alex felt. " 'Tis a very high honor, my lord."

Alex looked at Margaret, whose eyes were equally as huge in her face. "Wow. What do you think?"

"You ask me my opinion?"

"Of course I'm asking your opinion. Share and share alike, remember?"

"Well," she said, looking a bit stunned, "I just assumed you would—"

"Ask your opinion on matters that concern us both," Alex finished for her. "What do you say?"

She shook her head with wonder. "My sire would have fainted dead away at the thought."

Alex looked to his right where Jamie and Elizabeth sat. "Did you guys hear that?"

Jamie nodded. "Aye. It would be something to see, surely."

"Can you stay that long?"

Elizabeth exchanged a look with Jamie, then nodded to Alex. "We'd love to come."

"Then it's settled." Alex looked at the page. "Tell the king it would be our pleasure to be there."

The page nodded and dashed off. Alex settled back in his chair and let it sink in. He would be watching Richard of England be crowned for a second time. Talk about a story for the grandkids.

"Wow," he said.

"Aye, wow," Margaret agreed, reaching for his hand. She clutched it with hers. "I've never been to London. Have you?"

"Yes, but I imagine it had changed a bit when I saw it."

Margaret looked at him in faint surprise, then a very indulgent smile came over her face. "Oh, Alex, some day your mind will come fully clear. I'm just certain of it." She patted his arm. "I'm not worried, are you?"

His wife thought he was nuts. Great. "I'm just happy you're so patient with my insanity," he managed.

"How could I not be?" she asked.

Another page tugged on Alex's sleeve. "My lord Alexander, Lord Odo sends word."

It was the afternoon for messages it seemed. Where was a good administrative assistant when you needed one? Alex put on a patient smile.

"Sure, what is it?"

"He says the king prepares to leave within the hour."

"Well, then maybe we'll just take our leave of Tickhill at the same time," Alex said, looking at Margaret. "You're ready to get home, aren't you?"

She nodded. "More than."

The page looked shocked. "But, my lord, the bedding! Lord Odo has had his finest chamber prepared and reserved for you a bottle of his finest claret. All is in readiness."

Margaret had turned a pasty white. Alex almost reached over to push her head between her knees and tell her to keep breathing.

"Well," she said, her expression one of grim stoicism, "I suppose it must happen sometime."

Alex blinked. "Don't sound so thrilled."

She gritted her teeth. "I've seen mares bred, Alex. I've heard their screams and know what the bedding entails. And what I didn't already know, Lydia's ladies enlightened me on." She fingered the hilt of her dagger. "I'm prepared."

Alex knew the first thing he was going to do was relieve her of all her weapons before he made love to her. He leaned over and kissed her, and continued to kiss her until he felt her relax and begin to kiss him back. Then he pulled away.

"Forget everything you've heard and seen before now. It's going to be great."

She looked at him narrowly. "Are you lying?"

"Why would I lie?" It would be good, really good, if he could just keep her from killing him the first time. "I think you'll like it a lot."

She sighed. "Perhaps, though the thought of accomplishing the deed on Lydia's bed isn't all that appealing."

Accomplishing the deed? Alex looked to his right to see if Jamie had heard Margaret. Jamie was frowning thoughtfully off into space. Alex cleared his throat and Jamie shot him a brief glance.

"Flowers," he advised.

Alex grunted. Margaret would probably sneeze.

"You must have some romantic item to soften her heart," Jamie insisted softly, turning to him. "I would suggest wooing her to your bed, perhaps with a bit of verse or a song."

Well, dragging Baldric upstairs to provide verse was absolutely out of the question. He'd just have to find something else.

"You didn't bring anything I could borrow, did you?" Alex asked.

Jamie frowned. "And ruin my own chances with your sister?"

"Oh, give it up," Alex snorted. "As if you're really the one under the gun right now."

"Very well," Jamie said, sounding none too pleased about it. "But know that it is not without great reluctance that I do this."

"Right. You can gripe all you want about it later. Just help me out now, okay?"

Jamie grunted in agreement and Alex sighed in relief. Heaven only knew what sorts of things Jamie had brought with him, but Alex knew his sister's taste ran to poetry and love letters. Alex could only hope Margaret would be moved by a sonnet or two. He looked at her and smiled.

"There's Odo's finest claret to look forward to," he reminded her.

She sighed the sigh of a woman condemned to a fate only slightly better than death. "Very well, then."

Jamie started to cough.

Alex pounded his brother-in-law very ungently on the back, then turned to Lord Odo's page.

"Tell His Lordship we'd be honored." *And tell him to hurry up before Margaret changes her mind*, he added silently.

The page scampered off and Alex turned to his bride to try to reassure her only to find her busily gulping down Odo's second finest wine. Alex took the cup away.

"You'll want a clear head."

" 'Twas to dull the pain."

"It won't be as bad as you think."

"It had best not be."

Alex seconded his earlier decision to make sure she wasn't packing any steel when he took her to bed. What he wouldn't have given for a portable metal detector.

Before he could wish any more for that, the king rose and a mad scampering to bow and curtsy convulsed the company. Alex was grateful for the distraction. He'd been on the verge of thinking about the particulars of the wedding night, and just the thought of thinking about them was enough to send him right over the edge. Going over the edge would have to come later and hopefully he'd take Margaret right along with him.

Assuming she didn't skewer him first.

With Margaret of Falconberg, one just never knew.

Twenty-four

❧❦❧

THE MOANS ECHOED THROUGHOUT THE CASTLE. LORD Odo of Tickhill sat at his table, still recovering from the king's departure with a recently unearthed bottle of his very finest wine, and wondered at the volume and intensity of those moans.

What, by the saints, was Alexander doing to the girl?

Odo had squired with William of Falconberg, stood up for him at his wedding, and celebrated with him at the birth of each of his children. He'd mourned with him at the premature passing of his wife and grieved with him over the deaths of his sons. He'd also watched William waste away from his grief, leaving Margaret to fend for herself.

Odo had known, of course, just how long Margaret had kept up the ruse of her father being ill but alive. He'd done what he could secretly to aid her, for he'd always harbored a fatherly fondness for the girl who could best any of her brothers in a fair fight. And saints, what a woman she had become! Odo had held little private tournaments every now and then just to see if Margaret would come and humiliate the rest of the field. He'd never been disappointed. A pity she hadn't confided in him regarding Brackwald. He might have been able to help.

Then again, all he likely would have done was unwittingly expose her true state and thereby drive her to the altar sooner against her will. And what a man she would have missed out on.

Though at the moment, Odo was having less than charitable feelings toward Alexander of Seattle, lately of Falconberg. The moans were so intense, Odo couldn't decide if they were of pleasure or pain. The one thing he did know was that he needed to investigate. Far be it from him to intrude on another man's marriage bed, but he did feel a certain responsibility to Margaret and her happiness. Alexander could be strung up readily enough if need be.

He drained his cup, then rose and made his way from the great hall and up the stairs to his wife's solar. He'd seen the bed set up properly, a pair of tallow candles lit, and his finest claret set on the table with two goblets. And he'd managed to keep his wife from nipping at his heels about having her private solar used thusly.

He came to a dead halt at the top of the stairs. There, clustered about the door, were none other than his wife and all her ladies. Some were crouched, some were on tiptoes, but all had their ears pressed against the wood with all the enthusiasm of hungry leeches on a fat belly. As if they couldn't have heard the moans from down the stairs!

"By the saints," he hissed, "what do you?"

Lydia waved him to silence. "Hush," she said in a commanding whisper. "You distract us."

"I distract you?" he whispered back incredulously. "What is it you think you do to them?"

Lydia shot him a look of ire. "They're hardly attending us. By the saints, will you listen to them?"

Odo had no choice but to approach and listen. He leaned over his wife and pressed his ear to the wood.

"Is that good?" came a deep voice from inside the chamber.

"Oh, Alex," replied a higher, though very husky voice, " 'tis bliss! I never imagined . . . oh, by the saints!" This was followed by a gasp, then a moan of sheer pleasure.

Odo felt his cheeks flame. So he had spent his share of time as a squire with his ear pressed to various doors. And never mind that he'd also traveled to London as a young man and spent his share of nights in brothels where the sounds of pleasure fair echoed off the walls and ceilings. This was something else entirely.

"Ohhh," Margaret moaned again. "It surely cannot be any better than this."

"Oh, but it can. Here, how about this?"

Well, whatever he'd done to her had just set up an entirely new round of moans. Pleasure? Pain? He couldn't decide. Just the intensity alone was unsettling.

Odo could bear it no longer. He thought he either might expire from embarrassment on the spot, or be forced to carry his yipping wife off to their bedchamber posthaste to indulge in the images just listening to the goings-on inside inspired in him.

"Away from the door," he commanded softly. "Go on, all of you."

"But—" chorused the women.

"Husband—" warned his wife.

"Now!" he hissed sharply. "By the saints, women, leave them to their peace!"

Lydia and her ladies grumbled and muttered under their breaths, but they started off down the passageway just the same. Odo was tempted to linger, but another moan sent him scampering off after his wife and her women.

The poor child! The saints only knew what was happening to her!

MARGARET CLOSED HER eyes and flopped back against the pillows.

"Oh, my," she breathed.

"Good?"

"I'll let you know once I've recovered."

He laughed and leaned over to kiss her. "Your moans said it all."

"By the saints," she whispered, wondering if she would ever again have the strength to open her eyes. "How have I lived my life without that?"

"There's more."

"Is there?" she asked, bouncing back up enthusiastically. "Alex, this was a most marvelous gift."

"Well, you certainly sounded like you enjoyed it."

She smiled at him as she accepted the gold box. "How could I not? I've never partaken of anything so wonderful!"

She looked down and had to admit she was sorry to see there was but one little ball left.

Alex had presented her with the box after they'd retired to Lydia's solar. She'd half expected to have him assault her with kisses as a prelude to The Act, which she was certain would not be as pleasurable as he made it sound. Even though Elizabeth had promised it was very wonderful, Margaret had had her suspicions it was otherwise.

Instead, Alex had given her a box of pure gold, tied about with a ribbon made of a most marvelous fabric. There were even letters hammered into the box from the underside so they stood up. They were so perfectly formed, all she'd been able to do was gape at them in amazement.

"Godiva," Alex had explained.

"Godiva," she'd repeated in awe.

"Open it," he'd said.

She could hardly believe there was more to the gift, but she'd pulled away the ribbon, then lifted the lid carefully to find another sheaf of gold paper. She had fingered it lovingly.

" 'Tis beautiful," she'd said.

Alex had taken the paper away. "That's not the present."

Four little balls had been revealed. One covered with ground nuts, one white with brown stripes, one covered with dust, and a final one just a brown ball that didn't look all that appealing.

But then she'd sniffed.

And then she'd tasted.

She hadn't believed such moans could come from her own throat, but come they had. She'd thought she just might faint dead away from the glorious rush of pleasure that had coursed through her veins at the taste of the stuff on her tongue.

"Perhaps I should save the last," Margaret said, poking it carefully with her finger. It was the one covered in dust, though she now knew it was chocolate dust. "I think I need some time to recover from the first three."

"I think Jamie brought one more box, if that makes you feel any better."

Margaret looked at him in surprise. "And he's willing to part with it?"

Alex shrugged with a smile. "Consider it a wedding gift to the both of us. Besides, he can get more when they go back home."

"To Scotland."

"To 1998."

"Ah," Margaret said with a nod. She wasn't at all convinced that such a place, or a time, existed, but if she had been leaning toward such a conclusion, the very taste of this sweet paste might have convinced her.

Margaret replaced the lid with a faint twinge of regret. "I should save it," she said, setting the box on the table near the bed. Then she looked back at Alex. "For later."

He was stretched out on the bed, leaning up on his elbow. "There are other things we could do."

"Such as?"

He grinned at her. "Kiss."

She considered, then nodded. "I would like that."

"You'll like what comes after just as well, I promise."

She only shook her head.

"It's better than chocolate," he promised.

Margaret snorted before she could stop herself. "I cannot believe that."

Alex only laughed. "You'll see."

"Indeed, I shall. Very well, what will you have me do?"

"Come closer."

She inched closer to him.

"Now, lie down."

She was more than ready to do that. Somehow the chocolate had gone to her head and she was feeling rather dizzy.

And then Alex began to kiss her.

Her dizziness was joined by a growing fever. The longer he kissed her, the more feverish she began to feel. It was soon joined by a tingling feeling she couldn't identify, either.

"We could take off some of our clothes," Alex offered, lifting his head to gasp for air.

"Indeed," Margaret said, reaching for the laces of her gown. "I feel altogether flushed. I think it is the chocolate."

"It could be me, you know."

She considered that, then shook her head. "I think not. This is an entirely new feeling. I daresay I've kissed you enough in the past to know the difference."

"Margaret," he said, sounding faintly exasperated, "this wasn't just kissing. My hands were roaming all over your body."

She was just certain he was wrong, but there was no sense in not humoring him. She shed her clothes without thinking, then realized just what she'd done. She stood, very naked, at the side of the bed and stared at her also very naked, seemingly very eager husband.

"Well," she said lamely.

He crooked his finger at her. "Come here, lover."

"Maybe I should have that other piece of chocolate—"

"Save it. It'll take the place of a cigarette."

"Cigarette . . . ?"

"I'll explain later."

Well, there looked to be no avenue of escape. And besides, she was a Falconberg, and Falconbergs did not flee at the first sign of a good fight. Or a bad one, for that matter. And Margaret was a Falconberg and to be sure one of the bravest of the illustrious line.

So she went into her husband's arms, fell to the bed with him and found that his hands roaming over her bare body did cause heat in her, and a far different kind of heat than his little Godivas had.

"This may be a bit uncomfortable," he said, a goodly while later when he moved over her.

"It can't be," she said, pulling him to her. "It all feels so very goo—"

SIR ODO SAT at the top of the stairs, blocking the passage from his wife and her entourage. They'd done their best to overpower him, but he'd held firm. The moans had stopped quite a while ago. Either that was a good omen or a bad omen. He had no idea which.

Suddenly there was a howl of pain.

Then a huge crashing sound.

"My solar!" Lydia cried.

He caught her as she strove to push past him, then hauled her back onto his lap.

"I'm sure your furnishings have survived."

She didn't look to have believed him.

Odo saw the calculation come into her eyes and felt his gold begin to slip through his fingers. He knew there was naught he could do to halt it.

He sighed. "I'll see them replaced if not."

"I'll likely need new coverings for the chairs," Lydia said promptly.

Ah, how dearly this night had cost him! "Done," he conceded reluctantly.

"New thread for more wall hangings."

Odo closed his eyes, unable to face the mounting expenses. He leaned back against the stairwell and listened with half an ear to his wife's demands. Someone should have to pay for this trouble and it shouldn't have to be him.

He sat up with a start, then began to smile.

Lydia's merchants should have no trouble following his directions to the newly made Lord of Falconberg's purse.

Odo knew Lydia was still knee-deep in the listing forth of her demands, but he had ceased to listen. She could blather on 'til morning and it would affect him not at all. He began, however, to feel a bit of sympathy for young Alexander. This night would cost him a great deal.

Assuming, of course, that the lad survived the night. Odo frowned at the thought. He clutched his purse and prayed mightily that Alex would come from the bedding unscathed.

For there was complete silence in the solar, and Odo wondered if Margaret hadn't just done her husband in.

Twenty-five

✤✤✤

MARGARET WOKE TO THE SIGHT OF SUNSHINE STREAMING in the window. Ah, the weather would be fine today. It was the perfect accompaniment to the sunniness of her mood. Perhaps becoming intimately acquainted with her husband hadn't started out so well; the end results had been most satisfactory.

She shifted and groaned at the soreness in unaccustomed places.

"You can say that again," Alex mumbled. He lifted his head off the pillow next to hers, turned his face toward her, and smiled. "Mornin', wife."

"And a good morrow to you, husband," she said returning his smile. She lifted her hand and carefully touched his discolored eye. "My apologies."

He only snorted out a little laugh. "I'm only grateful you didn't have a blade at your disposal. You pack quite a punch, my love."

His eye was completely swollen shut and had taken on a decidedly unattractive smattering of dark colors: black, blue, but mostly lavender. In truth, though, he had no one to blame but himself. He'd warned her of a little discomfort, but she'd ached too much for him to pay him any heed. She had *not* expected that sharp, unrelenting sting. He was bloody lucky she'd only clouted him in the eye. If she'd had a blade handy, the saints only knew what might have happened.

She turned that over in her mind. He'd been thorough

enough in his search of her person before they retired to bed. She'd thought he was merely taking the opportunity to familiarize himself with her form, but now she could see that he'd been saving himself a sticking.

Well, he seemed none the worse for the wear. She trailed her fingers along the ridge of his bare shoulders and smiled at the sounds of pleasure he made.

"Would you have something to break your fast?" she asked.

"Maybe later."

She nodded. "Aye, I have to agree. I don't think I'm up to rising right now."

"I certainly am."

Margaret stared into a startlingly blue-green eye. There was a decided twinkle there.

"Well," she said, wondering just what he found so amusing, "then you go fetch us something."

"That's not what I'm talking about." His hand groped its way across the bed until it encountered her knee, then it investigated some more. He worked his way up until he'd captured her hand. He pulled it under the sheet. "Let me clear things up for you."

Obviously her fist in his eye hadn't cooled his ardor any, though the events of a very long, very pleasurable night should have told her as much. Amazingly enough, his fires seemingly still burned brightly even now.

"I see," she said.

"I think you do."

"I suppose I can think of less pleasing things to do first thing," she ventured.

"I'll bet you can."

He kissed her. Margaret was certain her mouth tasted as if a garrison had trooped through it during the night, but Alex seemed not to care. And, to be sure, she found that she cared even less what condition his was in. His mouth worked a magic on her that not even chocolate could equal.

And as for the rest . . . she'd bluntly told him that she

was certain nothing he could ever do would outdo what
those dark balls of sin had. She'd survived the night only
to have to take back her words. Godiva could not hold its
own against Alexander of Falconberg when it came to
leaving her convulsing with all-consuming pleasure.

"Oh," she said, as his callused hands moved purposefully over her body.

"What, no moans?" he teased, lifting his head to smile
down at her. "I'm insulted."

"Then I suppose," she said sweetly, "you must needs
try harder to wring them from me."

"That sounds like a challenge."

She lifted one eyebrow. "Take it as you will."

"That *definitely* sounds like a challenge," he laughed,
then bent himself back to his work.

She didn't think anything could equal his last night's
work, but she found that she was wrong. As he took her
and made her his yet again, she heard herself cry out and
was powerless to stop the sound. By the saints, the man
undid her!

He rolled away at length and gathered her to him. Margaret curled up in his arms and rested her head on his
shoulder.

"Think you," she began slowly, "that we've disturbed
the household?"

His laugh was a comforting rumble in his chest. "I
would imagine so."

"Hmmm," she said, tracing patterns on his chest with
her fingers. "Think you we should rise?"

"There's that word again—"

"I mean rise from the bed," she said, lifting her head
to glare down at him. It was only a halfhearted glare,
though. It was hard to take offense at teasing when it came
from a man who had just loved you so thoroughly.

Alex pulled her head back down to his shoulder.
"Maybe tomorrow."

"You mean to stay abed the entire day?"

"Works for me. Why, do you have a better idea?"

She lifted her head and looked down at him. "We could spend an hour or so in the lists."

He blinked. "You can't be serious."

"We could see to our gear."

His mouth fell open slightly. "You are serious."

She looked about her helplessly. "It feels so decadent to do nothing but stay abed."

"It's not decadent. It's our duty. I'm just sure that it's written somewhere that we have to stay in bed for at least a couple of days and make sure that our marriage is good and consummated."

"You don't think it has been already?"

"I'm not sure. When I can walk again, say in a week or so, I'll let you know. Until then, I think we have no choice but to keep at this until we're certain we've got it right. Besides," he said, pulling her head down and kissing her, "you're the countess of Falconberg. I'm sure there's someone seeing to your gear for you."

"And likely yours, too," she agreed.

"There are benefits to a title."

Indeed there were. And the best was that a title had made Alex her husband. She ran her fingers over his jaw, remembering the first time she'd had such an urge and how she'd denied herself the pleasure. It was odd that now she was able to indulge herself at will. She felt a surge of good feelings toward her husband and searched for a way to let him know of them.

"You showed well at the joust," she offered.

"Oh, my," he said, his eyes wide, "a compliment. Good thing I'm lying down or I'd probably be falling down."

"I'm being generous," she said. "After all, I did best you with the lance."

"You surprised the hell out of me," he corrected. "I was looking at Baldric waving that stupid pole with your headgear on it. I hardly saw you coming."

"You were in the dust. I was not."

He frowned at her. "If you'll remember, Lady Falconberg, I bested you with the sword."

She shrugged. "We all have our off days."

"Off days—" he spluttered.

She pulled away and looked at him with concern. "I should call for a meal. You look flushed."

"Of course I'm flushed! I beat you fairly and you won't admit defeat!"

"Alex, calm yourself," she said, sitting up. "Aye, a meal, before you do yourself an injury from lack of strength."

"Oh, no, you don't," he said, pulling her back down and rolling on top of her. He glared down at her. "Did you or did you not lose your sword thanks to my sending it flying out of your hands?"

"Well . . ." The feel of him stretched over her was exceedingly distracting. The man was naught but muscle. She ran her hands over his back, admiring the firmness of his skin. "Alex, where did you say you got these scars?"

"From a whip right before I had an extended stay in a Scottish dungeon, and you're changing the subject." He framed her face with his hands and frowned down at her. "Admit it, Margaret. You were defeated."

"I was distracted. You have the most arresting eyes, Alex."

"Margaret!"

"Tell me more of this Scottish dungeon."

"You wouldn't believe me. It was in the fifteenth century, and you're still changing the subject!"

She smiled sweetly. "You were distracted when I bested you. I will admit that I was distracted when you claim to have bested me."

He continued to glare down at her, then suddenly he laughed shortly. "You never will give in, will you?"

She shook her head. "Falconberg pride."

"Falconberg arrogance is more like it."

"Aye," she said, leaning up to kiss him hard on the lips. " 'Tis something you already possess in great abundance. My sire would have been pleased with you."

He laughed again, a somewhat helpless-sounding laugh, and dropped his head next to hers on her pillow. "Margaret, why is it I have the feeling I'll just never win against you?"

She patted him on the back. "I just wouldn't bother to try, were I you."

"Why should I? Every time I'm on the verge of it, you compliment me and it distracts me. I don't stand a chance."

"A wise man it is who knows his limitations."

He groaned and buried his face in her hair.

She stroked his back for several moments in silence, then cleared her throat.

"And what are your limitations on this . . . um . . ."

"Lovemaking?"

"Aye, that would be the word."

He didn't bother to lift his head. "You're grinding me into the ground, Meg. You know it, yet you keep on doing it."

She smiled. "Then 'tis a good thing you're such a sturdy fellow, is it not?"

He lifted his head and looked down at her, the light of battle simmering in his eye. "I'll need food first."

"I'll arrange it."

"You've thrown down the gauntlet, you know."

"Aye, I know."

"Food," he said, considering, "then a small nap. You'll want to take one, too."

"I will?"

"I'm sure of it." He rolled away with a groan. "I'm just sure of it," he repeated.

Margaret intended to bound out of bed, just to show him how rested she felt. Instead, she found herself on her feet but suddenly clinging to the foot post as seemingly every muscle in her body set up a clamoring protest. She drew a blanket around her and chanced a glance at her husband to see if he'd noticed.

His pillow was over his face, but the rest of him was shaking.

"Too much time abed," she announced as she hitched her way over to the door.

He shouted with laughter. Margaret jumped as she felt his pillow hit her square on the backside. She turned and glared at him.

"Disrespectful man," she muttered, then stuck her head out the door and bellowed for food.

BUT DISRESPECTFUL THOUGH he might have been, and seemingly lacking in the proper appreciation of her ability to best him on the field, Margaret had to admit he was a man without peer.

She had seen only the marriages about her and speculated on the misery endured in such unions. Instead, she found herself continually surprised by how pleasant a venture it had turned out to be.

They had returned to Falconberg soon after they were wed, to the undisguised relief of Lady Tickhill. Lord Odo had sent them off with another bottle of fine claret and a warning to Alex to expect visitors of the merchant kind within days. Margaret had shrugged it off, unsure why Odo seemed so pleased by that prospect, and unwilling to investigate further.

She had been too preoccupied with wondering how Alex might treat her once they reached home. She knew he wouldn't grind her beneath his heel, or at least she hoped she knew that, but all the same she'd wondered just how he would take over the running of her keep. Another man would have immediately shut her up in the solar and left her there to rot.

Of course, Alex was not just another man. Though she knew she shouldn't have been surprised, she always was to find herself at Alex's side during every moment of his day, seeing to the servants, conversing with their vassals, training the garrison.

And when Ralf's gold arrived, she'd been right there

next to him at the table, counting it. And then, surprisingly enough, he'd asked her what she thought they should do with it. He had deferred to each of her suggestions with an approving nod. His only request had been for a bit of it to spend as he saw fit. She had assumed he perhaps wanted a sword of his own, or another mount more suited to the rigors of jousting.

She'd been wrong.

Where he'd dredged up the idea she couldn't have said, but somewhere in that fogged brain of his, he had decided he had needed to woo her. Never mind that he'd already won her.

She'd hardly known how to take it.

It had begun in London. The journey there had been uneventful enough, merely a pleasant bit of travel with nights spent either at comfortable inns or under the stars. Margaret had been content merely to be with Alex wherever he chose to lay his head. Jamie and Elizabeth had been wonderful companions, full of stories about clan life, past and present. Margaret had even begun to accept their fanciful tales of their life in the future. They were such good souls, how could she not accept that slight failing in their mental state?

After reaching London, they had taken a pair of very fine chambers and settled in to wait for the king's coronation. She and Elizabeth had been taking their ease one afternoon when Alex had burst into the chamber with Jamie, both of their arms full of all manner of cloth and trailed by a handful of seamstresses. Alex had had a pair of gowns fashioned for her, gowns of such marvelous stuff that she could hardly keep her hands off herself as she wore them. It had almost been enough to convince her she should dress in a womanly fashion more often.

But it hadn't stopped there.

He'd seen to new hose and tunics for the both of them. He'd presented her with strange and exotic perfumes and foodstuffs. He'd had rings fashioned for her fingers and coverings fashioned for her hair.

And, of course, he'd presented her with a fine new dagger.

If she hadn't been in love with him before that, she would have been after she'd seen the firelight dancing along that perfectly fashioned edge.

"Damascus steel," he pointed out proudly.

How could a woman not love such a man?

So love him she had, more with each moment that passed. She loved the beauty of his face and form. She loved the sharpness of his logic that shone through despite the slight befuddlement of his wits over his past. She loved the ruthless light that came into his eye when he thought someone might be contemplating insulting him or, the saints forbid, her.

By the saints, she was fortunate she'd kidnapped him instead of Edward of Brackwald.

Twenty-six

ALEX SHIFTED IN THE SADDLE AND WONDERED IF HE would ever accustom himself to riding with as much ease as Margaret and Jamie seemed to. Maybe it had something to do with a long ride to London and back. Or it could just be that he had a twentieth-century butt that would never accustom itself to medieval travel.

Maybe they should have stayed longer in the city. It wasn't as if he hadn't had the money to pay for lodging. Edward had delivered Brackwald's ransom to Falconberg shortly after they'd returned there from Tickhill. Alex had barely had time to count it all before the time came to set out for London. Not that he'd minded that. The very thought of being in the same place where Richard of England would be recrowned was worth any number of saddle sores.

He hadn't been disappointed. Somehow he and Margaret, and Jamie and Elizabeth, had found themselves in great seats for the ceremony in Westminster. It was every bit as awe-inspiring as he'd imagined it, and much more so than any history book could ever have made it seem.

The only spooky thing had been walking through the Abbey and *not* seeing the graves he was accustomed to seeing. Jamie had been just as oblivious to it as Margaret was, but Alex had exchanged more than one startled glance with his sister.

"Look," Margaret said, interrupting his musings.

He followed her arm and smiled at the sight. "Home," he said with a sigh of relief.

"Aye," she said, returning his smile. "Home."

He'd never been so glad to see anything in his life. Though the trip south had been intensely interesting and seeing it from horseback rather than a speeding Jaguar had been educational, he was ready to be home. Maybe he'd work on building a tub for two. So it wouldn't be a Jacuzzi; a good soak was still nothing to take lightly.

" 'Tis pleasing to see no streams of smoke on the horizon," Margaret said as they cantered along.

"That's for sure."

Ralf hadn't been in London. The only words Alex had managed to say to Richard were "Congratulations, Sire," and "We'll send support to your army as soon as may be." Alex had used his title to his best advantage, pumping others for information and bullying where he had to, but the only report he had was that Ralf was due to arrive when Richard's fleet set sail for France. But where Ralf was keeping himself at present was a mystery and one Alex didn't want solved by seeing Falconberg going up in flames. That the skyline was clear was a great relief.

Maybe Ralf would actually do what the king had told him to do and go to France. Alex had serious doubts that would happen. If Ralf's gold resided in Margaret's cellar, Ralf was sure to follow close on its heels.

Well, there was nothing to do but prepare for it as best he could. Other than that, all he could do was enjoy being a newlywed.

And get busy building that king-size bathtub, of course.

THEY RODE INTO the bailey and Alex could only gape at the sight that greeted his eyes.

It was as if the entire shire had decided to show up for an extended stay. Tents, lean-tos, branches tied together worthy of any Swiss Family Robinson hut—they were all there.

And Sir George stood on the steps, positively beaming. Alex looked at Margaret.

"Any idea what this is?"

She looked as stunned as he. "I think perhaps they have come to have you dispense justice. 'Twas so in my sire's day."

"Well," Alex said, nonplussed. "It looks like things have been simmering for a while." He saw the tightening of her expression and winced. "I didn't mean that how it sounded."

She let out her breath slowly, then turned and smiled grimly at him. "I know, Alex. This is hardly your doing, nor is it your fault they wouldn't come to me before."

He swung down from his mount and held up his arms for her. "Come 'ere, wife," he said, pulling her down and into his arms. He held her tightly and bent his head to her ear. "Sometimes life really sucks, Margaret."

She put her face in the crook of his neck and merely stood in his embrace, holding on to him tightly. Alex closed his eyes and savored the feeling. Just what had he ever done to deserve this woman? She would never admit defeat, never admit hurt, never admit any weakness. But the fact that she stood with her arms around him was sign enough for him that she would accept comfort from him. It was enough.

"Let's go inside," he said softly. "I think we have enough time to at least hear some of these cases."

She lifted her head and met his gaze. "We?"

"Of course we," he said, tucking a stray strand of hair behind her ear. "What do I know of medieval justice? Just call me 'Alex the Figurehead.'"

She shook her head. "They'll not accept it from me."

"Well, they'll accept it from us."

"I likely shouldn't even be in the hall—"

He kissed away the rest of her words. "If I'm there, you're there. That's how this marriage works. With any luck Cook will have something good on the fire. Jamie's not exactly the best trail cook I've ever ridden with."

"I heard that slander," Jamie called from behind him. "I'd see you repaid, but I wouldn't want to humiliate you before your entire household."

Alex only laughed and put his arm around Margaret's shoulders. "Let's go do this and I'll deal with him later."

IT TURNED OUT to be a very long afternoon. After calming Amery and Baldric down, Alex had taken the time out for lunch. He'd known he would need it.

Then court was in session. There were several open-and-shut cases that didn't take long at all to solve. It was the more-complicated issues of property lines and water rights that forced him to adjourn for another snack and confer with Margaret and George in the solar. Never mind that it was all Falconberg land, there were still the grants Margaret's grandfather and father had given to those who worked Falconberg land for them. By the time George and Margaret had pulled out the original books and looked everything up, Alex's head was swimming with details.

"How does it feel to be back in the saddle?" Elizabeth asked, sitting down next to him and handing him one of the last Twinkies in the box.

"It makes me wish I'd paid more attention in that dry-as-dust property law class I took," he said, rubbing his forehead.

"Well, you're looking competent."

Alex looked at Margaret and George huddled over a thick pile of parchment. "There's the one who's competent. Don't ask me how she's managed to hold this all together with all these surly tenants."

"Welcome to being a landlord," Elizabeth said with a laugh, "in the truest sense of the word."

Alex smiled. "Strange as it may sound, I like it."

"It suits you."

Alex nodded and savored the laced-with-lard middle of the very last Twinkie. "I'm glad you guys could stay for a while."

"We wouldn't have missed it." Elizabeth smiled, then

looked away. "But we'll have to go eventually."

"I know."

She looked back at him and blinked rapidly. "I keep telling myself I won't do this."

Alex squeezed her hand. "You're just mourning the fact you won't have my closet to raid anymore. I understand it and accept it for what it's worth."

She punched him in the stomach. "Maybe I won't miss you after all," she said, rising.

"Why does everyone keep hitting me?" he gasped. "I live with brutal women."

"Ah-ha," Margaret said triumphantly. "Alex, come you here and look at this. We've found the original grant."

Alex pushed away his headache and limped over to ingest more details.

It promised to be an even longer evening than he'd feared.

But as he lay in bed with his wife a very long time later, he could only smile over the day's events. Who would have suspected that he'd find himself styled a medieval earl with his own people coming to him for justice? Maybe all that time spent either immersed in the law or hobnobbing with crooks had honed his sense of right and wrong. He turned over in his mind the stickier cases of the day, examining them again just to assure himself he had done the right thing.

"Alex," Margaret groaned, rolling away from him, "stop thinking and go to sleep."

"The wheels turning too loudly?"

"Saints, I can hardly sleep for the noise."

Alex laughed softly and rolled toward her to gather her back against him. "Sorry. I'll give it a rest."

"Aye, and give me one while you're at the task."

He kissed her hair and tried to relax. He felt her intertwine her fingers with his.

"Alex?"

"Hmmm?"

She was silent for so long, he thought she might have fallen asleep.

"You judged fairly today," she said finally.

He tightened his arms around her. "Thank you."

"Indeed," she continued slowly, "not even my grandsire could have walked so fine a line, and I always thought him the wisest man I'd ever known."

Well, he suspected there wasn't a much higher compliment in her book than that. He searched for several minutes for the right way to let her know he understood. In the end, all he could do was squeeze her hands.

"I love you," she whispered.

"Oh, Margaret," he said softly. He was afraid if he held her as tightly as he wanted to, he'd break her. "I love you, too."

She patted his hands. "Well, that's settled. Off to sleep with you, my lord. You've a full day tomorrow as well."

He smiled against her hair. Another tomorrow with Margaret of Falconberg. And countless other tomorrows after that.

It was almost too good to be true.

$Twenty$-$seven$

❧❀❧

MARGARET BOUNDED ENTHUSIASTICALLY UP THE STAIRS to look for her husband. What a fine morn it had been already. She'd had several successful goes at the quintain, Amery and young Ian had managed to break their fast without covering themselves and each other with food-stuffs, and Baldric had found his last rhyme without any aid. What would make the morning complete would be a few minutes of privacy with the man she loved, the light of her eyes and the joy of her heart—

"I can see how happy you are here, brother, but there is a part of me that cannot help but wonder how your choice will affect the future."

The sound of those words brought Margaret up short at the doorway to the solar. She pulled back into the shadows and frowned. That was Jamie speaking, but what could he possibly intend by such words?

"Jamie," Alex said with a deep sigh, "we've been over this before—"

"Aye, but have you—"

"I have. I have considered all the ramifications of my staying. I've considered them over and over again until I'm sick of considering. I've made my choice."

Ramifications. Margaret repeated the word to herself several times. It wasn't familiar, but surely had ominous overtones.

"Somehow," Alex continued, "I just have the feeling I won't be the first person to wake up in a different century and decide he was better off that way. Where do you think Baldric got all his limerick ideas? I doubt it was from a traveling minstrel of French origin.''

"But the changing of history—''

Alex laughed. "Oh, and you're one to talk!''

Margaret wondered what the expression was that Jamie wore to accompany his offended snort.

"A wee bit of wrong righting now and then hardly mars the fabric of history.''

"Beth told me just yesterday that your newly acquired taste for Barbados rum has necessitated more than one trip there for just pleasure.''

Jamie seemingly had no answer for that. The silence gave Margaret ample opportunity to consider Alex's words. And she had to admit that after spending a month with Elizabeth and Jamie, she was ready to concede that the rest of the family was certainly not daft. A group of more pleasant, rational people she had never before encountered. And if they weren't daft and could speak of these gates in the grass without smirking, it could mean only one thing: Alex had been telling her the truth from the start.

And this could only mean one thing: There truly was a place for him to return to, a place that was likely more interesting than her England and her keep. His keep. Their home together with its unraveled tapestries and leaking roof.

"But the fabric of time,'' Jamie said finally. "What of that?''

"What of it?''

"You're adding a thread where it doesn't belong, Alex. Your time is the twentieth century, not the twelfth. The reason I was able to go forward was because I escaped certain death. There was no more place for me in 1311. You still have a place in 1998.''

"For all you know I was destined to die in a car crash in another week.''

Margaret listened to them spout their strange words, and

for the first time wished she'd questioned Alex more thoroughly with perhaps a more open mind. What meant Jamie by the escaping of certain death? Did Alex indeed still have a place in another time?

She shook her head, stunned at the thought of such a thing being true and even more surprised that she was beginning to actually consider the possibility of it.

"That's another thing," Alex said. "I think your fabric-of-time idea has some serious holes in it."

"Where?" Jamie demanded. " 'Tis a most logical theory."

"Then explain this: You were supposed to die in 1311. You didn't, so you had to leave or you would have added a strand of life where one didn't belong. So how do you justify adding yourself into the twentieth century where you most certainly were not born?"

Jamie grunted, but it was a grunt of surprised dismay if she'd ever heard one.

"Well," he said, "to be sure I'll be giving that more thought."

She heard him rise and begin to pace. The footsteps stopped suddenly.

"How do we know I *wasn't* supposed to travel to the future?" Jamie demanded suddenly.

"The same way we don't know that I *wasn't* supposed to travel to 1194," Alex countered.

"Harumph," Jamie said. A chair creaked again under his weight. "There's something amiss with that, but damn me if I cannot divine it at present."

"Well, you get back to me when you have it figured out."

Margaret leaned against the wall and sighed. That was seemingly a crisis well avoided. There was no reason Alex couldn't stay in the past.

"By the saints," she muttered, "I've gone as daft as he has!"

"Aren't there things you'll miss?" Jamie asked, startling her. "Twentieth-century things?"

Margaret edged closer. That was a promising question if she'd ever heard one. Now she would hear Alex's list and determine for herself what it was he had given up for her sake.

"Miss?" Alex asked in a tone far too contemplative for her taste. "Sure I'll miss some things. I'll miss the Range Rover. I'll miss driving from one place to the next and arriving dry and able to walk without a hitch. I'll miss Twinkies."

Margaret had sampled a Twinkie and found it to be rather disgusting on the whole. She cared not for the coating it had left on the roof of her mouth. If that was the extent of Alex's desires, he was likely better off with her. Aye, she could hold her own against such foul pastries.

"What about ESPN?" Jamie asked. "The Lear? High-yield treasury notes?"

"That Forbes list has gone to your head, Jamie," Alex laughed. "I can't believe I'm listening to you talk about investments as if you'd been living with them your entire life."

"I'm a very fast learner," Jamie said, "and as such, it makes me wonder if you've considered that you'll be a great deal poorer here than you were in 1998."

Margaret considered that. To be sure these *treasury notes*, which sounded as if they were worth a great deal, were something to be concerned over. She chewed on her lip. This could mean trouble for her. Her coffers were never all that full. Full enough for her needs, but certainly not to overflowing. Though Ralf's contribution was substantial, was it enough to balance against treasury notes?

Then again, Alex was with her now. He would likely be able to collect rents some of her vassals hadn't been willing to pay her. That would certainly provide them with a luxury every now and again.

"Jamie, money isn't everything, as you well know. Sure I'll miss my comfortable, cushy lifestyle, but I guarantee you all that money means nothing if I have to give up Margaret to get it."

"Hmmm," was all Jamie answered.

Margaret felt her heart begin to lighten. It certainly sounded as if she was faring well against the lures of 1998. After all, how much more luxurious could it be than 1194? She had flues for her hearths. She had bedchambers with doors and feather pillows. Even the king would have been impressed with such largesse—which was the one reason she'd prayed he would never decide to come to Falconberg. The saints only knew what he might have decided would be a fine parting gift. She could well imagine him loading up his baggage wains with her mattresses and pillows. At least he wouldn't have been tempted by the wall hangings.

"I wonder," Jamie mused, "how you would feel if you returned home for a brief visit."

Alex laughed shortly. "Jamie, are you trying to talk me out of staying? I figured that you, of anyone, would be on my side on this."

"It isn't that I'm not. Indeed, I understand well the choice you have made."

"Then you have regrets?"

Jamie was so silent, Margaret was hard pressed not to peer inside the chamber and see what his expression was.

"Regrets? Nay, I have none. I would not trade my life with Elizabeth for anything. But 'tis not of me we speak."

"And you think I'm any less able than you to handle living in a different century?"

Indeed, Margaret added silently. Alex certainly seemed to adapt with alacrity to whatever Fate handed him. He obviously thought so, too, given the highly offended tone he'd taken.

"What I mean to say," Jamie said, "is that I came from a time very much like this one—"

"I know what you meant—" Alex interrupted.

"—and 'tis far easier to go from hardship to luxury than from the ease and comfort of your former life to—"

"What kind of pansy do you think I am?" Alex exploded. "I can live without a satellite dish!"

"Can you?"

Margaret heard furniture begin to take tumbles. Well, no matter whose dignity was being protected, she had no intention of having her solar destroyed by two such large men. If they wanted to kill each other, they could do it outside. She strode into the chamber and bellowed her command for them to cease.

They ignored her.

Alex was obviously bent on assuring Jamie that he was no pansy—whatever that meant, but she suspected it wasn't all that complimentary—and Jamie seemed just as determined to convince Alex that he was. Margaret clapped her hands, waved her arms, shouted at the top of her lungs for them to stop their foolishness. The only result was Jamie and Alex smashing through a chair and Alex demolishing what Jamie hadn't when Jamie heaved Alex off him.

"Here, this might help."

Margaret turned to find Elizabeth standing behind her holding a pitcher of water.

"Fresh water?" Margaret asked doubtfully. "Seems a shame to waste it thusly."

"It's probably better that way in the long run," Elizabeth said with a smile. "Drenched is one thing. Drenched with cesspool water is another."

Margaret had to agree, though she did so reluctantly. She took the pitcher and watched the two overgrown oafs who currently rolled about in the rushes at the foot of her favorite chair. She didn't dare let them go on any longer. She positioned herself so that she wouldn't splash the wood overmuch, avoided the thrashing of two sets of well-fashioned legs, and waited until both heads were well within drenching distance. Then she very deliberately up-ended the pitcher of water over them.

"What the hell—"

"By all the bloody saints—"

Margaret looked calmly down at the outraged males staring at her.

"You were nigh onto ruining what poor seats I have. If you must engage in such childish antics, do so outside."

Alex rolled to his feet, then shook himself like a dog, splattering her person and her good chair with water. Margaret wiped the water off with the sleeve of her tunic, then glared at her husband.

"Finished?"

"No," he said shortly. "Come on, Jamie. I'll deal with you outside."

"There are other things we should discuss," Jamie said, gingerly touching his cut lip. "Ramifications you may not have yet considered." He heaved himself to his feet, gave Elizabeth a pat, and followed Alex out the door.

Margaret looked at her newly made sister-in-law and grimaced. "I like not that word he continues to use. Ramifications. Surely no good can come of such a word."

"Nothing that either of us wants to dwell on, I'm sure," Elizabeth agreed. "I promised Amery and Ian I'd tell them a story, and Amery wanted you to come. Will you?"

"Gladly," Margaret said. It would take her mind off Jamie's unsettling words.

"What was that all about, anyway?"

"Jamie called Alex a pansy."

Elizabeth whistled softly. "Alex couldn't have been happy about that."

Margaret gestured toward the ruined chair. "That tells the tale well enough."

Elizabeth laughed. "Well, they'll work it out I'm sure. Let's go take our minds off it for a while. There'll be bruises to tend later."

Margaret followed Elizabeth from the solar. Perhaps listening to Elizabeth spin a tale or two would take her mind off more than Alex's bruises. She feared she might not be able to forget Jamie's words. Then she shook her head and decided not to let them unsettle her. Even if all the foolishness were true and Alex had come from a different time than hers, hers was surely far more attractive. There were luxuries aplenty in her castle. Why, her cook was the most highly skilled for leagues. Even Baldric, daft though he might be, could spin a tale worthy of any king's pleasure.

Aye, she had enough to offer him. Ramifications be damned.

$\mathcal{T}$wenty-eight

❧❦❧

ALEX STOOD ATOP THE BATTLEMENTS AND LOOKED OUT over Falconberg soil. In his wildest dreams he'd never imagined he would wind up in twelfth-century England wearing the title of earl of Falconberg. Somehow it sounded just a little more impressive than a doctor of jurisprudence. The rest of his family would certainly have been impressed.

His family. Alex dragged his hand through his hair and sighed. Not seeing them was something he had outright avoided thinking about before. After all, what had been the point? He'd resigned himself to never seeing them again and that had been that. But that had been before his conversation with Jamie late last night.

They'd been sitting in front of the fire innocently enough, nursing their post-wrestling injuries. All the talk of the twentieth century had made Alex wish that there was a way to go back and see his parents one last time and introduce them to Margaret. Alex might have continued to keep that in the wishful-thinking category if Jamie hadn't said there was likely a way he could manage it.

Damn him anyway.

"It has to do with the land," Jamie had said. "It seems that I can come and go as I please through these gates."

"And bringing me Ding-Dongs wouldn't qualify for a task in the past?" Alex had asked with a smile.

But Jamie hadn't smiled back. It might have been because of his split lip, but Alex suspected it was because the topic was too serious for joking.

They had talked far into the night. Alex hadn't liked what he'd heard, but he could see the logic in it all. Jamie's ancestors had lived for centuries in Scotland. That he should be tied to it in some elemental way was perfectly believable.

Not being able to bend the direction of the gates to one's will was another story, however. Not that he had any proof of it, either. Good grief, he hadn't even been shooting for England.

At least Jamie hadn't tried to reach for his plaid again. Alex suspected he'd cured his brother-in-law of his Fabric of Time lecture once and for all. All he knew was that if he'd had to listen to Jamie's "each thread has a purpose, and if a body pulls one here, the pattern of the fabric will be marred" spiel one more time, he would have screamed. Jamie still hadn't come up with a decent answer as to what had happened when he'd added himself *to* the twentieth century, but Alex suspected he was working frantically on it.

In any case, Jamie had said Alex and Margaret could travel with Jamie and Elizabeth forward to the twentieth century, then return home to the twelfth on their own, but that would be it. No frequent-flier miles. No popping back and forth for holidays. Jamie could get them to Scotland; they could get themselves home. Jamie had no answer for just exactly how Alex should determine which century he should be in. Alex could only think it through logically for himself. Margaret was here. What other reason did he need than that to remain?

Besides, he liked medieval England. He liked packing a sword. Truth be told, he liked being called "my lord" and knowing that people were depending on him to defend them. It came with its headaches, but the pluses were definitely attractive and he certainly had good training legally for the job. Besides, England would be a fascinating place historically for the next few decades, at least for the time he'd be alive. No nasty plagues or major wars. If he played his cards right, he could be in the thick of the whole Magna Carta business. He could make a difference.

And that didn't even cover the most important attraction in 1194: Margaret.

Though it would be nice to see his parents one last time to say goodbye. They should have the chance to meet Margaret. She should have the chance to see them.

"Alex?"

Alex jumped when he realized Margaret had come to stand next to him. "Sorry," he said with half a laugh. "I was thinking."

She looked at him solemnly. "Ramifications?"

He smiled and pulled her into his arms. "Yes, as a matter of fact."

She was silent, but hugged him more tightly.

"Do you want to know what I was thinking?"

"I'm afraid to," she said, her words muffled against his tunic.

He pressed a gentle kiss against her hair then put his lips to her ear. "I was thinking that I could ask nothing more of life than what it's already given me."

She lifted her head and looked at him gravely. "In truth?"

"In truth," he said, with a smile. "But that wasn't the most important thing."

He could have sworn she was bracing herself to hear something awful. "What would that be?" she asked.

"Everything I want I have right here in my arms."

He watched her digest that, then felt her relief in the relaxing of her rigid stance.

"The saints be praised for your good sense."

He laughed. "That's all I get for such a flowery sentiment?"

"What else would you have, my lord?"

"My lecherous imagination is running rampant," he said, "and I'll tell you all about it in a minute. I want to ask you something first."

"Aye?"

"I was wondering," he began, then he realized how very much he wanted what he was about to ask, "well, what I would really like is for you to meet my family."

She blinked. "But I have. Jamie and Elizabeth—"

"No," he said, "I mean the rest of my family."

She froze. "In Seattle?"

"We'll go to Scotland. They'll come to us."

She stepped back and looked at him closely. "Will they?"

"If everything goes well."

"And we'll be stepping through the blades of grass?"

She asked it without any inflection of disbelief and only a minor amount of lip-pursing. Alex couldn't help but smile. He could hardly wait to see her expression the first time she saw a modern invention. Jamie would have fingerprints all over his house from Margaret touching everything to make sure it was real.

"Yes," he said, realizing she was waiting for his answer. "That's exactly what we'll be doing."

She was considering it. Then she looked at him very carefully.

"Can we get back home?"

He couldn't lie. "I'm almost positive of it."

"This means much to you."

"I don't know that I'll ever see my family again. And I would very much like them to meet you."

"And you believe this will happen? This traveling to the future?"

"I know it will."

She put her arms around him and held on tightly. "Then I will go with you."

"You won't regret it."

She sighed. "I hope not."

Alex held her and looked out over Falconberg soil—soil that was now under his care and prayed that he wasn't doing something colossally stupid. They would pop back to the twentieth century, he would say his goodbyes, then they would come home and live out the rest of their lives in happiness.

Alex tightened his arms around his wife and began to make a list in his head of all the things he would need to bring back with him, beginning with several prescriptions of penicillin and ending with a case or two of Twinkies. Hopefully Beast would survive being used as a packhorse and the faery ring wouldn't strip him of his comfort food on the return trip.

MARGARET SURVEYED HER gear. Sword, mail, bow and quarels, and a handful of knives to hide on various parts of her person. Cook had been instructed to pack enough food for a brief journey. Now all that was left to do was wait for the morrow.

She'd already given the tidings to Baldric. They hadn't been well received. He had been highly offended that he wouldn't be taken along to immortalize any possible heroic deeds in verse. She'd promised him a detailed report when she returned, but she wasn't sure if that had satisfied him or not. He'd gone into hiding almost immediately, either to sulk or to shore up his strength for hours of creative effort upon her return.

Amery hadn't been told yet. Separation from Alex would be hard on the lad, even if they were gone only a few days. Margaret had decided the kindest thing they could do was tell him just before they departed. Even so, the boy seemed to know some mischief was afoot. He'd been raging about for a pair of days now, using his newly discovered word "nay" as many times as humanly possible.

"I see you've finished your preparations."

Margaret turned around to find her captain standing just outside the doorway.

"Aye," she said, uncertain what she should tell him. "We won't be gone long."

"Indeed."

" 'Tis merely a trip to see a few sights," Margaret said

defensively. "To show Alex a bit more of England."

George snorted. "I know exactly what you're about, Margaret. You needn't make up a tale to appease me."

"And what is it you think you know, good sir?"

George left his post in the passageway and came across the chamber to stand next to her. "I believe him," he said softly. "I believe he came from a year far in the future. I have had several talks with Alex and with Lord Jamie. They are honest men."

"Daft, you mean to say."

"Nay, I believe them to have all their wits about them. I daresay you'll see it all soon enough for yourself."

"I'll see nothing but countryside and the embarrassed face of my lord when he realizes his tale isn't true."

George smiled and put his hand on her shoulder briefly. "I envy you. I would give much to see what you'll see."

Margaret felt a distinct chill go down her spine, and it was far colder than the wind that leaked through the cracks in her shutters. She had the feeling, and 'twas a dread certainty indeed, that Alex had spoken the truth and she would be stepping through a blade of grass on the morrow into a world she had never before imagined. It was to be sure the stuff of legends. Faeries and elves did such things, not humankind. Yet there she was, on the brink of doing the selfsame thing. For a moment she wished with all her might that she might take someone of her own household, someone who would understand her uncertainty. She looked at George.

"Come, if you wish," she offered. *At least I won't be alone then.*

George shook his head with a smile. "Nay, girl, my place is here. What need have I to see the future? Alex has told me tales enough to keep my poor head spinning for years." He smiled again and stepped away. "I'll keep watch here for you while you're gone." He walked to the door, then paused and turned. "There is one thing, though."

Margaret felt affection well up in her. George had never

once asked her for anything, yet how often she had relied on him to serve and guide her. Aye, she would do whatever she could for him.

"Anything," she said.

"I'd like a baseball."

"A *what*?" She had expected steel or delicacies, or perhaps even to have Baldric locked in the dungeon while she was gone, but this foreign-sounding object? Never.

"A baseball. Ask Alex. He'll know all about it."

Margaret grunted. She didn't doubt Alex could spout a great deal of nonsense about such a thing, but anything else would be something she would just have to reserve judgment on.

"Be careful," George added, then turned and disappeared into the passageway before she could say anything else.

She turned back to her gear and stared at it, trying to decide if it was enough to take. For all she knew, they'd end up facing a score of bandits in some forest and it would be up to her to save their lives. The likelihood of them arriving any place where they might find anything as ridiculous as a *baseball* was very far-fetched. She paused, considered, then made her decision.

She turned away and went in search of another knife.

Twenty-nine

❦

"HOUSTON, WE HAVE A PROBLEM."

Alex continued to cinch Beast's saddle. "Whatever it is, it can be fixed later."

"Actually," Elizabeth said, "I think you'll want to take a look at this now."

Alex sighed, gave the straps one last tug, then turned around to see what else the morning could throw at him. He frowned. "What's this?"

"I think it's what it looks like," Elizabeth said dryly.

Margaret was in deep discussion with George, no doubt giving him a very long list of her last-minute instructions. That Alex didn't have a problem with. It was the group standing next to her that threatened to give him gray hairs.

Baldric was dressed for travel. Alex recognized the gear: the long, flowing, bardly cloak and the beat-up carpetbag made from remnants of tapestries Baldric had no doubt worked his magic on previously. Obviously the bard hadn't been in hiding to pout; he'd been in hiding to pack.

Amery was also dressed in his finest traveling apparel: sturdy leather boots and a little coat Elizabeth had put together for him. He wore his woobie swathed around his shoulders and head in a manner worthy of the most important sheik. Amery clutched his pillow with one hand and Frances's skirts with the other.

Or, rather, Frances's cloak with the other. Alex felt his frown deepen at the sight of Amery's keeper also seemingly prepared for a formidable journey. She was blushing miserably—which had been her condition the last time she'd been talked into going along for the ride by Baldric. The old man could be very persuasive when it suited him.

And then there was Joel, standing next to Baldric and clutching Alex's gear.

"You forgot your mail, my lord," he huffed, struggling to keep himself and all Alex's warrior paraphernalia upright and occupying the same space. "I brought it, as well as other things I thought you'd be needin'."

"But—" Alex spluttered.

"You'll have need of me," Joel plunged on. "A great lord such as yourself shouldn't be traveling about without his squire."

"But we aren't going all that far—"

"One never knows how far the road will take him," Baldric announced. "One also never knows the adventures he might have along the way. 'Tis only right that I come along to record any such occurrences."

"I really don't think—"

"You can't be leavin' us behind," Frances blurted out, then clamped her lips shut and blushed some more. She stared at the ground intently.

Alex looked at Margaret. She shrugged, then turned back to George and started up with her list again. Alex shook his head, then looked at his sister.

"This isn't going to work."

Elizabeth smiled. "It would probably be better not to bring them. If you try, Jamie will give you his Don't Mar the Fabric of Time lecture again."

"Holes and all."

"He's overlooking them."

He sighed. Maybe time was weaving a cloth none of them could understand right now. But he couldn't help but wonder just what sort of challenges his little fan club might present to the Chief Weaver.

"We will not be left behind," Baldric repeated, in his bardliest tone. He stuck his chin out, and the stiffness of the grizzled gray beard was enough to warn Alex resistance would be futile.

Alex looked at Elizabeth. "Well, it's not like they'd be living in the twentieth century. It'd just be a little visit."

She shrugged. "It's your call."

Alex smiled weakly. "It would certainly give Baldric some new material."

"That alone would be worth it. I'll go see what's keeping Jamie." She patted him on the shoulder, then went inside the hall.

Alex watched her go, feeling a pang of grief. He didn't want to think about missing his family. He was doing the right thing. He looked at Margaret and felt the surety wash over him again. They were meant to be together. The century didn't matter. Maybe Jamie would get back more often than he thought.

Alex looked at Joel. "I'll take the sword, Joel. The rest you can take back upstairs."

"But, my lord!"

"We're just out for a little ride, kid. No need of heavy gear."

"As you say, my lord," Joel said doubtfully.

Alex watched Joel set the sword down and casually drape a tunic over it, but not until he'd done what he obviously considered a fine job of hiding most of Alex's gear under the clothing. Alex didn't feel up to arguing so he didn't say anything. Instead, he went to see what sorts of things Margaret was drumming into poor George's head.

"—sure to see that Sir Richard does *not* take the night watch. Ever he falls asleep and more than once he's awoken only to find he has cut himself on his blade."

"Margaret," George said with a smile, "trust me. I will see that things run smoothly in your absence."

Margaret didn't look all that convinced. "I could perhaps go over the garrison list with you once more. . . ."

Alex smiled dryly at George's long-suffering sigh. "My love," he said, taking her by the arm and tugging gently, "George will be just fine. We'll be back in a few days, hardly long enough for anyone to notice we've been gone.''

"He's right," George said. "All will be well. You'll see."

Margaret sighed and allowed Alex to pull her close. "He wants a baseball, Alex. Whatever that is."

Alex smiled at George. "No problem." He looked at his wife's full battle gear. "I don't think you'll need your mail, Meg."

She pursed her lips. "I'm the only one with enough sense to wear it. The saints only know where we'll truly wind up. At least one of us should have some protection."

Alex could see various hiltlike lumps under her surcoat and noted the two daggers peeping out of each boot. Well, no one could ever say the woman was unprepared. He pressed a kiss on her forehead.

"Whatever you want, Meg. I'm just happy you're coming."

She grunted, then turned away and called out orders for horses to be rounded up for Baldric and the rest.

Alex looked at George. "We'll be back soon."

"I wish you good fortune with the gate."

"Well, it always seems to work for Jamie. We shouldn't have any trouble getting home this time. I mean," he said, realizing his choice of words, "we shouldn't have any trouble getting to *Jamie's* home."

George ignored his slip. "I cannot lie and say I do not envy you a bit."

"You could come. The rest of the castle seems hell-bent on it."

George shook his head. "I have yet work here in my time, Alex. I will stay and see it finished."

"Geez, George, we'll be home before you know it."

"I hope so." George embraced him briefly. "A safe journey to you then, my friend."

Alex nodded, then turned away before he embarrassed himself by blubbering. Jamie and Elizabeth were standing by their horses. Jamie was frowning at Alex's entourage, and Alex quickly looked elsewhere to avoid the inevitable lecture. Margaret was, unfortunately, nowhere to be seen.

"She's gone back inside," Baldric announced. "Best find her so we can be on our way. I've a need of new fodder for my verses!"

Heaven help us all, Alex thought to himself as he went inside the hall. Margaret wasn't in the kitchen, wasn't in her solar, and wasn't in their bedchamber. Alex headed toward the roof. It was her favorite place to go and brood. This wasn't a good sign.

She was standing where he suspected she'd be standing, looking out over Falconberg soil. Alex came to a halt beside her and leaned his elbows on the wall.

"Ready?" he asked.

She shook her head.

"Scared?" he asked softly.

She met his gaze. "Aye," she admitted reluctantly. "Nigh onto weeping." She looked back over her land. "I fear I'll never see it again. Assuming," she said with a dark look thrown his way, "that your tale is true and I find myself in some other century."

Alex smiled. "Seeing is believing, my love."

She snorted in a most unladylike manner.

Alex laughed in spite of himself. "Oh, Margaret, you are priceless. What would I do without you?"

"You'd have no one to torment with your foolishness."

Alex put his arm around her shoulders and drew her close in spite of her mail and the hilts of her daggers that dug into his side.

"Everything will be all right, Meg. You'll see."

She relaxed against him, but her gaze was fixed on her land. "Alex," she said softly.

"Yes, my love."

"I fear I'll never stand in this place again." She shivered. "That I'll never again feel this rock under my fingers." She looked at him, then. "Don't you feel it?"

Alex shoved aside his own unease. There was no reason they couldn't get back home. He and Jamie had done it when they'd gone back to fifteenth-century Scotland to take care of business. They'd come home just as easily as if they'd been out for a little stroll in the woods. There was no reason he and Margaret couldn't return to the same place in time. This was their home. That was enough.

"We'll be back," he said. "I think a person's always nervous before a long trip. You imagine up in your head all sorts of terrible outcomes. It's perfectly normal."

She didn't look convinced, but she nodded just the same. "Then let us be off. I'm anxious to see for myself finally that you are not a bit off in the head." She turned him toward the door. "At least you are wearing your sword. I compliment you on that show of good sense."

Alex knew he wouldn't get more out of her than that. He proceeded her down to the great hall, then took her hand. Cook and her staff stood at the edge of the hallway leading to the kitchens. Alex waved.

"We'll be back soon," he said firmly.

And they would. He would say his goodbyes, gather up what gear he thought he might need over the course of his life, and then they would come home. This was where he belonged. He smiled at the sight of the little balls of thread lining the walls. At least Baldric wouldn't do any damage over the next few days. He tightened his hand around Margaret's. She looked at him.

"Just a friendly hello," he managed.

She pursed her lips, but said nothing.

The company was mounted in the courtyard. Alex gave George a smart salute.

"See you in a few days."

"Godspeed, my lord."

Alex caught Jamie's frown as he took Beast's reins from one of the stableboys.

"What?" he asked defensively.

" 'Tis something of a large group," Jamie noted.

"It's a visit, Jamie. Everyone will survive, including the fabric of time."

Jamie didn't look all that convinced, but he said no more.

Alex mounted and rode with Margaret through the gates. The portcullis slammed home behind the group with an air of finality.

"Damn it," Alex muttered, "give me a break! Nothing's going to go wrong."

"Alex?"

Alex looked at his wife, who clearly had resurrected the idea that he'd lost all his marbles.

"Just talking to myself," he offered.

"Hmmm," she said, nodding. "I see."

"I do it a lot when I'm stressed out."

She smiled briefly. "I will not torment you if we travel no farther than Brackwald. You've nothing to fear from me. Well," she added, "perhaps a small bit of teasing."

"I feel better already."

"I thought you might."

Alex couldn't help but smile. Nagging feelings be damned. He had all he needed right next to him. It was just nerves. It had been a while since he'd been on the hot seat, so to speak. He'd certainly had his share of jitters in court over the years. This was just the same thing.

He blew out a breath in relief. That had to be it. He was taking five people into a time that wasn't their own, and it was just giving him a little performance anxiety. Who could blame him? For all he knew, Frances would have hysterics, and Baldric would unravel every bit of clothing he had and run screaming into the village pub naked. Heaven only knew what Margaret would do—probably turn her sword his direction and hack him to bits.

By the time they had traveled a mile or so, he had himself completely under control and had stopped thinking about his nerves and started thinking about how he was going to handle the inevitable group freak-out. Amery was too young to understand what he'd see, but Frances and Joel would no doubt understand a great deal. He planned to bribe them into behaving with junk food. Baldric was pretty much an unknown quantity, but Alex suspected he could be distracted with a few throw rugs.

It was Margaret who had him worried. She was wearing more weapons than he'd thought she'd owned. What would she do the first time she caught an eyeful of his Ranger Rover? Advance with blade bared?

And then he found himself with little time to speculate anymore. They had reached the faery ring. He looked at Margaret to judge her reaction. Her face was completely impassive. Either she was winning the war against teasing him, or she was scared spitless. He imagined it was probably the latter, and it probably had everything to do with the feeling of magic in the air.

There was no doubt in Alex's mind that they would wind back on Jamie's land. He certainly hadn't felt this kind of tremor in the air when he'd come to the ring with just Beast and his key phrases.

"Everybody inside," Jamie said, holding back until the rest of them were crammed inside the ring.

Alex looked at his brother-in-law and clutched his reins tightly. "Think this will work?"

"Of course," Jamie said with a grin. "I'm in sore need of a Jacuzzi and some brownies. I daresay the gate knows that."

"Will you get us back to the right year?"

"We can hope," Jamie said with another smile.

"Great," Alex muttered. "Our illustrious tour guide isn't sure of the destination or the year. Maybe I should have brought that mail after all." At least he had the comforting weight of William of Falconberg's sword on his hip. But what did he need with protection? He was with Jamie and, no matter what Jamie had said, that would be enough to get them back to the twentieth century. It had to be enough. Alex had goodbyes to say.

He looked at his wife. She was as white as a sheet. "Margaret?" he called softly.

Her eyes were glued to the sky. "It begins to snow," she whispered.

That certainly seemed to be the case. They had ridden out under blue skies. Those skies were cloudy now. And the surrounding countryside was blanketed with a good inch of snow.

Alex looked at his sister. Her expression was one of intense relief. She smiled at him.

"Looks like it worked," she said.

Alex nodded and turned to meet his wife's startled eyes. "Dorothy," he said, "I don't think we're in Kansas anymore."

Margaret drew her sword.

Alex sighed.

He had the feeling it was going to be a very long afternoon.

Thirty

MARGARET COULD HARDLY BELIEVE HER EYES. ONE MO-
ment she was staring up at blue sky, the next the sky had
filled with clouds, all sound had ceased and snow was
falling upon her upturned face. If this wasn't witchcraft,
she had no idea what was. She looked at her husband and
wondered if he was all a part of this, too. Should she
plunge her blade through his heart and save herself before
she traveled any further down this disastrous path that
surely led only to evil? She drew her blade with a shaking
hand.

"Uh-oh," Alex said. "This is bad."

Margaret felt her palms grow damp. She gripped her
sword all the harder. "What wickedness is this?" she demanded. Her voice was shrill even to her own ears.

Alex reached out to touch her. "Margaret—"

Margaret pulled her mount back and raised her blade
against her husband. "Don't touch me. I think I do not
know you as you really are, my lord."

"Margaret, I told you there was a gate—"

"Cease!" she shouted. "I'll hear no more of your babble!"

"Lady Margaret," Jamie said quietly, "I can understand—"

"Nay, you cannot!" She looked about her frantically
for some avenue of escape. She was being dragged to the
saints only knew where by these people who had made a

pact with the Devil. It was the only explanation that made sense.

They had all turned to look at her. Even Baldric was looking at her as if she'd just lost what remained of her wits. Amery was reaching for Alex, his eyes wide with unease.

They were all in league together. Why she hadn't seen it before, she did not know. Talk of the future had been nothing but a ploy to lure her from the keep and carry her off to their place of madness. She had to escape before it was too late for her. Obviously the rest of her company had succumbed to Alex's folly. She resheathed her sword and jerked on her reins.

Stop and give this more thought.

That was her common sense speaking; she recognized the coolness of the tone. She scowled and pulled until her horse was backing up out of the faery ring. Her common sense had obviously not served her thus far. 'Twas best she pay it no more heed.

'Tis but your unease that troubles you.

"Be silent!" she exclaimed, willing the voice away. She wheeled her horse around and set heels to his flanks. The sooner she was away from Alex and his daft family, the better.

"Margaret, wait!"

She spared a glance over her shoulder. At least only Alex followed her. She could take him easily.

You forget that he bested you at Tickhill with the sword—

"Only because I allowed it," she snapped. "And who asked you?"

"Margaret, damn it, stop!"

She could hear Alex gaining on her. She ducked into the forest in an effort to slow his progress. The snow was less there, which suited her well. Her mount was sure-footed, but even the most surefooted mount could take a tumble. She had no intentions of being crushed under her gelding before she could escape somewhere safe and make her plans. First, though, she would have to elude Alex.

Assuming he was still Alex. Had something foul in the faery ring possessed him while she looked away?

Oh, by the saints, Margaret...

"Enough!" she snarled. She would have clapped her hands over her ears, but the bloody voice was coming from inside her head. "I have two perfectly good eyes. I know what I've seen!"

Alex continued to gain ground. Margaret pushed her mount as fast as she dared. Without warning, the forest ended and she faced an open glen, the like of which she'd never seen before. She would have stopped and gaped if she'd had the time.

There was a large castle immediately before her. She didn't bother to consider it as a place of refuge. No doubt it was inhabited by souls as daft and wicked as Jamie and Alex. She would just have to continue on.

She'd barely thundered past the bailey gates when she found Alex by her side. He had hold of her reins before she knew what he intended.

"Nay!" she cried, trying to jerk them away from him.

"Margaret, calm down!" Alex shouted. "It's okay!"

He had control of her mount. She wouldn't travel as fast on foot, but she could escape just the same. She dismounted as gracefully as her mail would allow, then fled.

Alex caught her by the shoulder. She clouted him a good one as he spun her around. At least clutching the side of his head forced him to release her. Margaret could hardly believe she was going to have to do this, but she saw she had no choice. The man she loved, the man she had given her body to so many times over the past few weeks, had been overcome by some foul force. Likely the kindest thing she could do was finish him before he suffered anymore.

She drew her sword.

"What are you *doing*?" Alex demanded, backing away.

Margaret advanced. "If you'll not yield him back to me,

foul demon, I'll finish you off." She waved her sword. "And I do not jest."

"I can see that. Margaret, it's just _me_."

"Ha," she said derisively. "You fool me not. Prepare to meet your Master, Spawn of Darkness."

"Oh, hell," the demon said, with a sigh. "Have it your way, then."

Margaret didn't waste any more time with pleasantries. She lashed out at the creature who had once been her husband, but found that her thrusting wasn't as enthusiastic as it should have been. Perhaps he was sapping her strength with some wicked magic. She gave herself a hard shake and attacked again with more vigor. That wasn't much more successful. To her surprise, she found that she had little stomach for the deed. It would have been a simpler thing if perhaps the creature facing her hadn't looked so much like Alex. Or if it hadn't fought like Alex. Or if she hadn't fancied she saw her husband looking at her from out of the those blue-green eyes.

She pushed aside her foolish thoughts. Alex was no more and 'twas obvious to her that the only way she would return home was to slay this foul beast and free herself of his nefarious spell. She gathered strength from deep within and concentrated on her swordplay.

They fought for what seemed to her hours. The demon did no more than defend himself. Obviously, he planned to possess her when she admitted defeat. Well, that would never happen. Perhaps when she saw Alex in heaven he would thank her for what she prepared to do.

"Are you finished?" the demon asked politely, pausing to lean on his sword.

"Are you dead?"

That seemed to be answer enough for him. He lifted his sword and fended off her halfhearted attack.

Margaret realized it was just that. She tried to muster up more enthusiasm for the task. But the plain truth was, the more she crossed blades with the creature facing her, the more her head cleared. She began to doubt her doubts.

Out of the corner of her eye, she noted that Jamie and Elizabeth were standing nearby, holding their horses' reins. With a sudden move, Margaret caught the demon who had been her husband in the gut with her foot and sent him sprawling onto his backside. She stepped back a pace and used the opportunity to glance at Alex's family.

Elizabeth stood there calmly with a half smile playing around her mouth. She didn't look possessed. Margaret had never seen anyone in the throes of possession, but she'd heard it entailed a great deal of frothing at the mouth and vile swearing. Elizabeth was doing neither.

Margaret looked at Jamie. He was wearing the same amused smile his wife was, but she saw understanding in his eyes. She put her questions to him over the past weeks, and he'd seemed honest enough in his answers. He'd even told her of his own "journey" into the future and how it had startled him. She'd listened politely at the time, pitying Elizabeth for having a husband who indulged in such ridiculous imaginings.

Now she began to wonder if she hadn't been the one to suffer from ridiculous imaginings.

"Damn it to hell, Margaret," the demon groused as it heaved itself to its feet, "that's dirty fighting."

Foul cursing, Margaret noted. But no frothing at the mouth. She stared closely at the man facing her and gave the whole business more thought. It certainly looked like Alex. It definitely swore like Alex. She dropped her sword point to the ground and leaned on the hilt. It seemed incredible, but she thought she just might have made an error in judgment.

"Alex?" she asked.

He clapped his hand to his head. "Of course!" he bellowed. "Who the hell else would it be?"

She felt her eyes narrow of their own accord. "You've a mouth foul enough for a demon."

"You haven't heard anything yet," he grumbled. He rubbed his head, then winced. "You whacked me!"

"I did what I had to do."

Jamie cleared his throat. "I think we'll head up to the keep. You children come along when you've finished with your play."

Margaret watched them go, taking her mount and Alex's along with them. Then she turned back to her husband. She reached out and poked him in the chest.

"Alex?" she asked again, just to make sure.

In answer, he slipped his hand under her hair and hauled her to him. Before she could protest, he had captured her mouth in a searing kiss. She could only clutch the hilt of her sword and pray Alex would continue to hold her up as her knees were nigh onto buckling. He pulled away and Margaret felt her lips trembling. She put her hand over them so he wouldn't see. He took her hand away and kissed her again, a sweet, gentle kiss that almost brought tears to her eyes.

"I love you," he whispered. "Thank you for not killing me."

The sting of tears came now from embarrassment. "What have I done?" she moaned, burying her face in the crook of his neck.

"We call it 'freaking out,' " he said, sounding almost amused. "Everyone does it at some point in their lives."

"I've made a fool of myself."

"We're a great family to do it in front of. We all have very short memories. Besides, Jamie's done it a few times himself."

She lifted her head. "And you?"

"Never," he said with a smile. "I'm always in complete control."

She could find nothing to say to salvage her dignity, so she merely rested her forehead against his shoulder and sighed.

"You want to go inside now?"

She chewed her lip for a moment. "I'm not sure."

"I'll be right there with you."

She considered. "Making it that much easier for me to bury a blade in you."

His laugh was a comforting rumble in his chest. "If I didn't know I didn't already have enough hands to hold all of them, I'd relieve you of all your blades to avoid just that."

She didn't move. She couldn't. The saints only knew what else awaited her in this strange, snow-covered world of his. She knew they'd changed worlds. The landscape around her was one she'd never seen before.

Alex stroked her hair. "It's okay, Margaret. Think of it as an exciting adventure."

She grunted. "Oh, joy."

He laughed and pulled away to kiss her firmly on the mouth. "You'll be just fine. Why don't you put away your sword and let's go inside. I bet there'll be a fire going. Maybe some treats in the kitchen." He stepped back and held out his hand. "Will you come?"

She took a firm grip on her sword, then slowly put her other hand in his.

"You won't need that," he said with a gentle smile.

"How do you know what awaits inside?" she demanded. "The saints only know what might have overrun the keep in your absence."

"The only thing that might attack you would be something my little brother had grown under his bed."

"All the more reason to be prepared."

He squeezed her hand. "Margaret, nothing is going to hurt you inside."

"You don't sound all that sure, husband."

He took a deep breath. "There are several things that will probably surprise you at first. Over eight hundred years have passed between the time we left this morning and the time we're in now. Man has made a few interesting inventions."

"Such as?"

"I'll show you as we go."

It wasn't a good answer, but she suspected she wouldn't have a better one. She reluctantly put up her sword and let her husband lead her up toward the keep. While they walked, she allowed herself to speculate on what she might see inside.

Perhaps man had learned to fashion more beautiful tapestries. Likely the hearths had remained the same, but perhaps they were larger and produced better heat. As proud as she was of her own, she had to admit the only way to stay warm was to stand very close to the fire, as most of the heat found its way up into the flue. Future fare, though, was something she'd already sampled and found it to be much worse than what Cook produced, except of course, for those Godiva balls.

Well, she could think of no other realm in which there could have been much progress made. After all, what did man need with more than a good mount, a fairly laid table, and a soft, goosefeather mattress?

"I daresay," she began, "that things could not have changed all that . . . much . . ."

She froze. There, near to the door stood the most horrendous thing she'd ever seen. It was a cart, a covered cart with wheels as tall as her boots. It wore a black, shiny substance that reflected back her image as clearly as any polished mirror she'd ever seen.

"That's the Range Rover," Alex said, sounding very satisfied. "It's like a baggage wain, only it's more comfortable."

Margaret couldn't pull her eyes from the beast. "Where are the horses?"

"Inside it."

Margaret looked at her husband. He was grinning like a fool.

"You are not amusing," she stated.

"Aren't I?"

"Nay, my lord. Not in the slightest."

He pulled her toward the hall. "See what you think when we get inside."

Margaret took a deep breath as she entered the great hall. Well, this looked a bit familiar. Tapestries lined the walls and they were seemingly well fashioned—at least what she could tell from just inside the doorway. Baldric seemed to find them to his liking for he was running his hands over one and making approving noises.

Jamie's hearths were massive and he, too, had flues to carry the smoke away. There was a raised dais at the back of the hall with a very fine lord's table. Near the hearth sat a grouping of chairs. All in all, it looked to be a rather ordinary place. She glanced casually at the torches on the wall and then down at the stone beneath her feet.

It was then she began to see that things were perhaps a bit different in Jamie's keep.

There were no rushes on the floor. The stone was flat and well-laid, but there was nothing covering it to soak up the refuse of living. That was another strange thing. There were no remains from any meals littering the floor that she could see. No well-gnawed bones. No puddles of ale and other unmentionable substances.

Margaret sniffed. No stench of living either, if her nose told the tale true. Indeed, the place smelled very pleasant. Perhaps Alex's world was a cleaner place.

She sniffed again. "Ah," she said, her nose finding this new fragrance very much to its liking. "Jamie's cook has been at the fire."

"I smell brownies," Alex said, his own nose quivering in the air. "With any luck it'll be Joshua who's been cooking and not Zachary."

"Joshua?"

"Jamie's minstrel. He's very good at desserts."

"Jamie has a minstrel here in your world?"

"He came from the 1300s, like Jamie. He's English. You'll probably like him."

More traveling through blades of grass, she surmised. She shook her head. Either she had died and gone to a very earthy heaven, she had lost her mind completely, or she had indeed traveled to the future.

She wasn't sure which of the alternatives frightened her more.

She followed Alex across the great hall to what she assumed were the kitchens. She could hear the babble of voices, hearty laughter, and the sounds of cooking trappings banging together. It was the most reassuring thing she'd heard all day.

She paused before she reached the kitchen. The torches on the wall weren't torches. The fire was smooth, as if it were frozen in time. Indeed, she could almost fancy she saw fire flickering within the frozen fire.

"What . . . ?" she stammered.

"Lightbulb," Alex said. "It takes the place of candles. I'll tell you all about it later. Let's go eat first. We'll both feel better after a good snack."

Margaret nodded and let him pull her along, but she could hardly tear her gaze from those strange fires. Lightbulbs. 'Twas an odd term.

She stopped dead in her tracks at the entrance to the kitchens.

It was a large chamber, indeed a bit larger than her own humble place of cookery. There was a table in the midst of the room and benches set close for comfortable seating. But there was no hearth set into the wall, no fire with pots set to boiling over it, no barrels with grains and salted meat. The walls were lined with odd looking trunks set in at impossible angles and a pair of the very large boxes were covered with the same shiny substance that covered Alex's rovering baggage wain.

Margaret thought to ask where they kept the food, then she saw that there were dark brown items piled high on a plate.

"Brownies," Alex announced with satisfaction.

"Chocolate?" she asked.

"Oh, yeah." He nodded, dragging her forward.

As sinful as the Godiva balls, but chewier. Margaret worked her way through four or five, and found her nerves to be quite calmed by the aftereffects.

"Introduce me before my heart blows up," a voice said from across the room.

Margaret looked up in mid-brownie bite to find a

younger version of Alex standing across the table from her.

"My wife," Alex said, throwing a very proprietary arm around her shoulders, "Margaret. Margaret, that's Zachary, my younger brother."

"Wife?" Zachary choked, his eyes bugging out.

"You snooze, you lose," Alex said, sounding exceptionally smug.

"She's wearing mail," Zachary said, with undisguised admiration. "And a sword. Wow."

Well, she knew that word and it was a sure sign of a compliment. Margaret smiled, feeling better than she had all morning.

"And she knows how to use it," Alex warned, "so don't cross her. Or me, for that matter."

"Maybe she'd like to go sight-seeing," Zachary said, seemingly oblivious to the tightening of Alex's arm around her.

Margaret felt Alex shift, then heard the unmistakable sound of sword coming from scabbard. She watched in amazement as her husband brandished his sword at his brother.

"Don't even think about it."

"I'm sure Margaret can make up her own mind," Zachary insisted.

Alex turned his sword on her. "Don't you even think about it," he warned.

"I could take her sight-seeing," another man offered. Margaret looked at the man standing next to Jamie. He resembled Jamie so strongly, she had to assume he was Jamie's brother. "Patrick MacLeod," he said, with a low bow, "at your service, my lady."

"Nay, let it be me," another man said, leaping up from the table. He went down on bended knee. "Joshua MacLeod, minstrel to the Laird James MacLeod."

"Well," Margaret said, quite overcome.

"By the very saints in heaven," Joshua said, beating his breast with his fist, "I daresay I never thought to see another rival my lady Elizabeth for beauty, but I thought awrong! She, with the glory of the sun, and you, my lady Margaret, with the glory of the moon! Oh, blessed saints, my poor eyes are overcome with the beauty that surrounds me on all sides! Indeed, I should be the one to take you and show you the sights, lady, that I might gaze upon your loveliness and compose lays worthy of your beauty.''

Margaret could only gape at him in astonishment.

"I made the brownies, too," Joshua added.

Margaret factored that bit of news into her thinking. A minstrel who could also make concoctions worthy of a king's palate. Perhaps the twentieth century would be more to her liking than she thought. She opened her mouth to bargain away her presence for another plate of the food-stuffs only to find herself being pulled toward the door.

"*I'll* take her," Alex bellowed as he dragged her along behind him. "We're going to go get settled in."

Margaret smiled to herself as she followed her grumbling husband up the stairs. She counted on her free hand three men who had vied for her attentions, and that didn't include the snarling man who was cursing all three heartily as he made his way up the stairs.

The future was shaping up to be a very nice place indeed.

Thirty-one

❧✦❧

ALEX WOKE TO COMPLETE DARKNESS. WELL, IT WAS OB-
viously too early to get up. He wondered if opening his
eyes might shed more light on the time, then realized his
eyes were open. Definitely too early to get up.

He rolled toward Margaret only to flop his arm over an
empty bed. He squinted at the numbers on his alarm clock,
half surprised at how easy it had been to reaccustom himself to looking for it. 4:30. So Margaret had finally eluded
him long enough to go exploring. Alex shuddered to think
about what she'd gotten into already while he'd been
sleeping so peacefully. Hopefully she wasn't wandering
around outside the keep, tripping over gates in the grass.

He sat up with a jerk, then fumbled for the bedside
lamp. Margaret's sword was still propped up against the
chair where she'd left it the night before. He lay back with
a sigh of relief. One, she was still there. Two, she'd obviously given up on poking things with her blade to test
their mettle before she touched them.

He crawled from the bed and managed to find rumpled
sweats to put on. His search for slippers was futile, so he
settled for socks. Ah, the comforts of modern life.

He almost took the socks back off again. No sense in
spoiling himself.

He shut his bedroom door and looked down the hallway.
Jamie's study door was open. Alex knew what trouble he'd
gotten himself into by loitering there, so he quickly walked
down the hall to save his wife from the same. He stopped

at the doorway. He couldn't help but just stand there and smile at what he saw.

Margaret was sitting in Jamie's chair with a dagger in one hand and a book in the other. She was wearing a heavy sweater, boxer shorts, wool socks, and Snoopy slippers— all things filched from his armoire. Alex sighed. He was doomed to live with women who found his clothes much more interesting than their own. Margaret had a blanket draped over one leg, but the other was bare and hooked over the arm of the chair. Snoopy's ears flopped as she swung her leg back and forth. She read with complete concentration, absently reaching up to scratch the side of her head with the hilt of her dagger.

At least she'd pared down her arsenal to just a dagger. Alex had wondered there for a while if Jamie's hall would survive what Margaret was packing. This was the first time in two days he hadn't seen her roaming the hall with her sword bared and ready.

After brownies that first day, he'd managed to get her upstairs and down for a little nap. He'd figured she needed it and he'd known he needed it. He'd fallen asleep in spite of his intentions to watch over her, then woken only to find her in the bathroom, poking her sword down the toilet.

Things hadn't improved much from there.

Margaret had eaten lunch with one hand while investigating—at sword's length of course—everything in Jamie's kitchen. Alex had barely stopped her from sticking the blade into an electrical outlet. After that narrow brush with death, she'd herded Frances, Amery, Joel, and Baldric into a little group with the efficiency of a sheepdog and tried to keep them behind her as she scoped out the rest of the hall. It hadn't lasted long. Amery had escaped up to young Ian's room to fall into raptures over the best FAO Schwartz had to offer. Frances had begun trailing Elizabeth like a shadow and was soon seen to be up to her elbows in cookie dough. Baldric had sized up Joshua, then challenged him to a contest of verses. Joshua had opened with a Beatles' lyric and Baldric had countered with "Two,

Four, Six, Eight, Who do we all love to hate? Brackwald, Brackwald, Yeech!''

Alex had quickly left them to it.

Joel had remained by his side like the dutiful squire he was, clutching Alex's folded surcoat and taking in everything he saw with wide eyes.

So had passed Day One in the future. Day Two had begun promptly at dawn, and only that late because Alex had spent most of the night making love to his wife to keep her in bed. Where she came by her energy he didn't know, but she was up with the sun, preparing another assault on the twentieth century. The only difference was, she left behind her mail and her sword. But the dagger had been used liberally, followed by her fingers. And followed then by her questions, which were endless.

Alex had hardly known what to expect of his wife when he'd decided to return for a visit. Uncertainty? Unease?

As he stood and watched her devour a book and a movie at the same time, he realized he had misjudged her. She was fearless. He'd known that, but he hadn't known just how deep the trait ran. She assaulted his world with the same force she did her own. How he could have expected anything less, he didn't know.

She jumped in her chair, startling him. He looked at the TV screen and saw The Blob about to overtake and consume yet another victim.

''Yikes,'' Alex said, with a shiver.

Faster than he could follow, she had her dagger by the tip of the blade and her arm poised to fling it at him. He held up his hands in surrender.

''Just me,'' he said, ready to duck.

She looked at him narrowly. ''Come to drag me back to bed?''

''You didn't complain last night.''

She flipped her dagger up and caught it by the hilt on the way down, then laid it on the arm of the chair. ''Indeed, I didn't. 'Twas a most pleasant way to pass the time.

Then again," she added, with another glance at the TV, "I knew not what I was missing here."

"I've been replaced by a B movie," Alex said, walking over to her. "I'm insulted." He bent and kissed the top of her head. "What else have you watched?"

"*The Wizard of Oz,* though I tell you, Alex, I cared not a whit for that one witch. A most unpleasant creature. But," she said, brightening, "the next play is one called *Invasion of the Body Snatchers.* They have claimed it to be most entertaining."

Right, and if she saw that, she'd never look at any of them the same way again. He knew he'd never looked at Donald Sutherland the same way afterward.

"Why don't we go back to bed?" Alex suggested, reaching for the remote.

"Oh, nay," she said, batting his hand away, "The Blob has yet things to ingest, no doubt. And I haven't finished this manuscript yet. 'Tis most interesting, though I surely don't believe some of the things I've seen."

Alex glanced at the book now in her lap. She was halfway through *A Pictorial History of the Twentieth Century.*

"This business of the atomic bomb," she said with a shake of her head. "It seems most unsporting." She flipped back through pages until she found one showing the destruction of Hiroshima. "And to think there are so many of them just waiting to be exploded on unsuspecting folk."

"Not all man's inventions have been good ones."

"I can see that. Now," she said, turning back to the page she'd been studying, "who decided what the moon looked like up close?"

He smiled. "No one decided. Man flew up there and took a picture."

She frowned at him. "Impossible. Who has that kind of strength?"

"They blasted the men off the Earth with a rocket with enough fuel to get them there and back." He smiled at her look of skepticism. "They landed on the moon, took a few pictures, picked up a few rocks, and flew home.''

She snorted. '' 'Tis a tale only Baldric could imagine up in his twisted mind.''

''No, it's really true. In fact, that's how my parents are going to get here.''

''By flying?''

''Exactly.''

''Impossible.''

''It's true.''

She paused and considered. ''Can I see inside one of the beasts?''

''Maybe. I'll see what I can arrange. *If*,'' he added, ''you come back to bed with me now.''

She was torn, he could see that. Then she looked up at him. ''May I read now in bed?''

''We'll see how long you manage to concentrate,'' he promised.

''I am always in control of myself,'' she said primly, closing the book around her finger to keep her place and rising with dignity.

''Ha,'' he said, remembering all too well just how undone she'd been the night before—before she'd managed to sneak from his bed to watch TV.

''I allowed you to distract me.''

''Lying isn't nice, Meg.''

She stuck her nose in the air and took her Snoopy-covered feet down the hallway. ''Try as you will, my lord, I'll not be bested by you.''

Well, that sounded like a challenge, and one he wasn't going to pass up.

SEVERAL HOURS, AND a distraction or two later, Alex stood next to his Ranger Rover with keys in hand and questioned the wisdom of what he currently contemplated. Margaret was staring at his vehicle with the same expression she used while sizing up an unsavory bug in her flour barrels. He walked over to her and began to frisk her again. She scowled at him.

"I've brought nothing with me."

"I'm just groping you for the fun of it," he lied, bending to peer into her boots. Finding them comfortingly empty, he straightened and smiled at her. "Let's check under that tunic one more time—"

"Enough," she said crossly. "I gave you my word I would not stick anything into this beast of yours."

"It's not that I don't trust you. It's just that you haven't heard the noise it makes."

Alex looked behind his wife to find the rest of the household gathered on the steps watching with great interest. Alex was hoping to slip away before Amery noticed anything besides that Tonka truck he was fondling. Leaving the rest of them behind didn't look to be a problem. Baldric was busily unraveling a thrift-store sweater, probably gearing up for another round with Joshua. Elizabeth had Frances under control, and Jamie was trying to lure Joel away by promising a lesson in swordplay. Joel had remained unimpressed until Jamie had brought out a six-foot Claymore he'd unearthed during the reconstruction of the hall. There had been lots of little goodies like that, and Jamie had tried to distract Joel with them one by one. Alex watched as his squire promptly turned from him and followed the Claymore into the garden like a charmed snake.

"I'll pop the hood and turn it on," Alex said, dragging his attention back to the problem at hand. "Just don't, and I mean do *not*, stick anything—fingers or blades—into the engine when it's running."

Margaret looked ready to protest, so Alex gave it to her straight.

"The engine will grab your hand, pull it in, and chew it off."

She tucked her hands under her arms.

"Or your hair," he added, hoping to impress upon her just how dangerous it was. "Suck your head right off before you knew what was happening."

She took a pace back and looked at the Range Rover with new respect.

Alex started the engine up, then popped the hood. He held out his hand to her.

"Come look. The noise is just a lot of metal and things grinding."

"And the horses?"

"It's how they used to measure the power of the car. Horsepower. How many horses it would take to power the car. Get it?"

She nodded, then pulled her hand from his and tucked it back under her arm. "Fascinating."

"Wanna go for a ride?"

She looked at him with wide eyes. "Get inside it?"

"The passenger part is perfectly safe."

"As you say, husband."

Alex shut the hood and put her into the passenger seat. He hoped he'd removed all her hardware. The first time Jamie had gotten into a car, he'd cut his way out of the seat belt to escape. Alex hoped to avoid that, though he wondered why he bothered. It wasn't as if he'd be needing the car in the past.

"Okay," he said, getting in and shutting the door. "Now all we do is put it in gear and it goes."

"Without horses," she said, sounding awestruck.

Alex almost said "it sure beats a saddle," but he stopped himself just in time. There was something to be said for riding a horse. It certainly could be a more scenic way to travel.

Margaret seemed to take the whole thing fairly well. And when it started to rain, she put her hand under the windshield to feel it, then blinked in surprise when the rain hit the glass. Alex watched her consider that, then sit back and digest.

"It has its advantages," he conceded.

"So I see," she murmured.

It was a short trip to the village. Alex parked, then opened Margaret's door for her. She looked past him to a little antique shop.

"By the saints, what is that?" she asked, stretching out her hands and walking to the window.

Alex looked in the display window and tried to second-guess what she was gaping at. "Um, which thing?"

She ran her hands over the window. "This. This huge piece of glass." She looked stunned. "How do they fashion it so smoothly? And how does it remain here in spite of the storms?"

Alex shrugged helplessly. "They've just gotten better at it over the years."

"Hmmm," she said, and pulled away. " 'Tis a most amazing thing."

But she didn't look all that happy about it. Alex decided on distraction. She was probably tired with all the excitement of the last couple of days. He would show her around, feed her lunch, then take her home for another nap. And maybe he would manage to keep his hands to himself long enough to let her sleep this time.

And so they wandered from shop to shop. Alex stopped the moment she showed any interest at all and made mental notes of the things that pleased her. Beast could carry a few surprises home for them. Alex planned on having a lot of anniversaries to need presents for.

After ten minutes in a bookstore, she begged to go.

" 'Tis more than I can bear," she said, stumbling out into the street. "By the saints, Alex, a man could read forever and never read it all."

"That's probably true."

"Let us find an inn and beg a meal," she said, putting her arms around him. "I think I need something substantial."

"I know just the place."

He drove her to an inn at the far end of the village. It was the first place Jamie and Elizabeth had come after their trip forward in time. If there was anyone who could put Margaret at ease in 1998, it was the innkeeper with nerves of steel, Roddy MacLeod.

"Why, Alexander," Roddy said, opening the door with

a broad smile. " 'Tis a pleasure to see you, my lad."

"My lord Falconberg," Margaret corrected automatically, but her eyes were already searching out the entryway for new discoveries.

Alex met Roddy's startled eyes and smiled. "I'm afraid she's right. This is my wife, Margaret of Falconberg."

"Countess," Margaret added, easing past Roddy.

Roddy only smiled the smile of a man who'd ceased to be surprised by anything.

"A trip through the forest then?"

"Faery ring."

Roddy chuckled. "Ah, Laird Jamie is a one for stirring up mischief, is he not?"

"Well, this at least was good mischief. I never would have met Margaret otherwise."

"We were just about to sit down for a wee bite. Care to join us?"

"If it wouldn't be any trouble."

"Not at all. Who wouldn't be pleased to have an earl and his countess for a late lunch?"

They sat at Roddy's table with his wife and a couple of his sons, and Alex relaxed and smiled at the relating of village gossip. He'd spent quite a bit of time in Roddy's inn after Elizabeth's return, and it felt very much like home.

"Off with ye, lads," Roddy said, waving his sons away after lunch. "See to the table, then finish your other chores."

"I've a thing or two to see to myself," Roddy's wife said, rising and leaving her sons to the dishes.

"Let's take our ease in the parlor," Roddy said, rising. "If it pleases Your Lordship?"

Alex smiled at the teasing and nodded regally for Roddy's benefit.

They hadn't had but a cup of tea before Margaret looked at Roddy.

"Who is king in this day?"

Alex hid his smile behind his cup. He'd heard in glorious detail Jamie's reaction to the political situation. "I think she'll take this news better than Jamie did," he offered.

Roddy took a deep breath. "There is no king, my lady. At least not yet."

Margaret frowned. "What nonsense is this?"

" 'Tis a queen who sits the throne." He looked at Alex. "I'm certain I've said that before."

"And had Jamie threaten anarchy, no doubt," Alex added.

"A queen," Margaret said, smiling. "Why, 'tis a fine thing indeed."

"There have been several queens before her," Roddy added. "Ruling as ably as men, to be sure."

"Of course," Margaret said, as if anything else was unthinkable.

Alex smiled at the sight of her smugness. It was the first real pleasure he'd seen her take in the day. He should have brought her to Roddy's sooner.

"I believe such strong women likely began with Eleanor of Acquitaine," Roddy postulated, "even though she wasn't the sole ruler. 'Tis said she was a most imposing woman."

"Aye, she seemed that way to me the last time I saw her," Margaret agreed.

Roddy seemed momentarily startled, then shrugged it aside and plunged into glorious recountings of the English monarchy. Alex only listened with half an ear. He couldn't take his eyes from his wife. He'd once called her intoxicating. Now, he wondered if that did her justice. She stole his breath. Watching her sitting in that well-worn chair in an inn listening to tales that would happen long after she had died, Alex could hardly bear it. It was all he could do not to throw Roddy out of his own solar and take Margaret right there before the fireplace.

"Alex, you're flushed."

Alex found Margaret watching him, a frown wrinkling her perfect brow.

"Are you unwell?"

"In need of a nap, I think," he offered. "When you're ready to go."

Maybe he would do better to nap right where he was. He certainly didn't want to waste any time with it later.

To think he would have this woman for the rest of his life.

He'd done nothing to deserve her, but unrepentant pirate that he was, he had no intentions of giving her up on that technicality. She was his, damn it.

And he'd do whatever he had to to keep her.

Thirty-two

MARGARET STOOD AT THE ENTRANCE TO THE KITCHEN and stared bleakly at the green numbers on the microwave that gave faint illumination to the chamber. Another modern invention. Another miracle she would be depriving Alex of. He hadn't said as much, but she was certain his thinking ran along the same lines. In another few days he would come with her to the faery ring, step through the blades of grass, and leave behind him a life of comfort and wonder.

She walked into the kitchen, trailing her hand over whatever she encountered: cabinets that held foodstuffs up off the floor, the cooling box that kept perishables fresh long past when they should have given themselves over to mold, the stove that provided instant fire on command. The last still gave her chills when she thought on it. Though Alex claimed that an invisible substance was brought into the stove through metal tubes, and it was a very natural and logical thing, she couldn't help but feel as if someone worked magic in her presence each time a flame leaped to life. How stunned Cook would have been at the sight of such a thing.

Margaret stopped at the table and rested her hands on its sturdy, worn surface. Though she'd only eaten a handful of meals at this board, they had been fine ones, made even more so by the company. She had grown very fond of Jamie and Elizabeth, and even the other members of Jamie's household had made a favorable impression upon her. It seemed a terrible thing to pull Alex from his family, especially when he had the chance to see his parents. They were set to arrive the following week.

Her heart grew heavier at the thought of that. She could pull him away from the companionship of his sister and though it would grieve her, it wasn't anything that didn't happen in her day. Sisters were sent as brides to other keeps, or other countries for that matter, and to be sure some of them never saw their homeland again. But to ask him to give up his parents was something else.

She left the kitchen and made her way across the great hall to the stairs. She shook her head as she mounted them to the upper floor. Even the stairs were better fashioned here, smooth and well laid. And with more room for stepping. Margaret now wondered how she ever made it down hers at home without plunging down to her death. And Alex's feet were to be sure larger than hers.

Yet another item of interest for him to leave behind.

She walked down the passageway to Jamie's solar, her feet dragging. She managed to light one of the little lamps on the desk before she sat down heavily in Jamie's chair and dropped her face into her hands. Saints, but she could hardly bear to do what she knew she had to. With a groan, she leaned back against the chair and closed her eyes against the truth.

She could not stay.

And she could not ask Alex to come back with her.

She'd thought she could, at first. Her first pair of days in the future she'd been certain of it. After all, even though the future had very interesting enticements, so did London. There were still wonders to be seen and sampled in her century.

And then had come the Range Rover. As Margaret had traveled a fair distance in the rain yet remained perfectly dry and comfortable, she began to see that perhaps the future could indeed offer simple comforts that she could not hope to match. That had unsettled her, but she'd convinced herself soon enough that Alex could stand to be out in the elements more. It would be good for him.

And then she'd seen the glass on the merchant's shop window. It had been at that moment that she realized just what she was asking him to give up. By the saints, she didn't even own panes of glass for her windows! The one poor bit of the stuff she had was tucked into a place of honor in that pitiful outbuilding her grandsire had dubbed the chapel.

It occurred to her that if she'd spent more time there, perhaps on her knees, she might not have found herself in her current state of hell.

Smooth, clear glass. Shops that brought every wonder imaginable practically to a man's gates. Television that brought tidings from near and far straight into a man's keep. Strange and marvelous foodstuffs. Saints, even Godiva balls whenever a body had a hankering for one!

How could she possibly ask him to leave all that for the barbaric conditions of 1194?

He had a life here, a life that had to be lived. And she had a life there, a life that she couldn't escape. She could not turn her back on her responsibilities. Now, knowing what he had here, neither could she ask him to share in those responsibilities.

"Margaret?"

She nearly jumped from her skin. She whipped around to face her husband. "Aye?"

He smiled sleepily from the door. "I missed you. Come back to bed."

Ah, by the saints, she should have run while he was still asleep! But how could she have, when this was precisely what she'd waited for? One last chance to lay with the man she loved more than life itself.

She rose and fair threw herself into his arms. She clung to him and memorized exactly how it felt to held by those strong arms, to hear the sound of his voice rough against her ear, to know that he loved her as much as she loved him.

"Love me," she said, blindly seeking his mouth with her own. "Love me now, Alex."

Bless the man, he never had to hear that twice. Before she could squeak, he had swept her up into his arms and was stalking down the passageway. Margaret threw her arms around his neck and held on. She had to remember everything about him, every detail of his touch, of his smell, of his voice. It would be the only thing to give her comfort as she lived out the rest of her life without him.

He laid her on the bed, then stretched out next to her. His touch was so gentle and loving she might have wept had she not been so busy touching him in return, reminding herself a last time of the shape and feel of his form.

She did weep, though, as he made love to her, for she knew it would be the last time. To be sure, it was the most perfect joining of their bodies to date, and she couldn't help but feel as if their souls had been joined as well. Perhaps that was a good thing. After she'd lived her life and he'd lived his, they would meet up again in some better world and love yet again.

He rolled away and gathered her to him. "Don't go anywhere else tonight," he murmured as he lifted her face for his kiss.

She could only nod, for she wouldn't lie with words.

"I love you, Meg," he whispered.

"And I love you," she said, fighting her tears. "And I'll never stop."

"Neither will I," he said, giving her a gentle squeeze. "Let's sleep for a little, okay?"

"As you will, husband."

She waited until she felt him drift off. Once she was sure he wouldn't stir, she rose. She drew on his sweater, boxers, and woolen socks. That done silently enough, she retrieved her sword, the dagger he'd bought her in London, and then paused. She looked at his jeans lying over the arm of a chair, then shrugged and put them on. He could buy more. These she would treasure as if they'd been fashioned of gold.

She retrieved the missive she'd written him and left it on the chair next to the fire. Cowardly, aye, but she knew if she told him of her plan he would never agree to it. It was best she make the choice for him.

She gathered up the rest of her blades, then left the chamber. She put on her boots outside his door, then paused. It was tempting to take one last look at the souls she planned to leave behind, but what good would that serve? It would not change her mind about leaving, and it would not change her plan to leave them behind.

Amery would be safer here. Alex could adopt him and treat him as his own son. Frances already had taken to 1998 cooking styles and was happily installed in a chamber of her own. Joel could not be persuaded to leave his beloved master and that was as it should be.

Baldric worried her, for she knew he liked it well when she was there to listen to his verses, but she'd also watched him the night before sitting next to Joshua as Joshua made magic with words on some type of television screen. "A rhyming program that is Windows 95 compatible," Baldric had announced with a beatific smile. Margaret knew not the meaning of that, but she suspected Baldric would be far better off with his large white box than he would be with her.

Nay, 'twas best she leave them be, those souls she loved best. She clomped down the steps, cursing as she continued to have to hitch up Alex's jeans. She should have filched a belt while she was at it.

She left the hall before she could think better of it. The remainder of her gear she had stowed in the stables. Alex had asked about it, but she'd done no more than to lie and tell him she'd pressed Joel into seeing to it.

Once she'd reached the stables, she removed Alex's sweater and carefully placed it in her saddlebag. She donned her own padded undertunic, then slipped into her mail shirt. Once her horse was saddled, she left the stables and mounted in Jamie's courtyard. She gave the keep one last look, then put her heels to her mount and rode out the front gate.

She didn't look back.

ALEX WOKE, SATED and exhausted. Good grief, if making love with Margaret got any better than it was at present, it would kill him. But what a way to go.

He rolled toward his wife only to find her place empty. He sat up slowly and rubbed his eyes. Maybe once they got home he would actually wake up and find her still in bed. The lures of the twentieth century were obviously too much for her. Heaven only knew what she'd found to watch on TV. He listened carefully. He didn't hear any giggling, so it was a safe bet she hadn't found any Jerry Lewis reruns. For as long as he'd known her he'd never heard her giggle until the night before.

It had been all the more surprising given her mood. He wasn't up to speculating why she'd seemed depressed after their trip to the village. Weariness was certainly one answer. She couldn't have slept more than a few hours each night for the past few nights. He briefly considered hormones, then decided that wasn't a safe place for him to loiter. He certainly didn't want another chauvinist lecture from his sister when he brought it up. Maybe he could convince his wife to have a substantial nap that afternoon.

He stumbled to the bathroom, then returned, relieved and a bit more awake. Well, his boxers and sweater were gone, but his Snoopy slippers were still there. Alex reached for his jeans only to realize they weren't there anymore. Wonderful. Now the woman was starting to steal his pants, too.

Alex pulled on sweats, put on his slippers, and headed for Jamie's study to rescue his wife from whatever B movie currently held her captive.

But she wasn't in Jamie's study.

"Okay," he said slowly, frowning. "No TV, no books. Breakfast?"

It didn't sound like a bad idea on the whole, so he

headed downstairs for the kitchen. Jamie was at the table, plowing through a bowl of porridge he'd no doubt made himself. Elizabeth wasn't a morning person and she certainly wasn't an oatmeal kind of gal, so Jamie had been forced to see to his own breakfasts. Jamie looked up at him and shoved the pot and another bowl across the table.

"Saved some for you and Margaret," he said around a mouthful of mush.

"I thought she'd be here already."

Jamie shook his head. "Haven't seen her."

Alex frowned. "She's not upstairs."

"Maybe she went for a walk."

"Yeah," Alex said, feeling unaccountably relieved. "And with any luck she stayed away from the forest."

"A body can hope."

Alex ate half a dozen spoonfuls of porridge straight from the pan, then left the kitchen to grab his coat and shoes fit for a Scottish spring. He was halfway out into the hallway when he realized something.

Her sword was gone.

He whipped around and stared into his bedroom. Her sword was gone, along with the small collection of knives she'd been storing on top of an end table. Alex walked across the room slowly, wondering absently in the back of his mind why it was he had the overwhelming urge to throw up.

There was a note sitting on the table. Alex reached for it with hands that weren't the slightest bit steady.

My beloved Alex,

I cannot stay and I cannot ask you to return with me. I know what it is to lose your Family and I cannot have you give yours up when there is a way I can prevent it. And I cannot beg you to come now that I know What you would be Giving Up. I have no Panes of Glass for my windows!

*I leave my Heart in your hands. Return it to me when
we both reach that Far Better World to come. I will
await your Pleasure there.*

Margaret

Alex stared at the letter in horror. The blood thundered
in his ears, and he thought he just might lose it. He had
never lost it. Never. No matter what murkiness he'd found
himself in, no matter what losses he'd sustained, never
once had he lost control of himself. But now he thought
he might be on the verge of it. He knew his mouth was
open and his breath was coming in gasps and his blood
was still pounding in his ears. It was the only way he knew
he was still alive.

She'd left him.

"Alex!"

Alex felt a heavy hand come down hard on his shoulder
and he was spun around forcibly.

He looked at Jamie and found no words to express the
raging cyclone of emotion inside him.

"You were screaming," Jamie said grimly.

"Was I?" Alex rasped.

"Aye. What are the tidings?"

Alex shoved the note at his brother-in-law. He shut his
mouth to avoid any other verbal indications of his terror.

"Alex, I've no idea what to say—"

Alex shook off Jamie's hand. His sanity returned with
a rush. "Doesn't matter. I'll just gather up the crew and
we'll head for the faery ring. I'll be there two hours behind
her."

"Alex, I cannot guarantee that 'twill wor—"

"Don't," Alex said sharply. "Don't even say it." He
pushed past Jamie and started to yell. "Baldric! Joel!
Frances, pack up Amery and let's get going!"

Alex shoved past Jamie and dug around in his armoire
for a clean pair of jeans. He shucked off his sweats with
shaking hands. He jerked his clothes on, put on his boots

and took a last look around his room. Joel was in charge of his sword, so that was something off his list. He would have liked to have been a bit more prepared as far as taking things with him went, but there was no time for it now. Perhaps this was for the best. He'd go back to 1194 the same way he had the first time—with only the clothes on his back.

It took him almost an hour to get everyone loaded up, and by then he was almost frantic. Elizabeth and Jamie stood on the steps, watching with matching expressions of grief.

Once Alex had everyone mounted, he walked back up the steps and embraced his brother-in-law.

"Come if you can," he said hoarsely. "I'll miss you."

"Alex," Jamie said slowly, "I don't think—"

"Enough!" Alex exclaimed. He pulled away. "I will get back to her. I _will_ and nothing you can say will stop me."

Jamie sighed, then nodded. "As you will, brother. A good journey to you."

Alex embraced his sister. She was crying and he was on the verge of it. He pulled back, kissed her soundly, then walked away without a backward glance. He mounted, then led his little group through the gates and back toward the pond and the faery ring.

He would get back. Anything else was out of the question. Margaret was his life. Without her he might as well be dead and that was something the Gatekeeper of Time had to realize.

And if he didn't realize it, Alex would take a blade to him.

Thirty-three

❧❦❧

ELIZABETH STOOD AT THE THRESHOLD OF HER HALL WITH her husband by her side and stared at the gate her brother had ridden through only a few moments earlier.

"It won't work, will it?" she asked softly.

Jamie's arm came around her shoulders. "I think not, my love."

"Oh, Jamie," Elizabeth said, leaning her head against his shoulder. "I feel so responsible for this. If we hadn't asked Alex to come back, they would still be together in her time."

"He's his own man, Beth. He chose to come."

"But he didn't choose for her to leave without him."

"Nay, he didn't." Jamie sighed. "He could have gone back with her if they'd gone together. I'm fairly certain of that. 'Tis her place in her time that would have drawn them back."

"What was she thinking?" Elizabeth asked, wishing she could bang Alex and Margaret's heads together and knock sense into both of them. "Doesn't she realize how much he loves her?"

"Ah, but I daresay 'tis precisely for that reason that she left."

Elizabeth looked up at her husband and frowned. "How do you figure?"

Jamie smiled, pained. " 'Tis an age of marvels we live in, Beth. Margaret said herself that she couldn't pull Alex from them."

"What kind of wimp does she think he is? He can live without the Range Rover!"

Jamie drew her into his arms and hugged her. "Och, my bonny Beth, you judge her too harshly. She knows he loves her, else she would have left while he was awake. She knew he would try to follow her. She merely wishes him to be well and happy, and she likely fears he will not be in her time."

"The twentieth century isn't all it's cracked up to be."

He laughed then. "And now you'll tell me that you didn't come fair to fainting with relief when you realized you'd be birthing your bairns in a hospital, not in my bed."

"Well . . ."

"Or that you were happy to see my days of lifting cattle and riding the borders to be finished."

Elizabeth rested her cheek against her husband's chest and held on to him. She certainly couldn't deny she had been happy to come back home. Or how grateful she was to have him and the hospital down the road both in the same century. She was fortunate and she knew it.

By the same token, she honestly couldn't blame Margaret for her choice, because it was probably the same choice she would have made in her shoes.

" 'Twas a most unselfish thing she did, Beth," Jamie murmured.

"It was a colossally stupid thing she did," Elizabeth whispered. "He'll never survive it."

"He'll have to."

Elizabeth looked up at him. "Does she have things still to take care of, do you think?"

"Aye, I'd imagine so."

"We could try to take Alex back with us some other time." She nodded. "Yes, that's it. Let's go back with him, Jamie."

"Beth," he said softly, lifting his hand to brush her hair back from her face, "there is no guarantee. You know that as well as I do. What if we arrive too soon and she knows him not?''

''She'll fall in love with him anyway.''

''She won't let him past the door. And if we arrive much later, who's to say what will have happened? Besides, we have no more business in medieval England.''

''You don't know that,'' she said, but even as she said it, she knew he did know. Whatever part of Jamie's soul was tied up to the land was the same part of his soul that knew where he was needed. ''We could make a special trip.''

''And what happened when we made that unnecessary trip to Barbados? And, aye, I freely admit that was my doing.''

They'd barely escaped with their lives, but Elizabeth wasn't about to give him the satisfaction of that answer.

''And what about trying to see Jesse again?'' Jamie asked softly. ''Think on that, Beth, if the other fails to convince you.''

That was a trip she couldn't even bear to think about, much less discuss with Jamie. She'd had a bad feeling about it, and so had he, but she'd gone with him because he had so desperately wanted to see his son again.

She sighed. ''Well, we could at least go look up a few things in the library. If nothing else, we can assure him she never married again and that she had a good life.''

''Aye,'' Jamie said gently, ''we could do that much.''

Elizabeth took her husband's hand and again felt a wash of gratitude that she could do as much.

Her heart broke that Alex would never have that chance again.

''MY LORD, I fear young Amery has needs he must take care of,'' Frances ventured hesitantly. ''He complains most fiercely.''

Alex stared at Amery and saw that was indeed the case. The kid was kicking up a major fuss. Alex found it in him to wonder why he hadn't noticed it before.

"All right," he said, staring up at the sky. "Just don't go outside the ring."

Amery's sigh of relief at the emptying of his bladder should have teased a smile from even the most hard-hearted of men. Alex would have smiled if he could have, but he couldn't. He was too numb.

Alex, I don't think it will work.

Jamie had tried to tell him. Alex hadn't wanted to believe it.

He *still* didn't want to believe it. He would get them home if it killed him to do it.

"Let's concentrate," he said, focusing all his mental energy on Margaret's castle. "Think about home."

"Food," Amery demanded.

"Yes, Cook's pasties," Alex agreed.

"Lucky Charms," Amery countered.

"Here, Amery," Frances said, soothingly. "Here's a Ding-Dong. Just as good, aye?"

Alex stared at the Ding-Dong with growing horror. Maybe that was what was keeping them in the twentieth century. He fell from his horse, snatched the treat from Frances, and flung it into the forest.

"Any more?" he demanded.

She was quaking in her slippers. She pointed to her saddlebag.

Alex threw an entire stash of junk food outside the faery ring to howls of protest from Amery. Alex ignored him and turned on Joel.

"What about you? Got any contraband?"

Joel's eyes were big as saucers. With a shaking hand, he drew forth a dagger that Jamie had obviously given him. Well, it wasn't a Swiss Army knife so Alex let it pass. He turned to Baldric. The clicking of knitting needles was like machine-gun fire in the stillness of the glade. Alex held out his hand.

"Hand them over."

Baldric looked down his nose at him from atop his horse. "Nay."

It had been Elizabeth's idea to teach Baldric to knit, damn her. It kept him away from her chenille throws, but it was also probably keeping them all away from the twelfth century.

"We have to leave them behind," Alex announced.

Baldric clicked more furiously. "I think not, my lord."

"Baldric," Alex warned.

Without warning, Baldric stuffed the needles down the front of his tunic. "Nay," he said petulantly. "They were a gift from the lady Elizabeth to me personally."

"The yarn, then."

Baldric clutched the ball of pale pink angora to his chest and looked at Alex in horror. "By the very saints of heaven, you've lost your wits!" he exclaimed.

"You're right!" Alex shouted back. "I've lost every last one of them, and they're all in a pile around me here in this damned faery ring! And you're not helping!"

Baldric huffed at him, thoroughly offended. "My poor string has nothing to do with this. 'Twas a gift made especially to me by the lady Elizabeth."

Which was seemingly tantamount to a gift from the queen herself, if the frequency of his repeating it was any indication.

"Hell," Alex growled.

Baldric pulled his needles back out and set back to work on what looked like it might turn into a scarf. "I don't know why we don't return to Lady Elizabeth's keep and wait there for our Margaret. She'll come when she's ready."

"She won't," Alex said, wishing that weren't the case.

"Of course she will," Baldric said firmly. "How will she get along without my verses? Surely she didn't leave me behind apurpose."

Oh, the logic of a bard with steel in his hands. Alex turned in time to see Amery roaming well outside the faery ring, gathering up all the junk food he could with his two chubby little hands and carrying it back to Frances's horse. Frances tried to stop him, but his protests were almost deafening. She gave up and bowed her head in shame.

Alex felt his irritation leave as quickly as it had come. These sweet souls weren't responsible for any of this. He looked up at his squire and managed a faint smile.

"It's okay, Joel. Sorry I yelled."

Joel nodded, his eyes still huge in his pale little face. Alex walked over to Frances and put his arms around her.

"I'm sorry, honey," he said, brushing his hand over her hair. "I'm not angry with you."

"I never meant to do wrong," she whispered, starting to cry.

"Oh, Frances," Alex said, patting her back, "you didn't do wrong. You're more than welcome to take whatever you want home with you. I guess maybe we should pack it in for the day. We'll try again tomorrow."

Frances looked up at him with tear-filled eyes. "Think you she returned to Falconberg, my lord?"

Well, that's what he'd thought at first. For the briefest of moments he wondered if she'd just tried and not succeeded. Maybe she was back at the keep wondering what was keeping him so long outside.

But as quickly as that thought came, it left. Margaret never did anything by halves. If she intended to return home, then return home she would.

"I think she did," he answered finally. "And we'll follow her just as soon as we can."

"Tomorrow?" Joel asked hopefully from behind him.

Alex looked up at the sky. It was very late in the afternoon. They'd been in the ring since midmorning and nothing had happened. It wasn't going to do any good to stay any longer. He could feel it. He had the same feeling of emptiness he'd had when he'd tried to get back to the twentieth century. But at least then he hadn't really had anything to get home to.

Unlike now.

"Yes, tomorrow," Alex said.

He helped Amery gather up all Frances's snacks, saw everyone mounted and settled, then turned back to the keep. Maybe it would work tomorrow. Maybe he would have to go alone. Maybe he would hop on a passing Pegasus and just fly there.

Unfortunately, all three sounded equally improbable.

HE SAW TO the horses himself after sending the rest of his little ragtag family back up to the keep. It was well past dark when he finally allowed himself to go inside. The smell of dinner hit him square in the nose, and he had a brief flash of regret that he wouldn't enjoy twentieth-century cooking again.

"No, that was a flash of joy," he corrected himself. Thank heavens he would only have to put up with twentieth-century cooking for one more night. He could slurp his way through one more of Jamie's breakfasts and then he'd be on his way home. He toyed with ideas of what he would do to his wife first. Making love was definitely high on the list, though equally appealing was the thought of spanking her until she couldn't sit. Barbaric, yes, but he was a medieval earl and he had a reputation to live up to. At least making a list of possibilities would give him something constructive to do with his time at the moment. By the time he got to Falconberg, he would have quite a selection to choose from and could take great pleasure in deciding where to start.

The kitchen was unusually quiet. Not even Amery and Ian were throwing food at each other. Frances and Joel looked up at him as one, their expressions troubled. Alex could feel the tension in the air and sensed that they were wanting him to say something comforting.

Alex sat down next to his brother. "Fiona stand you up, buddy?"

"How'd you know?" Zachary asked crossly.

"Dumb luck. And my unfailing belief that there is justice in the world." He helped himself to stew. "Smells good. Who cooked?"

"My own humble self," Jamie's brother said, smiling

faintly. "Enjoy it while you can. You'll probably not taste anything so fine for the rest of your life."

"Well, Patrick, I can hope," Alex returned, then applied himself to his meal. There was very little small talk going on, but he chalked it up to his family not knowing what to say about the events of the day. Alex finished three helpings of stew, downed several rolls, and looked around for dessert. He still wasn't hearing much chatter, so he threw everyone a grim smile. "I'm okay. We're going to try again tomorrow."

Well, that comment dropped straight onto the table with a thud. Alex looked around at his family.

"Really. It's okay."

"Alex," Jamie said, rising, "why don't you come upstairs for a minute. I think there's something you should read."

Alex waved him away. "I think I need dessert first."

Jamie sat back down slowly. "As you will, brother."

Joshua had made Boston cream pie. Alex helped himself to three pieces. Once he felt his blood sugar level was firmly in the black, he turned to Jamie.

"All right, lay it on me. Some piece of trivia to carry back to Margaret? English history I missed in college?"

Jamie wouldn't meet his eyes. "I daresay you wouldn't have been looking for this, brother."

The hairs on the back of his neck stood up, without his permission.

"What?" he demanded. "What did you find?"

Jamie rose without a word. Alex followed him from the kitchen, up the stairs, and down the hallway to Jamie's study. Jamie gestured to a chair, but Alex shook his head.

"Just give it to me straight."

Jamie handed him a book. "We found this this afternoon."

Alex looked at the cover of the book. *Medieval English History*. The very sight of it sent a wave of chills down his spine.

"Page ninety-six," Jamie offered.

Alex felt for a chair and lowered himself into it. He didn't like Jamie's tone of voice. It was so carefully neutral that Alex knew this had to be something bad.

In May of 1194 Margaret of Falconberg perished in an act of arson most historians consider perpetrated by Ralf of Brackwald. As King Richard had already departed for his French campaign, Lord Brackwald merely sent tidings of the misfortune to the king, along with a substantial deposit to the king's coffers and the offer to see to Falconberg lands. Apparently Richard had too many other things on his mind to worry about little fires at home. He granted Brackwald the charter. It is a testament to Brackwald's poor management that the lands were rendered almost uninhabitable within half a decade.

It is also interesting to note that though Margaret's husband, Alexander, is considered to have perished with her in the fire, no conclusive evidence was found to support that theory.

Alex shook his head. "This doesn't mean anything. I'll just get back in time to stop it."

"Alex," Jamie said quietly, "you cannot. It's already happened."

"Then I'll go back earlier! I'll get her out of there before Ralf can do this. Surely that much time hasn't passed since she left here."

"You cannot go back," Jamie insisted. "I tried to tell you before."

"You said we'd get back because Margaret's life was there!" Alex exclaimed.

"Exactly," Jamie said. "Her life."

"My life is with her."

Jamie took the book carefully from Alex's shaking hands. "Brother, I fear that may not be the case."

"And how the hell would you know?" Alex shouted. "Damn you, Jamie, how can you sit there so bloody calmly and tell me my wife is dead and there's not a damn thing I can do about it?''

Jamie leaned back against the desk. ''I'm hardly calm, Alex. I'm sick with grief for you.''

''Save it,'' Alex snapped, jumping to his feet. ''I don't need it. What I need is to get the hell home.''

Jamie caught him by the arm on his way by. ''Alex, wait—''

Alex didn't think, he just let his fist fly. It wasn't a fair fight, but he didn't care. By the time Alex realized Jamie wasn't throwing any return punches, his brother-in-law's lip was bleeding, one eye was rapidly swelling shut, and he wasn't breathing very well anymore. Alex found it in himself to finally stop swinging. He stumbled away and leaned, hunched over, with his hands on Jamie's desk.

''I'm sorry,'' he gasped. ''I don't know what came over me.''

Jamie rolled to his feet stiffly. ''Ah, well, I daresay I do. And I surely cannot blame you for your grief, Alex. The saints know I'd be feeling the same in your place.''

Alex wished he could dredge up some more fury. It would certainly be preferable to the flat despair that engulfed him.

''There has to be a way,'' Alex said hoarsely.

''Will you hear me now?'' Jamie asked.

Alex nodded. He threw himself down into Jamie's desk chair and waited for his brother-in-law to sit down carefully in the chair Margaret had inhabited so often.

''I forced the forest once,'' Jamie said, looking at Alex unflinchingly. ''I knew I shouldn't have, but I was arrogant enough to ignore what my heart told me.''

''So it can be done.''

''Aye. At least by me.''

''Go on.''

Jamie smiled, then winced and put his hand to his lip. ''I wanted to see Jesse and wee Megan. I wanted to see my grandchildren left so many years behind me.'' He paused, then lifted an eyebrow. ''Can you blame me?''

"Not in the least."

"I knew my time there was finished. Even so, I'd tried previously a time or two to wander into the forest and see if perhaps I could return."

"Without Elizabeth?"

Jamie winced. "Aye. They were idle fancies I knew she wouldn't approve of."

"Well, idiot, there was your mistake."

Jamie scowled at him. "I didn't want to risk her."

"Like she would have accepted that as an excuse!"

"Well," Jamie said, sounding slightly offended, "I thought it most logical at the time."

"And then?"

"And then I decided that I would bend the forest to my will, no matter the cost. I took Elizabeth with me and forced the gate."

"How?"

"Don't ask."

Alex lifted an eyebrow. "Not a pleasant experience, I take it."

"Very unpleasant," Jamie agreed. "But travel we did to Jesse's time only to find Megan in her grave by a pair of years and Jesse freshly laid out for his own coffin. My kin thought they'd seen a ghost, and Beth and I scarce made it back to the forest before they tried to burn us."

Alex felt his mouth drop open. "You've got to be kidding."

Jamie shook his head. "A clan legend is only well received when the legend doesn't make personal appearances, or so I'd say from my experience."

Alex frowned. "And you think if I try to force the gate, the same will happen to me?"

"You couldn't force the gate, Alex. Perhaps I could, to send you back, but I can guarantee you wouldn't like it. And I couldn't say what welcome you'd receive. You might arrive just in time to see Margaret perishing in the flames and be too late to save her."

Alex chewed on that, then dismissed it. "All right, you

said you could send me back. But would you?''

Jamie didn't move. ''I've never tried anything but the forest. 'Tis a fair sight more powerful than that wee ring in the grass.''

''You don't think it would work.''

''Nay, I do not.''

Alex took a deep breath. Well, so much for honesty. ''So,'' he said, letting out his breath slowly, ''either I make it on my own, or I don't go.''

''Aye. But consider what you might find.''

''Margaret dead.''

''And Brackwald accusing you of her murder.''

Alex laughed shortly, but he felt anything but humor. ''Now, that's the first thing you've said tonight that I've agreed with. He'd do that in a heartbeat.''

''And it isn't as if your King Richard will be about to see the matter settled fairly. If Ralf is as thick with the prince as he appeared, you would find your time as Lord of Falconberg to be very short indeed.''

''Hell.''

Jamie only nodded with a grim look.

''If only I could get back sooner.''

'' 'Tis a big *if*, brother.''

Alex stood, suddenly. ''It may be a big *if*, but it's all I have.''

''But, Alex—''

''I won't ask you to do it for me, Jamie. I'll do it myself, tonight. Keep the crew, won't you?''

Jamie's jaw went slack. ''You jest!''

He shook his head. ''They'll be better off here anyway.''

''They won't like it.''

''They might not, but I won't endanger them. You'll see they survive.''

Jamie considered that for a moment, then looked up at him. ''How will I account for them?''

Alex scribbled Tony DiSalvio's number on a scrap of paper. ''Call this guy. Tell him who you are, what you need, and that he owes me big. If he gives you any crap, tell him I went on an extended vacation, but left you a key to my safe deposit box and you're on your way to see what's in it. That'll scare him.''

Jamie rubbed his chin thoughtfully. ''You haven't told me much about your work in New York, Alex.''

''The less you know, the better off you are.''

''Piracy is a messy business.''

Alex snorted. ''Tell me about it. Take care of the kids. I think Joel can be bribed with the Claymore and Frances is already hooked on Beth. I worry about Amery, but I can't take him with me. I think he'll be okay with you.''

''And your bard?''

''Keep him supplied with yarn and you're set.''

Jamie stood, then came and embraced Alex. ''I hope you find your heart's desire,'' he said gruffly. He patted Alex on the back and left the room.

Alex sighed and shook his head.

So did he.

Thirty-four

❧❧

THE FIRST THING SHE SAW WAS FIRE.

Margaret could see the smoke filling the dawn sky even from the faery ring. She put her heels to her mount's side and raced toward home. Saints above, what mischief was this?

By the time she could see Falconberg in the distance, all she could see was blackened outer walls and tongues of fire licking them and flicking up into the air. Margaret dismounted in a daze, hardly able to believe her eyes.

Had we been there, we would be dead.

The thought occurred to her with a blinding flash. Following hard on its heels was the realization that whoever had done this was likely still in the area. She loosened her blade in its sheath and patted the daggers concealed on various parts of her person. Perhaps she wouldn't live to see sunset, but she'd make certain that many of Ralf's men didn't, either.

Ralf had to be behind it. She could think of no other who would purposely destroy everything she loved simply to spite her. Everything she and Alex loved, that was. Aye, Alex had loved her land as much as she did. This would have grieved him beyond belief. Perhaps it was for the best that she'd returned alone, though what she now had to return to was very little indeed.

She crept through the forest, her eyes open and her ears trained to the slightest sound. No birds chirped in the trees above her, but that could have been due to the smell of char that lay thick in the woods.

She drew up at the edge of the forest and gaped at the sight that greeted her eyes.

Ralf of Brackwald, a very disheveled and filthier-than-usual Ralf of Brackwald, currently sparred with his brother, whose face was blackened with soot. Edward's clothes hung on him in tatters.

"It should have been mine!" Ralf snarled.

"Richard gave it to Alexander, and there's not a bloody thing you can do about that!" Edward retorted, fending off his brother's attack. "You lost Falconberg and Margaret both."

"Ha," Ralf sneered. "I daresay I burned the bitch up in her bed, and her foreign lover as well. I barred the doors from the outside and burned up the entire household before they awoke. Think you the king won't award me the lands now just the same?"

"He won't once I tell him you admitted to the crime."

"As if you'll have the chance!" Ralf exclaimed, thrusting viciously. "You're just bloody lucky you weren't boarded up inside as well. But no matter. I'll send you to hell just the same."

Margaret found herself with her dagger in her hand. To be sure, it would have been more fitting to slay Ralf with her sword, but she didn't want to interfere with Edward's battle.

While she watched, she turned over in her mind what she'd just learned. If Ralf were to be believed, they all thought her dead. She wasn't sure what that might mean to her, but she *was* sure it deserved more thought.

Alex's gift of Damascus steel was a pleasant weight in her hand. She held the dagger by the tip of the blade and hefted it a time or two, judging from that what she thought its arc might be and how much strength she might have to put behind the throwing of it. No sense in not being prepared, should she need to fling it.

Edward was holding up admirably, but Ralf was faring

better. Margaret had to admit that, repulsive though he might have been as a man, Ralf was a passing good swordsman. No finesse and certainly no chivalry, but lethal in his brutality.

She began to see that Edward would not win. Try as he might, the man simply did not have the skill to best his brother. His judgment was faulty, his aim just the slightest bit off. And Margaret could see by his stance that he didn't have what it took, in the end, to finish off the whoreson facing him.

And just what should she do if Edward failed? Should she finish Ralf herself? He certainly deserved it. He'd slain many of her people and destroyed much of her property. If he lived, he would make the rest of her life hell. Without a keep to hide in, she might very well find herself on the end of his sword.

She put her shoulders back. She would do the deed herself. Should Edward fail.

She watched for another handful of moments. And she had to admit to herself that it came as no surprise when Edward found himself without a sword, flat on his back, with his brother looming over him with blade raised. Margaret could only blink at her good fortune, for she had the full breadth of Ralf's back to use as her target.

"Die, you woman," Ralf snarled.

The dagger left her hand and flew true, straight into his back, straight into his heart. He stiffened, as if in shock, then whirled around. Margaret pulled back into the shadows, but not before she met Ralf's startled eyes.

But before he could call out her name, he gurgled his last breath, then pitched forward into the mud.

Margaret toyed with the idea of striding out from the trees, hauling Edward up by his tunic front, and slapping him for not having learnt his craft better. But before she could do so, a very blackened, very weary George of Falconberg stumbled toward Edward and managed to pull the lad to his feet.

Margaret felt her eyes burn at the sight of her captain

alive still and seemingly unhurt. She watched as George looked at the dagger in Ralf's back, then froze as he recognized it. But before he could reach for it, Edward had snatched it out from the corpse.

"Oh, gift of life!" he exclaimed. "Sir George, may I keep this as token of your service to me?"

"Ah . . . er . . ."

"Many thanks," Edward said, slinging his arm around George. "Your dagger is what saved me and I will be forever in your debt. It will always have a place of honor in my house."

George only grunted. Margaret understood completely.

"I'm happy to see you alive and well. Now, what of the souls in the keep? Any survivors?" Edward asked.

"A few," George answered carefully.

"Lady Falconberg? Lord Alexander?"

"I think not. We'll need to search a bit more. Perhaps they were out for a brief ride and missed all the excitement."

Edward coughed, then leaned heavily on George. "Aye, the excitement of all the murders my brother committed," he said with a deep frown. "By the saints, I cannot help but rejoice that he is dead."

"My lord," George said, "let me help you to the keep. Then I will return and check the area for ruffians."

"Aye, who knows who roams the woods in these perilous times?"

"Who indeed," George said with a grunt.

Margaret watched them go, then found herself a comfortable tree to wait against. George knew she was nearby and would find her soon enough. Until then, she would give herself over to the contemplation of her situation. There were too many decisions to be made, and the saints surely knew she didn't have enough time for the making of them.

Falconberg was in ruins. It would take years and more gold than she had at her disposal to see it rebuilt. At least she and Alex had had the sense to hide Ralf's gold in the cellar.

But that was the least of her worries. Who knew how many souls had perished because of Ralf's treachery? For all she knew, she had no one left to see to, no one left to protect, no one left to lead. How could she defend the land her grandsire had left her if she had no keep? How could she safeguard her peasants if she had no place of refuge for them? It would be kinder to allow Edward to take a stewardship over her land. At least he would have the gold to see to it.

And what of herself? She had no place to sleep, no place to eat, no place to hide if an army came up against her. She was defenseless and exposed. Indeed, what would she be other than a burden to those around her? And a burden she could not bear to be.

They thought she was dead.

Her strand in the twelfth-century fabric of time was ended. For the first time since climbing into Alex's Range Rover, she felt her heart begin to lighten. They thought her dead. And if they thought her dead and she suddenly reappeared, wouldn't that mar the threads of history irreparably?

Heaven forbid she should do that.

"Margaret."

She whirled around to find George behind her. Without thinking, she hastened to him and threw her arms around him. Before she knew it, she had burst into tears.

"I know," he said, patting her back soothingly. "I know, Margaret. The keep was a fine one indeed."

She pulled back. "The keep? I was worried for you, you old fool!"

He blinked, his eyes very white against the sootiness of his face. "For me?"

"Of course for you!"

He smiled briefly. "I am singed, but unhurt. I cannot say the same for your hall."

Margaret shrugged, almost surprised at the ease with

which she did it. "Drafty old place. Were the casualties high?"

"Unfortunately, aye. Cook and a few of her helpers survived by descending into the cellars, but 'twas no small feat to get them out before the place burned to cinders."

"And the gold?"

"Still safe under the salted eels."

She smiled in satisfaction. "Then I don't regret my knife finding home in Ralf's heart."

George shook his head. "Nay, you shouldn't. He's done enough damage and hurt to warrant it." He looked around her, then back at her. "I don't see young Alexander."

"I left him behind."

"You what?" George exclaimed. "Margaret, what were you thinking?"

"I thought he would be better off in that future of his," she said defensively. "I was only thinking of him."

"Aye, and while you were at it, why didn't you think on how miserable he would be?"

"Well . . ."

"Think you he relishes the thought of his entire life without you?"

"I suppose I hadn't thought—"

"Aye, I'd say you hadn't thought at all!"

She stared at him and fumed. "You didn't see what I saw."

"Nay, but I've heard all about it. Wouldn't you give it up for him?"

She rolled her eyes, but found she had no reply for that one. She would have given up the future and everything in it if it had meant she could remain with Alexander of Falconberg and spend every night in his arms.

George stared at her for several moments in silence. "Can you return to him?"

She stiffened in surprise at the question. She'd thought it to be simple thing, but she realized she had no idea whether or not such a thing was possible without Jamie.

"I know not," she breathed. "By the saints, I never thought I'd need to!"

"Then you'd best give it some thought now."

"I will. After I've seen things settled here to my satisfaction."

"There's nothing to settle. They think you perished in the flames."

She put her hand on his arm. "George, 'tis my land. Land my sire gave to me and his sire to him. I cannot let it fall into ruin."

"Then give me your list of demands to give to Edward and I'll see them accomplished. I'll say they were your wishes before you died."

She nodded. "That is wise. Let us take ourselves off a bit and settle things between us. There is much I must think on." She walked a little ways off and cursed under her breath. "If only Edward hadn't made off with my dagger."

"I'll see that it has a place of honor in his household," George said dryly.

"Wonderful," she said with another roll of her eyes. "Well, let us see to the rest of my affairs."

She said it with a light heart, though in truth her heart was divided by joy and sorrow. She longed to return to Alex, to be sure, but it was a hard thought to think of never seeing her keep again.

Yet, what was left of her keep to see? An empty, charred shell?

And who was to say she couldn't see the place again in the future? Perhaps some wealthy soul would have taken it upon himself to put it back to rights.

Edward, for instance.

And Alex would surely miss having his title. There was no reason some conscientious soul couldn't stipulate that somewhere in the future the title of earl of Falconberg should be given over promptly to someone who could prove to be a direct descendent of the first earl of Falconberg. Or the earl himself, should he deign to show up in some future century.

And what a conscientious soul Edward could prove to be.

The more she thought about it, the more a plan began to take shape in her mind. When she and George had reached her horse, she was ready with her list of demands.

BY THE TIME she'd finished with George, the afternoon sun was low in the sky and they'd ingested most of the future food she'd managed to stash in her saddlebags. George wiped the last of the potato chips from the front of his shirt, then frowned at her.

"I'll never remember it all."

"Aye, you will, old man. And see that it's done. I'll read about it in some manuscript and know if you've failed me."

He shook his head. "I don't know that Edward will agree to it."

"He will if you tell him that you've seen my ghost and I've sworn to haunt him for the rest of his days if he strays one step from the tasks I've set for him."

"And you think he'll believe that?"

"Brackwalds are notoriously superstitious."

George smiled at that. "That they are, my girl. Very well. I'll see to your items."

Margaret pushed herself to her feet. "Well, then my task is done. I should be on my way."

He rose with a great creaking of joints. "Aye. Give that lad of yours a fond greeting for me."

"I'll do so. Oh," she said, reaching down into her saddlebag, "I have something for you." She pulled forth a clear cube of some strange material—plastic Alex had called it. She handed it to George. "Here. As promised."

George accepted it with same awe he likely would have used had she handed him the crown of England and the scepter to go with it.

"Wow," he breathed, holding it up so he could gaze at the ball inside the plastic cube. "The players have signed their names. Look, Margaret. Mariner signatures abound upon it!"

Margaret wondered if those mariners shouldn't have been spending more time on their ship than playing games. And why had they scrawled their signatures upon that ridiculous white ball where it would do them no good whatsoever?

Men, she thought with a snort. Who could understand them?

She took out the little velvet cloth that had accompanied the baseball and draped it over the clear box.

"Best you don't frighten others with it," she suggested.

"Oh, aye," George breathed, stroking the box reverently. "I'll keep it quite safe."

"I've no doubt you will. Now, don't become so enraptured of this ridiculous ball that you forget the tasks you must see to for me."

He nodded, then gave her a grave smile. "I'll not forget what you've demanded, Meg. But you'll thank Alex for this, won't you?"

"Aye, I will," she said, though in reality she hoped he didn't strangle her for it when she returned. He'd had several baseballs sitting in a drawer, but none of them with the little scrawls and certainly none of them in clear boxes. The one she'd chosen was likely very dear to him. Oh, well, 'twas but a small price to pay for George's happiness.

She resettled her saddlebags, then turned to George a final time. Now the time had come to bid him farewell, she hardly knew how to go about it. Here was a man who had been more than just the captain of her guard. He'd stood behind her when there was no one else there. He'd been a father to her when her own had left her all alone. How she would miss his grunts, the occasional tugs on the end of her braid, the glint in his eye when she'd done something exceptionally noteworthy. Nay, telling him goodbye was not something she could do.

He set aside his treasure, then reached out and pulled her gruffly into his arms.

"I'll miss you," he said, his voice cracking. He cleared his throat. "Won't have anyone to keep in line."

"You'll have Edward," she managed.

"And what sport is there in that? No spirit in the lad." He kissed her on both cheeks, then pushed her away. "Go on with you, girl. Think of me now and then."

Margaret looked at him with tears in her eyes. "You won't come?"

He shook his head with a small smile. "And who would be here to keep Edward in his place? Nay, girl, the future's no place for me. I have my baseball. 'Tis enough."

She knew there was nothing left to say, so she nodded stiffly and turned away. She didn't consider herself a coward, but she knew she had no choice but to leap onto her horse and flee. So she did, before she broke down and sobbed.

By the time she reached the faery ring, she could no longer see. Her tears had run in rivers down her cheeks, the neck of her cloak was sopping wet, and her nose was raw from where she'd rubbed it once too often.

She dismounted inside the faery ring and took off her mail. She put Alex's sweater back on and repacked her gear a final time. Then she put her arm over her horse's withers. She looked up to see the sky beginning to darken and wondered what it was she should do now.

She waited.

And when she grew uncomfortable, she decided an announcement was in order.

"I'm ready to go to Scotland now," she said, just in case the proper faeries were listening.

Still nothing.

"Back to Alex," she clarified.

Stars began to appear.

"Hell," she muttered.

She considered yet again her situation and wondered just what Jamie had done to pop them forward with such ease.

Indeed, when she'd reached the faery ring near his keep, she'd done nothing but ride inside it, determine that going back to Falconberg was what she had to do, and *poof!* she'd been there.

She tried thinking of Jamie's keep. She even said *poof* a few times.

It didn't help.

She felt herself begin to panic. She couldn't stay in 1194. There was no more place for her. Her life, as far as anyone there was concerned, was over. She would mar no fabric of time if she left. All the proper omens and portents were aligned, and there was nothing left for her but to return to Alex and live out her life in bliss.

She searched frantically through her memory, wondering if there might be a key phrase she had missed, some action of celestial import she might have overlooked.

Then she froze.

Then she smiled.

"Well," she said, "that should work."

And she raised herself up onto her toes.

Thirty-five

❧❧❧

ALEX STOOD ON JAMIE'S ROOF AND STARED OUT OVER the back of the house toward the pond. Toward the faery ring. Toward the one place that kept him from the woman he loved.

He was half tempted to ride out and pull up every bloody plant there. It would be a fitting revenge.

He sighed and watched the mountains take on deep afternoon shadows. It had been almost thirty-six hours since Margaret had left him. He'd been counting. He wondered how he would feel when he hit the million mark. Probably not any better than he felt right now. It was a good thing he'd never live that long. The thought of living the rest of his life alone made him sick to his stomach.

He'd gone back to the ring yesterday after he'd brought everyone back to the keep. He'd spent the night in the faery ring. He'd woken up, then looked up to see an exhaust trail of the rare jets that flew that far north.

Things hadn't improved much from there.

He'd finally come home earlier that afternoon. If he'd been thinking, he would have packed a snack the night before, but hadn't been thinking. He was thinking now. He'd been standing on the roof for almost an hour, trying to decide just what to take so he could camp out permanently near that bloody grouping of spores. He'd considered building a little shed. That would certainly keep him occupied for quite some time, but it also smacked of a permanence he didn't want to get involved in because he had no intentions of being stuck in the twentieth century that long. He'd finally settled for a great deal of camping gear and a cell phone so he could call home for supplies. Maybe tomorrow he'd set up camp. He couldn't stomach the thought of it tonight.

He left the roof and made his way down the steps, along the hallway, and down to the great hall. His family was gathered near the fire. Baldric was preparing some sort of entertainment, but Alex couldn't bring himself to stop and listen. It reminded him too much of all the times he'd done just that with Margaret.

He left the hall and walked through the gates. It was cold outside, but he only noticed it in an academic sort of way. His heart was so frozen he could hardly feel the rest of himself.

He made his way along the stream that ran near Jamie's house. He picked his way over rocks and found the path that ran along the lake. Nice lake. Tempting to throw himself into it, but maybe later. He continued on toward the little glade of rowan trees that sheltered the faery ring.

And that was when he began to hear voices.

"Losing it," he noted. It was to be expected, probably, since he saw his life stretching out before him as a barren wasteland of time without Margaret. But voices? So soon?

He stopped in midstep. Yes, that was definitely a voice.

"Pitiful," he said, with a shake of his head, then continued on his way.

He reached the clearing, came to a dead halt, and gaped. He rubbed his eyes, sure he was seeing things. He knew he was hearing things.

"There's no place like home. There's no place like home."

Margaret was standing in the middle of the faery ring up on her toes, clicking her heels together for all she was worth, her face scrunched up in intense concentration.

"There's no place like home."

Alex cleared his throat. He tried to speak, but all that came out was a strangled grunt.

Her eyes flew open. He watched as she almost pitched forward flat onto her face in surprise.

"Alex?"

He nodded.

"Oh, Alex!"

The next thing he knew, she was in his arms. He clutched her to him and backed away from the ring. He didn't want its nefarious tentacles snatching her away from him now that he had her back.

"Oh, Margaret," he whispered hoarsely, hardly able to keep on his feet from his relief. "Oh, Margaret!"

It was all he found himself able to say. He clutched her to him as hard as he dared, praying he wasn't hallucinating. The feeling of hot tears on his cheek was comforting, but it was the feeling of her tears on his neck that convinced him he wasn't dreaming.

"I thought I'd lost you," he rasped. "I thought I'd never see you again."

She only shook her head and held on to him more tightly.

They stood there until the sky was black and the stars had come out in full force.

Then Alex remembered his very long list and the agony he'd felt while making it. He pulled back from her, took her by the shoulders, and started to shake her.

"What were you thinking?" he thundered. "Damn you, Margaret of Falconberg, just what in the hell were you using for a brain?"

"I just thought—"

"Well, you damn well won't be doing that again any time soon!" he bellowed.

She only blinked at him. Then she started to smile. He saw nothing whatsoever humorous about the situation. In fact, he wasn't seeing anything much beyond red at the moment.

"You're glad to see me," she said.

He wasn't sure if more shaking was called for, or if he should just turn her over his knee right there.

And then he realized the enormity of it all.

"You're alive," he said, stunned.

"Aye, and a lucky thing it is, too. Had we been at Falconberg, neither of us would be so."

"Who started the fire?"

Her jaw went slack. "You know of the fire?"

"Jamie found it in a history book. I was frantic because I thought I couldn't get back to you before you were burned to cinders."

Her expression softened. "You endeavored to go back?"

"Of course I endeavored to go back!"

"Didn't succeed, obviously."

"Well, it wasn't for a lack of trying," he growled. He yanked her close again. "I'm really angry with you."

"Aye, I suspected you might be."

"I can't believe you left me. I can't believe the thought even crossed your mind."

She tightened her arms around him. "I couldn't ask you to leave all this—"

"Why does everyone think I'm such a pansy?" he exploded, pushing her back to arm's length. "I could have handled twelfth-century England! I would have made a damn good earl!"

"But the Range Rover—"

"I'm selling it tomorrow," he snapped. "Get used to the idea of walking, because that's the only way you're going to get anywhere from now on."

"Oh, Alex, you can't sell it. I like it well." She drew close again and patted his back. "One certainly arrives at his destination in a drier condition than on horseback."

Well, it obviously wasn't going to take her long to get used to the idea of travel by car. Alex scowled into her hair. She'd caused him an enormous amount of stress, ripped his heart out by its roots, and now she was calmly discussing his car as if she didn't have anything better to talk about.

"Let's go home," he grumbled. "I have business with your backside."

She blinked. "You do?"

"Spankings," he clarified. "Lots of them."

"I'd rather work this out in the lists, if it's all the same to you."

"It isn't and I don't want to."

"I won't be spanked."

He frowned at her. "I'm the earl."

She lifted one eyebrow. "And I am the countess and I will not be spanked." She snapped her fingers and her horse trotted over obediently. "Let's go home, Alex. I've eaten nothing all day but the *faux* food of yours I took with me, and I'm in sore need of something good."

Before Alex could protest, she had him by one hand and her horse by the other and was towing both of them back to the stables. She placed him on a handy bench while she tended her to her mount. Alex watched her put away her saddle gear, then watched some more as she brushed and fed her horse. The longer he watched, the more it sunk in just what had been given back to him. This stunning, courageous, *stubborn* woman was his. Forever. If he could just keep her away from gates in the grass.

"You're not leaving again, are you?" he asked quietly.

She put away the currycomb, then came out of the stall. She closed the door and leaned back against it.

"Nay," she said, just as quietly.

"You almost killed me, Meg. I couldn't take it again."

She looked at him gravely. "You do love me, don't you, Alex?"

He pursed his lips. "You can't mean to tell me it took you this long to finally figure that out."

She shook her head with a small smile. "I knew it all along."

"I would have gone back with you happily."

She came across to him and put her hand out to touch his cheek softly. "Aye, I know."

"I'll miss your hall."

"Aye. As will I."

He rose and pulled her gently against him. "I love you, Margaret. I just can't tell you how much."

"And I love you," she said, lifting her face and kissing him. "And it will take me many years to tell you how much."

He grunted. "Maybe by then I will have forgiven you for all the pain you've caused me over the past two days."

"I'll see you appeased."

"Damn right you will."

"Might I have a meal first?"

"Maybe. When I can bear to let you out of my arms."

"Alex," she said solemnly, "I'll never leave you again. Why would I, when my life is standing right here?"

"I wish you'd come to that conclusion two days ago."

She shook her head. "I had a work to finish in the past, Alex. And if you feed me, I'll tell you of it."

Alex grunted as he walked with her from the stables. "You're as bad as Jamie with your 'tasks in the past.' All I need in my life is two of you going at it."

She smiled brightly. "Who's to say you and I haven't more work to do in other times? I've a mind to see that first Queen Elizabeth. What a turbulent time that would be to—"

Alex cut her off with a kiss. And when he'd let her up long enough to catch her breath, he kissed her again. The very last thing he wanted to hear was more talk of time traveling.

"—and Mary with all her intrigues and lov—"

Well, it was either going to have to be his mouth or food silencing her at all times. And he wouldn't let her near Jamie. Heaven only knew what sorts of things the two of them would concoct together. He and Elizabeth didn't stand a chance. Maybe he would move Margaret somewhere far from all those damn gates—like Siberia. Africa. Australia. Alex turned the possibilities over in his mind until the rumbling of Margaret's stomach became too distracting.

"Food?" she gasped, when he released her mouth.

"Only if you stop talking about sixteenth-century political intrigues."

"Food, then perhaps an evening in Jamie's library," she said, tugging him toward the house. "I have a few things to search out."

"I'm the man of the house," he tried as she pulled him through the front door.

She completely ignored him.

"My word is law," he announced to his family as Margaret hauled him across the great hall.

They were all gaping at him, either because they couldn't believe whom he was being towed by, or because they couldn't believe he was stupid to believe what was coming out of his mouth.

"I am the earl!" he exclaimed desperately.

No one paid any attention to him. Amery bolted, screeching, from Elizabeth's lap and threw himself against Margaret. Frances and Joel ran just as quickly and wrapped themselves around her as tightly as humanly possible.

Baldric made her a low bow, then looked at Alex. "See?" he said, sounding supremely satisfied. "I told you she would return! How could she bear life without my verses?"

How, indeed, Alex wanted to say, but he was interrupted by Joshua throwing himself to his knees in front of Margaret.

"Ah, the moon no longer hides her face from us!" he exclaimed. "Now both my days and my nights are filled with heavenly visions of loveliness! I knew the Fates would not deny this humble maker of ballads such glorious inspiration—"

"Aye, to be sure," Margaret interrupted him. "I vow, Joshua, that such lays would sit better with me had I a plate of your brownies to soothe me."

"As you wish," Joshua said, leaping to his feet and rushing across the hall to the kitchen.

Margaret hugged the children clinging to her, shared

brief embraces with Jamie and Elizabeth, then looked at Alex. "Supper, perhaps? I daresay I smell stew coming from the kitchens."

Alex gave up trying to put his earlish foot down. He followed her meekly to the kitchen, stirring himself to shove Zachary a few feet away when his brother came too close to Margaret, then sat himself at the table and put his head down on the wood. He should have known from the beginning that Margaret would run roughshod over him. She'd done so from the first. How had he ever thought to hold his own against her, even in his own century?

He smiled against the wood. What did he care? He had her back and he was never going to let her go again. He would keep her near him by whatever means necessary.

"Chains," he said, lifting his head and looking at his assorted and collected family which was crowded into the kitchen and all babbling at once. They seemingly didn't have any interest in him.

"A set of shackles," he announced.

Baldric perked up a little at that, but soon turned back to the primary entertainment who was currently inhaling her dinner.

"Bungee cords," Alex said with a satisfied smile.

Thirty-six

❦❧

MARGARET SCRAPED THE BOTTOM OF HER DESSERT BOWL
and frowned. She looked at Elizabeth. "No more?"

"Sorry," Elizabeth said with a smile.

"What was this again?"

"Ice cream. Häagen-Dazs. Chocolate-chocolate-chip."

"Alex," Margaret said, waving her spoon at him,
"we'll need to hie ourselves off to the village first thing
on the morrow to procure more of this. 'Tis powerfully
delicious over brownies."

"Silken scarves," he replied, with a devilish glint in his
eye. "Or maybe just a good old-fashioned hemp rope."

Well, 'twas obvious her husband had taken more ice
cream than was good for him. She frowned at him, then
turned back to her waiting audience.

"The fire," Jamie prompted.

"Ah, the fire," she said with a nod. "It would appear
that Ralf shut up the doors, then put a torch to the keep.
I happened upon him readying himself to finish Edward
off—and to be sure Edward's swordplay was mightily
lacking—and buried my dagger in his heart."

Alex began to choke. Margaret pounded him on the back
and finished her tale.

"I had speech with Sir George after the fact and told
him of my wishes. He vowed to watch after Edward. I
gave him a baseball and the tale was finished."

"Baseball?" Alex asked.

Margaret looked at him with what she hoped was a confident air. "Aye, one of yours."

"Which one?"

"The one in the little clear box with all the scribblings upon it. George was most pleased with the gift."

Alex seemed to be torn between spluttering and choking, so she refrained from pounding him further on the back until he made up his mind which it would be.

"My Mariner's *signed* baseball?" he demanded finally, having gone very red in the face.

" 'Twas the only one I could find in the dark."

He looked to be on the verge of saying something truly unpleasant, then he suddenly laughed and leaned over to kiss her full on the mouth.

"Small price to pay," he said simply.

She heaved a silent sigh of relief that *that* hurdle was successfully overcome.

"Then you left your land to Edward of Brackwald," Jamie said, scratching his chin.

"Aye," she said, turning to her brother-in-law. "It seemed the most logical thing to do. And I told him he was to hold it in tru—"

She shut her mouth abruptly as she realized she was about to spill a part of the tale she had no desire for Alex to hear as yet. She looked at Elizabeth.

"We must have speech together."

"Okay," Elizabeth said, with a smile. "Whenever you want."

"Now."

Alex scowled at her. "Well, at least she isn't Jamie. You won't get any time traveling ideas from her."

"Ideas?" Jamie said, perking up. "I'm always open to a new idea or two."

Margaret left her husband bellowing at his brother-in-law and hastened with Elizabeth to the fire in the great hall.

"I need to travel to Falconberg," she said without preamble. "The castle is being held in trust for Alex."

Elizabeth didn't even blink, which raised Margaret's opinion of her to even greater heights.

"Sounds like fun. When shall we go?"

"I would go tonight, but I fear Alex would find that little to his liking."

"I'd imagine so," Elizabeth said, laughing. "And my mom and dad should be here in the morning, and you'll want to meet them."

"Within the se'nnight, then," Margaret said.

"I'll be happy to go with you."

Margaret nodded and set aside thoughts of her plans. She would meet Alex's parents on the morrow, and she could ill afford to make a poor impression. Waiting a few days to see Falconberg couldn't make much of a difference.

IT TOOK A good deal longer than a few days to see everything settled. It was the beginning of August before Margaret had her husband packed up and loaded themselves into the Range Rover. Jamie had volunteered the Jaguar for the trip, but Margaret had seen the reluctance with which he prepared to part with his beloved car, so she insisted the other would suit them well enough. Besides, the Range Rover held all manner of camping gear, and they would certainly need it.

Margaret adjusted her dark glasses against the glare of the unusually sunny August day and smiled at the sights of Scotland passing so quickly before her.

"Is there a purpose to this little trip?" Alex asked.

She hid her smile and put her hand on his leg. "Perhaps."

"Would it have anything to do with your request for 300,000 pounds sterling a few months ago?"

"It might. Then again, I might have just wanted to go shopping. Clothing is bloody expensive in your day, Alex."

He looked pointedly at her jeans and very worn T-shirt.

The shirt was something she had helped herself to from his armoire that very morning.

"Since you never wear anything I haven't broken in already," he said dryly, "I have to assume you're lying."

She only smiled pleasantly. "A woman is entitled to her secrets. It's part of our mystique."

"You watch too much TV."

"I read it in a book."

"Then you read too much." He scowled at her. "You were much easier to control eight centuries ago."

She snorted. "As if you ever controlled me."

He pursed his lips, but she could see it was in an effort to hide his smile. "Allow me my fantasies, okay?"

"Why indulge in fantasy, when reality is so marvelous?"

"Stop that, or I'll have to pull over and ravish you."

Yet another good reason to have brought the Range Rover. Fold-down backseats. Ah, but the future was a marvelous place.

"Later," she promised. "I'm anxious to reach our destination."

"No hints?"

"Keep traveling south, Alex. That's all you'll get from me."

"We're booked at hotels for the next two nights on our way south. Why did we bring camping stuff?"

She took off her sunglasses to better look at her husband. He drove with one hand on the wheel, one hand covering hers on his leg. He wore a dry smile, which he always did when he knew she was up to something. She had to admit to herself that he wore that smile quite often.

"You ask too many questions," she said lightly.

"And if I demand answers?"

"You won't have them until I'm ready for you to have them."

He sighed. "Henpecked. Abused. Trampled. Just put that on my headstone."

She snorted. "You are none of the above."

"And be sure to decorate it with pansies, my flower of choice."

She laughed. "Oh, Alex, I do love you."

"That's what you keep telling me. Now, why won't you just do the domestic goddess thing and cater to my every whim?"

"Because I am a countess and we do not cater to whims."

"Not even if I asked nicely?"

She shook her head. "How unhappy you would be if you found yourself pampered at every turn."

"I'm willing to risk it."

She smiled to herself. How pampered he was, and he knew it well. Though she would be the first to admit it ran both ways. She also knew he enjoyed the constant fight for control. He lorded over her and she countessed over him and their lives were perfectly blissful. The only thing which had troubled her at all was the nagging ache she felt for Falconberg. Jamie's keep was a marvel with all its modern inventions, and she had passed many happy hours there with Alex's family and their own. The Highlands were beautiful, and rugged, and wandering through them the past few months had been bliss.

But she missed her land.

That was taken care of now, though, and soon they would bring their own family back down and start up their own lives again. Falconberg was close enough that journeying to Scotland wouldn't be a problem. They'd made quick work of adopting Frances, Joel, and Amery. The children would surely wish to see their cousin Ian regularly. Jamie and Elizabeth could visit often, when they weren't wandering off through the centuries unwreaking havoc.

Assuming Alex was amenable to it.

But what if Alex cared not for her idea?

It was something she had refused to consider. Of course he would like it. He often spoke of his disappointment that the crown no longer recognized his title, which made it all the more difficult to lord it over her. He would be pleased with the way she'd spent such a staggering sum of his money.

Or so she hoped.

If not, she'd just made the largest mistake of her life.

TWO DAYS LATER Alex was wishing they'd hired a plane and wishing even more sincerely that Margaret would tell him where they were going. He'd tried to get a peak at her map, but she'd shoved it inside her shirt instantly. As if that would have stopped him. Fear of ruining her surprise was all that had kept him from it.

And if her jumpiness was any indication, it promised to be a whopper of a surprise.

He could have told that just from the price tag alone. It had taken a single phone call and a small shifting of minor assets to have the check cut for her, but he'd wondered what she'd found that was worth all that dough.

"Left," she said, interrupting his musings. "This is the road we must take."

Things were starting to look familiar. Then again, he'd felt for miles like he was near Falconberg. The lush, rolling hills and little hamlets had made him feel as if he'd gone back hundreds of years. What was strange, though, was the fact that he was seeing the countryside from the comfort of a car. It certainly hadn't given him much time to savor the view. Maybe there was something to be said for traveling on horseback.

He suddenly found that his foot had come off the gas and his jaw had gone slack.

Falconberg.

He could see it in the distance.

He looked at Margaret in shock. "Is that what I think it is?"

She was as pale as a ghost. She nodded with a jerk of her head.

Alex took hold of himself and continued up a road he'd certainly never ridden over before. The closer he came to the castle, the more he realized what was wrong with the picture.

"It's fixed," he said, blinking in surprise. He looked at his wife. "Did you do this?"

She shook her head. "Edward did. It was part of the promise George exacted from him."

Alex smiled. "That was well done. And what did you use as blackmail?"

"He was told my ghost would haunt him 'til the day he died if he failed in the task."

"And those Brackwalds always were a superstitious bunch."

"Aye, that they were."

Alex laughed and squeezed her hand. "You're something else."

"Aye, well . . ." she trailed off. "Don't make up your mind quite yet."

Alex pulled up short at the moat. The drawbridge was up. "I guess we could swim . . ."

The drawbridge was coming down.

Alex watched in surprise as it lowered itself completely, then he gaped at the sight of the portcullis being raised. He looked at Margaret.

"The current owner expecting us?"

"In a manner of speaking."

"Can we drive across?"

"Aye, I'm told the bridge will bear the weight of the car."

He took her word for it, drove across the bridge and through the barbican. He pulled to a stop in the bailey and just stared at the sight that greeted his eyes. So maybe the outbuildings needed some work. The chapel was intact, but now several headstones surrounded it. Alex was very tempted to go see whose they were, but that would have to wait. The owners probably wouldn't be too pleased to find him poking around their ancestors.

The lists were in great shape, though the road now divided what they once had been from land some diligent soul had turned into a garden. And what a garden it was.

"Bet they hire someone to deadhead those roses," he said with a nod at the vast field of colorful plant life.

"I imagine so," Margaret agreed with a nod. She got out of the car and waited for him.

Alex followed her, then took her hand. "Well, shall we go knock and see if anyone's home?"

She nodded. Her hands were as cold as ice.

"I'm sorry," he said quietly. "This must be hard to see someone else in your home."

It must have been especially hard because she didn't say anything, only quickened her pace. By the time they came to a teetering halt at the front door, they were almost running. Alex gave Margaret's hand a quick squeeze and smiled.

"Here goes nothing," he said, and knocked on the door.

No one answered.

He knocked again. Maybe they were an older couple and not all that spry. Or maybe the owner had been manning the drawbridge. He looked behind him but saw no one on top of the barbican. He turned back to the door and frowned.

"I don't think we're going to get in."

"You could try the key."

Alex watched as she pulled a key out of her pocket and held it up. He stared at it for several moments, trying to understand just what that meant. He looked at his wife. She wore the most neutral expression he had ever seen on her face.

Well, except for the absolute uncertainty shining in her eyes.

"Key?" he managed.

She nodded hesitantly.

"Key," he repeated, realization dawning on him. He felt himself beginning to smile. "You didn't."

She winced. "I did."

He laughed. He couldn't help himself. "You bought the castle?"

"And our titles, too," she admitted.

He could hardly believe it. "They were for sale?"

"Oh, not originally," she said, modestly, "you'd be surprised what all those years of dealing with Brackwalds can do for a woman."

Alex snatched her to him and hugged her so hard, he heard things popping.

"You wonderful woman," he said, kissing her hard on the mouth. "I can't believe you did this!"

"You're pleased?" she wheezed.

"Oh, Margaret," he said, shaking his head in wonder, "I'm thrilled. I've missed home."

"Have you?"

She looked as if he'd just given her a dump truck full of Damascus steel.

"How could I not?" he asked, smiling down at her. "I fell in love with you here. I jousted to keep this place for you. I thought I would spend the rest of my life tramping over this very soil with you. How could I not have missed it?"

She handed him the key. "Then welcome home, my lord."

He took it, fitted it to the lock, then put her hand over his.

"Let's open it together," he said with a smile.

They turned the lock and Alex pushed in the door. He strode into his home—straight into three inches of muck.

"The roof still leaks," she said, from behind him.

He laughed in spite of himself. "Hence the camping gear?"

"I thought it best."

Alex looked around and started calculating just how much money it would take to make the place livable. It should have made him queasy, but it didn't. He was too overwhelmed by what he was standing in and the fact that it was his.

Theirs.

He turned and faced his wife.

"Thank you," he said softly.

She smiled, a shy smile that made him itch to carry her off somewhere and give that smile a closer look.

"I'm happy you're pleased."

"I'm very pleased."

She pointed to the mantel over the hearth. There was a small box with a glass front.

"My knife," she said with a satisfied smile. "A Brackwald family heirloom they were most reluctant to part with."

"What did you *do* to them?" he asked hesitantly, half afraid to hear the answer.

She shrugged. "Money talks."

He laughed. "You're as bad as I am." He looked around the hall and felt as if he'd finally come home. It had been one hell of a journey to get there, but it was worth it. He smiled at his wife. "Is our bedroom still intact?"

She shook her head. "The keep is soundly built, but it's been uninhabited for quite some time. And the furnishings haven't survived very well. I'm certain George would have seen to it if he could have, but there was only so much he could do."

"He did a great job."

"There are headstones with our names out there," she continued. "I daresay he buried a few things we'll want to unearth."

Alex shuddered. "What a friend."

"You might find your baseball there. If he didn't take it to his own grave."

That would be an interesting sight. Alex contemplated the thought of finding a shovel, then decided maybe it was best left for another time. There were several more interesting things he could think of to do with his time at present and most of them included the shedding of clothes.

"How about a nap in the Range Rover?" he suggested.

"Why don't we spend an hour or so in the lists first?" she countered. "To get the feel of the place."

"I'd rather get the feel of—"

"Oh, by the saints," she said, with a laugh. "You've but one thing on your mind, my lord."

"You're right," he said, reaching for her.

"An hour," she said, backing away. "Unless His Lordship's old bones are too frail for such an activity."

He frowned at her. "Don't you want to nap?"

"I want to work up an appetite. Unless you fear the deed," she said, with a regretful sigh.

It was a blatant challenge and he knew it, but he wasn't going to pass it up. He tossed her the Range Rover keys, then paused at the front door while she continued on down the steps. He looked out over his bailey and could hardly believe he was back in the same place he'd left eight hundred years earlier, only now he had all the modern conveniences. Not that it would have mattered to him, but he wasn't going to look a gift horse in the mouth. His title, his keep, and his wife all in the same time period. It was too good to be true.

And Falconberg was certainly close enough for frequent visits with Jamie and Elizabeth. Alex suspected Joel might go into serious withdrawals if he couldn't fondle the Claymore at least every couple of months. And heaven help him if he couldn't get Baldric and Joshua together often for more of their brainstorming sessions. Alex wasn't sure the twentieth century was quite ready for a book collaboration by the two of them, but he didn't dare stand in their way. No, living this close to his baby sister and her family was truly a blessing, and one he wouldn't ever take for granted.

He watched Margaret dig in the back of the car, then saw her pull out two swords. He smiled at the sight of her, her hair in a braid down her back, striding toward him in jeans and boots, looking for all the world as if she'd always worn such clothes.

She tossed his sword at him, then drew hers, holding it up to the sun and watching the light flicker over the blade.

A woman in jeans and boots who could outfight any man in her century or his.

Except him, of course. But he wouldn't remind her of that too often. She might prove him wrong more times than his ego could take.

"Thinking of flowers to plant?" she asked sweetly. "Pansies, perhaps?"

He grinned at her. "You're just itching for a fight, aren't you?"

"Just don't miss your mark. These are my favorite jeans."

"Well, at least they're yours for a change."

She stuck her nose into the air, turned and strode off to the lists. Alex followed more slowly, enjoying the view and the anticipation of what was to come. How in the world had he ever deserved her? What had he done to merit the joy of her laughter, the strength of her convictions, the depth of her love? It was worth every moment of uncertainty, every moment of wanting but not having her, every moment of waiting for her to come into his life. He didn't deserve her, but he wasn't going to argue the point.

"Finished daydreaming?" she taunted.

He threw back his head and laughed for the sheer joy of it.

By the saints, what a woman!